NILIFF

The
REBEL

10657144

Also by Jaime Raven

The Madam
The Alibi
The Mother

The REBEL

JAIME RAVEN

avon.

This novel is entirely a work of fiction.
The names, characters and incidents portrayed in it are
the work of the author's imagination. Any resemblance to
actual persons, living or dead, events or localities is
entirely coincidental.

AVON

A division of HarperCollins*Publishers*
1 London Bridge Street,
London SE1 9GF

www.harpercollins.co.uk

A Paperback Original 2018

1

First published in Great Britain by
HarperCollins*Publishers* 2018

Copyright © Jaime Raven 2018

Jaime Raven asserts the moral right to
be identified as the author of this work

A catalogue record for this book is
available from the British Library

ISBN-13: 978-0-00-825349-3

Set in Minion by Palimpsest Book Production Limited,
Falkirk, Stirlingshire

Printed and bound in Great Britain by
Printed and bound by CPI Group (UK) Ltd, Croydon CR0 4YY

MIX
Paper from
responsible sources
FSC™ C007454

This book is produced from independently certified FSC™ paper
to ensure responsible forest management.

For more information visit: www.harpercollins.co.uk/green

All rights reserved. No part of this publication may be
reproduced, stored in a retrieval system, or transmitted,
in any form or by any means, electronic, mechanical,
photocopying, recording or otherwise, without the prior
permission of the publishers.

To the new arrivals, in order of age – Evelyn, Lucas, Adam and Ella. May they all have a happy life.

Swansong: a metaphorical phrase for a final gesture, effort, or performance before death or retirement.

PROLOGUE

It was a dry night so Terry Malone decided to walk home. He hoped it would give him time to sober up and get over the shock of what he'd been told.

The revelation had knocked him for six and even now, two hours later, he still couldn't get his mind around it.

It didn't help that he'd had too much champagne. He wasn't used to it. He preferred beer and whisky, but his boss had insisted on cracking open two bottles of Moët.

'Get it down you, lad,' Roy Slack had urged him back at the club. 'This is a big fucking deal and we have to celebrate.'

The West End was still buzzing even though it was almost midnight, but Terry was oblivious to the crowds and the incessant hum of the traffic.

Forty-five minutes. That was about how long it would take him to trek to his home across the river in Lambeth. Amy would be in bed, of course, but she wouldn't be asleep. Whenever he was this late she stayed awake and worried.

He supposed it was only to be expected. The wives and girlfriends of most of the other gang members were the same. Being a villain wasn't like being an accountant or a teacher or a bus driver. It was a tough, stressful business that entailed risk and uncertainty. And it put an awful lot of strain on families and friends.

Amy had become far more anxious since discovering she was pregnant four months ago. She kept asking him what would happen to her and the baby if he got shot, stabbed or banged up for years.

That was why Terry had been giving serious consideration to packing it in and going straight. It was also why he was dreading her reaction to tonight's bombshell revelation. The impact on their lives was going to be considerable and she was bound to freak out.

In all honesty he wouldn't blame her. He was struggling to come to terms with it himself and it was making his head spin.

When he reached Lambeth Bridge he broke his stride and sparked up a fag. From his pocket he took the letter that Slack had given to him. He read it through for the umpteenth time and once again he felt a flash of heat in his chest. The words were already embedded in his mind. They were shocking, life-changing, terrifying. And they sent a cold chill down his spine.

He put the letter back in his pocket and stood looking down on the inky black Thames, his heart thudding in his chest.

After a couple of minutes he decided that he wouldn't break the news to Amy for at least a couple of days. That'd give him time to take it all in and assess the implications. There was so much to think about, not least the kind of future he wanted for his unborn child.

He drew smoke deep into his lungs and reflected on what a momentous year it had already been.

Seven months ago he'd been pushing drugs for an Eastern European outfit in North London before its leaders became victims of the Met's latest crackdown on organised crime. Their arrests had caused chaos inside the organisation and allowed rival gangs to move in on the territory and the various businesses.

Just weeks later his mother had died, aged fifty-three, after a stroke. She'd managed to cling on in hospital for several days before taking her last breath.

Terry had been devastated and the future had looked truly bleak. But as one door closed another one had opened. He'd been approached by Roy Slack's people and invited to join the biggest and most ruthless firm in the capital.

He'd then met Amy in one of Slack's West End clubs. After only five dates he realised that he loved her and on the seventh date she'd announced that she was pregnant.

She'd thought he'd be angry and disappointed, but he couldn't have been happier. At twenty-six he was ready to be a father and was determined to make a good job of it.

He'd been telling himself that he would always be there for his son or daughter, and he'd try to give them a better start in life than the one he'd had.

But was that going to be possible given what he now knew?

It was one of the many questions that were piling up inside his head as he stood on the bridge and fought against the panic that was threatening to overwhelm him.

He felt a little better by the time he got home. The walk had flushed most of the alcohol through his system and his head had stopped spinning.

It was just after 1am when he let himself in through the front door of their terraced house, within walking distance of the Imperial War Museum.

He'd been renting it for two years and the location was perfect.

But now they'd have to move. After what he'd learned tonight there was no way that he and Amy could stay here. It just wouldn't be safe.

'Is that you, babe?' Amy called out.

'It is,' he replied, closing the door behind him. 'I'll be straight up.'

He took off his coat and went into the kitchen to pour himself a glass of water. He spotted two new glossy wedding magazines on the table where Amy had left them. The date had been set for January fourth, three months from now, but the details still had to be worked out.

He wanted a cheap and cheerful affair in a register office and a few drinks in the pub afterwards. But Amy had her heart set on something more elaborate, and so they were looking at a hotel do with a combined ceremony and reception for up to eighty people.

As Terry fingered the edge of one of the magazines more questions popped into his head.

Would their wedding plans have to be put on hold? Would Amy still want to marry him after he told her what Roy Slack had said? Was it fair not to break the news to her straight away?

'What's keeping you, babe?'

Her voice wrenched him out of himself and he hurriedly filled a glass with tap water. Then he took a long, deep breath, switched off the kitchen light and climbed the stairs.

Amy was sitting up against her pillows, her swollen breasts resting on the duvet, her long dark hair cascading over her shoulders.

She was the same age as him but looked at least five years younger. Her pale skin was flawless and her eyes were an electrifying blue.

He forced a smile and crossed the room to plant a kiss on her

4

lips. As always he felt a rush of affection for her. She was the first woman he had ever loved and he couldn't imagine ever being without her.

Since meeting her he had changed for the better. He'd mellowed and matured. He no longer kept trying to live up to his fearsome reputation as a short-tempered thug. Those days were behind him and he was glad of it.

He still sorted people out when ordered to do so but he no longer threw his weight around or started unnecessary fights just for the fun of it.

'You look done in, Terry,' Amy said. 'Is everything all right?'

'Sure it is,' he told her. 'I'm late because I had a meeting with the boss.'

'What about?'

'Oh, just business stuff. But he got me drinking champagne and it's gone straight to my head.'

She laughed. 'I have no sympathy. You know that bubbly doesn't agree with you.'

'Yeah, well, best to keep the boss sweet.'

He went into the en suite, cleaned his teeth and emptied his bladder. He was anxious not to get drawn into a conversation because he might just blurt out something he'd regret.

'I need to get some shut eye,' he said as he climbed into bed. 'I've got another early start in the morning.'

He gave her a cuddle and at the same time reached over to switch off the lamp.

'Are you sure you're OK?' Amy asked him. 'You don't seem your usual self.'

'I'm fine. Honest. Just dead tired.'

'Only I was hoping that maybe we could get it on. I've been so bloody horny all evening.'

Pregnancy had boosted Amy's libido to the point where it seemed she couldn't get enough of it, and normally he was only too eager to satisfy her craving. But right now a shag was out of the question. With what was going on inside his head he was sure he wouldn't even be able to get it up.

'It'll have to wait until morning, babe,' he said. 'I'm so knackered I know I'll disappoint you.'

'Why don't you let me work my magic then,' she said as she reached under the duvet.

But she failed to get a rise out of him and he was relieved when she gave up after thirty seconds and rolled over.

It wasn't long before she started snoring so he didn't have to pretend to be asleep. He was able to lie there on his back with his eyes wide open, his mind wrestling with a growing anxiety.

He was still awake an hour later when a chilling sound reached him from downstairs – the sound of the front door being smashed in.

He knew instinctively what was happening before the shouting started. It was a police raid and they were sure to be mob-handed.

He heard their boots pounding up the stairs and he felt the floor shudder.

Then the landing light went on and there was another crash as the door to one of the other rooms was rammed open.

'Armed police,' a voice called out. 'Stay where you are.'

But Terry was already on the move, throwing off the duvet and leaping off the bed.

As he fumbled for the lamp switch the bedroom door was flung open and Amy screamed.

Terry, naked and disoriented, spun round so fast that he lost his balance and lurched towards a police officer in full body armour who was standing in the doorway. The officer reacted by discharging two bullets in quick succession from his Glock 17 pistol.

Both shells slammed into Terry's chest and he was thrown onto the floor.

The last thing he heard was Amy screaming, but he died not knowing that she was in the throes of a painful miscarriage induced by shock.

The police officer, a man with three years' experience in the firearms unit, would later tell an investigation that he thought the suspect was attacking him.

The inquiry would also hear that the raid was one of a number that took place that night on the homes of individuals known to be involved in organised crime.

In Terry's house the team found a quantity of Class A drugs, a sawn-off shotgun and a total of ten thousand pounds in cash.

They also found a collection of documents and magazines pertaining to a wedding that would now never take place.

PART ONE

1

Laura

Two months later

The man in the dock had already been convicted and this afternoon he was going to be sentenced.

That was why I'd come along on what was supposed to be a rare day off. I wanted to see the bastard's face when the judge told him how many years he'd have to spend behind bars.

My colleagues and I were hoping for a long, long stretch. If he got less than twenty we'd be disappointed. With any luck he'd die in prison, and since he was in his mid-fifties there was every chance he would.

The man's name was Harry Fuller, and at his trial, which had ended a month ago, he'd been found guilty of a range of offences from extortion and money laundering to drug trafficking and people smuggling. These were committed during the five years he'd spent as head of one of London's most notorious crime gangs.

He had also been linked to at least six murders, but we hadn't come up with the evidence to charge him with those.

It was still a great result, though. We'd managed to succeed where others before us had failed. Harry Fuller had at last been well and truly nailed.

I was watching the proceedings from the packed public gallery and switching my gaze between the judge and Fuller. The judge had indicated that he was going to make a statement before passing sentence, and he was now consulting his notes before getting on with it.

As usual I was in awe of my surroundings: London's Central Criminal Court, more commonly known as the Old Bailey. I'd been here many times and it never failed to impress me. So many lives had been changed in this place and so many wrongs had been put right. For a copper like me it was nothing less than a shrine to the law and to the legal system.

I noticed that Fuller had spotted me and even across the courtroom I could see the devilish glint in his eyes.

I held his gaze, forcing myself not to waver. But it was hard not to be unnerved by the expression on his face. It reminded me of the old cliché that if looks could kill I'd be dead.

In appearance Fuller was the archetypal gangster, big and beefy with a bullet-shaped head and broken nose. But there was more to him than muscle and menace. He was also a shrewd businessman, and it was estimated that his firm had been turning over fifty million pounds a year.

Without him at the helm, the firm was already coming apart at the seams, and that was great because it had been one of our primary objectives.

It was DS Martin Weeks and I who had made the collar that day at Fuller's office in Stratford. I was the one who'd done the talking, and I would never forget Fuller's reaction when I'd showed him my warrant card and said, 'DI Laura Jefferson. I'm with

Scotland Yard's organised crime task force and I'm here to tell you that you're nicked.'

He'd raised his brow at me and the hint of a smile had played at the corners of his mouth.

'Well, what do you know?' he'd said, his voice dripping with contempt. 'I wondered if and when you lot would get around to me. But it's only fair to warn you that I won't be so easy to take down as those others you've collared.'

And he'd been right. But we'd got there in the end through an immense amount of effort and some good luck. Everyone had put in a ton of extra hours to ensure that we had a watertight case against the man.

'Here comes the moment of truth.'

The voice belonged to the woman who was sitting directly behind me and it snapped me back to the present.

I turned my attention to the judge who had finished checking his notes and was ready to speak. The court bailiff asked everyone to be quiet, which prompted about half a dozen people to loudly clear their throats.

The judge, who was in his early seventies, remained completely unfazed. He simply paused until a deafening silence descended on the courtroom.

Then he read out his statement in a voice that was slow and measured.

'I want to take this opportunity to commend those police officers who were responsible for bringing this case to trial,' he said. 'Organised crime is a shameful scar on this great city – indeed on the whole country. Men like the defendant have always acted with impunity, flaunting the law as they built their vast criminal empires. It's true to say that the situation has progressed from a serious problem into a large-scale crisis.

'That was why I was so pleased when Scotland Yard set up a special task force eighteen months ago to deal with it. And, as we learned during this trial, their successes so far have been nothing short of spectacular.

'Harry Fuller is the latest gangster whose reign has thankfully been brought to an ignominious end. And I'm sure he won't be the last thanks to the efforts of the task force.'

The judge paused to acknowledge my boss, Detective Chief Superintendent George Drummond, who was sitting in the well of the court with the prosecution team.

'I would like to put on record my thanks to all of those officers involved,' he said. 'And I want them to know that they have the support of every law-abiding person in this country. We appreciate that this work they're doing places them in considerable danger, and we can only hope and pray that no harm comes to them in the course of their investigations.'

The judge then turned to Harry Fuller and said, 'I've already warned you to expect a custodial sentence, Mr Fuller. It's clear that your crimes are such that I can show no mercy. For far too long you've acted as though you are above the law. But nobody is above the law, no matter how much power they wield or money they have.'

The judge paused again, twice as long this time, and then he told Fuller that he was going to spend at least thirty years in prison.

'Fucking brilliant,' I blurted out and everyone heard me, including Fuller, who shot me a look that told me he was as shocked as I was.

I curled a smile for his benefit, and he reacted by closing his eyes and blowing out his cheeks.

It was a far better result than any of us could have hoped for, and I was delighted because another vile gangster had been snared. But for the task force there would be no resting on its laurels.

Fuller was a terrific catch, but he wasn't in the same league as the villain who was going to be our next target.

After the sentencing came the inevitable media scrum outside the court.

Reporters, photographers and TV crews had turned out in force to get reactions from all the main players, including DCS Drummond.

The gaffer was surrounded the moment he appeared on the pavement. This was something I'd anticipated, which was why I'd hurried out of the building ahead of him.

I was now standing just far enough away to hear him read out a pre-prepared statement, but in a position where I couldn't be filmed or photographed.

'On behalf of Scotland Yard and the task force team, I'd like to say how pleased we are that the judge has seen fit to impose on Harry Fuller such a lengthy period of incarceration,' he said. 'We believe it to be wholly appropriate given the nature of the crimes the man has committed over a number of years.'

Unlike me, Drummond relished being in the spotlight. He always came across as supremely cool and self-assured. The fact that he looked like a film star dressed up as a copper no doubt helped to boost his confidence.

He was a fit-looking forty-eight year old, with chiselled features and dark, wavy hair. At six foot four he towered over his immediate colleagues and I'd never seen him dressed in anything other than a smart two-piece suit or uniform.

His statement was short and sweet, and when he was finished the first question came from a BBC reporter who asked, 'The judge drew particular attention to the task force that's under your command, detective chief superintendent. Can you just remind us exactly what your remit is?'

Drummond pursed his lips and nodded. 'The organised crime task force was set up to deliver a decisive blow to the hardened criminals who've infiltrated every area of society in London. We've been assigned a team of twenty dedicated detectives and thirty support staff, and we work in tandem with the National Crime Agency and Scotland Yard's specialist divisions.'

As Drummond continued he had to squint against the harsh light from a sun that sat low in the sky. It may have been bright, but there was no warmth in it. I could feel the cold December air through my overcoat and jumper.

It made me shiver, and I suddenly realised how much I was looking forward to the team get-together in the Rose and Crown. A few gin and tonics would soon warm me up.

Drummond had organised the do to celebrate the outcome of this latest case and it was due to kick off in a couple of hours, at five o'clock. But I was sure that my colleagues would start arriving earlier since the pub was only a short walk from the office at Scotland Yard.

As if on cue one of those colleagues suddenly appeared on the scene and when she saw me she came right over.

'I didn't expect to see you here,' Kate Chappell said. 'I thought you were on a day off.'

'I wouldn't have missed it for the world,' I said. 'The look on Fuller's face when he was told he was going down for thirty years was priceless.'

'I bet it was. I'm only sorry I missed it. I had a job over in Bermondsey that took longer than expected.'

Kate and I got on well, even though we didn't have much in

common. She was nine years older than me at forty-two and at least two stones heavier. Her hair was short and lifeless and about as hard to control as her weight.

She often joked that I was too pretty to be a copper and that it wasn't fair that I could eat like a horse and still be a size ten.

But I had a sneaking suspicion that she resented the fact that I outranked her. And if she did I wouldn't have blamed her because she was a better detective than most of those I'd worked with.

'Did you drive or come here by tube?' she asked me.

'Tube,' I said.

'Well, I've got a pool car that's parked around the corner. I can give you a lift to the pub, assuming you're coming along for the booze up.'

'Of course I am, which reminds me I ought to call Aidan to tell him what's happened.'

Kate gestured towards Drummond. 'I suspect your boyfriend already knows by now. Even before the governor's finished telling the world how great we are I reckon that everyone with a TV, radio or smartphone will know about the fate of that ghastly gobshite Harry Fuller.'

The DCS was now being asked to reveal details about the crime syndicate which the task force would set its sights on next, and Kate and I listened with interest.

'I won't be drawn into naming names,' Drummond said. 'But I believe it's an open secret that our aim now is to bring to justice this country's most feared and revered organised criminal. He knows who he is and I'm sure he knows that we're coming for him.'

2

Slack

It was the first time Roy Slack had heard himself described as the most feared and revered crime boss in the country, and it made him smile.

He knew it to be true, of course, just like he'd known for some time that the Old Bill were going to come after him with everything they had.

But he wasn't going to make it easy for them. In fact he intended to ensure that it was a move they would come to regret.

He turned his attention away from the huge flat-screen TV on his office wall and said to Danny Carver, 'Thirty frigging years. The poor sod might as well top himself because he won't ever be coming out.'

Danny was his most trusted enforcer, a fifty-five-year-old former mercenary whose nickname in the underworld was The Rottweiler. He was a thickset individual with a boxer's physique and a well-deserved reputation as a violent psychopath, qualities that made him perfect for the job he did.

'My money was on a fifteen stretch, boss,' he said. 'But we should have guessed the bastards would use the poor bugger to send a message to us.'

Slack nodded. Danny was right. This was a crude example of the police and the judicial system working together to show they meant business.

'The wankers are mistaken if they think it'll have me shitting in my pants,' Slack said. 'Harry Fuller was a fairly easy target, but I won't be.'

The two men, who were alone in the office, turned their attention back to the TV screen.

Sky News were reporting live from outside the Old Bailey and DCS George Drummond was still responding to questions. He was a smooth-looking bastard who clearly had an inflated opinion of himself.

Slack had met the man on two occasions and he knew their paths would cross again.

'Seems to me that what that bloke is saying amounts to a declaration of all-out war,' Danny said.

Slack leaned back in his padded leather chair and swung his shoes up onto the desk.

'That's exactly what it is, Danny,' he said. 'And if it's a war they want, then it's a war they're gonna get.'

He'd known what was coming ever since the Home Office announced a major new offensive against organised crime in London. It was essentially a political move over widespread concern that the problem had got out of hand.

There had been an epidemic of gun and knife crime in the capital, and during the past three years no less than thirty people had been murdered during gang turf wars.

The press had also been making a big thing of the fact that the annual cost of organised crime on the London economy was now running at billions of pounds.

The task force that was put together was well resourced and had managed to rack up some early successes, Harry Fuller being the biggest scalp so far.

Before him there was Paul Mason, who'd run the East London mob for five years. And before Mason there were the Romanian brothers – Stefan and Anton Severin – who were known as the kings of crack cocaine north of the Thames.

Slack didn't shed a tear for any of them. They were rivals, after all, and he'd been mopping up some of their business. But the downfall of such heavyweight villains was a sure sign that this time he couldn't afford to be complacent.

The task force presented a credible threat to his illicit empire, which was spread across all of South London, as well as the lucrative West End.

But clinging on to what he'd built up over many years wasn't the real driving force behind what he was planning.

And neither was fear of ending up behind bars like Harry Fuller and the others.

What Slack intended to do was motivated by something far more profound and much closer to his heart.

Revenge.

Slack hadn't yet told anyone what he planned to do but that was about to change because he was going to confide in Danny Carver. He needed Danny to help him put the wheels in motion.

Now that the Fuller trial had ended they'd be coming after him with all guns blazing.

There'd be raids on his businesses and the homes of his employees and associates. Surveillance would be stepped up, all his financial affairs would be probed like never before, and the bastards would cause as much disruption as possible to his operations.

They'd push and squeeze and threaten in their desperate search for something to use against him. And if they weren't successful then he wouldn't put it past them to fit him up.

They were probably expecting him to batten down the hatches before pissing off to his villa on the Costa del Sol. So they were going to get a big fucking shock when he retaliated by launching a pre-emptive strike.

'The slags won't know what's hit them, babe,' he said to the framed photo on his desk. 'Mine is going to be the loudest swan-song this city has ever heard.'

His late wife's smiling face stared back at him and brought a lump to his throat. Even after all this time he still found it hard to accept that Julie was gone.

The photo was taken on their honeymoon in Capri twenty-three years ago. They were standing together with the sea in the background and he had his arm around her shoulders.

She'd been at her most gorgeous then – blonde and tanned and slim, with a face that had squeezed his heart the moment he'd laid eyes on it.

Back then he hadn't been so bad looking himself. His hair had been thick and black and there'd been no fat on his frame or lines on his face.

Now, at the age of fifty-seven, his hair was grey and wispy and he had a gut the size of a rugby ball. Years of hard living were evident in the creases on his forehead and neck, and in the dark pouches beneath his eyes.

'You need to speak up, boss. I didn't catch what you just said.'

Danny's voice snapped him out of himself and he wrenched his attention away from the photo.

'Sorry, mate,' he said. 'I was miles away and mumbling to myself.'

Danny was sitting on the sofa below the window that offered up a view of the rooftops of Rotherhithe. He leaned forward and picked up the TV remote from the coffee table in front of him. He used it to mute the sound of the Sky News reporter who was summing up what had happened at the Old Bailey.

'This is serious shit, boss,' he said. 'So I think it's time you told me how the fuck you intend to respond.'

Slack clamped his lips together and nodded. 'You're right, Danny old son. But what I'm going to say is just between you and me, at least to start with. I don't want the other lads to freak out before the fun even begins.'

3

Laura

The media circus outside the court ended as quickly as it had begun. After giving his interview, DCS Drummond was whisked away in a car driven by someone from the Crown Prosecution Service.

Harry's Fuller's lawyer then made a brief statement announcing that they'd be appealing both the conviction and sentence, but he refused to answer any questions.

Kate and I were both on a high as we walked to her car. It was a terrific feeling knowing that we'd helped to end the career of another vicious mobster.

At times like this I realised why I loved being a copper. But it wasn't just the exhilarating sense of achievement. It was also another result in honour of my dear departed dad.

I knew he would have been proud of me, and it was such an awful shame that he couldn't tell me how much.

He was still alive back when I followed in his footsteps and joined the force twelve years ago. He'd risen to the rank of detective chief inspector in Lewisham CID, and he'd always been my inspiration.

'Policing is a noble profession, sweetheart,' he told me when I announced my intention to enrol on leaving university. 'But as you and your mother know only too well it'll take over your life. So you need to be one hundred per cent certain that it's what you want to do.'

'It is,' I said.

'In that case you'll have my full support. But promise me one thing, Laura. You'll always be true to the oath you'll take at the outset. If at any time you feel you can't, then pack it in and go work in a shop or a factory.'

He made a point of telling me that, because my first six months on the job coincided with a relentless wave of negative publicity for the police.

Corruption within the Met was being exposed on an almost weekly basis, and a lot of new recruits like myself became disillusioned.

But for me the scandals served only to strengthen my commitment and my resolve to be a good, honest copper like my father.

It wasn't as if I hadn't been aware that the Met in particular was infested with officers who were on the take. While at university a report was published that claimed there'd been a sharp increase in the number of officers dealing in drugs and abusing their power for 'sexual gratification'.

I'd since discovered myself that the force did indeed have its share of bad apples, but most officers walked a straight line and were a credit to the profession.

Of course, being above board and serving with distinction did not make it less likely that you'd come to harm in the line of duty.

My father found that out the night he opened his front door to a man who shot him three times in the chest.

Seven years on – with the killer still out there somewhere – the memory moves me to tears and gives rise to a blast of anger.

It's only about two miles from the Old Bailey to New Scotland Yard. But the traffic was murderous so it was slow going in Kate's pool car.

She took us via the Victoria Embankment and there was gridlock for much of the way.

We were passing under Waterloo Bridge when my mobile rang. It was Aidan.

'I gather congratulations are in order,' he said. 'I just heard it on the news. You must be pleased.'

'I'm over the moon,' I said. 'We all are, which is why we're going to the pub for a celebration drink.'

'You deserve it, hon. Have a great time.'

'Are you home already?'

'No, I've only just left the school. I'll grab a takeaway. Do you want me to get something for you?'

'No, don't worry. I'll sort myself out.'

Aidan was a teacher and worked in a big comprehensive near our home in Balham. We'd been together for four years, having been introduced by my matchmaking mother who was one of his colleagues.

'I'll see you when I see you then,' Aidan said. 'And try not to get too tipsy. There's still a big stain on the carpet from the last time you rolled in drunk.'

I laughed and told him that I loved him, then put the phone back in my shoulder bag.

'From the sound of it, things are still great on the home front,' Kate said.

I nodded. 'It couldn't be better. We're a good match, and thankfully Aidan's pretty understanding about all the unsocial hours and stuff.'

'You're lucky. I've come to the conclusion that good men are a dying breed.'

Kate had been bitter and cynical about men ever since I'd known her, but I had some sympathy. Her marriage came to a brutal end after only two years when she found her husband – a fellow detective working at the same station – in bed with another woman, for whom he promptly left her.

What compounded her suffering and humiliation was the fact that most of their colleagues had known he'd been having an affair for months and no one had told her.

But the sorry saga did not end there. Two months after walking out, her husband died in an accident outside his new home when he was struck by a car that mounted the pavement. So grief was suddenly added to Kate's emotional burden.

'Are you seeing anyone at the moment?' I asked tentatively.

She shook her head. 'I was going out with a bloke until a couple of weeks ago. He was some kind of financial adviser, and that was the problem. He kept trying to get me to part with money. When he said he could double my savings I realised he was a wrong 'un and told him to sod off.'

I couldn't help feeling sorry for her, but then it was a familiar story. I knew a couple of other middle-aged women who'd had similar experiences on the dating scene.

'I made the mistake of telling that lech Tony Marsden that I was single again,' Kate said. 'And he had the cheek to ask me if I wanted to go out for a drink with him.'

'What did you say?'

'I told him that I wasn't that bloody desperate and that he should be ashamed of himself.'

I grinned. 'I'm sure he's heard that before.'

'Maybe so, but the slimy toerag then said I didn't know what I was missing.'

We both laughed and I went on to tell her about how Marsden tried it on with me at the last Christmas do.

'It wouldn't be so bad if he wasn't by far the worst of a bad bunch,' I said.

Tony Marsden was another of the detective sergeants on the team. He was an opinionated prick who despite being married with a young son was known to play away with anyone who'd have him, including prostitutes.

It was no secret that he was addicted to gambling as well as illicit sex, and he had always struck me as a pretty dodgy character, the kind of copper my dad would have hated working with.

And it was just our rotten luck that Marsden should arrive at the Rose and Crown at the same time we did, after Kate had dropped off the pool car.

He was a squat, bullish man in his late thirties, with a florid complexion and fair hair that was as short as putting-green grass.

When he saw us approaching, he opened the door to the saloon bar and treated us to one of his lascivious smirks.

'Evening, ladies,' he said. 'I trust you'll both be on your best behaviour. If not then I can assure you that it won't be a problem, at least with me.'

'Grow up, for pity's sake,' I said as I brushed past him, noting that his suit carried the heavy stench of cigarette smoke.

Inside it looked like the start of a boy's night out, which was usually the case when the team got together socially. That was because Kate and I were two of only four women among the twenty detectives.

One of the others was Janet Dean, who was the same rank as me. She was already at the bar and waved when she spotted us.

Janet was in her late forties, and it was fair to say that she was the most unpopular member of the team. She was a miserable bitch most of the time and rarely attended social functions. When she did she tended to drink too much and slag people off.

'So what's your tipple, girls?' she said as we approached the bar. 'The booze is on the house so we might as well get stuck in.'

Her thin face was flushed and there was a wet patch on the front of her cream blouse. It was obvious she had already downed a few glasses of something.

I opted for a gin and tonic, and Kate had a white wine.

'I'm surprised you've graced us with your presence, Janet,' Kate said. 'I can't remember the last time you joined us for a drink.'

Janet lifted her shoulders and eyebrows at the same time.

'It's a special occasion,' she said. 'And besides, Ethan is spending a couple of days in Brighton working on the boat so I've got no reason to rush home.'

That was the other thing that people didn't like about Janet Dean. She too often boasted about how well off she and her husband were. They lived in a town house in Chelsea, owned two BMWs, and their latest acquisition was a cabin cruiser that was moored in Brighton marina.

Of course, their lifestyle wasn't funded by her copper's salary. Her husband worked for an investment company in the City, although she'd always been vague about exactly what he did, and kept schtum about how much he earned.

I was on my second G and T when DCS Drummond decided to propose a toast to the team's latest success.

'You've all done a great job and I'm proud of you,' he said. 'But make no mistake – things are about to get much tougher. Roy Slack is a master when it comes to evading prosecution. And there's no one who's as cautious as he is at avoiding surveillance. As you know from the intelligence packs you've been given, he uses unregistered mobiles and employs debugging devices in his home and office. He also has powerful friends and we suspect there are officers in the Met who are in his pocket. Those are among the people we aim to flush out during this investigation.'

We all knew it wasn't going to be easy. Slack was London's longest established crime boss and it was strongly believed that he had connections with senior officers, the Crown Prosecution Service and several MPs. It was one of the reasons he had managed to reign supreme for so long.

'When we get together tomorrow I'll give a full briefing on our approach,' Drummond said. 'But one of our main lines of enquiry will continue to be the disappearance of firearms officer Hugh Wallis. I still believe that it's highly likely that Slack had something to do with it, despite his denials.'

Officer Wallis had vanished while returning to his home in Shoreditch from a late shift just a week ago. His car was then found the next day parked behind a warehouse a few miles away in Stratford. The keys were still in the ignition.

No one had heard from him since his disappearance and no clues to his whereabouts had been offered up by traffic cameras and CCTV.

According to his wife there were no issues in his life that he might have decided to run away from. It was therefore feared that something bad had happened to him.

The task force had been alerted because Wallis had been involved in a joint operation that had been mounted three months ago with the NCA. Raids were carried out on the homes of twelve known villains, including a man named Terry Malone, who worked for Slack.

Wallis had shot Malone dead when he thought the guy was about to attack him. But there was a bit of a rumpus because Malone's girlfriend – who sadly miscarried during the raid – later claimed that Malone had not posed a threat, and that the officer had fired the three fatal shots because he panicked.

An investigation cleared Wallis and accepted that the action he took upon entering the couple's bedroom that night was justified.

But the decision caused a ripple of alarm within the criminal community and the word on the street was that Roy Slack's people had been using their contacts to try to find out the identity of the officer, which hadn't of course been made public.

Personally I had my doubts that Slack would be so stupid as to seek retribution against the police, especially on behalf of someone who was fairly low down the food chain within his organisation.

But as we would soon discover, the man was far more ruthless than his reputation had led us to believe.

And he had secrets that would turn out to be just as shocking as his actions.

4

Slack

It didn't take long for Roy Slack to reveal his plan to Danny Carver. It was a simple one, after all.

Danny's reaction was predictable. His jaw dropped and the colour retreated from his face.

'Is this a fucking joke, boss?' he said, his voice stretched thin with shock. 'Because if it ain't, then I think you might have lost your marbles.'

Slack stood up and stepped out from behind his desk. It was uncomfortably warm in the office so he slipped off his cardigan and threw it on the chair. His white shirt had dark patches of sweat under each armpit.

He crossed the room to the cabinet with the bottles of spirits on top.

'Care for a whisky, Danny?' he asked.

'Too bloody right I do,' Danny answered. 'And please make it a large one because I think I need it.'

Slack smiled to himself as he poured out triples of his finest malt, flown down from his favourite distillery in the Highlands.

He handed a glass to Danny. 'You've been with me a long time, mate, and you're the only person in this world who I'd trust with my life. It's why I've told you what I intend to do and it's the reason I'm now going to tell you why I want to do it.'

Danny's hard face fisted into a frown and he rolled out his bottom lip.

'Well, I'm all ears, boss,' he said.

Slack sat down beside him on the sofa and sipped at his whisky.

'I also need you to know that you're going to be well looked after whatever happens,' he said. 'I'm going to transfer a large sum of cash into your offshore account first thing in the morning. If the firm survives then you can stick around if you want to. If it doesn't you'll have the option to fuck off abroad and enjoy an early retirement.'

Danny's frown deepened and he tilted his head to one side.

'Sounds to me like you've given a lot of thought to this, boss,' he said.

Slack nodded. 'It's been rolling around inside my head for weeks. Now I can't wait to get on with it.'

Danny grinned, showing off his two gold teeth.

'Well, it sure is an insane idea,' he said. 'But for what it's worth I reckon the fuckers have it coming. Most of 'em are more crooked than we are.'

Slack knew he could depend on Danny not to fill his nappy at the thought of what was going to happen. They didn't call him The Rottweiler for nothing. He was a man of violence, a crazy fuck, who had maimed and killed more men than he could probably remember.

He was also fiercely loyal and had carried out heinous crimes on Slack's behalf without a second's thought. He was completely devoid of empathy and compassion.

For that reason Slack had absolutely no doubt that he would be able to count on him in the days and weeks ahead.

'So come on, boss,' Danny said. 'There's no way you'd be set on doing this just to hang on to what you've got. There has to be something else, something that you've been keeping close to your chest.'

So Slack told him, and for the first time since they'd met, Danny Carver was lost for words.

'So now you know everything,' Roy Slack said. 'And that's a privilege I won't grant to anyone else. The rest of the guys will be fed information as and when I deem it to be necessary.'

Danny was slow to respond and Slack could tell that he wasn't sure how. What he'd just been told had come as quite a shock, and he was shrewd enough to know that his world was about to be tilted on its axis.

'I'm determined to see this through for the reasons I've just given,' Slack said. 'So don't bother trying to talk me out of it. My mind's made up, and since I'm still head of this outfit I'll expect you to support me.'

Danny drained the whisky from his glass and found his voice.

'I won't try to talk you out of it, boss. Not because I know it'll be a waste of time, but because if I was in your shoes I'd be tempted to do something similar.'

Slack was pleased but not surprised. He and Danny were very much alike in the sense that they had no respect for authority and both harboured a simmering hatred for the police.

It went way back to those early years spent on a rough council estate in Peckham when the cops were their enemy.

As teenagers they were sucked into the gang culture and from there they embarked on a life of villainy.

They eventually went their separate ways. Slack stayed in London and built a reputation for himself as a hard, uncompromising gangster. He served his apprenticeship as a thief, a pimp, a drug dealer and an enforcer. And all that time he managed to stay out of jail by outsmarting the law.

But Danny wasn't so lucky. At eighteen he stabbed to death a man who came onto his girlfriend in a pub. He was convicted of murder and spent twelve years in prison. When released he went to work with a bunch of mercenaries in Libya. After a couple of years in that hellhole, he returned to London and offered his services to his old pal from Peckham.

Slack had been only too pleased to give him a job, and it wasn't long before Danny became his right-hand man.

'So have you got any questions, mate?' Slack asked as he got up from the sofa to pour some more drinks.

'I've got lots, boss,' Danny said. 'But they can wait. I'd rather we got down to business and you told me how we're going to get this party started.'

Slack poured two more whiskies and then sat back down on the sofa.

'It's already started, mate,' he said. 'Yesterday I spoke to our friend Carlos Cruz in Mexico. He owes me a big favour and I called it in.'

'What do you want from him?' Danny asked.

Slack took a deep breath and held it for a second before speaking.

'I want him to supply us with an assassin,' he said, as though that were quite a normal request to make. 'Someone who won't be on the radar of any law enforcement agency anywhere in Europe. As we all know the best and most prolific contract killers work for the Mexican cartels.'

'What was his response?'

'He told me he'd be only too happy to help and that he'd ring me this evening.'

Danny's brow peaked. 'So assuming he delivers, what'll be the next step?'

A slow smile spread across Slack's face. 'We then make use of the information that's been passed onto me by our mole inside the organised crime task force.'

5

Laura

The task force had a temporary base at New Scotland Yard because the building we usually occupied around the corner was being refurbished. But it suited me because the interior was fresh and modern, and there were spectacular views across the Thames. It was also much closer to the Rose and Crown and a couple of other cosy little watering holes.

I was among the first to leave the pub after four gin and tonics, a ham sandwich and a packet of cheese and onion crisps.

I would have stayed later if it had been Friday, but I had no intention of getting pissed on a Monday night.

I'd enjoyed myself, though. The banter, the camaraderie, the chance to talk about things other than work. Plus, I'd also managed to steer clear of Tony Marsden, who'd spent much of the time chatting up the buxom barmaid.

DCS Drummond had been on good form throughout and had taken particular pleasure in using the occasion to reveal some more good news – that the wife of our colleague, DI Dave Prentiss, had given birth to a baby boy that very afternoon, which was why he wasn't with us. Prentiss was one of the detectives I got on well with, so I was really happy for him.

After leaving the pub I walked to Embankment tube station and travelled south via the Northern Line to Balham where Aidan and I rented a house just off the High Road.

I got home shortly after nine o'clock. Aidan was watching the television in the living room and he was surprised to see me back so early.

'What happened?' he said. 'Did they run out of booze?'

I laughed. 'I didn't dare stay any longer. It was my day off, remember, and I had a couple of wines with lunch. One more alcoholic drink and no way will I be fit for work in the morning.'

He got up from his favourite armchair, pulled me into an embrace, and kissed me tenderly on the mouth.

As always it was just what I needed at the end of a day spent apart. His warm, minty breath and the feel of his body so close to mine gave rise to a familiar sense of gratitude for having him in my life.

I loved him beyond measure and I knew in my heart that I'd always be able to trust him. He wasn't like Tony Marsden or Kate Chappell's adulterous husband.

Having got my pulse racing, he helped me off with my coat and offered to make me a cup of coffee.

'Sit down and relax,' he said. 'Fancy a couple of chocolate biscuits?'

'Does the Pope believe in Christ?'

He gave me another kiss, this time on the forehead, and I watched him slide off into the kitchen.

He was wearing his 'comfy' uniform – a pair of black tracksuit bottoms and a baggy blue sweatshirt with more stains on it than a baby's bib.

I was the only person who ever got to see him like this. Whenever we had visitors he'd put on jeans and a smart jumper and pretend that he didn't live like a slob while at home.

But the truth was Aidan Bray was one of those men who looked pretty cool whatever they wore.

He was tall and trim with a sporty physique honed during regular sessions in the gym. But it was his face more than anything else that had attracted me to him in the first place. It was more interesting than handsome, and there was an openness to it that drew people in.

His eyes were large and green and set slightly too far apart. His cheeks dimpled when he smiled and his light brown hair was flecked with grey even though he was only thirty-three.

As he disappeared into the kitchen I realised yet again how lucky I was, certainly compared to Kate who had lost all faith in men, and was struggling to get her personal life back on track.

I dropped onto the sofa and exhaled a long breath. In front of me on the television a recorded episode of *A Place in the Sun* was drawing to a close. Aidan was a big fan, partly because he dreamt of moving to Spain one day to be nearer to his parents who'd retired to the Costa Blanca a few years ago.

I picked up the remote and turned to the BBC News Channel. Within thirty seconds they were running the Harry Fuller story and I watched DCS Drummond facing the media outside the Old Bailey.

'So tell me more about this bloke Roy Slack,' Aidan said as he re-entered the living room with my coffee. 'I gather you're gunning for him next.'

I looked up, surprised. 'Have they mentioned him by name on the news?'

'No. But he's been all over social media this evening and he was trending on Twitter when I last checked.'

The force was always careful not to name people until they were questioned or charged, especially those who had the means and clout to cause a fuss. The mainstream media also tended to be cautious for fear of litigation. But on the Internet it was a different matter and people didn't care about such things as libel and defamation.

Aidan handed me my coffee and biscuits and settled back into his armchair, waiting for me to answer his question.

He rarely asked me about my work and the characters we pursued because he knew that there was so much I couldn't tell him. He had only ever demonstrated a vague curiosity anyway, and that could more often than not be satisfied by reading the *Evening Standard*.

'Roy Slack can best be described as a tyrant who presides over this country's biggest criminal enterprise,' I explained. 'He's the closest we have to the old Mafia godfathers.'

Aidan didn't want a detailed character assessment of the man, just the lurid headlines. So that was what I gave him.

'Slack's whole life has been spent as a criminal but would you believe the bastard has never seen the inside of a prison cell?' I said. 'He's got a hand in every illicit pie across Central and South London. That includes drugs, extortion, fraud, prostitution, porn, money laundering – the lot.

'He's been the subject of intense investigations by the NCA and before them the Serious Organised Crime Agency. But he's kept a clean sheet, thanks to witness intimidation, bent coppers and by being more careful than any other villain out there. And he's still going from strength to strength after more than a decade at the top of his game. We now know that he's even established strong links with a notorious Mexican cartel that's flooding the whole of Europe with cocaine and heroin.'

'He sounds like quite a guy,' Aidan said. 'But you'd never guess it from the photos I've seen on the web. He looks like a kindly uncle who's ageing before his time.'

'Well, over the years a lot of people have learned to their cost that his appearance can be more than a little deceiving. He's a vicious bastard who surrounds himself with men who are even more vicious, including some nutter known at The Rottweiler.'

'What about his private life? Does he actually have one?'

'He lives well,' I said. 'But that's about all we know. He's got a fancy apartment overlooking the Thames, a big country house in Kent and a luxury villa in Spain – all paid for through legitimate businesses that are fronts for his dodgy activities.'

'Is it a family-run organisation?' Aidan asked.

I shook my head. 'If it was we're sure he would have retired by now and handed over the reins to a son or daughter. But if you ask me that's down to poetic justice.'

'What do you mean?'

'Well, he lost his wife ten years ago in a car crash. They never had children.'

'That's tough,' Aidan said. 'But even so it's hard to feel sorry for the guy.'

I didn't bother carrying on even though I could have revealed a lot more about Roy Slack. I could sense that Aidan had heard enough and, besides, it was only fair that we talked a bit about his day.

He jumped at the chance to tell me that he'd been asked to organise the staff Christmas party this year alongside my mother, who always got involved in her capacity as school secretary.

I feigned interest even though it wasn't something that I could get excited about. But at least it was a timely reminder that it wasn't all about me and the work I did. Too often I gave that impression whenever I got wrapped up in a case. I withdrew into myself and thought about little else. And I knew that wasn't fair on Aidan, even though he never complained.

To be sure Roy Slack and his minions were going to dominate my days for the foreseeable future, along with every other member of the task force.

I told myself that this time I would do my best to keep the investigation separate from my home life. I was determined not to let Aidan suffer in any way.

6

Slack

Danny Carver was a man of many talents. He was proficient in the use of most guns. He could strangle the toughest of men with his bare hands. He knew exactly how to torture someone to get them to cough up. And he could go days without sleep and still be a match for anyone in a street brawl.

But in recent years he had acquired a particular talent that didn't involve violence – and yet it had proved just as useful to Roy Slack.

Danny had become a computer geek. He wasn't up there with those cyber criminals who terrify the likes of governments, banks and big corporations. But his newfound skills had helped to develop new revenue streams for the firm through scams involving online fraud, hacking and identity theft. He'd also helped to make it difficult for the Old Bill to eavesdrop on their communications by installing sophisticated defence software in their mobiles and laptops.

It was therefore going to fall on Danny to get the ball rolling.

Slack took a sheet of paper from his desk drawer and held it up.

'This is a copy of the list I just told you about,' he said. 'It contains the names and contact details of every detective on the organised crime task force. Next to each individual there's a home address and the names of the people who are closest to them – wives, husbands, mothers, fathers, children, etcetera. Our mole has also provided me with a separate file containing photographs of most of those on the list. It's been uploaded as a password-protected page on the web.'

'So what is it you want me to do, boss?'

'To start with I want you to send an anonymous text message to every detective so they receive it at the same time. You have to make it impossible for the message to be traced back to us. Can you do that?'

Danny nodded. 'Piece of cake. So what'll be in the message?'

Slack handed the sheet of paper to Danny.

'I've written it there under the names. It's short and to the point and there's no way it can be misinterpreted.'

Danny read the message and gave a little whistle through his teeth.

'Well, if this fails to put the fear of God into the bastards then I don't know what will,' he said.

Slack's office was above a pub/restaurant the firm owned in Rotherhithe, a quiet suburb of South East London.

It was used as their base of operations and had round-the-clock security.

There was a meeting room next door and from its rear window you could see across the Thames to the spectacular skyline of

Canary Wharf. One of the high-rise buildings had been home to Slack for the past four years. It was where he stayed when he was in London, which these days was most of the time.

It was just after nine o'clock and usually when he was here this late he would go for a meal downstairs. But tonight he had no appetite – at least for food.

'Call Mike and let him know I'm ready to go home,' he said to Danny. 'And tell him I'll be making the usual stop along the way.'

Mike Walker was one of his regular drivers. Long gone were the days when Slack drove anywhere himself.

He put on his suit jacket while Danny made the call, and filled his pockets with his phone, wallet and pack of Havana cigars.

'Mike's warming up the car,' Danny said. 'He says he'll ring Jasmine to tell her you're on your way over.'

Slack nodded. 'That's terrific. The last job for you tonight is to tell the lads that I want them here for a meeting tomorrow at eleven o'clock. I need to warn them that the shit's about to hit the fan.'

They headed off in different directions – Danny to his house in Streatham and Slack to the home of his mistress in Vauxhall.

Jasmine Tinder lived in a flat he paid the rent on and it was an arrangement that suited them both. He wasn't interested in another long-term relationship because he knew that no bird could ever match up to his Julie.

But it didn't mean that his sex drive had hit the buffers, and so he made sure he got his end away on a regular basis. He was lucky in that the nature of his business meant that horny little muffins were always on tap.

Jasmine was one of several he currently had on the go, and the moment he entered the flat he realised yet again why she was his favourite.

'I was hoping you'd drop by, babe,' she said, licking her lips. 'The thought of you fucking me senseless has had me dripping between the legs for hours.'

She stood before him in nothing but a black bra and panties, a twenty-one-year-old sex siren from Manchester with metallic red hair, tits the size of melons and the face of an angel.

It was all part of an act, of course, a performance designed to get him excited. But it was exactly what he wanted. What he paid her for.

She took his hand and led him into the bedroom and as she started to slowly take off his clothes, his cock rose to the occasion.

Sex with Jasmine was always good, and it was the only time he never used a condom. He didn't have to because he'd had the snip years ago and he made sure she had regular check-ups at a private STD clinic.

He didn't try to drag it out because he had a lot on his mind and there was a risk he'd lose his erection. But it was no less enjoyable. He came inside her from behind and she did a pretty good job of faking her own orgasm.

His timing, as it turned out, was perfect because he'd just got his breath back when his mobile rang. He'd placed it on the bedside table, and as he picked it up he told Jasmine to leave the room.

'It is me, my friend,' Carlos Cruz said when he answered. 'Are you able to talk?'

'Give me a second,' Slack said as he pushed his back up against the headboard. His heart was still hammering and his face was drenched in sweat.

Cruz was probably calling from one of several homes he owned on the west coast of Mexico. It was from there he ran the infamous Sinaloa cartel, the one that the US government had described as the most powerful drug trafficking organisation in the world.

Cruz himself had approached Slack just over a year ago and offered to supply the firm with cocaine, crystal meth and heroin at a discount. He'd promised to undercut all other suppliers because they were eager to break into all the European markets. So far the guy had been true to his word and they'd both done well out of it.

'So does this relate to the conversation we had yesterday, Carlos?' Slack asked.

'Indeed it does, my friend. You have helped me, and so now I am prepared to help you. But this is still a business arrangement and the sum of money you have offered needs to be increased from two million dollars to three million. And that is non-negotiable. For that price the trigger will stay with you for up to two weeks. If you want to extend the contract it will cost more.'

Slack didn't balk at the figure. In fact he'd been prepared to pay a lot more. After all this was a job that required expertise and experience, and since the world's most experienced killers for hire were in Mexico it seemed like a sensible move.

'Your price is acceptable,' Slack said. 'But don't let me down, Carlos. If your operative doesn't live up to my expectations then it could be very damaging to our relationship.'

'Have no fear, my friend,' Carlos said. 'I have chosen well. The person I'm sending has been working exclusively for the cartel for about eight years, and in that time has carried out over fifty hits on our behalf.'

'That's mightily impressive,' Slack said.

'I'm glad you think so. You'll need to make all the arrangements at your end including accommodation, transport and weapons.'

'I'll sort it. So how soon can your man be here?'

'Late tomorrow should be possible.'

'Then I'll have him picked up at the airport.'

'That's great, but there's one thing you need to be aware of.'

'What's that?'

'The person whose services you are acquiring is a woman, not a man. She's the best in the business and goes by the name of Rosa Lopez, but the Mexican media have labelled her *La Asesina*, which in English means *The Slayer*.'

7

Rosa

Acapulco used to be one of Mexico's most popular tourist destinations, with its spectacular beaches and bustling nightlife.

Its heyday was in the 50s and 60s when it epitomised tropical glamour and became a playground for the rich and famous.

But over the last decade or so the glitter had turned to blood and it had become one of the most violent towns on the planet.

Rosa Lopez reflected on this as she prepared to leave her hotel room overlooking the bay.

She'd first come here twenty-two years ago when she was just six. It was the last vacation she ever had with her parents before they were slaughtered in their sleep.

The memories hadn't faded, and she still remembered how busy the beaches were then and how rare it was to see police officers on the streets. These days the beaches were often empty and the tourist areas were patrolled by heavily armed cops and soldiers.

But heightened levels of security had failed to stop the drug cartels from fighting each other for control of the smuggling routes along the Guerrero coast.

And it was this conflict that had brought Rosa back to the Pacific town.

She had arrived earlier by plane from Mexico City, and after checking in she'd had time for a short nap and a hot eucalyptus bubble bath.

Now she was ready to go to work. But before leaving the room she checked herself in the full-length mirror and nodded approvingly.

She was dressed to kill and that was deliberate because after the job was done she planned to visit one of the town's famous nightclubs.

She was wearing her tightest designer jeans, faded and low-slung on the hips, and a V-neck T-shirt that revealed most of her ample cleavage.

Her lipstick was garishly red and her hair hung loose about her shoulders.

Her aim, as always, was to stand out from the crowd, which required a degree of effort in venues that were loud and dark and filled with pussy.

Killing always made her juices flow and she had no intention of spending the night alone. She'd discovered long ago that the best way to wind down and relax was to have sex with a beautiful stranger.

'Time to hit the town,' she said to herself, as she draped a little red purse over her shoulder.

A few minutes later she was walking through the hotel's luxurious reception area to the sound of *Going Loco Down in Acapulco* by the Four Tops. It made her smile because it had been her father's favourite song and he'd played it constantly at their home in Culiacan. It was one of the reasons he'd been so keen to visit the place.

As previously arranged there was a car waiting for her in front of the hotel, the driver standing next to it, waiting to open the door for her. He was tall and dark-skinned, and wearing a black shirt over jeans. He introduced himself as Miguel.

The only thing she knew about him was that, like her, he worked for the Sinaloa cartel. Carlos Cruz, their boss, had given her his number and she'd called him from the hotel.

His face broke into a wide grin as she approached.

'I have heard many things about you, Miss Lopez,' he said in Spanish as his eyes gave her the once-over. 'And I can see that the tales of your beauty were not exaggerated.'

She got this a lot from the men she encountered and it used to drive her crazy. Now she just ignored it.

'There's no time for small talk,' she said sharply. 'Just get me to where we're going.'

His smile vanished and he quickly opened the rear door for her to climb inside.

As soon as they were on the move, she said, 'So tell me what I need to know.'

She already knew that there were two targets and they were top lieutenants in the Los Zetas cartel, which had been at war with the Sinaloa cartel for some time.

Carlos wanted them taken out because a month ago they had given the order for a local politician and his entire family to be murdered. The man, his wife and their two teenage daughters had had their throats cut and were then beheaded. Video footage of it happening had been then posted on the Internet.

'The pair have been under surveillance throughout the day,' Miguel said. 'They are now at a restaurant on Avenue Escencia. The place is busy and the two are sitting next to a window with a view of the ocean.'

50

Rosa had seen photographs of the two men and had committed their faces to memory. They were both in their early thirties and were known as a pair of brutal enforcers whose speciality was torture.

'Is there anyone looking out for them?' she asked.

He nodded. 'There's one minder. A few minutes ago he was sitting on a wall to the left of the entrance. He's wearing a dark suit and if he moves I'll be informed.'

Rosa was impressed. It was always good to know well in advance what to expect.

'I'm taking you to a side road a few hundred yards from the restaurant,' Miguel said. 'We'll be there in about ten minutes. It's where the motorcycle you requested has been parked. Everything else you asked for is in the trunk.'

'Sounds good,' Rosa said, looking at her watch. 'With luck it'll all be over within half an hour.'

Rosa was driven to a narrow, unlit road that looked as though it was rarely used. There were no properties nearby, and the darkness was oppressive, as though it carried weight.

A motorcycle was resting up against a hedge. It was an old Honda Cargo 150 and the engine was still warm. Rosa had been riding motorbikes for years and she was familiar with the controls.

Miguel handed her the key and said, 'It was picked up earlier today and is in a very good condition.'

From the trunk of his car he took out a helmet, a one-piece leather motorcycle suit, gloves, and a small rucksack containing a Glock 19 machine pistol and a commando knife.

Rosa slipped into the suit and heaved the rucksack onto her back.

Miguel then told her how to get to the restaurant and she mounted the bike.

'I wish you luck, Miss Lopez,' he said. 'But I am sure that you won't need it.'

The restaurant was set back from the main road and was clearly a popular establishment. The lighting inside was subdued and there was a parking area in front with about a dozen cars.

Rosa spotted the bodyguard straight away. He was sitting on a low wall smoking a cigarette and he was the only person in sight.

She brought the bike to a halt against the kerb just a couple of yards away from him.

He stood up stiffly to attention as she dismounted. She'd already removed the commando knife from the rucksack and with her back to the guy she unzipped her suit top and reached for it with her gloved hand.

She then used the element of surprise to her advantage by whirling around and rushing at him.

Before he could react she plunged the knife deep into his stomach with a fierce upward thrust.

His eyes ballooned in their sockets and he staggered backwards, allowing Rosa to withdraw the knife and stab him in the chest. It sent him sprawling over the wall and onto a patch of grass where his body convulsed in a death shudder.

She then threw the knife onto the ground next to him and took the pistol from the rucksack, which she simply discarded.

Without a moment's hesitation she burst into the restaurant. It was about half full and there was soft music playing in the background.

Heads turned towards her as she strode across the room with her pistol arm raised. But she stayed focused on the two men at the far table next to the window.

As soon as they realised what was happening, they both jumped to their feet, which made it less likely that Rosa would miss them.

She took aim and let loose with the machine pistol. Amid screams all around her she watched as the bullets tore into her victims, spraying blood over the window and the white tablecloth between them.

Both men hit the floor like bags of cement and she shot them several more times for good measure.

Then she turned around and fired a few more rounds into the ceiling so that none of the customers or staff would be tempted to approach her.

But she needn't have worried because those who hadn't already dashed out of the restaurant were cowering under the tables.

Outside, she dropped the gun, mounted the bike, and with a screech of rubber she made her escape.

It was another job well done and she was pleased with herself.

Five minutes later she was back in the car, having removed the helmet and leather suit.

She told Miguel that it had gone without a hitch and that the two Los Zetas enforcers were dead.

'Carlos will be pleased,' he said. 'You did well. Now I will take you back to your hotel.'

'I'm not going back yet,' she said. 'I want you to drop me off at a nightclub that you know will be lively tonight. I need to wind down.'

His response to this was to laugh.

'You are a strange one, Miss Lopez. I've never known anyone to want to party straight after committing murder.'

Rosa ignored him and looked out the window. She didn't need someone to tell her that she was strange. After all, anyone who made a living killing people could not, by any stretch of the imagination, be right in the head.

But it was OK because she was happy with herself and life was good. She was never troubled by the constraints of a conscience or the burden of a moral compass. It made everything so much easier.

When she was detained in a juvenile detention centre after her first murder she saw three counsellors and they all agreed that her traumatic childhood was to blame for her damaged soul – as if that hadn't always been strikingly obvious.

'There's a nightclub I can recommend,' Miguel said. 'It's always busy, especially in the run-up to Christmas.'

'Then take me there,' she said.

On the way she phoned Carlos as arranged.

'It's done,' she said. 'You'll have no more trouble from those two.'

'You are a star, Rosa,' he said. 'I knew I could trust you not to let me down.'

'I'll stay over tonight and head back in the morning.'

'Well, actually there's been a change of plan,' he said. 'You've got a new assignment. It's in London of all places and there's a big bonus in it for you.'

'How big?'

'Half a million dollars.'

'That's a lot of money, Carlos.'

'This job is special, Rosa. And you could be there for a while.'

After he'd filled her in, she said, 'I've always wanted to go to London. When do they want me there?'

'Tomorrow. So you'll need to get moving. We have a private jet on standby at Acapulco airport. Flight time to Mexico City is just over an hour. There's a British Airways flight to London at eleven ten. A first class ticket's been reserved. Think you can make it?'

'Of course.'

'Good. Then buy whatever you need at the airport or when you get there.'

Rosa's job for the cartel involved a lot of travel, usually within Mexico and the States. But in recent years she'd also had assignments in Canada, Columbia and Brazil. This would be her first trip to Europe and there was no way she was going to turn it down.

'Call me when you're in Mexico City and I'll give you more details,' Cruz said.

After hanging up she told Miguel that she'd be going back to the hotel after all, but only to pack. She then wanted him to take her to the airport. A late night was now out of the question. She was disappointed, for sure, but that was the nature of the game she was in. Business always had to come before pleasure.

8

Laura

I felt pretty good the next morning, so I was glad I hadn't drunk too much the night before.

It was another cold day and the sky over London was a nauseous grey.

Aidan and I left the house together before heading in different directions. On the way to the tube station I popped into Sainsbury's to get a card to mark the birth of Dave Prentiss's baby. While there I noticed that Harry Fuller's jail sentence featured on the front pages of most of the newspapers. The headlines made for pleasant reading:

London gangster gets 30 years
End of the road for Mr Big
Crime boss set to die in prison

I bought a copy of the *Mail*, which devoted two inside pages to the story. There was a detailed account of what was said in court, plus quotes from various people, including DCS Drummond, the Met Commissioner and the Mayor of London.

There were also a couple of sidebar articles. One, written by the paper's chief crime reporter, summarised Fuller's criminal career and outlined the extent of his nefarious activities.

The other focused on the task force and our previous successes investigating Paul Mason and the Severin brothers. It also made a carefully worded reference to our next target and threw caution to the wind by naming him.

We understand the task force will now investigate several other high-profile individuals who've been linked to organised crime. Among them is businessman Roy Slack who runs a number of clubs, restaurants and import companies across London. He has always denied any involvement in criminal activities but has been interviewed by police on a number of occasions. Most recently he was questioned about the disappearance of firearms officer Hugh Wallis, who shot and killed a man during a raid several months ago. The man, Terry Malone, was a known criminal and was employed by Mr Slack . . .

It was all positive publicity for us, I thought, and it was sure to make Slack and his people nervous.

I wondered what extra precautions he'd be taking to protect himself and his businesses. Or would he believe that he was powerful enough and savvy enough to ride it out?

After all, he'd managed to get away with it for so long. Year after year the Met had tried and failed to breach his defences. So maybe he'd actually come to believe that he was invincible.

The thought of it made me smile because it brought to mind another famous gangster who reckoned he was too smart for the forces of law and order.

His name was Al Capone, and he ended up in America's notorious Alcatraz prison.

I was among the last of the team to arrive at the office because of delays on the Northern Line. But the morning briefing was still a way off so it wasn't a problem.

Some of the detectives were nursing hangovers, including Tony Marsden and Janet Dean. Marsden was sallow-faced and unshaven, and his tie hung at his throat in a loose knot.

Janet, on the other hand, was smartly dressed in a dark blue suit that seemed sober to the point of austere. But the heavy make-up failed to conceal the dark crescents under her tired eyes.

By contrast Dave Prentiss was positively glowing. He was an affable, portly guy with a smile that produced deep creases around his eyes. His desk was already covered in baby cards and I gave him mine.

'Congratulations, Dave,' I said, kissing his cheek. 'Have you named him yet?'

'We have. He's Josh.'

'Good choice. And how's Karen?'

'She's great. She'll be coming home tomorrow.'

'I'm surprised you've come in.'

'Well, I'd rather be here than sitting at home. I'm taking next week off to help Karen out and get to know the little one.'

Baby talk always reminded me that my own biological clock was ticking away. It was an issue I tried not to think about too often because it made me anxious and confused.

The fact was Aidan and I had been trying for a baby for six months and I hadn't yet conceived, which was troubling. So far we hadn't told our parents we were trying because we wanted it to be a surprise when it did happen, along with the announcement of our wedding plans.

We were both of the view that it was easier to pretend that we had no plans in place to start a family and get married anytime soon. That way we wouldn't come under intense pressure, especially from my mother, who was desperate for a grandchild.

Prentiss held up his phone to show me a photo of the baby a few hours after the birth.

'He's gorgeous,' I said and couldn't help feeling a little broody.

Drummond chose that moment to clap his hands in order to get everyone's attention, and it came as a welcome distraction.

He stood at one end of the large, open-plan office between two whiteboards. Pinned to the boards were various photos and documents relating to Roy Slack and his organisation.

The photos were of Slack and some of his henchmen, including Danny Carver, Frank Piper and Terry Malone, the man killed when police raided his home in Lambeth. There was also a picture of Hugh Wallis, the missing firearms officer who shot Malone.

The documents contained snippets of information that had already been gathered, including biographical notes and a breakdown of the legitimate businesses that were in Slack's name and through which he laundered money.

The impression given in the media was that we were starting this investigation from scratch. But that wasn't so. A small group of detectives and support staff had been working on it for months while the rest of us concentrated on the Harry Fuller case.

Drummond began the briefing with another verbal pat on the back for us all.

'I've just come from a meeting with the Commissioner,' he said. 'He wants you all to know that you're doing a cracking job. But now we have to work even harder to keep up the momentum.'

In some ways Drummond reminded me of my father. There was an aura about him, a sense of control and power that inspired confidence and loyalty among his staff.

'This scumbag is our next target,' he said, pointing to a picture of Roy Slack. 'Our mission won't be complete until he's banged up and his organisation lies in ruins. But it's not going to be a pushover. We estimate that Slack has over a hundred people working for him full time and he's therefore able to distance himself from the day-to-day stuff.

'Also, there's still a hell of a lot we don't know about his operations. With the others we were able to gather a fair amount of intelligence. We had someone undercover in Paul Mason's outfit and we managed to turn two of Fuller's guys so they fed us inside information.

'But so far all attempts to infiltrate Slack's mob have failed because anyone even suspected of doing the dirty either disappears or turns up dead.'

Drummond then went on to outline our approach to the investigation. He talked enthusiastically about tactics and strategy and read out a list of priorities. He took questions and invited us to put forward constructive ideas.

It turned into one of those meetings that draws everyone together, and the longer it went on the more excited everyone became. We were all eager to get on with the job, to use all the skills and resources to depose another crime lord.

There was a look of determination on the faces of the officers around me. I was aware of a restless energy that was almost palpable. Everyone was feeling optimistic about the case and the mood in the room was buoyant.

But then suddenly something weird happened and it changed everything in the blink of an eye.

The mobile phones of every detective in the room pinged or vibrated at the same time, signalling an incoming text message.

I'd never known it to happen before and it took us all by surprise. Even Drummond stopped speaking mid-sentence and a frown creased his brow.

Kate Chappell, who was standing next to me, was the first to open up the message and read it because she'd been holding her phone in her hand.

And judging by the look on her face I knew it was something serious.

The message did indeed contain a serious threat, and it sent a ripple of unease around the room.

I read it through twice and felt an icy knot form in my stomach.

Kate Chappell was the first to react, her voice tight with stress. 'This has to be someone's idea of a sick joke,' she said.

Drummond was the next to speak, and it sounded like he was struggling to keep his composure. His face was firm and stoic, but his eyes were dull with shock.

'First I need to know who among you has received this text,' he said. 'So would those who have please raise your hands?'

There were fifteen detectives in the room and five support staff. Only the detectives put up their hands.

Drummond twisted his lips in thought and shook his head.

'Now there's no need for anyone to panic,' he said. 'My gut tells me that DS Chappell is right and that this is a nasty, pointless prank. Hopefully it won't take us long to confirm that once the techies find out who the sender is.'

But I for one wasn't reassured by his words. It was an anonymous text and whoever had sent it would have covered his or her tracks. Plus, I didn't feel that the threat contained in the text could be dismissed so easily.

I read it again as the air around me began to oscillate with tension:

I demand that the organised crime task force be disbanded. I know that Scotland Yard chiefs will ignore me so I'm calling on you and all the other detectives attached to the unit to step back from it. Those of you who refuse will suffer the consequences and either you or those close to you, including family members, will be killed. You are advised to take this seriously. Do not make the mistake of treating it as an empty threat.

Most of us tried to reply to the text but we all got the same message back – that the recipient could not be contacted.

The message threw up a ton of questions, and not just the obvious one of whether we should take it seriously. If it wasn't a prank then was it conceivable that the threat would actually be carried out? Would this person really go so far as to launch a murderous campaign against a team of police officers and their families?

It was the stuff of nightmares, but in the age of rampant terrorism it wouldn't come as such a massive shock if it did happen. London was already on high alert following ISIS-inspired attacks on coppers in the streets.

But this had nothing to do with terrorists. I was sure of that. And so too was Tony Marsden.

'I reckon this is the work of some villain who wants to put the frighteners on us,' he said, loud enough for everyone to hear. 'And the main suspect has to be Roy fucking Slack.'

'Let's not jump the gun,' Drummond said. 'Anyone could have sent it.'

'But surely it must be someone with a vested interest, guv,' Marsden persisted. 'And the timing of it points to him.'

'Tony's right, sir,' Dave Prentiss said. 'It's just the kind of thing the bugger would do to stir things up. He's desperate to throw us off track, if only to give him time to come up with ways to keep us from bringing him down.'

A thought occurred to me and I said, 'What worries me is that whoever sent this has all of our personal phone numbers. Now that can only mean one of two things – the personnel files have been hacked or someone leaked them.'

It was suddenly obvious to everyone that even if this did turn out to be a prank, it still gave serious cause for concern.

'I need to refer this upstairs to the Commissioner,' Drummond said. 'In the meantime I don't want anyone outside this office to learn about this. That includes families and friends. And call those detectives who aren't here to find out if they've also received this message.'

He told us to crack on with our jobs as though nothing had changed. But that was wishful thinking on his part. Everything had changed and it was impossible to concentrate on anything other than the words contained in the message.

. . . those of you who refuse will suffer the consequences and either you or those close to you, including family members, will be killed . . .

9

Slack

So the die was cast, and Roy Slack wondered how long it would be before the cops came knocking on his door.

He was sure to be their prime suspect, but since there was no hard evidence linking him to the message all he had to do was deny knowing anything about it.

Before sending the text, Danny had asked him if he was sure it was the road he wanted to go down.

'I've never been so sure of anything in my life,' he'd told him. 'The bastards have got this coming. And it won't be enough to kill a couple of detectives. I want to put the Met itself on the spot. I want the world to see what a useless bunch of tossers they really are. And this is the only way I can think of doing that in the time I have left.'

That conversation had taken place an hour ago. Now Slack and his eight top lieutenants were sat around the long table in the conference room above the pub in Rotherhithe. These were the men who effectively ran his businesses. They carried out his orders and were paid handsomely for their loyalty. There was a hierarchy of sorts and even an organisational chart.

Danny Carver was second-in-command and had a roving remit. The others oversaw different parts of the operation. Frank Piper took care of the drugs. Billy Lightfoot was in charge of the clubs and restaurants. Adam Clarke ran the brothels and protection rackets. Clive Miller looked after the warehouses – and so on.

Below them was a small army of enforcers, bean counters, lawyers, bent coppers and a bevy of corrupt local authority officials.

Slack kicked off the meeting by telling them what they already knew – that they were now in the Old Bill's line of fire.

Frank Piper voiced the concerns of all of them when he said, 'After what's happened to Fuller and the others we're all worried, boss. The bastards are really gonna put the squeeze on us.'

Slack leaned forward, elbows on the table, and a spark of irritation flashed in his eyes.

'There's no need to get your bollocks in a twist, Frank,' he said. 'We've known for a while that this was coming and we've already put some measures in place to protect ourselves. You guys just have to keep your nerve and avoid making any stupid mistakes.'

He wasn't going to tell Piper and the others what he planned to do and why. It'd serve no useful purpose. Unlike Danny they wouldn't understand and they couldn't be trusted not to turn against him when the killings began and the pressure really stacked up.

He didn't care if they refused to believe that he wasn't responsible. All he cared about now was using this opportunity to go out with a bang, and to punish the Old Bill for what they had done to him.

It was why he was willing to shell out three million dollars to a Mexican drugs baron in order to get the job done.

Throughout his life he'd been in conflict with the police. He blamed them for what happened to his Julie and the last straw came when they killed Terry Malone.

It was the reason he hated them with every fibre of his being. And why he wanted to settle the score before it was too late.

Slack did not like having to lie to his crew, but he felt he had to. If he told them the truth then they'd go into panic mode and start deserting the firm like it was a sinking ship.

In time that wouldn't matter, but he didn't want to give the Old Bill the satisfaction of seeing his empire fall apart too early in the game.

Danny Carver played his part in reassuring the others that the firm would be able to weather the storm that was coming. He put on an act that was worthy of an Oscar, inspired in part by the £500k that had been transferred earlier into his offshore bank account, and the promise that another £500k would be sent in a week's time.

Danny was a realist, after all. He could see that events had conspired to bring about the end of an era.

Slack had filled him in on the conversation he'd had last night with Carlos Cruz and the information he had subsequently gleaned through Google about the Mexican contract killer nicknamed 'The Slayer'.

'Seems like she's the stuff of legend, Danny,' he'd said. 'The media are not even sure she really exists.'

Slack had spent an hour on his laptop and had learned that The Slayer was one of a number of notorious female assassins who were working or had worked for the Mexican cartels.

And from the sound of it they were a right bunch of blood-thirsty crazies. Dubbed *Las Flacas* (The Skinny Ones), they were now commonplace in the major cartels. They were considered ideal *sicarias* (hired killers) because they were young, beautiful, reckless, and attracted less attention than their male counterparts.

One glamorous hit-woman known as Juana made headlines in 2016 when, after being arrested, she confessed to having sex with the beheaded corpses of her victims and to drinking their blood.

Others included *La Güera Loca*, or 'The Crazy Blonde' who had appeared in a video posted online in which she'd beheaded a man with a machete. She was currently one of the most wanted women in Mexico.

And then there was the infamous Maria Lopez, or *La Tosca* – 'The Tough One' – who was caught in 2011 and went on to own up to twenty murders.

'Our girl has more than twice that number of kills to her credit,' Slack had told Danny. 'She calls herself Rosa Lopez, but Cruz says it's not her real name. He says she's the best in the business but he wouldn't tell me anything else about her.'

'I don't think there's anything more you need to know, boss,' Danny had said. 'For the job you want her to do she sounds fucking perfect.'

10

Rosa

While Slack was holding court in Rotherhithe, Rosa Lopez was just over halfway through her flight to London.

She'd managed a few hours' sleep, disturbed as usual by the same recurring dream that took her back to that morning twenty-two years ago when she walked into her parents' bedroom and found them lying on their blood-covered sheets.

She tried to wake them and when she couldn't she just lay on the bed between them, crying and screaming until Mr Torres from next door broke in and discovered the carnage.

The dream was always so chillingly vivid and it served as a constant reminder of the event that changed the course of her life.

She was told later that her mother and father had each been shot twice from close range by an assassin or assassins who almost certainly used a silenced pistol. It was never established how they'd got into the house in the dead of night, but she did find out why.

Her father had been a drugs dealer for a local gang and had been targeted by his own people who accused him of stealing money from them. In order to make an example of him they decided to kill his wife at the same time.

Rosa was adopted by her father's sister Teresa and her husband Enrique. But she hardly knew her aunt and had never met Enrique before the day they came to collect her.

For a while they were kind and considerate and made an effort to make her feel comfortable. But it didn't last long. Teresa had three other older children and Rosa soon got the impression that the family regretted taking her in.

Enrique first came to her bedroom two nights after her seventh birthday. He kissed her on the mouth and touched her between the legs, making her promise not to tell anyone.

The next time, a week later, he made her touch his penis and told her what to do with it.

Soon he was raping her on a regular basis and when she cried he slapped her and pinched her cheeks and threatened to strangle her if she didn't act like she enjoyed it.

It was obvious that her aunt knew about it and chose to turn a blind eye. But then she was also afraid of Enrique because he was a violent, controlling man with a fierce temper.

The abuse carried on for four years, during which time she was farmed out on occasion to Enrique's perverted friends.

Then, just three days before her eleventh birthday, Rosa decided she'd had enough.

They were sitting around the kitchen table eating dinner – Rosa, Enrique, Teresa and their youngest son Pedro.

When Rosa was handed the bread knife and told to slice the loaf, she was gripped by a sudden rage so fierce that it propelled her out of her chair. A second later she was lunging at Enrique and thrusting the knife into his chest.

He fell back on his chair and she went down with him. Before

Teresa and Pedro could pull her off she managed to stab him twice more – in the mouth and in the right eye socket.

Enrique died before the ambulance arrived and Rosa spent the next seven years in juvenile prison where she learned that life is cheap and you have to be strong to survive.

She cultivated friendships with seasoned criminals, especially those with ties to the cartels. And through them she eventually learned the identity of the man who had murdered her parents.

His name was Antonio Garcia and she swore that one day she would get her revenge.

That day came shortly after she was released at the age of eighteen. She tracked Garcia down to a house in Durango and stalked him for several days. He was arriving home late one evening when she decided to strike. She rushed up behind him just as he was opening his front door. She shoved the muzzle of a gun into his back and ordered him to go inside where she quickly rendered him unconscious with a blow to the head.

When he woke up five minutes later he was handcuffed to a chair and that was where he stayed throughout the night while Rosa systematically tortured him.

She forced him to tell her the name of the man who had got him to kill her parents and before he died she cut off his penis and both his ears.

A week later Rosa walked into a bar in Camargo and put three bullets into the head of the gang boss who had ordered the hit on her parents.

After that she was snapped up by the Sinaloa cartel. She helped move drugs, committed robberies and got involved in kidnappings. But it was soon obvious that her real forte lie in killing people. She had a natural aptitude for it, and over time they started calling her The Slayer.

But she didn't mind. In fact she found it rather flattering. And neither did she mind that behind her back she was also described as a psychopath.

It was true, after all. And it was no doubt why she enjoyed doing what she did.

And why she was so looking forward to what lay ahead in London.

11

Laura

The air of enthusiasm that had prevailed at the start of the day quickly evaporated. In its place there grew a stifling sense of foreboding.

The thoughts of everyone on the task force were dominated by the anonymous text message and its chilling warning.

As hard as I tried I just couldn't get it out of my mind. The job we did was often a test of sanity, but I felt that we were now being tested to the limit.

At lunchtime word came back from the experts in the cyber-crime unit that they were unable to trace the source of the message, which was what we'd expected.

Anyone can send an anonymous text or email through apps that can be downloaded from the Internet or websites that offer it as a service.

DCS Drummond also reported back on a brief conversation he'd had with the Commissioner.

'His view is that we shouldn't take it too seriously,' Drummond said. 'It isn't the first time that officers in the Met have received threats of this kind and he's sure that it won't be the last. His advice is to be extra vigilant and at the same time raise the issue with those we interview as part of the investigation into Roy Slack's mob.'

It was true that police officers were often threatened. Early on during the investigation into Harry Fuller, a man called my mobile and left a voice message threatening to rape me if I didn't stop pursuing the gang boss. It gave me a shock, and I was dismayed to discover he'd used a burner phone so he couldn't be traced.

But his threat just did not ring true so I didn't lose any sleep over it.

However, this latest threat was different and far more unusual. It had been sent to a whole team of detectives and to my knowledge that had never happened before. It also referred to our families, and that made it all the more alarming. Was it really possible that Aidan and my own mother were in danger? Did I need to warn them? Or was it best not to scare them since we still couldn't be sure this wasn't just a prank?

Amongst the detectives, Dave Prentiss appeared to be the most affected by it, presumably because he had only just become a father.

When a group of us gathered in the canteen for a sandwich lunch, he told us he'd been searching Google for stories about serious attacks on the police and what he'd found out had clearly worried him.

'I didn't realise there had been so many, especially in the States,' he said.

He mentioned the case of a former soldier who shot five cops dead in Dallas in 2016. The same year gunmen in Mexico's western state of Michoacán shot down a police helicopter, killing the pilot and three officers. And as recently as February 2017, a plot was uncovered to assassinate eight officers with the Pecos Valley Drug Task Force in the US state of New Mexico.

'This is scary stuff,' Prentiss said. 'It's as though nutters everywhere have declared open season on us.'

It might have been an exaggeration, but Prentiss did have a point. There had never been a time when coppers had felt so vulnerable. That was why the debate as to whether all officers in the UK should carry weapons was heating up again.

I had always been opposed to it, along with the majority of my colleagues in the Met, but in view of this new threat I began to wonder if I'd feel safer with a gun strapped to my waistband.

The afternoon was spent getting our act together and deciding who would do what in the weeks ahead. But it was difficult to focus because of the threat.

My thoughts kept turning to Aidan and my mother and I succumbed to the urge to text them both to make sure they were all right. Aidan replied with, 'Why wouldn't I be?' But I didn't respond for fear of making him suspicious.

Get a grip, I told myself. Aidan and Mum are OK. They're safe. So stop worrying about them and get on with the job.

We needed to familiarise ourselves with the various files on the system relating to Roy Slack's firm.

While we'd been tied up with the Harry Fuller case most of the information had been updated. Surveillance reports and financial records had been added, along with more photos and notes on members of Slack's inner circle.

Needless to say no new evidence linking Slack to any criminal activities had emerged. But then he hadn't been subjected to the kind of scrutiny and pressure that we were about to apply.

I spent the best part of an hour studying everything we had on Slack, and making copious notes along the way.

Included in the paperwork was the interview that was conducted just under a week ago following the disappearance of firearms officer Hugh Wallis who shot and killed Slack's employee Terry Malone.

Slack, accompanied by one of his high-flying lawyers, presented the officers with a cast-iron alibi for the period when Wallis vanished. He insisted he had not asked his people to seek out the identity of the firearms officer after the shooting and claimed Malone had been employed as a bouncer with the security company he ran.

He was asked why Malone had a shotgun and drugs in his house, to which he replied, 'You should ask him that question. Oh, but you can't, can you, because you murdered the poor bugger and at the same time killed his unborn baby.'

What had happened that night was indeed unfortunate and it was questionable as to whether Wallis had made the right call. But the inquiry into the incident had given him the benefit of the doubt.

However, the manner of Malone's death might well have prompted someone to seek revenge against Wallis. And since Malone had no living relatives, suspicion had fallen on Slack.

But if he had arranged for Wallis to be kidnapped and killed, then I was sure we would never be able to prove it.

The story was always the same with Roy Slack. He managed to avoid any link between himself and the dirty deeds carried out on his behalf.

I had never interviewed or questioned the man myself but those who had had generally formed similar opinions of him. He was smart, they said, and paranoid. And he treated all police officers with utter contempt.

The profile we'd been building also included descriptions provided by underworld figures who had dared to tell us what they knew about him.

Certain words cropped up repeatedly. They were: *cruel*, *brutal*, *heartless*, *tyrannical* and *vicious*.

Reading back through all the stuff we had on the guy, I found myself hoping to God that he wasn't the person who had sent the text. Because if it was him then I feared that there was a good chance it wasn't just an empty threat.

12

Slack

Everything was in hand for Rosa Lopez's arrival. The plane was due to touch down at Heathrow just after four o'clock and Danny was going to pick her up.

He would then drive her to the hotel she'd been booked into before taking her to the pub where Slack would meet her. There she'd be given a detailed briefing and the equipment that she'd requested via Carlos Cruz, which included weapons.

Before then Slack had some business to attend to in Dulwich. It was something he'd been putting off for a week because he'd had other things to deal with. But now seemed like a good time to get it done, since he had to go out anyway in order to rendezvous with The Slayer.

Before leaving the building he had lunch in the pub's restaurant with some of the lads. After a few wines and beers with their steaks, they were more willing to express their fears about what was happening.

'Most of my days are now spent making sure the plods are not watching or listening to me,' Frank Piper said. 'I know that a couple of Harry Fuller's guys came unstuck because they didn't know that the task force had placed bugs in their homes and tracking devices in their cars.'

'They were fucking careless,' Danny Carver said. 'It's not that hard to stop the snooping if you know how to.'

'And we do know how to,' Slack said. 'That's why they've struggled to get close to us.'

But he could see that whatever he told Piper and the others it was not going to ease their anxiety. So after a while he gave up trying and focused on his meal.

At three o'clock he told Mike Walker to bring the car around the front.

'We're going to the house in Park Crescent,' he said. 'And you need to make bloody sure we're not followed.'

It's only about six miles from Rotherhithe to Dulwich, but the route Mike took to get there added two miles to the journey.

He used to be a cabbie so he knew the area like the back of his hand. There was no way the Old Bill could have tailed them without being spotted.

Dulwich was one of the more serene parts of South London with a picturesque park and a famous college. It was also a good place to invest in property, which was why Slack had bought the house in Park Crescent a few years ago.

It was one of four the firm owned south of the river and three were being rented out. They'd been purchased through fake companies so they wouldn't fall victim to seizure warrants if ever he was arrested and charged with an offence. The place in Park Crescent was currently occupied by two of his most reliable crew members – Johnny Devonshire and Pat Knowles. He let them live there for free because the place was frequently used for all kinds of activities, including the storage of drugs and stolen goods, clandestine meetings with corrupt coppers and officials, and as a safe house for those who needed to drop out of sight for a while.

It was a detached property close to the hospital, with an integral garage and a small front garden enclosed by high hedges that provided a degree of privacy.

Johnny and Pat were expecting him and, as the car pulled up at the kerb, the front door was opened and they both stepped outside.

They were tall, muscle-bound hard cases, and had worked as a team since sharing a prison cell at the Scrubs some years ago.

Slack told Mike to wait in the car while he got out to shake hands with Johnny and Pat.

'Good to see you, boss,' Pat said. 'We weren't sure you'd ever manage to get here.'

He shrugged. 'It's been hectic guys. Plus, I was playing safe because the Old Bill have been watching me.'

He entered the house and took off his overcoat, which he handed to Johnny.

'Any problems with our lodger?' he asked.

Johnny shook his head. 'None at all. We've been feeding him sleeping pills so he's been as quiet as a mouse.'

'Right. Well after tonight he'll be off your hands.'

Slack walked along the corridor to the door that led to the basement.

'I'll go down and sort him by myself,' he said. 'Do me a favour and put the kettle on. I'm sure I'll fancy a cuppa when I've finished.'

He pulled the door open and stepped inside. The light was already on and as he descended the stairs he felt his pulse quicken.

The basement was large and gloomy and was often packed with

illicit contraband. But now it was virtually empty except for the man who was sitting on a bare mattress with his back to the wall and one hand cuffed to a metal ring secured to the floor.

He was a sinewy guy with a crew cut and a face half covered with stubble. Pale and glassy-eyed, he was wearing a roll-neck sweater and jeans.

There were two blankets next to him on the mattress and the air around him stank of shit.

He opened his mouth to say something, but Slack spoke first as his face morphed into a mask of pure hatred.

'So you're the trigger-happy cunt who murdered both my son and unborn grandchild,' he said.

It was the first time he'd laid eyes on Hugh Wallis since arranging for Danny and a couple of the other lads to snatch him.

That was a week ago, shortly after one of the bent coppers on the firm's payroll had leaked his identity.

He'd been brought here to await his punishment, which Slack had been determined to administer himself.

'Please let me go,' Wallis pleaded, his eyes wide and bloodshot. 'I have a family, for Christ's sake.'

Slack made a sneering shape with his mouth.

'Do you know who I am?' he yelled.

Wallis nodded and a tear streaked down his right cheek.

'You're Roy Slack.'

'That's right. And I'm here to pay you back for killing Terry Malone when there was no need. And you did it only a few hours after I broke the news to him that I was his dad. That can't be allowed to go unpunished.'

Wallis tried to respond, but Slack held up his hand to stop him.

'I don't want to hear what you have to say. This is not a fucking court of law where you get to plead your case. As far as I'm concerned you're as guilty as sin. Terry's girlfriend was there, as you know. She told everyone what happened. But your lot chose to believe you over her and that ain't right.'

Wallis pulled himself up on one knee and started pleading for his life.

Slack responded by stepping forward and saying, 'You should count yourself lucky that you're not being tortured. As much as I'd like to make you suffer I haven't got the time to piss around.'

He thrust his right hand into his trouser pocket and when he pulled it out he was clutching a brass knuckle-duster with spikes.

The fear shone out of the copper's eyes as Slack clenched his jaw and bared his teeth.

'You took my son away from me before I had a chance to get to know him,' he said. 'I had big plans for that boy and you fucked them up. And because you're a copper you thought you'd get away with it. Well, you were wrong.'

The first blow tore a chunk out of Wallis's arm as he raised it to shield his face. He screamed and toppled onto his back.

Slack jumped onto the mattress and started aiming kicks at the man's head. Wallis was too weak to put up a fight. He tried to roll onto his side and bring his legs up against his chest, but he wasn't quick enough.

Slack dropped down heavily on top of him, and sat astride his stomach. And then he let rip with the knuckleduster, his weapon of choice for the past thirty years.

He smashed it against his victim's face, head and throat, tearing flesh and crushing bone and teeth. And he didn't let up for a full two minutes, by which time Wallis was unrecognisable. And he was dead.

He'd made a right mess, though, and there was blood everywhere, including on his hands and shirt. But that wasn't a problem because there was a wardrobe full of spare clobber upstairs.

He dragged himself to his feet and used his hanky to wipe his blood and prints from the knuckle-duster, which he then slipped back in his pocket.

He paused to look down at his victim, or, rather, what was left of him.

'That was for you, Terry my son,' he said. 'The bastard got what he deserved.'

Slack walked back up the stairs where Johnny and Pat were waiting for him in the hallway.

'I'm ready for that tea now,' Slack said.

'Is the guy sorted, boss?' Pat asked him.

Slack nodded, a little breathless. 'It's time to call the clean-up crew. I want the body to disappear, along with every last trace of the cunt.'

13

Laura

There was another briefing at four o'clock. By then our approach to the new investigation was taking shape.

Tasks had been assigned and everyone had been brought up to speed on what intel the Met had on Roy Slack's firm.

There was a lot of hearsay and speculation, along with a list of all the known faces who worked for him. Most of them had criminal records and violent reputations. But what was lacking was hard, incriminating evidence against them and their boss.

There had been some successes over the past few years. Two of the firm's drug dealers had been caught red-handed and sent down, but had refused to say who they were working for. And a major haul of cocaine from Mexico – with a street value of ten million pounds – was intercepted on a ship at Dover. But although we were certain it belonged to Slack and came from his cartel partners, we couldn't prove it.

The London gangs had managed to grow and prosper partly because of the huge cuts imposed by successive governments on police manpower and resources. The Met in particular had often been stretched to breaking point.

But it was a different story now with the task force initiative and the government's determination to get on top of the problem.

The tide had turned in our favour and we were now getting results. Of course there was no way we could ever entirely eliminate organised crime in the capital, but at least we could inflict enormous damage and reassure the public that we were doing our job.

And my job in respect of this new case was to focus on the main man – Roy Slack. It was the same brief I'd had on the last investigation, which was why I'd been one of the two officers sent to arrest Harry Fuller, the other being Martin Weeks.

This time Drummond had teamed me up with Kate Chappell because Martin had since moved over to the National Crime Agency. I was happy with that; Kate too.

'I want you to dig up as much as you can on Slack's private life,' Drummond said to both of us. 'For instance, we know he has at least one mistress. But are there others and can we get anything out of them? And what about his enemies? I'm struck by the fact that in the past so little was done to squeeze them for information. So draw up a list of those you think we should talk to.'

He told us to arrange for surveillance to be stepped up on Slack and his top henchmen.

'We've been watching his flat in Canary Wharf and his office in Rotherhithe,' he said. 'But it hasn't been round-the-clock because we've been short of people. From now on we need to know where he is and what he's up to 24/7.'

'What about the text message and the threat to kill us all?' I said. 'Shouldn't we go and ask him if he knows anything about that?'

Drummond shook his head. 'I don't see the point at this stage. Even if he did arrange for it to be sent he'll only deny it.'

'But we could use it as an excuse to seize his phone and laptop.'

'We had him in under a week ago after Officer Wallis disappeared,' Drummond said. 'As you know he was questioned for several hours and his properties were searched. If we haul him in again this soon without any solid new evidence then his lawyers will go ape-shit. So I think we should hold fire until we have something concrete to confront him with. Besides, the techies are still trying to find out where the message came from and it's only fair to give them more time.'

I wasn't happy with that and I could tell I wasn't the only one. The threat we had all received was still hanging over our heads like a dark cloud – and there seemed no prospect of it going away anytime soon.

On the way home I saw my first Christmas tree. It lit up the window of a charity shop close to the tube station in Balham.

The big day was still three weeks away but the city was already gearing up for it. This year Aidan and I had made plans to spend it with his parents in Spain. The flights were booked and I was really looking forward to it. Usually we stayed home and had my mother round, but she'd made arrangements to spend Christmas with her best friend Sylvia who lived in the New Forest.

Mum had also arranged to come round to our house this evening and I'd completely forgotten. It wasn't until I walked in and saw her sitting at the kitchen table that I remembered.

It was six o'clock and Aidan had already sorted the dinner – cheese-filled jacket potatoes – and he'd even poured me a glass of white wine.

'You forgot I was coming, didn't you?' Mum said as I leaned over to kiss her. 'I could tell from your face.'

'It's your imagination,' I said. 'I've been looking forward to seeing you.'

She grinned and I wondered why I ever bothered lying to her. She could read me like a book.

I took off my coat and gave Aidan a quick cuddle.

'Looks like you've had a tough day,' Mum said. 'Is everything all right?'

I'd decided on the way home to adhere to Drummond's instruction and not to mention the threatening message, at least until the techies had spent more time looking into it. It was best they didn't know. Mum, especially, would be unnerved by it.

'We launched a new investigation this morning,' I said. 'That's always a bit stressful. It means reading lots of files and attending long, drawn-out meetings.'

'Aidan's been telling me about it, and I saw your boss on the news,' Mum said. 'I'm really proud of you, Laura, and I know your father would be too.'

As she spoke I could see the glint of unshed tears in her eyes. The mere mention of my father always provoked an emotional reaction even after all this time. She had never really come to terms with his death and that was why she hadn't been able to move on. She wore grief like a chain around her neck and the weight of it showed on her face.

She was fifty-eight but looked much older. Her eyes, which peered out through thick-rimmed glasses, had lost their sparkle, and her skin was stretched too tight across her bones. It was as though the life had been sucked out of her.

I walked over and gave her another kiss on the forehead.

'It's nice of you to say that, Mum. It means a lot.'

And then I quickly tried to lighten the mood by changing the subject. I told her about Dave Prentiss becoming a father. I knew she'd be interested because she'd met him not so long ago. I'd agreed to go along to the school to give a talk about careers in the police force, but had to pull out at the last minute. Dave had done me a favour by stepping in.

'They've named him Josh,' I said. 'And he's so cute.'

It did the trick. My Mum smiled and said, 'What a coincidence. My neighbour became a grandmother yesterday as well.'

Babies were her favourite subject and she stuck with it as Aidan served up the potatoes. We both waited for the inevitable question and it wasn't long in coming.

'So have you two given any more thought to getting married and starting a family?'

It was always so tempting to tell her the truth, but now wasn't the time to start building her hopes up, especially if, God forbid, I wasn't able to have children.

'I keep telling you, Mum,' I said. 'You'll be the first to know when we do. I promise. We just want to wait for a while and concentrate on our careers. There's no hurry, after all.'

She kept her eyes on me and pointed her fork at Aidan.

'Well, let me tell you, young lady,' she said. 'You've struck gold with this one, and if I was in your shoes I'd tie him down with a wedding ring and children so he can't get away.'

Aidan couldn't help but laugh as he reached across the table and placed a hand over my mother's.

'There's no way I would ever leave your daughter,' he said. 'She's the best darn thing that's ever happened to me.'

Aidan had a knack for saying things that stirred my emotions and made me want to make love to him. And if my mother hadn't been with us I would have dragged him upstairs to the bedroom and done just that.

Instead it was going to have to wait until after he had taken her home.

But as always she was keen to be off as soon as she'd finished dinner.

'Are you sure you don't want a coffee?' I asked her.

She shook her head. 'It's almost seven and you know I like to be in bed by eight during the week. But thank you for a lovely evening.'

'It's been our pleasure,' Aidan said, as he pushed back his chair and stood up.

At that moment his mobile pinged with an incoming text message. It was lying next to me on the table so I picked it up and handed it to him.

While he checked it I started clearing the dishes but then stopped suddenly when I heard him gasp.

'What's wrong?' I said, turning back to him with a plate in each hand.

He looked up, his eyes bulging, his mouth agape.

'What in Christ's name does this mean?' he said and held the phone towards me.

I put the plates down and grabbed the phone. And as I started reading the text every muscle in my body went still.

This morning I sent the following message to every detective on the organised crime task force. Thought you should know.

It was the same message with the same unambiguous threat.

'Is this for real, Laura?' Aidan asked, thrusting his chin towards my mother. 'Are our lives in danger?'

14

Slack

He was on his second pint when Danny called him on his mobile.

'I'm sorry for the delay, boss. The plane got stuck in a holding pattern over the airport for ages. Then we had to contend with the bloody rush hour.'

'Where are you now?'

'I'm just checking her into the hotel. What about you?'

'I'm in the pub. Arrived about half an hour ago.'

'Great. We should be there in ten minutes.'

It was why that particular hotel had been chosen. It needed to be within walking distance of the pub.

'What about the second text message?' Slack said. 'Did it get sent?'

'It did. I had confirmation a few minutes ago.'

The second message had been Danny's idea. He'd come up with it late last night as a way of raising the fear factor even before the killings began. It was sent to those people close to the detectives whose phone numbers they'd been able to obtain.

'Just so you know, boss, I've not had a chance to talk to Jack about the gear,' Danny said.

'Don't worry. He's taken delivery of everything and it's all out the back.'

Jack Pickering was the pub landlord and he worked for Slack who owned the building. There was a yard at the rear with a lock-up garage that the firm made extensive use of. It was the perfect place to store the stuff that Rosa Lopez needed to do her job.

After hanging up, Slack sipped at his beer and looked out the window. The evening rush hour was over, but in this part of Lambeth the roads were still busy.

It had taken them almost an hour to get here from Dulwich – a distance of about four miles. On the way he'd told Mike to drive past the house where Terry Malone had lived and died.

It had made him feel sad and yet pleased with himself at the same time. Sad because of what had happened to Terry and pleased because he'd been able to avenge his untimely death.

He didn't give a toss about that gun-toting copper or his family. The bastard determined his own fate when he shot a defenceless Terry in cold blood.

Just six months ago Slack wouldn't have cared. He'd never met Terry and had no idea that he'd worked for the Romanians in North London before the gang's leaders were snared by the task force.

But then, out of the blue, he got a call from an old girlfriend who was in Guy's Hospital having suffered a severe stroke.

Chloe Malone had begged him to visit her, saying she had something important to tell him. So he'd gone along out of curiosity and she'd revealed that just after they'd split up twenty-six years ago she'd discovered she was pregnant. Eight months later she gave birth to a boy.

'He's your son, Roy,' she'd told him. 'I want you to know now because there have been serious complications and I might have only days to live. And Terry needs someone to look out for him, otherwise he'll end up dead or in jail.'

She'd gone on to say that she didn't tell him about the baby because their relationship had ended badly after he decided to dump her for another woman.

'It would never have worked out,' she'd said. 'You would have wanted the baby but not me. I was sure that you would have made my life a misery or even taken steps to get rid of me.'

To say that he'd been shocked would have been a gross understatement. The revelation had shaken him to the core. He was angry with her even though he knew that what she'd said was true.

Their affair had lasted five months. It was fun but he'd never loved her and when someone better came along he dropped her like a hot brick.

Before he left the hospital she gave him a letter she'd written to Terry in which she disclosed that Slack was his father.

'I'm not going to tell him before I die,' she'd said. 'That wouldn't be fair, if you decide that you want nothing to do with him. But if you do want to be part of his life then show him the letter.'

Three days later she passed away and for weeks afterwards he wasn't sure what to do or whether or not to even believe her.

So he made enquiries, found out that Terry was looking for work, and got the lads to recruit him onto the firm. Then he took steps to secretly obtain samples of his DNA, which confirmed what Chloe had said.

That was when it really hit home that he had a son. The effect on him was profound. Julie had never been able to conceive and he had always wanted a child.

So he came to a decision. He would promote the lad within

the firm and get to know him. And then when he felt the time was right he would drop the bombshell and show him Chloe's letter.

After that he would groom Terry to be his successor. The idea pleased and excited him, and suddenly he had a purpose in life other than making money.

But then something happened that changed everything and that was why he confided in Terry that night in the club.

He gave him the letter from his mother and told him that he wanted him to eventually take charge of the firm. And he told him why his plan had been brought forward.

Naturally the lad reacted as though he'd received a jolt of electricity. But Slack had assured him that he had what it took and that it was meant to be.

'So go home and think about it, son,' he'd said. 'Your mother asked me to look out for you and that's exactly what I plan to do. You and my grandchild will have a bright and prosperous future. And you'll want for nothing.'

They were the last words he said to Terry. Hours later the lad was dead.

Rosa Lopez was not what he was expecting. The eyes of everyone in the saloon bar were drawn towards her as she came in ahead of Danny who held the door open for her.

Slack felt the urge to whistle as she walked towards where he was sitting in an alcove next to the window.

She was disarmingly attractive, with thick, lustrous black hair and naturally olive skin. Her face was smooth and narrow, and she moved with the sinewy grace of a catwalk model.

She had on a smart leather jacket with a fleece lining that looked brand new and probably was. It was open at the front and underneath she was wearing torn jeans and a tight brown sweater.

She was slim but endowed in all the right places, and it struck him that she was so unlike any of the contract killers he had ever come across.

Rosa Lopez was stunning, and he reckoned she probably stood out even among the beautiful *sicarias* in Latin America. He found it strange that someone so young and beautiful could be a sadistic killer. He wondered if she had been born a psychopath or whether events in her life had turned her into one.

As she approached, he held out his hand and introduced himself. She smiled and it lit up her face, but there was something unconvincing about it.

'Welcome to London,' he said. 'I've heard a lot about you.'

'Not too much I hope,' she replied.

She spoke perfect English with only the faintest trace of an accent.

'Please take a seat,' he said. 'Danny will get the drinks in.'

'Just an orange juice for me,' she said, sitting down opposite him without removing her coat. 'I never touch alcohol when I'm on an assignment.'

'Very sensible of you,' Slack said.

As Danny went off to the bar, Slack studied the woman who had come all the way from Mexico. Her eyes were the colour of dark chocolate and there was no emotion in them. In fact they quite unnerved him.

'How was the journey?' he asked.

'Very pleasant. But then it usually is when one travels first class.'

'And is the hotel to your liking?'

She shrugged. 'Not really. It's cheap and cheerful, but that's OK because I understand it was chosen for its location. And anyway I'm not here on vacation.'

'That's true enough,' Slack said. 'And can I take it that your boss made you aware of how unusual this job is?'

'It's not that unusual, Mr Slack. I've taken out plenty of police officers over the years. Once I killed three in a single day and in different locations. I'm not in the least bit intimidated by the scale of this assignment.'

Slack was impressed. He could see now why Carlos Cruz had sent her and why she was so highly rated. She had the one essential attribute of all successful contract killers; she was not troubled by the conventional standards of morality.

Danny came back to the table with their drinks and Slack was struck by a jarring thought. To the other customers they no doubt looked like normal people, friends enjoying an evening out. But in reality they were the opposite of normal. Between them they had carried out scores of abhorrent crimes and were planning to commit many more.

Rosa suggested they steer clear of small talk and get straight down to business. So Slack told her about the organised crime task force and the text messages that had been sent to the detectives and their immediate family members.

Rosa raised her brow. 'And do you really think that killing some detectives will stop the rest of them coming after you?'

He grinned. 'Not at all. But that's not why I'm doing it. This is just the opening salvo in a war I've declared against London's police. I want to start by making them think it's just about the task force. That'll confuse and unsettle them before the real fun begins.'

At this point he took a mobile phone and a buff-coloured envelope from his pocket and handed them to her.

'It's an unregistered phone and you can use it to contact me and Danny,' he said. 'Our numbers have been programmed in and we have your number. The envelope contains the list of targets. Names, addresses and contact details of the detectives and their loved ones. There's also a link to a website on which we've uploaded photographs of all the officers and many of the family members.'

'Where did the information come from?' Rosa asked.

'There's someone on the task force who's working for us.'

Rosa picked up the envelope, folded it and slipped it into the inside pocket of her jacket along with the phone.

'The stuff you requested is in the lock-up garage at the rear of these premises,' he said. 'It's in a secure position and you'll be given a key to access it when you need to. When you've finished your drink we'll show it to you. Now have you got any questions?'

She drank some of her juice, then wet her upper lip with her tongue.

'I've got two questions,' she said. 'I'd like to know how long you expect me to stay and how many people you want me to kill.'

Slack leaned towards her. 'Under the deal with your boss I have you for two weeks. I'd like you to carry out the hits at a rate of one a day, although I do appreciate that it might not be possible. And, if I'm not otherwise disposed, I might well ask Cruz to extend the contract. It all depends how much fun I'm having.'

The garage behind the pub was set back from the road. Danny unlocked it and raised the door, and Slack and Rosa followed him inside.

In front of them was a motorbike with leathers and a helmet on the seat. Saddlebags were attached either side of the seat.

'We were told only that you wanted two wheels,' Danny said. 'Is this thing OK?'

She looked it over and nodded. 'It looks perfectly fine.'

'Good. There's a bunch of fake stick-on number plates in the left-side saddlebag. Change them as often as you need to avoid street traffic cameras.'

On the table to the right of it there was an iPad, a takedown sniper rifle in an open briefcase, a pistol with silencer attached, a large knife, a garrotte with plastic handles, and five mobile phones.

'These are all burner phones so you can dump them after you use them,' Slack said. 'It means you don't have to use the phone I've already given you. The iPad has been set up so you're ready to go online.'

Rosa stepped forward and ran her hands over the weapons.

'You've been very thorough,' she said.

'That's because like you we're pros,' Slack told her.

Danny then handed her the key to the garage. It was attached to a plastic keyring that enclosed a photo of the pub's exterior and the words: *Three Crowns, Vauxhall*. They then stepped outside, and Rosa locked up.

'Would you like another drink?' Slack asked her.

She shook her head. 'No, thank you. I need to go back to the hotel to start planning. And since this is my first time in London I have to get my bearings.'

'Well, if there's anything else you need you only have to ask.'

'There is something I need to know,' she said. 'Do you want to be the one who decides who I target and when? Or are you leaving that to me?'

'That's your call, Rosa,' he said. 'You have the names and plenty of information on all of them. The only thing I ask is that you don't hang around.'

'No problem,' she said. 'All being well I'll start tomorrow.'

15

Laura

'I can't believe you weren't going to tell me about this threat,' Aidan said, and the words hissed through his teeth. 'I had a right to know and so did your mum.'

It was an hour since Aidan had opened up the message and still the atmosphere in our house was taut with tension.

Aidan was angry as well as shocked and my mother was a bag of nerves. Her reaction was completely understandable because the same message had been sent to her mobile, which had been on silent mode in her handbag. She discovered it only after I asked her to check the phone.

To make matters worse I'd received calls from two colleagues informing me that their family members had also received the message.

'I didn't want to worry you,' I said lamely. 'And the gaffer ordered us not to tell anyone about it.'

'But I'm not anyone, Laura,' Aidan said. 'I'm your partner and I have a right to know if my life is being threatened.'

'But we can't be sure it's not just some vile prank,' I said. 'We therefore have to be careful not to create unnecessary alarm.'

'So you and your colleagues decided that the best course of action was to keep quiet and ignore it.'

'No, not at all. It's being looked into to determine whether it's a credible threat.'

'And while you do that you think it's all right to leave us in the dark. Is that it?'

I didn't answer, just stood there in the middle of the kitchen, the breath trapped in my lungs.

'Well, whoever is behind it obviously knew that you wouldn't tell us,' he went on. 'And the fact that they have our private numbers suggests to me that this is not the work of some harmless prankster.'

I couldn't disagree with him on that point so I didn't try.

'I'm really sorry I didn't tell you about it,' I said, looking from Aidan to my mother who was still sitting at the table twirling a hanky between her fingers. 'I wish now that I had.'

'So what should we do?' my mother said, her voice cracking with emotion. 'Is it going to be safe for us to carry on as normal?'

'Of course it is, Mum,' I said. 'Lots of people make threats and most times that's all they turn out to be.'

My father's face pushed itself into my thoughts suddenly and I wished he was here with us now. He'd know how best to handle the situation, how to respond to the genuine fears being expressed by my mother and Aidan.

It was difficult for me because I was just as worried as they were, and just as creeped out by what was happening.

Aidan had already asked me who we thought was responsible and I'd told him we had no idea. Now he jumped to his own conclusion.

'That man Roy Slack must be behind this,' he said. 'It stands to reason. The task force has made it known it intends to smash up his empire. So he's resorting to desperate measures to stop it.'

'We can't be sure it's him,' I said.

'Well, has he been arrested or even questioned? And if not, then why not?'

I should have been able to reassure them that they had nothing to worry about but I couldn't. Instead I was as anxious as they were and a knot of dread was growing in my stomach.

I feared that this might well be the start of something bad . . . something that we wouldn't be able to control.

16

Laura

When the alarm went off I was already awake, and had been for most of the night.

Aidan stirred and groaned beside me, and as per our morning routine neither of us moved much for about five minutes.

Then, without saying a word, I hauled myself out of bed and into the en suite. That was his cue to get up and go downstairs to make the teas.

Under the hot shower I reflected on the previous evening and how awkward it had been.

My mother had stayed until nine o'clock – well past her bedtime – and would probably have slept in the spare room if she'd had a change of clothes.

The anonymous message had really upset her and she had convinced herself that she was about to become the victim of a crazed killer. Aidan had worked with me to try to allay her fears but she'd kept shaking her head and insisting that we couldn't possibly know what was going to happen.

And she was right, which was why the situation was so worrying.

Aidan's anger had gradually subsided during the course of the evening, and when he returned from taking Mum home, he opened a fresh bottle of wine, filled two glasses, and got me to sit next to him on the sofa.

'Your mum's not here now so it's time to be brutally honest with me, Laura,' he'd said. 'I want to know how concerned we should be about this threat, given that your team are going after some of the city's most powerful criminals.'

So I'd told him what I honestly believed – that this was now a threat that had to be taken very seriously, and I was pretty sure my superiors would agree with me.

We'd talked about it until after midnight, and I'd been wide awake when we'd finally climbed into bed.

Aidan had dropped off fairly quickly, but for me it wasn't so easy. I was too rattled and the adrenalin continued to pump through my veins at a rate of knots.

So now I was tired as well as anxious, and that was no way to start a new day.

Our mornings were always a rush so we didn't have time for another conversation about the death threat. But Aidan made me promise to call or text him if there were any significant developments during the day.

Before we parted we hugged each other and it was longer and tighter than usual.

'Stay safe, sweetheart,' he said, and his words sent a shudder along my spine.

That was probably the moment when I fully realised just how unsettled I'd become.

Before leaving Aidan, I asked him to keep an eye on my mother in school. I then called her on the way to the station and actually felt relieved when she answered.

She said she was already in her office but admitted to getting very little sleep during the night.

'I'll keep you updated on what's going on,' I said. 'But please try not to worry. You'll be fine.'

'It's not me I'm worried about, Laura. It's you. I keep thinking about your father and how easy it was for his killer to get to him. I wouldn't want to live if the same thing happened to you.'

'It won't and you have to believe that.'

'How can I if you stay on this task force?'

'Stepping back from it is not an option, Mum. You know that.'

'Well then, don't tell me not to worry.'

On the tube I couldn't stop thinking about what she'd said and I could feel the anxiety building up inside me. By the time I got to the Yard my head was spinning and a cold sweat had settled on my skin.

Once in the office it soon became apparent that close family members of the other detectives were also freaking out.

'The wife's shit scared,' Tony Marsden said to a group gathered around the coffee machine. 'She was in tears all night and this morning she told me that she wanted me to get re-assigned.'

'Well, my husband reckons we should all stop working until we know who's behind it.' This from DI Gloria Stanford, who was one of the newest recruits to the team.

Even DCS Drummond had a story to tell. His wife was visiting relatives in Scotland when she called him from there to say she'd received the message.

'I tried telling her it was probably a prank but she wouldn't have it,' he said. 'She got quite upset.'

It was quickly established that the message had been sent to the partners or immediate family members of all the detectives. These included husbands, wives, boyfriends, girlfriends, mothers, fathers and a couple of grown-up children.

Among those who took it really badly was Dave Prentiss's wife, Karen. Prentiss, who was on his day off, phoned in to say that she became hysterical when she opened the message while breast-feeding their new baby in the hospital.

It was all very disturbing and no one really knew what to make of it. Drummond told us the Commissioner had been informed and he'd been in contact with the Home Secretary.

The cyber-crime unit had been working through the night to try to get a handle on who had sent the text.

'They're also trying to find out how this person or persons could have obtained so many private phone numbers,' he said. 'And obviously until they have the answer we're all under suspicion of leaking them.'

This was to be expected but it nevertheless came as a shock. I didn't want to believe that one or more members of the team might be corrupt.

Kate Chappell asked Drummond if we'd be offered any form of protection, to which he replied, 'That's not at all feasible. There are far too many of us and the Met's already stretched because of the high-level terror threat against our people on the streets.'

'So what do you expect us to do, guv?' she said.

Drummond's voice took on a hard edge. 'That's a stupid question, detective. What I expect you all to do is your job, no matter how tough it gets.'

It was a sobering reminder to all of us that as police officers we could not step back from the firing line. We had no choice but to stand firm regardless of how many death threats came our way.

But it was different for our loved ones and I felt compelled to remind Drummond of this.

'What about our families, sir?' I said. 'Will they get protection?'

'Let's not get ahead of ourselves, DI Jefferson,' he said. 'We still can't be certain that this isn't just some nutcase making mischief. So there's no way the Commissioner will sanction personal protection for so many people.'

'But surely we now have to treat this as a credible threat, sir.'

He nodded. 'And we will, but our response has to be measured and carefully considered. We can't just pluck scores of officers out of the air so that they can act as round-the-clock bodyguards for individuals. That'd be a mega commitment – especially if this drags on for weeks – and we simply don't have the manpower and resources.'

He was making a valid point and we all knew it. Protecting people deemed to be at risk was extremely labour intensive and it wasn't always effective. There had been numerous instances over the years where people had been attacked and even killed despite being under police guard.

Drummond rounded off the meeting by asking for a list of all possible suspects.

'In response to this latest development we need to question the most likely suspects,' he said. 'I'm guessing Roy Slack will be at the top of the list. But include all other villains who will know that it's only a matter of time before we come after them. And check the database to see if anything like this has happened before. There'll be more than a few loonies out there who've got form for wasting our time by making outrageous threats and demands.'

If anything the meeting had served only to increase my sense

104

of unease. It was as though a grenade had been lobbed into the room and no one knew what to do with it.

It hadn't yet gone off and we were hoping it was a fake. But there was no way we could ignore it, because if it wasn't a fake then it had the potential to cause an awful lot of damage.

17

Rosa

Rosa stood naked in front of the window, her body flushed from the heat of the shower.

Her room was four floors up and overlooked a busy street full of shops. She could hear the tuneless chorus of blaring horns and people's voices.

It reminded her of Mexico City. It was less chaotic, but just as frenetic.

London had, for a long time, been on her list of places she wanted to visit. But her first impression was not a favourable one. It was dirtier than she'd expected and the buildings were bland and weary-looking.

But maybe that was because this was an insalubrious area and she would have to cross the River Thames to sample London's real delights.

This morning the city was draped in billowy clouds but at least it wasn't raining.

The time was just after eleven o'clock. She'd slept late partly because of the jet lag, but mostly because she'd sat up until the early hours preparing for her mission.

There was a lot to do in a short space of time. But she was used to working quickly. More often than not she was expected to carry out hits with barely twenty-four hours' notice.

She had gone through the list that Roy Slack had given her and checked the website containing the photographs of most of the targets. She'd then used the iPad to search for the individuals online.

There wasn't much information on the detectives, who, for obvious reasons, preferred to keep a low profile, but most of the relatives and partners on the list had a presence on Facebook, Twitter and various other social media sites. This enabled Rosa to compile a wealth of useful facts and figures.

She'd then run all the addresses through Google Earth and transferred some of the images of their homes to the phone she'd been given.

At 4am she'd gone through the names again, cross-referencing them against all the other information.

The names of the detectives were typed in a bold, black font and their ranks were included. The boss was a DCS George Drummond. Underneath his name was his wife's name.

Below him there were several DCIs, and then some DIs, DSs and DCs.

Rosa had circled six names with her pen – Graham Nash, George Drummond, Phil Warren, Laura Jefferson, Dave Prentiss and Gloria Stanford. She'd chosen them for several reasons – they were all based south of the river, they all had husbands, wives or partners who were named, and they all lived in a house and not a flat, which made them more vulnerable.

Before crawling into bed, Rosa had selected her first victim.

She'd also come to the conclusion that with so many victims to choose from this assignment was going to be pretty straight-forward.

She started the day as she always did, with two cups of strong black coffee. Then she dressed in a light-grey tank top and jeans.

She'd worked out a plan for the day ahead. First she would go and get something to eat because she'd missed breakfast in the hotel's small dining room.

Then she'd visit a few stores to buy some things, including clothes, because the few she'd brought with her were for warmer climes.

She would purchase everything using the debit and credit cards that identified her as Maria Rodriquez, which was one of the false names she operated under.

Then she'd go to the garage behind the pub and take the motorbike for a spin. She planned to visit several locations, including the home of her first victim so she'd know exactly where to go later. Then she'd return to the hotel to do some more research before getting ready and going to work.

She wanted the first hit to go smoothly in order to impress the client, who was clearly paying Carlos Cruz a significant amount of money over and above the half million she was going to get.

Since the meeting in the pub she hadn't given much thought to Roy Slack, although he did strike her as someone who was past his prime.

She knew how powerful and ruthless he was from the many online news stories. But she'd sensed in his eyes an expression at odds with a demeanour that reeked of malevolence.

She had seen the same look in the eyes of a few ageing cartel bosses when they were suddenly confronted with the grim truth that they were mortal after all.

She had no idea what was behind Slack's decision to embark on a killing spree that in her opinion would achieve very little other than creating a pile of blood-soaked corpses.

It was the kind of thing they did in Mexico, usually as an act of revenge against rivals or groups of people who spoke out against them.

So perhaps it was revenge that was motivating Roy Slack. The truth was she would probably never know. But as long as she got paid for her services she really didn't care.

18

Laura

It was 3pm and Kate Chappell and I were on our way to Roy Slack's business HQ in Rotherhithe. A team of uniformed officers were in a van behind us. We knew that Slack was there because he'd been under surveillance since this morning.

We were armed with a warrant to search the premises and seize his phone and any computers. We'd also obtained warrants to search his flat and the homes and offices of other villains who we reckoned might be responsible for the death threats.

It'd be the second time in a week that the police had descended on Slack's place, and for that reason I wasn't optimistic about finding any incriminating evidence.

But Drummond had told us that it would be enough at this stage just to get a sense of whether he knew something.

'And use it as an excuse to mark his card,' Drummond had said. 'Tell him that his days are numbered and he'll soon be following Harry Fuller into the dock at the Old Bailey. In other words do your best to unnerve him.'

We were dropping in unannounced, but that didn't mean he

wouldn't be expecting us. It was quite possible that he'd already been tipped off that we were coming and was therefore prepared.

It was a horrible thought that there might be a rat on the team, but it had to be a distinct possibility given that all our private phone numbers had been leaked.

The Southside Arms was sandwiched between two apartment buildings close to the riverfront in Rotherhithe. It boasted two bars and a large restaurant.

There were three floors above it and Roy Slack's office was on the top floor. Access was either through the pub or through a door to the side that had a video intercom and a security camera.

As we came to a stop in front of the building I was the first onto the pavement followed by six uniforms and Kate.

'I'll take the side door,' I told her. 'You go through the pub.'

I was about to give instructions to the uniforms when the side door opened and a man stepped out onto the pavement. He raised a hand towards me, palm facing out.

'There's no need to go storming inside like a fucking army,' he said. 'There are people in there enjoying their lunch.'

He was at once familiar to me from the many photos I'd seen. His name was Danny Carver, but in the underworld he was known as The Rottweiler.

'I'm Detective Inspector Laura Jefferson from the organised crime task force and I'm here to speak to Roy Slack,' I said. 'I also have a warrant to search his office.'

He smiled then, flashing a couple of gold teeth that made him look like a pirate.

'Well, you're in luck, my love,' he said. 'He's upstairs, and he'll be happy to answer your questions, whatever they're about.'

It was not the reaction I'd expected, but I didn't let that faze me.

As I stepped towards him I was struck by how big and ugly he was. He had a barrel-chest beneath a black T-shirt and thick arms adorned with tattoos. His dark hair was short and spiky and his broken nose was pressed flat against the rest of his face.

'Were you expecting us?' I asked when I stood facing him.

'How could we have possibly known you were coming?' he said, grinning. 'You didn't have the good manners to tell us.'

I turned to look at Kate and she rolled her eyes. It was all too obvious that they'd been forewarned, and that concerned me.

I instructed two uniforms to wait outside and question anyone who left the building, then told Carver to take us upstairs to his boss.

It felt like an anti-climax. I'd been bracing myself for a loud, hostile reception, but instead we were being treated like welcome guests. That in itself was a bad omen. Either Slack had nothing to hide or he'd hidden it where he knew we would never find it.

'So what goes on up here?' I said as we mounted the stairs.

Carver, who was ahead of me, spoke without turning.

'This is the hub of Mr Slack's business empire,' he said. 'From here he oversees the running of his restaurants, pubs, clubs and property portfolio.'

'So what about all the other stuff he's involved in?' I asked.

He stopped walking and turned to face me, a frown gathering on his brow.

'You've lost me,' he said. 'What other stuff are you talking about?'

Jesus, I thought. This creep knows how to play it cool.

'I'm talking about the businesses that bring in the real

112

money – like the drugs and prostitution and smuggling and so forth.'

His lips stretched into another mirthless grin.

'Nice try, my love. But you lot really need to accept that you've been barking up the wrong tree for years. My boss is a legitimate businessman. He's not a gangster. If he was I'm sure that even half-wits like you would have been able to prove it by now.'

Our eyes locked briefly and I could see he wanted me to respond. But when I didn't he shrugged his shoulders and carried on up the stairs.

I stared at his back and told myself that when Roy Slack was eventually taken down I'd do all I could to make sure that this cocky bastard was right there alongside him.

On the top floor there was a carpeted corridor with two open doors on either side.

We followed Carver past a small kitchen and then a room containing a long conference table.

The walls were painted a soft grey and there were a few hanging prints of old London.

There was no sign of life until we got to the last room on the right. Slack's office. He was sitting behind a large mahogany desk wearing a white open-neck shirt that was too tight across his chest and stomach.

Carver stood to one side and waved me into the room. Kate followed, but I gestured for the uniforms to wait outside in the corridor. Then I whipped out my ID and showed it to Slack.

'DI Laura Jefferson,' I said. 'I'm here with DS Kate Chappell.'

'And let me guess,' he said. 'You're with the organised crime task force.'

I nodded. 'We are.'

'Well, you didn't waste any time did you? Fresh from putting poor Harry Fuller away you've decided to get back to harassing me.'

'We need to ask you a few questions, Mr Slack,' I said. 'And for your information we have a warrant to search this office and seize your phones and computers.'

His eyebrows knitted together.

'This sounds serious,' he said. 'Should I call my lawyer?'

'That's up to you. But if you choose to we'll have to conduct the interview at the Yard.'

He shrugged. 'In that case I'll listen to what you have to say and then decide.' He indicated the two chairs in front of the desk. 'You'd better sit down then. Would you like Danny to get you something to drink? Tea or coffee?'

'No thanks,' I said for both of us.

Once seated, I took out my notebook and flipped it open. While doing so I studied the man behind the desk who seemed to be more relaxed than he should have been.

Every one of his fifty-seven years was etched in his face. His complexion was unhealthy and sallow, and red veins laced the whites of his eyes.

He looked unwell to me, but even so there was a quiet, brooding intensity about him that told me he was still a force to be reckoned with.

'So fire away, detective inspector,' he said. 'What's brought you people back here so soon after the last visit? If it's to ask me again where that firearms officer is, well, my answer's the same: I haven't the foggiest idea.'

I decided to get straight to the point and said, 'This has nothing to do with Officer Wallis. It's about an anonymous text message that's been sent to all the detectives on the task force, along with members of our families.'

'Is that so?'

'It is. The sender says he wants the task force to be disbanded and calls on the detectives to step back from it.'

I paused there to gauge his reaction. But there wasn't one. His expression didn't change.

'That sounds pretty innocuous,' he said. 'What the fuck has it got to do with me?'

'The message goes on to say that if we refuse to step back then we'll be killed,' I said.

He gave a little whistle. 'I can see why you're in a flap. But I still don't know what it has to do with me.'

'I'd have thought that was obvious,' I said. 'You more than anyone has a good reason to want to see the task force disbanded and the investigation into your activities halted or at least disrupted.'

His eyes tightened. 'And do you really think I'm stupid enough to make things worse for myself by killing coppers?' he said, his voice rising. 'Give me some credit, love. I've got nothing to do with any anonymous threats so you're wasting your time and mine.'

'Then you won't mind if we check your phones and computers, both here and at your flat.'

He shrugged and pointed to a mobile phone lying on the desk.

'There's my phone,' he said. 'It's unregistered but I've had it a couple of weeks and in that time I've not sent a single text. And the laptop's over there on the cabinet. I use it to stay across my businesses. You can take it with you but I want it back once you've checked it.'

'Is that your only phone?' I asked.

'It is. I don't make many calls. And that's my only laptop.'

'So there are no others at your flat?'

'Go see for yourself. I'll call security and tell them to let you in. And please tell your people not to make a mess like they did last time.'

I felt a flash of anger. The guy was playing us. He had no doubt taken steps to ensure that we wouldn't find anything on the phone and computer that could be used against him.

'So let's be clear, Mr Slack,' I said. 'You're saying you know nothing about these death threats?'

'That's exactly what I'm saying. There are plenty of people out there who are shit scared of you and might be tempted to make threats. But I'm not one of them.'

'Well, you can rest assured that you're not the only one we're talking to.'

He gave a derisive snort. 'But I suppose I'm the prime suspect.'

I allowed the corners of my mouth to lift in a smile.

'Of course you are,' I said. 'And with good reason. You know we've turned our attention on you so your days as London's Mr Big are numbered.'

He laughed then and I felt my hackles rise.

'Listen to me,' he snarled. 'You no-good cunts have been trying to stitch me up for years. You've caused me no end of grief and for that reason I don't give a monkey's if some nutjob is threatening to kill a bunch of you. As far as I'm concerned you're all scum and if the threats are carried out then I'll be cracking open the champers.'

It was all I could do not to throw myself across the desk and dig my fingers into his eyes. But somehow I managed to repress the rage that rose up inside me. I forced myself to keep a neutral face, but I couldn't stop my body from shaking or my heart from pounding against my rib cage.

Slack continued to stare at me unflinchingly, and I stared right back.

116

The silence stretched between us for about ten seconds. And then a sneer rose on his face and he said, 'I'm not going to say anymore so you can bring those clowns in now and search the place. When you're finished I want you to fuck off and take note of the fact that I won't be so accommodating if you show up again.'

I didn't say anything because I didn't trust myself not to go too far. What Slack had said was vile and unwarranted, but he hadn't committed a crime.

So we went through the motions, searching not just his office but also the other rooms on the top floor. And while we did that the smug bastard and his gold-toothed henchman went downstairs to the pub to have a late lunch and a drink.

When we left there we took Slack's phone and laptop with us, but I knew there'd be nothing on them of interest to us.

'So what do you think?' Kate said as we got back in the car.

'I think that man is a sorry excuse for a human being,' I answered. 'And I think there's a good chance he's behind this. But I don't know how the hell we'll be able to prove it.'

19

Rosa

It was just after 6pm and Rosa was ready to go to work. But, as she was about to leave the hotel room, a news item on the television caught her eye.

CNN were reporting on the murder of a journalist back home in Sinaloa.

'Award-winning reporter Antonia Castillo was shot dead in the street as he got out of his car,' the anchor was saying. 'Mr Castillo was famed for his coverage of drug cartel activities. He's the ninth reporter to have been murdered in Mexico this year alone.'

Rosa couldn't help but smile. Castillo had been pissing off Carlos Cruz for some time and his death had been on the cards. If she hadn't been five and a half thousand miles away in London she might well have been the one assigned to get rid of him.

She wasn't complaining, though. This was a dream job. An all-expenses paid trip to a European capital. The chance to stock up on designer clothes at some of the world's most famous stores. And then there were the targets who were going to be sitting ducks, plus the huge fee, of course.

The money from this job would take her savings to over three million dollars. That was enough to retire on. But she wouldn't be doing that anytime soon because killing made her feel good and gave meaning to her life. She enjoyed the thrill of it, the power, the sense of absolute control. She couldn't imagine lying on a beach every day or doing some crappy job just to alleviate the boredom.

CNN moved onto another story so she switched off the TV and checked herself in the mirror.

Her hair was gathered up and pinned at the back and over it she'd put on a woollen hat pulled down over her ears. Under her leather jacket she was wearing the navy polo sweater and black jeans she'd bought earlier, along with a new pair of dark trainers.

Satisfied with her appearance, she left the room, went downstairs, and exited the hotel.

The air outside was raw and she was glad to see that the street was heaving with traffic and pedestrians. She'd decided to strike at the tail end of the rush hour. She wanted to make it as hard as possible for the cops to spot her going to and from her victim's house.

She knew that extreme caution was necessary in a city with over half a million surveillance cameras. She'd spotted plenty of them while checking out the various locations today and she'd try to avoid them where possible.

She walked briskly to the pub, which was only a couple of hundred yards from the hotel. She let herself into the garage at the rear and got to work.

The first thing she did was remove her coat and slip into the two-piece motorcycle suit. Then she picked up the pistol she'd chosen for the first hit and put it inside the jacket. Finally, she picked up the helmet and rolled the bike outside, locking the door behind her.

She wheeled the bike out onto the road and got on it. Before placing the helmet on her head she made a call using one of the burner phones that Slack had given to her. She'd put the number in earlier so that she wouldn't have to memorise it.

It rang three times before being answered.

'Hello.'

It was a woman's voice and Rosa assumed it must be the victim's wife.

'Is Detective Inspector Prentiss there?' she asked. 'It's the office here.'

'He is but I'll have to get him,' the woman said. 'Who shall I say is calling?'

Rosa abruptly ended the call, turned off the phone and dropped it on the ground where she smashed it beneath her trainer.

Then she put on the helmet and fired up the bike.

It was a relief to know that DI Dave Prentiss was at home. He would be her first victim and hopefully he'd be dead within the hour. That would give Rosa plenty of time to make a night of it in London's famous West End.

With luck she might even get herself laid.

Dave Prentiss lived in a quiet street in Battersea, less than a mile from the hotel in Vauxhall.

He had just become a father, information gleaned from his wife's most recent social media posts. Rosa therefore stopped on the way to the house to buy a bunch of flowers.

She'd also decided that if it was the wife who answered the door then she'd be the one to die. After all, the brief was to kill the detectives or the family members and loved ones whose names were on the list she'd been given.

She'd seen photos of both husband and wife so she wasn't going to make a mistake.

Navigating her way through the heaving South London traffic was easy now that she had the hang of riding on the left side of the road. The number of motorcyclists surprised her, but it worked in her favour. She could move around the city without drawing attention to herself and that was going to be important in the days ahead.

She left the bike two streets away from the house where she knew there were no CCTV cameras. She removed the helmet but left the hat on as she moved towards the house carrying the bunch of flowers, lowering her head whenever she passed another pedestrian.

It was a terraced house and the small front garden was enclosed by hedges on either side, which was perfect. As she approached it she was pleased to see that the street was empty.

There were lights on inside the house and a car on the driveway.

Rosa's body was rigid, her jaw clenched, as she walked up to the front door.

She filled her lungs with air and held the flowers in front of her face. With the other hand she pulled the gun from inside her jacket. Then she rang the bell.

She heard movement inside after only a couple of seconds, and suddenly the door was pulled open.

Dave Prentiss appeared and she saw his smiling face through the flowers. As soon as he started to speak she squeezed the trigger. The bullet popped as it exited through the silencer and ploughed into his chest.

He fell backwards into the hallway, blood spurting from the wound like an industrial sprinkler.

Rosa lowered the flowers, took aim, and fired two more shots into the cop's face.

Job done, she slipped the gun back into the jacket and turned away from her blood-drenched victim.

As she headed back down the driveway she heard a baby start to cry somewhere in the house. But it didn't cause her to break her stride as she calmly walked away from the house.

She dropped the flowers into a trash can at the end of the street.

PART TWO

20

Laura

I was in the office when the call came through at just after seven thirty. I'd decided to work late so that I could be around when the techies finished going through Roy Slack's phone and laptop.

It was Drummond who took the call and he came straight out of his office and summoned everyone together. There were seven of us – four detectives and three support staff – and we gathered around him with a shared sense of anticipation.

From the look on the boss's face it seemed obvious that he had some bad news to impart. His skin was the colour of sour milk and his bottom lip appeared to be trembling.

He stood with his head slightly forward, shoulders curved, and rubbed a palm across his forehead. When he spoke his voice was shaking and I could tell that he was fighting to calm it.

'Something terrible has just happened,' he said, and then paused for a couple of seconds before continuing. 'Dave Prentiss has been shot and I'm afraid . . . I'm afraid he's dead.'

I felt my heart crumble in my chest and a cold flush went over my skin. I heard someone gasp and someone else swore.

'It occurred at his home in Battersea,' Drummond went on. 'The killer struck when Dave opened his front door.'

My throat tightened with shock, and the question I wanted to ask wouldn't come out. I started shaking my head, finding it hard to grasp what Drummond had said.

Surely it must be a mistake, I told myself. Dave can't be dead. I saw him yesterday, gave him a card and congratulated him on the birth of his baby.

Behind me one of the female support staff gave an anguished cry and burst into tears. Drummond looked at her and the lines between his eyes deepened.

I cleared my throat and found my voice.

'What else do you know, guv?' I said.

He hunched his shoulders. 'Not much at this stage except that his wife and child were at the house when it happened but they're unharmed. And there's no sign of the perp. I'm going straight there now.'

'I'd like to come with you,' I blurted out.

He nodded. 'Fine. The rest of you start bashing the phones. Inform your colleagues before they hear it on the news and get them all in. Also, liaise with Wandsworth nick. They've assigned a DCI Resnick to the case. He's already at the scene.'

Drummond signalled for me to get ready, then went back into his office to get his coat. But for several seconds I couldn't move. It felt like a large stone was crushing my chest.

Someone placed a hand on my shoulder and said, 'Are you OK, Laura?'

I turned. It was Janet Dean and her face had lost all its colour.

'I can't believe it,' I said. 'This is so bad.'

'I know. It's awful.'

126

I breathed in deep through my nostrils and tried to compose myself.

'I have a horrible feeling that this is just the start,' I said. 'And that it wasn't an empty threat after all.'

Janet stared at me and I noticed that her lips had gone white around the edges.

'Let's just hope and pray that you're wrong, Laura,' she said. 'Because if you're not then God only knows how we're going to stop it from happening again.'

I sat in the back of the patrol car with Drummond as we raced towards Battersea. The siren wailed and the traffic parted to let us through.

Drummond's phone was stuck to his ear so we didn't get a chance to talk. He had conversations with various people, including the Commissioner and the commanding officer at Wandsworth, on whose patch the killing had taken place.

The murder of any police officer always sparks a wave of disquiet. But what had happened to Dave Prentiss was going to have massive implications for the Met and indeed for the country.

It sounded like he was the victim of a cold-blooded assassination, and gut instinct was telling me that it was committed by, or on behalf of, the person who sent us the death threat.

I didn't believe that it was a coincidence, and I gathered from what Drummond was telling everyone that he didn't either.

I had never seen him so rattled, but that was understandable. Prentiss was one of twenty detectives under his command and we'd all received the same text message warning us to stop working for the task force.

I feared now that it was indeed just the start . . . that there would be more murders if we didn't yield to the demand.

And that our close friends and family members would be among the victims.

The street was filled with police cars, and their flashing lights were reflected in the windows of the small terraced houses.

I'd never been to Prentiss's house before and when we pulled up outside it my first thought was how nice it was. But then the sight of all the uniforms on the driveway hit me like a cattle prod and robbed me of air. As I stepped out of the car onto the pavement I felt an icy chill in my stomach.

Drummond came and stood beside me and asked me if I was all right.

'Not really, guv,' I said. 'But I'm glad I'm here. I need to see this.'

He was about to say something else when a tall man in a white forensic suit appeared and introduced himself as DCI Bob Resnick. He looked about fifty and had dark, wavy hair.

'I was told that you were coming, sir,' he said to Drummond. 'I understand that Dave Prentiss was on your task force.'

'That's right,' Drummond said. 'So what have you got?'

He told us what we already knew, that Prentiss had been shot dead when he opened his front door to someone.

'His wife was upstairs with her new baby when the doorbell rang,' he said. 'She said her husband went to answer it. She didn't even know he'd been murdered until she came downstairs a couple of minutes later to see why he wasn't responding to her calls. She found him in the hallway.'

'Did she not hear the shots?' Drummond asked.

'She says there weren't any, which leads me to believe that the killer used a gun with a silencer. And that suggests it was the work of a pro.'

'How many shots were fired?' I asked.

'Three. A bullet in the chest and two in the face. So be warned – he's not a pretty sight.'

As he spoke I could feel the horror closing in around me and bile rose in my throat.

In my mind's eye I saw Prentiss as he'd been the day before. The proud father, all smiles as he showed me a picture of his baby. Little Josh. The boy would now grow up never knowing his father who was shot on the day he was brought home from hospital.

I just couldn't fathom the mentality behind such a vicious, mindless act. It was an appalling tragedy that was going to have an impact on so many lives.

Resnick was now telling us that Karen Prentiss and her baby were in the neighbour's house and naturally she was in a terrible state.

Around us the air buzzed and crackled with radio chatter. Officers were whispering to each other, their faces stiff with shock.

'We'll need to liaise closely on this one,' Resnick said. 'It's possible, or perhaps even likely, that DI Prentiss was targeted because he was on your task force. Have you any idea who might have done it or paid someone to do it?'

After a brief hesitation, Drummond said, 'There's something you need to know and I fear it's related to this.'

'Really?'

So Drummond told him about the threat and even showed him the message on his own phone.

'We were instructed by the Commissioner to keep it to ourselves,' he said. 'But then yesterday evening the message was forwarded to our family members and people who are close to us.'

'Holy Christ,' Resnick said. 'That's fucking scary.'

He gave himself a moment to take in what he'd been told and then asked us if we were ready to view the body. Drummond said we were but first we had to slip on the white suits and shoe covers.

The scene in the hallway sucked the breath out of my lungs. Dave Prentiss's body was covered with a sheet and when it was pulled back I saw that most of his face had been blown away.

He was sprawled on his back with his arms stretched out above him. The sheer, brutal sadness of what I was seeing brought me out in a cold sweat. I just didn't want to imagine what it had been like for his wife when she came down the stairs and found him.

I'd encountered a disturbing number of murder victims during my time on the force. Men, women and children who'd been shot, stabbed, beaten and burned. But I'd never felt as traumatised as I did now. This was the first time I'd stood looking down at the body of someone I'd actually known. And it was a totally different experience. I had to fight the urge to give in to my emotions and cry, or throw up, or run back to the car. It wasn't easy, but I stood my ground and focused on keeping my breath steady and even.

'Mrs Prentiss started screaming when she saw him and then ran into the street to get help,' Resnick said. 'It was a neighbour who called the three nines. We've started going door-to-door, but so far we haven't found anyone who saw anything.'

'What about CCTV cameras?' Drummond asked.

Resnick shook his head. 'There are none in this street and I expect the nearest one will be on the main road, which is a bugger.'

He then told us that to get into the house we'd have to go through the kitchen so I tore my gaze away from the body and followed him and Drummond around the side of the house.

It was all so surreal and upsetting, and I found it hard to concentrate.

Inside it was a perfectly normal house except for the ghostlike figures and the low, strained conversations.

In every room there were things that had been bought for the baby. A cot, packs of nappies, a Moses basket, neatly folded vests and rompers.

There was a lead weight in my heart and it got heavier when we walked into the living room and I saw framed photos of Prentiss and his wife on the mantelpiece.

'This must be hard for you guys,' Resnick said. 'I gather DI Prentiss was popular among his colleagues.'

'Indeed he was,' Drummond said. 'He took today off so that he could pick his wife and baby up from the hospital.'

'Will you want to speak to her, sir?'

Drummond nodded. 'Of course. I can't say I'm looking forward to it, though.'

'I'll come with you, guv,' I said. 'Karen knows me. We've met a couple of times.'

Just then my phone pinged with an incoming text. I was going to ignore it because I assumed it was Aidan checking to see where I was. But then a similar sound came from Drummond's pocket, and he said, 'Let's hope it's a coincidence.'

A moment later we discovered that it wasn't: the same message had been sent to both of us.

21

Slack

The BBC News Channel was the first to break the story. A young female presenter suddenly adopted a solemn expression and said, 'We're getting reports that a police officer has been shot dead in London. He hasn't yet been named, but we understand he was at home in Battersea with his wife when he was gunned down on his doorstep.'

Roy Slack had been glued to the TV screen since Rosa had called him an hour ago to inform him that she'd claimed her first victim.

'It's done,' she'd said, her voice clipped and devoid of emotion. 'Tune into the news for the details.'

And that was all she had said before hanging up.

While waiting for the story to appear, Slack had phoned Danny to get him to send another message to the detectives. After telling him what to put in it he'd poured himself another Scotch and lit one of his Cuban cigars.

Now he sat with his feet up on the coffee table and savoured the warm sense of satisfaction that washed through him. His mission was properly underway now and there was no turning back.

For him revenge had always been sweet, but this time it was going to be sweeter than ever. Those smug, self-righteous detectives who were coming after him were going to pay for the sins of all those who'd gone before them.

And he was going to relish their suffering and the turmoil it was going to create.

Killing Hugh Wallis would never have been enough. This wasn't about individuals. Wallis had been sent to Terry's house by those above him, so they were just as culpable. And so were the slags who had covered up the crime by concluding that Terry was responsible for his own death.

It was just another example of the rank hypocrisy that prevailed inside the Met. As far as he was concerned Scotland Yard was a swamp filled with vermin. The coppers who weren't corrupt were guided by a sickening sense of moral superiority. They were obsessed with bringing down villains who provided services that were much in demand. But they spent far less time and effort going after rapists, muggers, wife beaters, child molesters and jihadist fanatics who infested the capital.

Men like Harry Fuller did not deserve to go to prison for thirty years while paedophiles were as a rule sentenced to less than half that.

Slack's own father had died in prison after he was stitched up by coppers who planted a gun in his car. They did it because they knew he was part of an armed gang that robbed a jewellers, but hadn't been able to prove it. Ryan Slack, who was just fifty-four, was three months into his sentence when he got into a fight and suffered a fatal stab wound.

Years later Slack was given another reason to hate the Old

Bill after he was hauled in for questioning for the third time in a month. His wife was furious. She'd decided to drive to Camberwell nick to give the detectives a piece of her mind. On the way she'd smashed head-on into another car while overtaking a bus.

Everyone said that Julie had herself to blame but that wasn't how Slack saw it. If the coppers hadn't taken him in that day then she would in all probability still be alive.

Over the years the bastards had blighted his life. Now, at last, it was payback time.

The apartment was filling up with cigar smoke so Slack decided to go out onto the balcony. But first he topped up the Scotch and slipped on a cardigan.

It was a cold but calm night, and a slice of moon peeked through the clouds, silent and pale.

The view he had of South London was spectacular, and it was the main reason he'd splashed out two million quid on the apartment. From here he could see much of the territory he controlled. But it meant far more to him than that.

It was where he'd grown up. Where his father was buried. Where Julie was cremated. Where his son was murdered and where his grandchild was denied the gift of life.

There was a time when he'd dreamt of moving away. He'd promised Julie that once he had enough dosh in the bank they'd retire to a place where they could live out their lives drinking cocktails and enjoying the sun.

But no matter how much wealth he accumulated it was never enough to entice him away from the business. And that was something he bitterly regretted.

After she died he went on to make enough money to buy a

134

house in Kent, a villa in Spain and a luxurious apartment here at Canary Wharf.

But he had come to realise a long time ago that without someone to share them with they were just meaningless possessions.

He hardly ever stayed in Kent or went to Spain because being in those big properties served only to compound his loneliness.

That was why he stayed in London most of the time. He was able to keep busy and surround himself with people. Plus, he got to enjoy the view as often as he wanted.

Tonight the city seemed even brighter and noisier than usual. Lights were going up for Christmas all over the place and there was a constant wail of police sirens.

He looked over towards Battersea as he drew on his cigar and tried to imagine the chaotic scene outside the copper's house. The street would be swarming with police, forensic suits, reporters, and members of the public.

Most of them wouldn't yet know that it was the first of many. But they soon would, and then it'd be the start of a nightmare for all those cunts at Scotland Yard.

Slack knew that there was no way they'd disband the task force or allow any detectives to willingly step away from it. But that was the whole point of the exercise. He'd wanted them to be in an impossible position from the start. And he'd aimed to achieve that with the text messages – by forcing them to ignore the death threats. Now in the eyes of the public they would have to share some responsibility for the killings, and it was certain to fuel the crisis they were about to face.

He had every confidence in Rosa Lopez, and not just because of her fearsome reputation. There was something about her that set her apart from other people. It was an intangible quality that was impossible to define and yet marked her out as a grade-A psycho. And it told him that she would approach the task she'd been given with gusto, that the more people she killed the better she would feel about herself.

He was also pretty sure that in the unlikely event that she was caught she wouldn't dob him in for fear of upsetting her boss back in Mexico.

But even if she did it wouldn't matter that much so long as she'd racked up enough kills by then to have made it all worthwhile.

He raised his glass of Scotch in a toast to the woman they called The Slayer, the only person who could give him what he wanted before he bailed out.

'There's a lot riding on your beautiful shoulders,' he said aloud. 'Please don't let me down, Rosa. Pay the bastards back for what they did to the only people who ever meant anything to me.'

He gulped down the rest of his drink and suddenly found himself fantasising about the woman. He pictured her in the hotel room thinking through the plan for her next hit. But, rather than hunched over a desk, she was lying on the bed with her legs apart and her mouth open.

She was indeed exceptionally horny, and none of his mistresses, including Jasmine, could compare. Given the chance he'd willingly pay a king's ransom to spend the night with her.

22

Rosa

Rosa did not plan to stay cooped up in her hotel room. Having dispensed with detective Dave Prentiss she was ready to party.

Some of the world's most celebrated gay clubs were in London, and no way was she going to miss the opportunity to visit at least a few of them during her stay in the city.

She'd been denied the chance to let her hair down in Acapulco, so she felt she deserved it now. She had already selected her next victim and carried out all the necessary research. So there was no need to spend the evening formulating a plan.

That first kill had been a breeze, but she anticipated that from now on things would get a little more difficult. She was OK with that, even welcomed the challenge, because there was only so much the cops could do to protect themselves.

In Mexico every police officer, journalist and judge knew they were potential targets of one or more of the cartels. Some went to extraordinary lengths to try to ensure they stayed safe. They hired armed bodyguards, moved house, cut themselves off from the rest of the world. But ninety-nine per cent of the time they still ended up dead.

Rosa had learned from experience that every line of defence could be breached. Usually it was down to human error or underestimating the guile of the assassin.

Rosa was proud of the fact that she had never failed an assignment, no matter how difficult it had appeared at the outset. She had a work ethic that put her peers to shame and would have made her an asset to any terrorist organisation.

Having spent so many years killing people she couldn't imagine doing anything else for a living.

Before his death her father had started sharing all the hopes and dreams he'd had for his only child. But those memories had been distilled by the passage of time so she couldn't remember what he wanted her to be.

Of one thing she was certain, though – that neither of her parents would have been proud of the fact that she had turned into a killing machine. And that she'd earned the dubious distinction of being rated as the best in the business.

An hour after leaving the hotel Rosa walked into a lively little nightclub in the heart of London's West End.

The place was heaving with men and women who all seemed to be in their twenties and thirties. Some were gyrating on the dance floor while others were standing at the bar or sitting at little round tables. Rosa was delighted to see that a good many were by themselves. No doubt they were hoping to get lucky just as she was.

Back at the hotel she had replaced the navy polo sweater with a tight pink T-shirt and the black jeans with her favourite pair of designer ones.

She knew she looked a million dollars and so she wasn't at all surprised that she drew so much attention as she walked purposefully up to the bar.

A couple of women smiled at her and she smiled back. One guy in a string vest and white arse-hugging shorts blew her a kiss and she returned the gesture.

At the bar she dug into her shoulder bag for some cash and ordered a tonic with ice and lemon.

In response to the look the barman gave her, she said, 'Alcohol makes me crazy. Too much too soon and I'll be ripping off my clothes and dancing on the table tops before the night is over.'

The barman laughed, but someone behind her said, 'Well, I for one don't think that would be such a bad thing.'

Rosa turned and found herself looking into the smiling face of a stunning woman in a white blouse that hugged her slim form. She had fair hair cut in a boyish style and beautiful eyes under thick long lashes.

'My name is Alice,' she said. 'As soon as you walked in I knew that I had to buy you a drink. And after what I've just heard I'm really hoping you're going to let me.'

Rosa could not believe her luck. She'd struck gold with this pretty little thing and in record time.

'I'm Maria,' she said, pushing the fringe out of her eyes. 'And of course you can buy me a drink but only if you allow me to buy the next one.'

Alice's smile got wider and her white teeth positively sparkled.

'Are you sure you don't want a vodka with that tonic?' she said.

'I'm sure.'

Alice turned to the barman and said, 'A tonic for this lovely lady and the usual for me, Henry,' she said. 'And you can put it on my tab.'

'So you're a regular here,' Rosa said.

Alice nodded. 'I work in London and I'm lucky enough to have my own flat here. But I'm guessing that this is your first visit to the Vichy Lounge.'

'It's my first visit to London,' Rosa said.

'Wow. From your accent I take it you're Spanish.'

'Mexican.'

'Well, your English is perfect.'

'I spent many hours studying,' she said. 'It's a beautiful language.'

'I'm glad you think so. But yours is so much more sexy.'

Rosa laughed. 'So tell me about yourself, Alice. If we're going to spend the rest of the evening together then I'd like to know more about you.'

Alice took a step closer to Rosa and touched her arm. Rosa felt her pulse quicken and she started to imagine Alice's body up against her own. They were about the same height but Alice was less curvy with small, pert breasts and pale skin.

'I'm twenty-four years old and work for my father's advertising agency,' Alice said. 'I went with boys up until the age of nineteen and then realised why they never did anything for me in the sack. I've recently come out of a long-term relationship with a bitch who cheated on me and for the foreseeable future I plan on staying single and having a bloody good time.'

It was Rosa's turn then and the lies came naturally. She was twenty-three and worked for the Mexican government's tourism department. She was in London to promote her country at various travel seminars.

'And while I'm here I thought I'd find out if it's true that English women are among the world's best lovers.'

It was all so easy, Rosa thought. But since they were both after the same thing there was no reason for it not to be.

The rest of the evening went spectacularly well. They retreated to a booth where the banter continued and Alice turned out to be one of the most flirty and tactile women she had met in a long time.

Desire was already thick in Rosa's veins before they kissed for the first time. Alice's lips were warm and salty and her mouth tasted pleasantly of vodka with a dash of mint.

Rosa stuck with the tonic and enjoyed watching Alice getting slowly drunk.

They had a couple of dances and at one point Rosa slipped her hand under Alice's blouse and felt her nipples harden. She knew then that this was all leading up to the perfect end to a perfect day.

At 11pm Alice invited Rosa back to her apartment.

'It's a short cab ride from here,' she said. 'And from the bedroom there's a fantastic view of Hyde Park.'

Rosa's luck just kept getting better. She was relieved that she didn't have to take Alice back to the hotel, and not only because it was a shithole. There was always a risk that she would see something that she shouldn't. It had happened once before in Miami Beach when a girl who spent the night in her suite opened a drawer and found a machine pistol and a photo of the man Rosa had gone there to assassinate.

Rosa had been forced to kill the girl by slitting her throat, which was a shame. But there was no risk of that happening to beautiful Alice in her own apartment.

23

Laura

Needless to say I did not intend to go home to bed. There was no way I'd be able to sleep anyway.

By the time I left the crime scene in Battersea, I was completely shell-shocked. I'd almost broken down while talking to Karen Prentiss. The poor woman had been in a terrible state and had barely been able to speak to us. She just kept repeating her husband's name and saying she couldn't believe what had happened. And all the time she'd clung onto her baby for dear life and he'd cried along with her.

On the way back to the Yard I called Aidan who'd been desperately trying to contact me. He'd seen the story on the news and had assumed it was connected to the death threat.

'Your mother turned up here a while ago,' he said, before I could get a word in. 'She's been in tears and is fucking terrified.'

My mum had met Dave Prentiss, of course, from the time he came to the school. So it didn't surprise me that she was getting even more worked up.

I couldn't lie to Aidan so I told him that we'd received another message. This one had simply said: You now know that it wasn't an empty threat. Interestingly the latest text had not been sent to him or my mother, which probably meant that only the task force detectives had received it.

'I won't be coming home tonight,' I said. 'I have to go back to the office.'

Aidan drew in a loud breath. 'So what if the killer turns up on our doorstep? Shouldn't we be given some kind of protection?'

'That's something I'll be pushing for, Aidan. I promise. In the meantime don't answer the door to anyone you don't know.'

'But this is crazy. We shouldn't be living in fear like this.'

'I realise that and I can assure you that everything possible is being done to find out who's behind this.'

His voice cracked with fury. 'That's the type of thing you say to the media, Laura. Not to me.'

DCS Drummond was sitting next to me in the back seat of the patrol car and I was sure that he could hear what Aidan was saying.

'I'm sorry, Aidan,' I said, wishing I'd held off calling him until I was back in the office. 'But please stay calm and try not to worry. It's extremely unlikely that the killer will strike again tonight.'

'And is that supposed to reassure me and your mum?'

'Look, I really do understand how you must feel,' I said. 'All I can do is to ask the local station to send a patrol car round to watch the house. I'll call them straight away.'

'Well, I appreciate that, Laura and so does your mum. She's staying here for the night.'

'That's good. But I have to go. You should both try to get some sleep. I'll ring when I can with an update.'

We said our goodbyes and I severed the connection.

'I'm sorry about that, guv, but my boyfriend is really worried.'

'There's no need to apologise,' Drummond said. 'He's right to be worried. We all are. And arranging for a car to watch the house is a good idea.' He pulled out his phone. 'In fact let me do it for you. I'll call control and get them to send marked cars to the homes of all the detectives, including my own.'

'I thought your wife was away in Scotland, guv,' I said.

'She got back earlier this evening. I think she might have gone straight to bed and doesn't know yet about the shooting.'

While Drummond made the call I looked out of the window. My heart was booming in my ears. I was struggling to get a handle on my emotions. Dark thoughts were swirling through my head, each one adding to my anxiety.

Dave Prentiss's murder. The warning that more of us were going to be targeted. The fear in Aidan's voice. The fact that the killer was now on the loose in London. For all I knew he was already standing outside our house in Balham. Ready and waiting for an opportunity to kill Aidan. Or perhaps he would go after my mother next. Strike when she appeared at a window or left for work in the morning.

The thought of it was burning me up inside, making me feel sick. Surely more needed to be done to protect them. To keep them from being killed.

Getting marked cars to park outside our homes was only a short-term measure. It couldn't go on indefinitely. But protecting all the detectives and our families was going to be a huge problem, given that we couldn't all stay indoors until the threat went away.

As Drummond had pointed out earlier, providing round-the-clock protection for everyone would be a mega commitment. Small teams of officers would have to be assigned to each individual and for us detectives that would be completely impractical. We simply wouldn't be able to do our jobs.

And the same would go for our loved ones. Would Aidan be able to teach? Would the school even want him to turn up for work, knowing he was on a killer's hit list?

We had all been hoping and praying that we were dealing with an empty threat. That we wouldn't have to confront all those difficult-to-solve issues. But now we knew it was real and that meant we had to deal with it, along with the inevitable tsunami of fear and panic.

'We need to pull in all the likely suspects,' Drummond said, coming off the phone. 'And that includes the villains who have the clout to hire a contract killer. It's my firm belief that Dave Prentiss was murdered by a pro.'

'It has to be possible that the killer is the same person who sent the messages,' I said.

Drummond nodded. 'I agree it's possible, but I think it's unlikely. This doesn't feel like the work of a one-man-band to me. It has to be someone like Roy Slack. He's got the motive, the bottle and the money to pay someone to do his dirty work.'

'There was nothing incriminating on his phones or laptop, guv,' I said. 'In fact they'd hardly been used. And we had a good look round his office and flat.'

'The guy's not stupid. He wouldn't be sending the messages himself anyway and he'd have made damn sure there's nothing to link him to them.'

'I reckon that will apply to every face we put in the frame,' I said.

'Exactly. Which is why we have a serious fucking problem. We can't give in to the absurd demand, but at the same time there'll be public outrage if more of us are killed. The pressure will be like nothing we've ever experienced.'

'So how do we handle it, guv?' I said.

He shrugged. 'We do the only thing we can do and that's our very best. We drop everything else we're doing and concentrate on finding the bastard responsible. We question every villain and every snout in London. It'll mean working in tandem with Resnick and his team and any other division that gets drawn into it. And we do whatever we can to protect ourselves and our families.'

'That's a tall order, guv.'

He turned to look at me and his expression caused my stomach to do a swift somersault.

'Don't you think I know that, Laura?' he said, and he didn't try to disguise the tremor in his voice. 'Why do you think I'm shitting bricks?'

The Met was used to dealing with the big events, including those appalling atrocities committed by terrorists. But the murder of Dave Prentiss was greeted with total shock and disbelief.

By midnight everyone knew about the threat to his colleagues and their loved ones. Inevitably it was leaked to the media and during the early hours it became part of the blanket coverage on the news channels.

Every member of the task force came into the office and Drummond briefed them on what had happened in Battersea. There was an outpouring of grief, followed by a verbal commitment to hunt down those responsible, whatever the risks. The reaction was predictable because it was all so close to home. But the outward displays of solidarity and determination masked an underlying fear that everybody felt. I could see it in their eyes and hear it in their voices. Indeed, most of the detectives said their loved ones had reacted badly, just as Aidan had.

At the briefing, Drummond announced that marked patrol

cars would take up position outside the homes of everyone who had received the death threat. He also said that all potential suspects were to be hauled in for questioning.

But there were so many questions that he couldn't answer. Like what would happen if the killings continued? What level of protection, if any, would be provided? Would detectives be allowed to resign from the task force and take up other duties? Would the top brass actually consider suspending the organised crime investigations? And what was being done to track down the rat within our midst?

There were five television monitors in the room and it was hard to ignore the footage that appeared. There were shots of the Prentiss house, the uniforms and forensic suits gathered in front of it. There were also several shots of Dave Prentiss and constant references to the fact that his wife had only just given birth.

'Scotland Yard is saying very little at this stage,' the Sky News presenter said. 'But there are reports that Detective Inspector Prentiss and other officers attached to the organised crime task force had received anonymous text messages containing death threats. We'll bring you more as and when we get it.'

As the morning progressed I kept thinking that I would wake up from a terrible nightmare. But it wasn't to be.

As dawn broke over London I was convinced that the new day was going to bring more pain and heartache.

At six o'clock in the morning I had the dubious pleasure of interviewing Roy Slack again. He was amongst a bunch of high-profile villains who were rounded up across London overnight.

They included members of gangs that were on the task force's target list and individuals who fitted the profile of a contract killer. Their names were provided by the Met's Intelligence Unit and it was surprising how many there were and how many I'd never heard of.

Among them were those suspected of gang-related murders, those who'd served time for gun crimes, and former soldiers and mercenaries who had made names for themselves in the underworld.

One name stood out. Danny Carver. The Rottweiler. He was being questioned by officers at Streatham who had descended on his house in the early hours.

His boss had a lawyer with him this time – a fat, sweaty man named Darren Peacock – and the process was much more formal. We were in an interview room and Kate Chappell and I were facing Slack and Peacock across a table. The interview was being recorded and Slack had been read his rights.

We were late getting started because Peacock had only just turned up and he clearly wasn't happy about being dragged out of bed.

'I would like to state at the outset that I shall be lodging a formal complaint on behalf of my client,' Peacock said. 'It's clear he's the victim of an extreme case of police harassment. This is the third time in a week that he's been questioned. And it was totally out of order to wrench him from his bed at four o'clock in the morning.'

'The points you raise are noted, Mr Peacock,' I said. 'But a police officer was shot dead at his home last night. As you probably know, his name was Dave Prentiss and he was a member of the organised crime task force that has just launched an investigation into your client's business affairs. For that reason it was deemed necessary to arrest him as quickly as possible along with a number of other individuals.'

Slack seemed far less stressed than his brief, whose face was shiny with sweat. He sat there, calm and composed, in a V-neck sweater that revealed a thatch of grey hairs on his chest. Sandpaper stubble coated his jaw, and there was plenty of baggage beneath his watery eyes.

'My client had nothing to do with that poor man's death,' Peacock said. 'He was at home in his flat when it happened. You can confirm it by speaking to the concierge at the block and by checking the security cameras there.'

The ghost of a smile crossed Slack's face and he said, 'But you know that already, Detective Jefferson, because you've got my flat under surveillance.'

I gave him a closed-mouth grin.

'No one has accused you of actually carrying out the murder,' I said. 'I'm sure the days when you allowed your own hands to get dirty are long gone. But we believe the shooter was acting on behalf of someone who paid him. The same someone who's behind the death threat text messages. And you need to convince us that it isn't you.'

'My client doesn't have to convince you of anything,' Peacock said. 'The onus is on you to back up your suspicions and accusations with proof and it's obvious that you can't. You've already seized his phones and computer and come up with sod all as I understand it. So it's simply not good enough to claim that he's so anxious to stop you probing his affairs that he would resort to slaughtering police officers.'

'You're talking as though your client is an upstanding member of the community,' I said. 'But we all know that he's a ruthless gangster who's almost certainly been directly or indirectly responsible for dozens of killings over the years.'

Slack's smile got bigger but his lawyer affected an expression of pure outrage.

'May I remind you, officer, that despite the best efforts of the Metropolitan Police, Mr Slack has never been convicted of any crime,' Peacock said. 'What's more, you've never produced a shred of evidence linking him to any criminal activity.'

'He's been extremely lucky,' I said. 'But his luck is about to run out.' I turned to Slack. 'Isn't that why you're in a panic, Roy? You realise that this time we really mean business and that we won't stop until you're behind bars? So this is a desperate bid to cling onto your empire. You actually believe in the legend you've created – that you're this godfather-like figure who controls a big part of London and is above the law.

'In that respect you're just like the Richardson brothers and the Kray twins who were here before you. They also thought they could get away with anything, including murder, until they were standing in the dock at the Old Bailey.'

Slack chuckled. 'Nice little speech, detective. But you're way off the mark. The truth is I don't give a fuck about my so-called empire and I've no reason to be concerned about your investigation. None of it matters to me anymore and that's because I'm not going to be around for much longer.'

'So does that mean you're planning to do a runner?' I said. 'Move away to that fancy villa you've got down in Spain?'

Before answering he took a slow, deliberate breath and fixed me with a stare that was so intense I could almost feel it.

'No, Detective Jefferson,' he said, slowly. 'It means that I've been given at most six months to live.'

His lawyer was obviously just as surprised as I was. He started to speak, but Slack waved a hand to stop him.

'It's true,' Slack said. 'I have stage three pancreatic cancer. It was diagnosed just over three months ago and by then it was too late to do anything about. The doctors said it was inoperable.'

'That's bollocks,' I said. 'You don't look ill.'

Although in truth he didn't look a picture of health either. I remembered it was the impression I got when I first laid eyes on him the day before.

'That's the problem with this form of cancer,' he said. 'You often don't get any symptoms at the start. I'm only now beginning to suffer from back pain, weight loss and a bit of jaundice.'

Kate leaned forward and said, 'So are you having any treatment?'

He shrugged. 'I take tablets to control the pain, but that's about it. They offered me chemo but said it would only extend my life for a few months so I didn't see the point.'

'I'll need the contact details for your doctor,' I said. 'We'll have to check this out.'

'His number's on my phone and you've still got that,' he said.

'So why didn't you tell me about this yesterday?' I asked him.

He pursed his lips. 'There was no reason to. I thought that you would realise I had nothing to do with the death threats and leave me alone.'

'So who else is aware of this?'

'Nobody, and I'd like it to stay that way. In the time I've got left I have to offload the businesses or close them down. If it gets out that I'm on my last legs it'll only make things more difficult.'

It was certainly a turn up for the books. Something I hadn't expected. Jesus.

There was a long pause while I tried to get my head around it. I looked at Kate and her face posed a question: *What the hell do we do now?*

I clamped my lips together and raised my brow, as if to say: *I don't really know.*

Peacock leaned forward and whispered something in Slack's ear. Slack shook his head and patted the lawyer's hand.

Peacock then turned to me and said, 'In view of what we've just been told I really feel that this interview should be concluded. It's now even more evident that my client is not the person you're looking for. You can't seriously believe that he would risk his liberty by killing police officers – or even arranging for them to be killed – when his own life is almost over.'

It was a fair point to make but I wasn't yet ready to go along with it. After all, Roy Slack was a vicious criminal, a man of violence, so how could we be sure that he wouldn't embark on a murderous spree even with a death sentence hanging over his own head?

'We'll call it quits for now then,' I said to Slack. 'I'll make enquiries with your doctor and speak to my superiors. But despite what you've told us you still remain a suspect.'

Slack and his lawyer stood up together and Slack shook his head.

'You know what I hate about you fucking coppers,' he said, looking from me to Kate. 'You spend millions hounding people like me while letting scumbags who you know are terrorists roam around London plotting to kill innocent people. You should be ashamed of your fucking selves.'

And on that note he stormed out of the interview room with his fat lawyer trailing after him.

24

Laura

Roy Slack's bombshell revelation became one of the main talking points during the rest of the morning. Drummond refused to believe it until I'd spoken to the guy's doctor at St Thomas's Hospital who confirmed it.

'Mr Slack has asked me to provide you with all the information you require,' consultant oncologist Peter Merrick told me. 'I'm afraid that what my patient has told you is the truth. His pancreatic cancer will soon be at stage four and his life expectancy is no more than six months. But I suspect he'll be dead long before then as his condition has begun to deteriorate quite noticeably.'

It was hugely significant, not just because it raised a question as to whether he remained a suspect in respect of the death threats, but also because we'd need to work out where the investigation into his firm went from here. Who would take over the reins? Would he wind down any of his illicit operations in addition to the legit businesses? Would his demise lead to a power struggle between rival gangs?

I found it hard to feel sorry for Slack. It seemed he was going to part this world without being punished for a life of crime. He'd built up and run one of London's most powerful criminal empires. He'd been heavily involved in drugs, extortion, prostitution and money laundering. He'd established partnerships with Eastern European people smuggling gangs and at least one notorious Mexican crime cartel.

He had caused so much misery for so many people, but he'd be going to his grave content in the knowledge that he had got away with it. Two fingers up to the law. To all those officers in the Met who'd been unable to bring him down. It was wrong. Scandalous. Ridiculous.

Like hearing that a child killer has committed suicide in his prison cell while awaiting trial.

I rang Aidan just after seven o'clock and he told me that both he and my mother were going into work.

'We can't just sit at home all day worrying,' he said. 'For all we know this could go on for weeks.'

It was a frightening thought but I tried to play it down by telling him that it was very unlikely. I knew there would be no point urging him to stay at home behind locked doors. He'd already made it clear that he wasn't prepared to.

He confirmed that a marked police car had been parked outside the house during the night but had disappeared about an hour ago.

'They'll come back later,' I said. 'And in the meantime I'll see if I can get them to station a car outside the school.'

I then told him I'd stay in touch throughout the day and hung up.

There was so much going on that it was impossible for me to focus on any one thing. The morning papers, reviewed on the news channels, were all leading with Dave Prentiss's murder. But they had gone to press before the media got wind of the death threat messages. Now it was an even bigger story and views were being expressed, and questions were being asked.

A politician interviewed on Sky News said it was essential that the Met did not close down the organised crime task force.

'It would be like surrendering to terrorists,' he said. 'We cannot afford to let that happen.'

A prominent media pundit made a comment on the BBC that was picked out as a sound bite by every other news programme.

'The police are there to catch criminals and protect the public,' she said. 'But who protects them when they become the targets?'

It was a question that resonated with all of us and the Home Secretary himself tried to answer it when he was confronted by reporters.

'This has come as a profound shock,' he said. 'The murder of Detective Inspector Prentiss is being given the utmost priority. You can be sure that we will find whoever is responsible and bring them to justice. And we will also do whatever we can to protect other detectives and their families who've been threatened.'

Drummond got us all together again after he'd had a meeting with the Commissioner and other top brass. He announced that he'd be taking part in a press conference later in the morning and that the option of winding up the task force and suspending investigations into organised crime would not even be a consideration.

'You must all realise that despite what has happened to DI Prentiss we can't possibly throw in the towel,' he said. 'It would be like an army walking away from a war because a soldier has been killed. And make no mistake; we are at war with the criminals who are adopting terror tactics in order to remain in power.'

Janet Dean asked him if detectives would be allowed to transfer out of the task force. His answer was a categoric no.

'It would be a major sign of weakness,' he said. 'And it would damage the credibility of the entire force. Once such a precedent is set who knows where it would lead?'

He then invited everyone to update him on all the interviews that had been conducted and the tasks that had been set. I was up first and began by playing the video recording of the interview with Roy Slack.

'For those of you who don't already know, his oncology consultant has confirmed that what he said is true. Plus, I've done some checking online. Pancreatic cancer has one of the highest mortality rates of all major cancers. It's also difficult to spot in the early stages because often there aren't any symptoms until after it's become inoperable.'

'So do we rule him out as a suspect on the basis that he'll soon be dead?' Drummond asked. 'Even though he has a strong motive for wanting to see us disband the task force and leave him alone?'

'Absolutely not,' I said. 'It could be that he wants to go out with a bang. Pay us back for hounding him over the years.'

Drummond mulled this over. 'That's an interesting theory, but the guy has had an easier ride than most villains. He's always managed to stay one step ahead of us and he's never been banged up. I can't imagine that he bears grudges that are so strong they would compel him to do something like this.'

'Then perhaps it's someone else in his firm who's behind it,' Kate said. 'Maybe the person who'll be taking over from him wants to make life hard for us.'

'But he told us that nobody knows about his condition,' I pointed out.

Kate shrugged. 'Well, he could be wrong, or he could be lying.'

'It wouldn't surprise me if Danny Carver was being lined up to assume control,' I said. 'By all accounts he's the closest Slack has to a family and he's also a complete psycho.'

'He was questioned by detectives in Streatham,' Drummond said. 'He's insisting he knows nothing about the threats. And we know that he was in his house when the murder was committed because he's one of those we've just put under surveillance.'

We were getting the same feedback from the teams who were interviewing all the other suspects who'd been rounded up. They all had alibis and they all denied any knowledge of the threats.

'We have to keep plugging away,' Drummond said. 'Laura, you and Kate stay with Slack. He's still my prime suspect despite the sob story. And let's get access to everyone else's phone records and online communications. And we need search warrants for all their properties.'

'What about us and our families, sir?' DCI Graham Nash said. 'Will we be getting protection? My wife runs a bookshop in Clapham, and she's insisting on going to work even though I've advised her against it.'

'I can understand your concerns because we're all in the same boat,' Drummond responded. 'The Commissioner has agreed that we can continue to station a patrol car outside each of our homes overnight.'

'That's not nearly enough, sir,' Nash said.

Drummond nodded. 'I agree, but it's a start. And while we wait to see what else can be done I strongly suggest that you tell your wives, husbands and partners to be on their guard and to report anything that strikes them as suspicious.'

It wasn't what I'd been hoping to hear, but it was what I'd expected. The issue of protection would have to be decided at the highest level and after a whole range of factors had been considered.

The Met did not have access to unlimited resources and manpower. Staffing levels were at their lowest for years and detective numbers had fallen dramatically. Plus, hundreds of officers were already involved in protection and surveillance duties as part of the severe terror alert that was in place across the country. Drummond had said earlier that we couldn't expect every one of us to be given twenty-four hour protection. There were nineteen detectives on the task force, now that Prentiss wasn't included, and the number of family members and friends who had received the death threat totalled twenty-eight. Personal round-the-clock protection for all of us would require at least 250 officers working to a rota.

The sheer scale of such an operation, on top of everything else that was going on, was mind-blowing.

25

Rosa

She woke to the soft touch of Alice's fingers between her legs.

'I thought that would stir you,' Alice said. 'I was hoping we could have a little play before we both have to get up and go to work.'

Rosa was on her back. She turned to look at the face of the woman she was sharing the bed with. Alice Green, she'd said her name was, and she'd turned out to be a real star performer between the sheets.

In the early morning light coming through the windows she looked as good as she had the night before. Eyes wide and innocent. Lips enticingly moist. Skin so soft and clear that you just wanted to lick it.

She was everything that Rosa found desirable in a woman. It was no wonder the sex had been so good. So delicious.

'I've been awake for ages just staring at you,' Alice said. 'My God you're so beautiful. I can't believe I struck so lucky last night.'

'I'm the lucky one,' Rosa said. 'If the taxi driver hadn't recommended that particular club I would never have met you.'

The memories came flooding back. Leaving the club. The cab ride to the apartment building close to Hyde Park. Undressing each other the moment they entered Alice's luxurious apartment. Then falling on the king-size bed. Kissing. Sucking. Stroking. Licking. Probing. Going at it with total abandon.

Rosa had felt electrified by Alice's stunning body, her unbridled passion, the things she did with her lovely tongue. It had been as though neither of them had made love for a long time and that was what had made it so good. So special.

With Rosa it was all about the sex. Always. She didn't have what it took to form an emotional attachment with anyone. So all she could do was make the most of what did provide at least some semblance of meaning to her life. Such as the thrill of the kill. The power she wielded. The feel of another woman's lips.

For most people it wouldn't be enough. For some it would be more than they could ever hope for. So Rosa wasn't complaining. She never complained. It was partly because she didn't believe for a single second that she would live to a ripe old age. Eventually she would make a mistake and the cops would catch up with her. Or she'd become a target herself and fall victim to someone who was more cunning than she was.

So what was the point in fretting over what was lacking in her life? Best to cling onto what she had going for her and enjoy it while it lasted.

'It's eight thirty,' Alice said. 'The good thing about working for my dad is that nobody complains if I turn up late. So what do you say to us giving each other a couple more orgasms?'

Rosa moaned with pleasure as Alice inserted a finger into her dripping vagina.

'I can't think of a better way to start the day,' she replied.

The morning sex lasted just over half an hour and it was more than satisfying. Rosa came twice, squirting her juices over the sheets. Then she experienced a full-blown orgasm that made her blood sizzle.

Afterwards, they showered together before Alice gave her a quick tour of the apartment, which had to be worth a fortune.

'I know what you're thinking,' Alice said. 'That I'm a poor little rich girl living off her dad's generosity. Well, I suppose I am but there's nothing I can do about it so I don't bother trying.'

Rosa laughed. 'I think you're lovely, Alice. And that's despite the fact that you're a beautiful, sexy, spoilt little rich girl.'

They dressed together next to the window that offered up a view of Hyde Park. Rosa had got her bearings by now and she knew that beyond the park was South London. Vauxhall. Battersea. The area controlled by the man who was paying her to kill people.

She'd be going back there soon. Back to the hotel. Back to the garage containing the motorcycle and the weapons. Then to the place where she intended to claim her next victim.

'Oh, that's awful,' Alice said suddenly.

Rosa saw that she was staring at the wall-mounted TV that she'd just switched on using a remote control. A news anchor was telling viewers that a police officer had been murdered the previous evening on his own doorstep.

'Who the hell would do such a thing?' Alice said. 'It's so horrible.'

Rosa wondered how Alice would react if she knew that the woman who had just licked her vagina was the person responsible. The thought made her want to smile, but she decided it wouldn't be appropriate.

'This sort of thing happens all too frequently in Mexico,' Rosa said. 'There are murders every day. The drug cartels do terrible things. They're a law unto themselves. Nobody is safe. Especially the police.'

'I've heard about that,' Alice said. 'And I saw a documentary

161

that claimed your country is, like, one of the most violent places on earth.'

'It's true,' Rosa said, and she had to resist the temptation to reveal what had happened to her own parents. Alice didn't need to know. Nobody did. It was her cross to bear.

A photo appeared on the screen. The victim. Detective Inspector Dave Prentiss. Shot dead execution-style at his home in Battersea, according to the anchor. The police were appealing for witnesses. And there was concern that other officers and their families had been threatened.

There was another TV in the kitchen, and Alice turned it on as she made coffee and toast.

'Will I see you again?' she asked Rosa. 'I'd really like to.'

'Well, I'm free tonight if you are,' Rosa said.

Alice grinned. 'Of course I am. We can go out or you can come straight here.'

'Why don't we meet at the club again? I really enjoyed dancing with you.'

Alice giggled like a child. 'That's a great idea.'

Rosa wrote down Alice's mobile number and gave the other woman hers.

Then their attention was drawn back to the TV. Coverage of a press conference. All about the murder of detective Prentiss and the threats against his colleagues on the organised crime task force.

A man identified on screen as Metropolitan Police Commissioner John Saunders was saying, 'Our thoughts are with Detective Inspector Prentiss's wife and newborn baby. This is a shocking crime and I can assure you it will not go unpunished.'

Rosa held back another smile. *That's where you're wrong, Mr Commissioner. You have no idea who killed him. Not a clue. You'll be looking in all the wrong places. Chasing the wrong people. Working yourselves into a frenzy because you'll be wondering who will be the next victim. And not even Roy Slack knows that. Only I do, which is why this is going to be such an easy assignment. I have choices. Options. If one plan falls apart I just have to move on to the next.*

'Oh, Jesus, did you hear that?' Alice said. 'The poor man's wife has only just had a baby. That's so tragic.'

Indeed it was, Rosa thought. But then tragedy was part of life. Part of the whole goddamn cycle we were all caught up in. It couldn't be avoided, so there was no point making a deal of it. You just have to move on. Put it behind you. Accept that everything happens for a reason.

It was what they drummed into her after she found the blood-spattered bodies of her mother and father. And it was what she'd believed to be true ever since.

She was back in the hotel room by eleven o'clock. After changing out of last night's clothes she spent the next couple of hours in her bra and panties going over the notes she'd made the previous day.

She crossed Dave Prentiss off the list of names she'd been given and reminded herself how she intended to approach the next two hits.

At the same time she worked out contingencies, knowing that she would probably have to adapt her plans as she went along. She could no longer predict where her targets would be because now they would all be worried and therefore taking precautions.

She left the TV on, tuned to the news, and nothing she heard gave her cause for concern. And neither did it make her feel guilty. That was a pointless emotion, which in her line of work could not be indulged.

So what if the detective she'd shot had just become a father? She hadn't known the guy so why should she care?

163

Plus, it was Roy Slack who bore responsibility for what had happened and for what was going to happen. He had issued the death sentences. She was simply acting on his instructions, upholding her end of the contract.

But she wondered how many killings he'd allow her to carry out before he called a halt. Did he have the balls to let it go to double figures? If he didn't stop her, and she stayed for two weeks, that would be fourteen hits if she managed one a day, which was, in all honesty, pushing it.

By Mexican standards it wasn't a lot. The murder rate in Tijuana alone was three a day. A year ago, during the course of just one week, thirty people were executed – ten cops, twelve cartel members and eight soldiers. And it wasn't uncommon for the authorities there to uncover mass graves where all the victims had been decapitated.

But this was London. Not Tijuana. And not Mexico. And although it was evident that Roy Slack did not have much of a conscience, she wasn't sure he had enough ice in his veins to let it go too far.

Carlos Cruz, on the other hand, had once got his people to slaughter an entire police unit of twenty men and women because none of them was prepared to take a bribe.

Rosa still couldn't figure out why Slack thought that what he was doing was a good idea. Surely he would eventually come to his senses and realise that it could only be counter-productive in the long term. Even if the police never discovered that he was the man behind it, the repercussions for the city's gangs were going to be dramatic.

The TV caught her eye again. The Met Commissioner was back and making a statement outside Scotland Yard.

'After a meeting with the Home Secretary I would like to dispel rumours that we are prepared to close down the operations of the organised crime task force,' he said. 'This will not happen despite the threats that have this morning been made public. The task force is now working with the Murder Investigation Team, the Counter Terrorism Command and the National Crime Agency in a bid to find those who are seeking to scare this great police force of ours into submission.'

Rosa crossed the room and switched off the TV. She'd seen enough. She checked her watch and decided that it was time she went back to work. But before getting dressed she had one call to make and the number was among those on the list in front of her.

When a woman answered, she said, 'Is that Mrs Marion Nash?'

'Er, yes. Who's calling?'

'It's the BBC here, Mrs Nash,' Rosa said. 'As the wife of one of the detectives on the organised crime task force we wondered if you would care to comment on what is happening.'

'Oh no. I don't think I should.'

'But it's true, isn't it, that you also received the text message containing the death threat?'

'Well, er, yes, but . . .'

'Has it prevented you from going to work or carrying on as normal?'

'No it hasn't. I'm in work now and I'm busy so I really have to go. Sorry. You should call the police press office.'

Marion Nash hung up and Rosa turned off her own phone and removed the battery. She'd found out what she needed to know. The wife of DCI Graham Nash had shown a degree of courage and defiance by going to work in the bookshop she ran in Clapham.

Sadly for her it would prove to be a costly mistake.

26

Slack

Roy Slack was back in his apartment and he was on a high. The opening notes of his swansong were already reverberating across the city. The reaction was off the scale. Shock. Incredulity. Condemnation.

The Old Bill were feeling the pain and it was only day one. It cheered him to think how much more they would have to endure before this was finally over.

He still didn't know when that would be. But he did know that he'd make sure he got his money's worth out of Rosa Lopez. He would measure the success of the venture by how many people she killed and how their deaths impacted the Met and everyone who worked within it.

He wanted them to suffer both collectively and individually. He wanted to provoke panic and fear and confusion. He wanted to see desperation in the eyes of senior officers when they addressed the public and gave interviews. He wasn't going to be satisfied unless the consequences were devastating. And he was sure they would be.

He was watching the news from the comfort of his padded leather armchair, switching between channels while drinking coffee and smoking a cigar.

The cops had let him walk because they'd known that they weren't going to charge him with anything. How could they? There was no evidence. Nothing at all to connect him to the murder of DI Prentiss or the text messages.

He hadn't planned on telling them about the cancer just yet, but he'd seen it as the only way of stopping the bitch from wasting his time. And it'd worked. He'd probably still be in the interview room if he hadn't fessed up.

But he wasn't sure how he felt about his condition no longer being a secret. Before today he'd only told two people – Terry Malone and Danny Carver. Telling Terry on the night he was shot dead had been hard. It was only weeks after he'd been given the news himself.

Pancreatic cancer.

As soon as the doctor told him he knew that he wouldn't have long to live. Years before his own mother had been given the same diagnosis and so he'd learned all about it, including the fact that in some cases it can be hereditary.

She might have lived for up to six months if she hadn't decided to spare herself and everyone around her a lot of agony and distress by taking her own life.

Slack had already made up his own mind to follow her example, and sooner rather than later. But instead of taking an overdose he would use the pistol he kept in the hidden safe along with his trusty knuckleduster and the laptop and phones that he didn't want the police to get their hands on.

The safe also contained the suicide letter he had already written. It was in an envelope marked *Metropolitan Police*.

In the note he made it clear that he was responsible for the bloodbath. And he put the blame squarely on the shoulders of the Met for what they'd done to his father, his wife, his son and his grandchild.

He wouldn't be around to see their reaction, of course. But at least he'd die in the knowledge that the bastards would never forget him.

Or the fact that he'd made them pay a heavy price for what they'd done.

Danny called as soon as the police in Streatham released him. He'd been held for five hours and his flat had been turned upside down.

'They took a couple of phones and a tablet,' he said. 'But don't worry – they're not the ones I use. Those are well hidden.'

They compared notes on their respective interviews and agreed the cops were clueless.

'I told them about my condition,' Slack said. 'I asked them not to share the info but it doesn't mean they won't.'

'I don't think it matters considering where this is all going,' Danny said.

'I agree, but I'd like to keep it from the lads as long as possible.'

'Fair enough, but they're pretty anxious after all that's happened. I've spread the word that we'll meet up later. I just need to give 'em a time.'

'Let's say seven o'clock at the office,' Slack said. 'I'll have dinner downstairs afterwards.'

'OK, I'll arrange it.'

'And one other thing. I'm gonna want you to send another message to the detectives.'

'Saying what?'

'I'll tell you when I see you.'

Slack hung up and called Mike. He told him to come and pick him up at six thrity. That gave him plenty of time to shower and change.

He finished his coffee and left what remained of his cigar in the ashtray. He was heading for the bathroom when a text came through on his phone. It was from Rosa, and it caused the hairs on the back of his neck to stand to attention.

Number two taken care of in Clapham. News will break soon.

27

Laura

Emotions were running high in the office. Everyone was tired and tearful, and each person was dealing with the shock in his or her own way.

It wasn't as though we could withdraw into ourselves and grieve for one of our own. We had to stay on top of things, stay focused, do our jobs . . . even though we were reeling from Dave Prentiss's murder.

Kate Chappell was among those who were struggling to cope. When I went into the toilets I found her staring at herself in the mirror, her eyes beaten red from crying.

'I don't know how they can expect us to carry on as normal,' she said. 'Dave's been murdered, for Christ's sake. Anyone of us could be next.'

'The alternative is to give in to the maniac who's behind it,' I said, placing a hand on her shoulder. 'And we can't let that happen.'

She took a tissue from her jacket pocket and dabbed at her eyes.

'But this is not like anything we've faced before, Laura. Dave wasn't picked at random like when a terrorist attacks a uniform in the street. He was deliberately targeted. The killer knew his name, where he lived, when he'd be home.'

We looked at each other in the mirror.

'So what do you think we should do?' I asked.

She sucked on her bottom lip. 'I think the task force operations should be suspended while this is investigated by other divisions. And if they won't go for that upstairs then we should be given the option of stepping away from it. It's not fair to make us carry on like this. I can't be the only person who's scared to leave this building and go home.'

She wasn't. I knew that. Several other detectives had told me that they too were nervous about going home. One had already called his wife to tell her to pick up their two sons from school and go straight to his parents' house.

Kate drew a sharp breath and threw her tissue in the bin.

'I'm sick and tired of bad things happening,' she said. 'And I can't help thinking that my life would have been so much better, and far less dramatic, if I'd never joined the police.'

I cocked my head to one side and frowned.

'Do you really mean that?'

She turned towards me and her features tightened.

'Damn right I do. I married late because I was so busy doing this job that I forgot to have a social life. And when I did finally get hitched it was to a copper who turned out to be a cheating bastard. If he hadn't died in an accident I swear I would have killed him myself.'

She started sobbing again so I put my arms around her and gave her a hug.

I managed not to cry along with her, but it required a large amount of willpower. Inside I was just as fearful and confused, although I hadn't got to the stage where I was wishing I'd never joined the force. If anything I felt an even stronger sense of responsibility, not only to my colleagues, but also to the public. We were the last line of defence and we couldn't back away from any challenge or threat, no matter how severe. But would I still feel the same way if the killings continued? That was a question I wasn't able to answer.

Aidan rang to say he was at home and that my mother was with him.

'She's still scared, Laura,' he said. 'So I've told her to stay here tonight.'

I swallowed hard. Pinched the bridge of my nose. Didn't know what to say to ease his fears.

'We've been watching the news,' he said. 'They're saying the killer's still out there.'

'That's right,' I said. 'But the investigation has only just begun. We're hoping—'

He cut me off. 'Look, be straight with me, hon. Do you have any idea who's doing this?'

'We have a bunch of suspects,' I said.

'So that's a no then.'

'I didn't say that, Aidan.'

'You didn't have to. What about that man Slack, the gangster?'

'He was arrested and I questioned him myself,' I said.

'Then why have I just heard on the news that he's been released without charge, along with others?'

'We know he didn't kill Dave Prentiss because he's under surveillance. But although it's possible he paid someone to do it we can't charge him unless we can prove it, and right now we can't. Plus, we haven't uncovered any link between him and the text messages.'

He gave an exasperated sigh and his tone became less combative.

'I don't want it to sound like I'm having a go at you, Laura,' he said. 'But try to put yourself in our position. It was bad enough when we received the message. But now we know that this nutter has every intention of carrying out his threat.'

'I'm in the same position as you and mum,' I said. 'So I do know how you feel. And if I could just make it all go away by waving a magic wand I would. But it's going to take time. And, just so you know, there are discussions taking place at the highest level about protection for everyone concerned.'

He left it a couple of beats before responding, and I heard my mother in the background asking him when I'd be coming home.

'Tell her I hope to be home in a few hours,' I said. 'I'm desperately in need of a shower and some sleep.'

'Well, whatever time you get here I'll be up,' he said. 'And please take care of yourself.'

When I came off the phone I had to resist a sudden urge to drop everything and rush straight home. I wanted to be with Aidan and my mum. They were the two most important people in my life and they were at risk from a deranged killer or killers.

What if one of them was going to be the next target? Or both of them for that matter? How would I ever forgive myself, knowing that I hadn't done more to protect them?

But we were all faced with the same dilemma – and none of us knew how to respond to it.

Drummond called us together for another update. Frustration lent an edge to his voice as he announced that all the faces we'd brought in for questioning had either been released or would be soon.

'We've got sweet fuck all,' he said. 'We're still sifting through phone records and computers but I'm not optimistic.'

He told us the National Crime Agency was concentrating on foreign crime gangs who were operating in London – the Russian Mafia, the Mexican cartel that had links to Slack's mob, and the Eastern European outfits.

'Meanwhile we'll continue to focus on the home-grown firms,' he said. 'Another list of names is about to be circulated so let's get cracking on it.'

He went on to say that a new shift pattern was being drawn up so that we could take turns to catch up on lost sleep.

He then returned to the subject of protection and said he'd put in a request for armed officers to accompany detectives during the day.

'Those of you who are authorised to carry weapons will hopefully be able to arm yourselves with a handgun,' he said.

That included me. I had attended the firearms course as part of a ten-month secondment to the Met's Specialist Protection Command. My job there was to be a close protection officer for visiting dignitaries and politicians. But I'd never felt comfortable in the role and had thankfully never had to pull the trigger on my Glock pistol.

So it actually came as a huge relief when they offered me a position with the task force and I was able to move straight over.

I was still pondering the unappealing idea of carrying a gun again when Drummond's mobile rang and he stopped speaking to answer it. As he listened he gestured for the rest of us to be quiet by raising his hand.

And so we watched as his face ran through a gauntlet of emotions, from vague curiosity to shock to total disbelief. Then he turned his back on us to respond to whatever he'd been told.

It was obvious to us all by then that something had happened.

Something that the boss hadn't expected. He finally ended the call and turned to face us again, and a hard lump formed in my throat as he struggled to regain his composure. Before he spoke his eyes swept the room and for some reason settled on DCI Nash.

Then, in a voice that was strangely shaky, he said, 'Can you come into my office for a moment, Nash?' To the rest of us, he added, 'Stay where you are. I need to brief you on a development.'

Graham Nash wore a deep frown as he stood up and followed the gaffer into his office, closing the door behind him. Seconds later a horrible cry came from inside the room and my heart leapt.

28

Rosa

She had four hours to kill before meeting up with Alice at the Vichy Lounge. Time then to make preparations for the next hit before getting ready.

She was really looking forward to her night out. The dancing. The sex. The uncomplicated intimacy. It was the perfect way to come down from what was in effect the ultimate high.

Every killing affected her like a drug. The racing heartbeat. The soaring metabolism. The rising blood pressure. The surge of adrenalin.

Afterwards she always felt the need to relax and recharge her batteries. And there was no better way to do that than by letting her hair down and having a good time.

It usually included a fair amount of alcohol – her favourite drinks being tequila cocktails and champagne. But this assignment wasn't over so she had to keep a clear head.

She was now sitting in front of the iPad, waiting for it to power up, while nibbling on a pre-packaged ham sandwich.

She was delighted with the way things were going. Two hits in two days and she hadn't encountered a single problem.

Marion Nash had been an easy target. Just as easy as Dave Prentiss had been. Rosa's mind carried her back through the sequence of events. Everything had gone according to plan.

When she'd left the hotel room it had been almost dark outside. On the way to pick up the bike from the garage she'd popped into a charity shop where she'd paid a few pounds for a man's heavy black overcoat. It was two sizes too big but perfect for what she'd wanted it for. She'd sat on it during the short ride to Clapham.

The tiny independent bookshop run by Mrs Nash was right on the High Street. Rosa had parked the bike in a quiet street nearby that was not covered by any CCTV cameras. There she'd slipped the coat over her leather suit, put the helmet in one of the saddlebags, and replaced it with her own baseball cap.

The evening was cold and damp and everyone she passed had been in a hurry to get where they were going. No one paid any attention to the figure in the long coat and cap who could have been a man or a woman.

She'd stood watching the shop for the best part of twenty minutes from a doorway across the street. Through the window she'd been able to see Mrs Nash, and it was clear that the woman was working alone.

Only one customer entered the shop during that time: a young man in a raincoat who only spent a few minutes in there before leaving without buying a book.

Seconds after he'd gone Rosa had made her move. Head down, overcoat collar pulled up, she'd crossed the road between the slow-moving traffic.

A bell had rung as she'd entered the shop. Mrs Nash, a tall, middle-aged woman with dyed blonde hair, had been standing behind the counter.

Rosa had lifted her head just far enough to scan the interior and spot the single surveillance camera on the far wall. Having located its position she avoided looking at it as she moved between head-high bookshelves towards the counter.

'Hello there,' Mrs Nash had said, as she approached. 'Can I be of assistance?'

Rosa had smiled at her while at the same time drawing the silenced pistol from inside the coat. She'd then pulled the trigger twice before the woman even had time to react.

Both bullets had smashed into her chest and thrown her against the wall behind her. She'd slid to the floor as blood poured from the wounds onto her bright-green blouse.

Rosa had then stepped behind the counter to make sure that her victim was dead. And that was when she'd spotted the sleek black digital video recorder beneath the counter, the machine that no doubt stored the surveillance camera footage. It was a stupid place to put it and it took Rosa just seconds to unplug it from the mains and walk out of the shop with it under her arm.

The DVR had fitted snugly in one of the saddlebags and on the way back to the garage she'd dumped that and the overcoat in a commercial wheelie bin in front of a car park.

Now as she reflected on the completion of another successful job, the corners of her mouth lifted in a satisfied smirk. She was on a roll, for sure. Carlos would be pleased and so would the client. She now had to hope that the rest of the assignment went just as smoothly. If so, then she could start to think about ways of spending some of the half million dollars she was being paid.

29

Laura

There was no easy way to break the news to us so Drummond didn't attempt to.

But before speaking to us he called DI Phil Warren into his office and got him to sit with a very distraught Graham Nash. Warren was Nash's closest friend on the task force and they often worked together as a pair.

After the boss had closed his door on them he told us that Nash's wife Marion had been shot dead in her bookshop on Clapham High Street.

'It's believed to have happened about two hours ago,' Drummond said. 'Her body was found lying behind the counter by a customer. The senior investigating officer at the scene has only just discovered that she was Graham's wife and one of the people who received the death threat.'

There was a long, heavy silence during which nobody spoke or moved. We were all shocked and paralysed. My mind raced along with my heart. I thought about the death threat we had all received.

. . . I'm calling on you and the other detectives attached to the unit to step back from it. Those of you who refuse will suffer the consequences and either you or those close to you, including family members, will be killed . . .

Oh God.

First Dave Prentiss. Now Graham Nash's wife, Marion. I couldn't believe it. Didn't want to believe it.

My mind seemed to shut down for a time and I was only half aware of what was going on around me. I heard more than one person sobbing. I felt my own tears threaten, but I squeezed my eyes closed and fought them back.

Suddenly there was a burst of activity in the room. Phones started ringing. People started talking and moving. Drummond's strident voice rose above the sounds, telling us all to stay calm.

Time appeared to stand still for a while, but a lot actually happened. Drummond dispatched himself to the crime scene in Clapham, this time with Tony Marsden in tow.

DCI Nash, who was a total wreck, was escorted out of the room by Warren and two support staffers. I had no idea where they were taking him.

Janet Dean sat beside me and broke down and someone switched on the TV monitors so that we heard that reports were coming in of another fatal shooting in London.

I just sat behind my desk as the anger and anxiety balled like a fist inside me. I was trying to decide what to do when the Commissioner himself suddenly appeared in the office.

John Saunders was a tall, lean man with a thin face and pinched features. He was meticulously dressed in his uniform and he immediately seized our attention.

'DCS Drummond has appraised me of the situation by phone,' he said. 'He's asked me to tell you that he'll be back as soon as he's spoken to the SOI in Clapham and checked the scene for himself. He'd like you all to stay here so that he can brief you on his return. I realise that this is a difficult time, but it's essential that we hold it together and don't weaken our resolve in response to these terrible events.'

To his credit the man didn't retreat when questions were fired at him about what protection would be provided for the rest of us.

But instead of listening to his answers I reached for the phone on my desk. I wanted to know that Aidan was all right. I also had to tell him there had been another murder – and that I wouldn't be coming home any time soon after all.

30

Slack

On the way to the office Slack tapped out a message on one of his burner phones.

Call me on this number

Five minutes later his mobile rang and he answered it.

'Can you talk?' he said.

The voice on the other end of the line was barely above a whisper.

'I can now. I've been trying to contact you, Roy.'

'I know, but I've been busy. Where are you now?'

'At the Yard. Just outside the office.'

'So tell me what you know about the Clapham killing.'

'But surely you already know that the victim was the wife of one of the detectives. Everyone here is gutted.'

'Good. So any sign that the Met is about to roll over and close down the task force?'

'Are you fucking insane? It's never going to happen and you must know it.'

He laughed. 'That's exactly what I wanted to hear.'

'I don't get it. This is madness. You have to stop it.'

'Don't tell me you've suddenly developed a conscience,' he said. 'You've never given a shit about your colleagues before.'

'But this is different. When I gave you the list of names and contact details you didn't tell me what you were going to do with it. If I'd known you were going to start killing people I would never have done it.'

'You had no fucking choice,' he snapped. 'It was either that or I was gonna let it be known that you've been on my payroll for the past five years and that a while back you were involved in the murder of a police officer. So stop whinging and stay the fucking course. If you don't I'll see to it that you spend the rest of your life in a cell.'

'But I don't understand what you're hoping to achieve by doing this. It won't stop the Met from going after the firm. You're still the prime suspect despite your denials. And why are you so set on seeing the task force wound up if you're not going to be around for much longer? It makes no sense to me.'

'It has nothing to do with the task force or the firm,' he said. 'This is me getting my own back against your lot for all the grief I've suffered over the years. I want revenge before I die.'

He waited for a response, but all he heard was a sharp intake of breath.

'There are things that have been done to me that you know nothing about,' he said. 'But eventually it'll become clear to you and everyone else. In the meantime stop pretending that you care about your colleagues and do what you're paid to do – which is whatever I say.'

Slack pressed his thumb against the call-end icon and heaved an almighty sigh.

Bent coppers never ceased to amaze him. They were happy to

take the bung and shaft their mates. And yet at the same time they tried to convince themselves that they were still good people.

Fucking pathetic.

It was another reason he hated the Old Bill so much. They were hypocritical slags who had fewer morals than most of the people they pursued.

The meeting got underway as soon as he arrived at the office, and he found it hard not to feel sorry for the men sitting with him around the table. They were his loyal lieutenants, after all. Several of them – Frank Piper, Adam Clarke and Johnny Lightfoot – had been with him for years. And they had done their bit to ensure that the firm thrived and prospered.

But they now faced an uncertain future through no fault of their own.

After he was gone the firm would in all likelihood fall apart. Danny had made it clear that he wasn't going to hang around with a view to taking over. As soon as Slack gave him the go-ahead – and the rest of the money he'd been promised – he was going to flee to South America and carve out a new life for himself.

The rest of the lads were going to be left to pick up the pieces. And that wasn't going to be easy. The Old Bill would no doubt seek their own form of retribution after the bloodbath finally ended and they got wind of his suicide note.

Piper and the others were going to find it hard to convince anyone that they hadn't known that their boss had ordered the killings. The cops might well accuse them of being involved. And even if there were no formal charges, the lads were going to be in for a rough ride.

But none of this stopped Slack from lying through his teeth when he was asked if he knew anything about the murder of DI

Dave Prentiss and the threats against other members of the task force and their families. The media hadn't yet linked these with the murder in Clapham earlier in the evening.

'Believe me, I'm as much in the dark as you are,' Slack said, sounding as sincere as an evangelist. 'I don't know who's behind it. So I can only assume it's one of the other outfits, probably the Russians. They know the task force will be going after them as well.'

It was a plausible enough explanation and the guys appeared to accept it. But then why wouldn't they? Slack had always been up front with them in the past and he had looked after their interests. They also knew that to question his honesty was a sure way to wind up in hospital.

The thing was, he didn't feel that he owed them anything beyond what they'd already had from him. Under his leadership they had made pots of money. It was how they could afford to live in fancy houses and drive around in flash cars.

It'd be different if they were family. But they weren't. Thanks to the Old Bill he didn't have a family.

The meeting was constructive only in the sense that they covered a lot of ground. It was agreed that while they were under unusually high levels of police surveillance they would put the brakes on some of the operations, including the riskier aspects of the drugs distribution network and the collection of protection money.

'It'll cost us a fucking fortune,' Frank Piper said, his voice stretched with tension.

Slack nodded. 'I realise that, but it can't be helped while all this shit's going down.'

Slack ended the meeting with more lies about how he had their interests at heart and how he was confident the task force would not topple the firm.

He wasn't feeling well suddenly and he knew that if he didn't take his medication it was going to get a lot worse. There was already a pain at the base of his spine and it would soon work its way up his back.

The problem was he'd left his tablets at the flat so it meant skipping dinner and heading straight back there.

'Go downstairs and enjoy yourselves lads,' he said. 'I have some business to attend to so I won't be joining you.'

After they'd left the meeting room he asked Danny to join him in his office and there he explained why he couldn't hang around.

'I'll be fine once I've dosed myself up,' he said.

He dictated a short text message that he wanted Danny to send to the task force detectives. Then, before leaving the office, he sent a text to the phone he'd given to Rosa Lopez.

Good work so far. I'm adding another name to the list. Deal with this one asap. Details to follow.

31

Laura

Aidan reacted to the news of Marion Nash's murder by saying, 'Oh God. This is terrifying.'

I told him that I didn't have the details and that I wasn't sure when I'd be home.

'I don't know what's going to happen.' I said. 'Things are moving so fast we can barely keep up.'

I had never been in this position before. None of us had. We were not only police officers. We were also victims. And so were those who were close to us. It made it difficult to know how to respond.

'You should go and get some sleep,' I said to Aidan. 'Don't wait up for me. And please do what you can to make mum feel safe.'

As I hung up, my throat got tight. It was becoming harder for me to keep a lid on my emotions. Coppers were supposed to remain detached and objective. Calm under pressure. But, under the circumstances, that simply wasn't possible.

The fear was bunching up inside me and I was feeling emotionally raw. Two people were dead – one a close colleague and friend, the other the wife of another colleague.

I'd met Marion Nash on several occasions. And her husband had never tired of telling the rest of us how she had given up her job as a librarian to open her own bookshop. Her only son had flown the nest so she had put her heart and soul into making it a success.

Her death was indeed a terrible, pointless tragedy. The second in less than twenty-four hours. That in itself was enough to make the blood curdle.

It told us that we were dealing with a cold, calculating killer. A true professional. Someone who planned ahead. Someone who researched his victims and knew where they would be at any given time.

I thought it sensible to assume that the assassin was male. Most contract killers were, certainly in this part of the world. In South America and Mexico it was different. There women were just as likely to be gang leaders and hired guns.

But in Europe and the US it was a male-dominated profession. Some hitmen even advertised their services on the dark web. Many of those were rank amateurs, though, and they were often hired by men and women who wanted their spouses or business partners bumped off. They usually ended up getting caught and their subsequent trials were becoming regular features in tabloid newspapers.

But the real pros managed to ply their trade for years while raking in huge amounts of money. They were the guys who crime lords like Roy Slack turned to when they wanted one or more executions to be carried out cleanly and efficiently. They were like ghosts who appeared only when they were summoned and then disappeared again after their work was done.

It was possible that the killer now on the rampage in London had been brought in from abroad. If so then it was doubtful that he had ever appeared on the radars of any of our law enforcement agencies.

It would therefore be difficult, if not impossible, to identify him.

So the only way we stood a chance of catching the bastard was if he made a mistake.

And how likely was that?

Before leaving the office, the Commissioner assured everyone that a plan would be drawn up to provide protection for all of us. But he reiterated what he had announced publicly – that the task force operations would not be suspended.

'We cannot give in to this lunatic's demand,' he said. 'If we do there's no telling what will happen. He might well turn his attention to one of the other task forces or specialist units. Would we then be expected to close those down as well?'

It was a point I hadn't considered because I'd been assuming that the motive for the threats and the murders was simply to halt our investigation into Roy Slack's firm. If there was more to it than that then I couldn't for the life of me think what it could be.

I was still of the view that Slack had a hand in what was happening, either alone or as part of a consortium of crime syndicates that had got together to fight back against the Met.

After all, across the various divisions we'd inflicted considerable damage on the London underworld during the past couple of years. It was therefore conceivable that they were now aiming to cause fear and panic within our ranks in an attempt to limit our effectiveness.

This was an issue we discussed among ourselves while waiting for Drummond and Tony Marsden to return. When they did, at just after eleven o'clock, they both wore sombre expressions. Drummond explained in heartbreaking detail what had happened in Clapham. How the killer had entered the shop and fired two bullets into Marion Nash's chest while she stood behind the counter.

'None of the people working in neighbouring premises heard gunfire,' he said. 'That suggests a silencer was used. We'll know for sure if it was the same weapon after forensics have checked it.'

But there was no doubt in any of our minds that it would be the same gun.

'There's a single surveillance camera in the shop, but the killer took the digital video recorder with him,' Drummond continued. 'CCTV cameras in the street have still to be checked.'

DS Marsden then told us that Graham Nash had been taken to the crime scene at his own insistence. He had identified his wife and was now at home.

'He's obviously in a very bad way,' Marsden said. 'We've managed to contact their son, and Graham has a brother who's flying in from Dublin as we speak.'

We were all far too shocked and exhausted to carry on working in any meaningful way so Drummond told us to go home and get some sleep. The office would be manned by a handful of support staff who were on the night shift.

But as soon as he finished speaking there came a further shock. It arrived in the form of another text message on the phones of all the detectives. And once again it made us realise that we had absolutely no control over the situation we found ourselves in.

Next time it could be you or someone you love. You know what you have to do to stay safe. And by the way, any officers assigned to protect you will themselves become targets.

32

Rosa

This time they returned to Alice's apartment just before midnight. They'd spent the evening dancing and smooching at the Vichy Lounge, and not once did Rosa think about the assignment. Instead she gave into a passion that consumed every bit of her mind and body and left no room for anything else.

The pretty young Londoner had that effect on her. Rosa could not recall the last time she'd been with someone with whom she felt so compatible.

They were lying on their backs now, having spent the last hour feasting on each other's flesh. Above the bed the glow from a scented candle flickered on the ceiling.

'I'm really going to miss you when you go back to Mexico,' Alice said.

Rosa had told her she'd be in London for two weeks, and they had even talked about doing some other stuff together. With the weekend approaching, Alice had offered to show her around the city. She'd mentioned Oxford Street, Covent Garden, Hyde Park, Trafalgar Square. These were all places that Rosa had heard of and the prospect of visiting them excited her. So too did the thought of sharing the experiences with Alice. It wasn't something that Rosa usually did because she rarely stayed anywhere longer than one or two nights.

'I'd like to see Buckingham Palace,' Rosa said. 'I've seen so many pictures of it.'

Alice giggled. 'Then that will be the first stop on our tour. Shall we do it on Sunday? Please say yes.'

Rosa giggled back. 'I don't see why not.'

They fell silent as sleep crept up on them. Alice was the first to drop off and her breathing became heavier. Rosa succumbed shortly after and as soon as the darkness claimed her so too did the nightmare.

There are three men in the room with her. Two of them are strangers. The third is Enrique, her adoptive father.

He's told her that they're his friends and that they've been looking forward to meeting her.

'They didn't believe me when I told them what a beautiful little girl you are,' he says. 'So that's why I've brought you here to their home. So that they can see for themselves.'

Rosa has only just turned eight years old and she's scared. She thinks she knows what is going to happen to her. The men are going to do horrible things to her and make her do things to them. And if she tries to resist or starts to cry she'll be hurt.

Enrique usually slaps her face or pinches her cheek so hard it brings tears to her eyes. Sometimes he says that if she doesn't behave he'll drive her deep into the forest and leave her there all alone.

Once she said that she was going to tell her aunt and in response he threatened to burn her eyes out with a cigarette.

So she no longer resists or cries or tells him to stop.

192

But this is the first time he's introduced her to anyone and she suspects it's because her aunt is in hospital having something called an appendix taken out of her body.

'My friends have given me money to buy you some gifts,' Enrique says. 'So I want you to show them how grateful you are. Do you understand?'

Rosa nods. Of course she understands, despite her tender age.

'That's great,' Enrique says. 'Now we will all watch while you take off your clothes.'

Rosa woke up with a start, her face covered in sweat, her heart pounding in her chest.

She hadn't had that particular dream for a while. But it was always there, lurking inside her mind, a reminder of one of the defining events in her young life. It was when Enrique started sharing her with his friends in return for money, none of which he gave to her.

It happened many times after that. Sometimes it seemed as if she could still feel the pain they inflicted with their hands and teeth and hard cocks.

She got out of bed as quietly as possible so as not to wake Alice, then padded naked into the bathroom and splashed cold water onto her face.

Some of her nightmares were more vivid than others. And a few, like the one she'd just had, were so real that it was like reliving the experience.

After a couple of minutes she climbed back into bed. Alice was still out cold, and her chest was rising and falling with every breath.

Rosa stretched out and closed her eyes, but this time sleep did not come easily. Her mind was suddenly too active and she couldn't stop her thoughts from shifting to her assignment. And the next target.

She had worked everything out earlier in the hotel. The approach. The escape. The method of execution.

The person she had chosen appeared third on the list that Roy Slack had given to her. The photo she had seen was burned onto her retinas.

The victim's name was Laura Jefferson, and she was a detective inspector on the organised crime task force. She had a boyfriend named Aidan and a mother named Ruth, and they were also on the list.

Laura Jefferson was a very attractive woman. She had kind eyes and a sensuous mouth.

It seemed a shame to Rosa that by this time tomorrow she'd be dead.

33

Laura

A clap of thunder woke me on Friday morning. When I rolled onto my side I discovered that I was alone in the bed.

The LED light on the digital clock told me it was 6am It meant that I'd managed about three hours of fragmented sleep.

Aidan had been awake when I'd arrived home at just after one. We had talked for a while as my mother snored in the next room.

He told me how worried she was and how he had managed to persuade her to take the day off and drive to Ringwood in the New Forest where she could spend the weekend with her best friend, Sylvia Jones.

I'd said it was a great idea even though the thought of her having to flee her home because she was scared made me shiver.

They were both sitting at the kitchen table when I shuffled in wearing my towelling robe. Mum was already dressed and she told me she had made arrangements with Sylvia.

'Are you sure that you don't mind me going, Laura?' she asked me. 'Nobody will know I'm there so I'll be safe.'

Her words triggered a blitz of emotions in me. Guilt. Fear. Shock. A raging sense of impotence.

How could this be happening to my mother? To us? To one of the largest police forces in the world?

It beggared belief, and yet here we were. Living in fear. Wondering who would be next to die.

'Are you all right, Laura?'

Aidan's voice snapped me out of myself. I told him I was fine. Just not quite awake.

Then I hugged my mum and told her that I wanted her to go to Sylvia's.

'It's the sensible thing to do,' I said. 'I wish I could go with you.'

'I'm sure Sylvia wouldn't mind,' she said.

I shook my head. 'It's not possible, Mum. I have to stay here to help find whoever is doing this. And I swear to you that we will. It's only a matter of time. We're throwing everything at it. Hundreds of officers are working on the case.'

She already knew almost as much as I did about the murder of Marion Nash. The TV was playing in the background, tuned to the breakfast news on the BBC.

The link between the two killings had been established and they were showing photographs of Mrs Nash and Dave Prentiss. There were also exterior shots of the bookstore in Clapham and a short interview with the Commissioner outside Scotland Yard.

'I can confirm that Mrs Nash was the wife of a detective chief inspector on the organised crime task force,' he said. 'And that she was among those who received the death threat text message.'

In answer to a question from a reporter he was forced to admit that Mrs Nash had not been provided with personal police protection.

'The issue of how to protect those individuals at risk is being considered as a matter of extreme urgency,' he said. 'There will be a press conference later this morning when we'll be giving more details about the investigation.'

The Commissioner looked exhausted and I doubted that he'd had any sleep.

After his interview they put up a photo of Marion Nash with her husband, which looked as though it had been taken some years ago. My thoughts shifted to Graham and my heart went out to him. How on earth would he cope? His life had been callously ripped apart.

The three of us watched the news in silence for a few minutes and then Mum said that she needed to go home and pack a bag before driving to Ringwood.

Aidan said he would take her and that he'd shower when he got back. Unlike my mother, he intended to go to work at the school.

Neither of us could hold back the tears as we said our goodbyes. I hadn't seen Mum this distressed in a long time and it really got to me. But I was glad she was going to Ringwood. It was going to be a huge weight off my shoulders. She'd be perfectly safe there. I was sure of that.

After they'd gone I finished the coffee and did a quick tour of the house, checking the windows and doors. The place wasn't as secure as it should have been. There was no burglar alarm. No motion-detector lights at the front and back.

The wall at the bottom of the small rear garden was only about five feet high and backed onto an unlit alley that ran between the houses.

Clearly I hadn't paid enough attention to security and as a police officer I should have. I recalled that when we moved in the landlord had said that he was happy for us to install an alarm and outside lights. But we hadn't bothered to, partly because we were never sure from one year to the next how long we'd stay. Our intention had always been to buy our own house or flat in a less expensive area.

As I stepped into the shower I made a mental note to arrange for a locksmith to come round at the weekend to make the front and back doors more secure.

We would also put up motion-detector lights that would come on if the man who had murdered Dave Prentiss and Marion Nash decided to approach our house.

Thunder rolled across the sky as I made my way into work. Rain showers lashed the streets, and I was forced to hail a cab from the tube station for the last leg of the journey.

When I walked into the office at nine o'clock it was throbbing with activity. A new whiteboard had been set up with photos of Mrs Nash and the crime scene in Clapham.

My stomach pitched when I saw the poor woman lying on the floor in a pool of her own blood.

'I've never known anything like this,' Tony Marsden said as he came and stood beside me. 'We need to catch this fucker before we all end up like that.'

As sensitive as ever, I thought. But he was right. This couldn't go on.

He looked at me and a line creased his forehead.

'My money is still on Roy Slack,' he said. 'He's the only villain out there who would dare to take it this far. We all know he thinks he owns this city and that he's more ruthless than any of the other gang bosses.'

'My gut's telling me the same thing,' I said. 'But we also know that the guy's smart enough to make sure we won't be able to prove anything.'

A fire grew in his eyes. 'If it was up to me I'd do what the scumbag obviously did to that firearms officer, Hugh Wallis. Just lift him off the street and make him disappear.'

There was nothing worse than knowing, or at least strongly suspecting, that someone was guilty of a crime and not being able to do anything about it.

At nine thirty, Drummond started the first briefing of the day. He began by announcing that four detectives, including Janet Dean, had not turned up this morning. Janet was claiming that she had a hospital appointment. The others said they were having to deal with distraught family members.

I was surprised that so many of the team had actually come in. The eyes of everyone in the room were glazed and haunted. It was clear that trauma and exhaustion were taking their toll.

There had been a couple of developments overnight. Forensics had confirmed that the same gun had been used to kill both Dave Prentiss and Marion Nash. And some CCTV footage showed the killer entering and leaving the bookshop. It was poor quality, though, and therefore not very helpful. As we viewed it on the monitors, I felt my blood surge.

Drummond provided a commentary. 'It's from a street camera about thirty metres from the shop. You can see the figure in a long dark overcoat and baseball cap walking into shot from across the road. He pauses briefly outside the shop and then goes in. Just two minutes later he comes out and crosses back over the road. Unfortunately there are no cameras covering the other side. The next person to enter the shop discovered the body.'

Drummond then put up a couple of freeze frames showing magnified images of the figure in the overcoat. But they were far too blurry to distinguish any features and it was impossible even to tell if it was a man or a woman.

'We're about to release this to the media,' he said. 'Maybe we'll get lucky and it turns out someone saw where this person went.'

Drummond then said he was about to have a meeting with the Commissioner and other senior officers to discuss the latest text message that had come through last night, telling us that any officers assigned to protect us would also be targeted.

'The situation is going from bad to worse,' he said. 'So until it's decided how we respond to this I don't want anybody going anywhere by themselves. A list of all the civilians who received the original text has been passed on to uniform who will be contacting them about their individual situations. We'll do everything we can to make them safe.'

We were then told that the Commissioner had sanctioned the carrying of firearms by those officers who were authorised to use them.

That was all I needed to hear. As soon as the briefing was over I went to pick up a gun. At the same time I picked up a Taser for good measure and slipped it into my bag.

The pistol I signed out was a Glock 17, and I wore it now in a holster around my waist, cowboy style. It provided a degree of comfort even though I hoped I would never have to use it.

Despite everything that was happening, Drummond said he wanted us to continue doing our jobs. The emphasis had changed, of course. In the short term at least we were no longer focused on breaking up Roy Slack's empire and finding evidence to bring charges relating to his involvement in organised crime.

Now we had to devote ourselves entirely to the task of finding out who was behind the murders and the threats. Other units within the Met were doing the same – the Murder Investigation

Teams in Battersea and Clapham, the National Crime Agency, and the Cyber Crime division.

My remit continued to be to concentrate on Slack himself and to look for chinks in his armour. I started by getting an update from the team who were keeping him under surveillance.

I learned that he left his apartment at Canary Wharf at about six thirty the previous evening and went to his office in Rotherhithe where it appeared he had a meeting with some of the main faces in his organisation.

We hadn't managed to plant any listening devices in the building so we did not know what was discussed. But we could guess.

When Slack left there he went straight back to his apartment and he was still there apparently.

I wondered if it was worth going to see him again, to question him about Marion Nash's murder. Probably not, I decided. He would just tell me that he didn't do it and had no idea who did.

I was aware that a couple of the team were coming round to the view that he might not be involved after all. I'd heard them talking. They weren't convinced that someone with terminal cancer would unleash a pointless firestorm that would jeopardise their freedom during the final months of their life.

It was a reasonable explanation and one that I felt would gain traction if we weren't able to link him soon to what was going on.

But I was with Tony Marsden in believing that Slack should remain firmly in the frame. And it wasn't just because of his track record as a cruel and cold-blooded gang leader. It was also down to his attitude and demeanour on those two occasions when I'd interviewed him. Plus, the way he'd looked at me as he'd answered my questions – like he wanted me to know that he was hiding a huge secret. And challenging me to find out what it was.

Well, I had never been one to shy away from a challenge. So as I started wading once again through the file we had on Slack, it was with a new sense of urgency. I was searching for something, anything, that might have been missed.

An hour later, my eyes strained from staring into the computer screen, I spotted something. It was in the notes relating to Terry Malone, the villain shot dead during the raid on his home by firearms officer Hugh Wallis, who had since disappeared. Malone had been working as a bouncer for Slack at the time.

What intrigued me was a brief reference to a remark made by a police informant who attended Malone's funeral. He claimed that during the wake in a pub he overhead Slack say that Malone's death was 'the final straw'.

I was surprised that this hadn't been picked up by those officers who'd questioned Slack about Wallis's disappearance. It certainly hadn't been mentioned during the formal interview.

But in the context of what was happening now I felt that it could be hugely significant.

And therefore I intended to follow it up.

34

Rosa

'You'll never believe this,' Alice said. 'There's been another murder in London.'

Rosa sat up in the bed and rubbed at her eyes with her fingers. She'd been waiting for Alice to return from the kitchen where she'd gone to make some coffee.

'It's another bad one,' Alice went on, placing Rosa's mug next to her on the bedside table. 'This time it was a woman and she was married to a detective who worked with the one who was shot the night before.'

Rosa let her jaw drop to give the impression that she was surprised.

'That's terrible,' she said.

'I know.' Alice sounded visibly upset. 'It's most certainly not what someone on their first visit to this city should have to wake up to.'

Rosa forced a grin.

'I'm used to it, Alice. You're forgetting that I'm from Mexico.

Murders take place all over the country every day of the week. Believe me, nothing that happens here will shock me.'

'That's not the point,' Alice said, as she got back into bed. 'I want you to be impressed by this country, this city. If you are then you're more likely to come back.'

It was such a sweet thing to say and Rosa was touched. She wondered if most English girls were as warm and open as Alice.

'Do you mind if I switch the television on?' Alice asked.

'Of course not.'

It was ten o'clock and they had already had sex, which had been just as good as the time before and the time before that.

Rosa had told Alice that she was due to attend a meeting at midday. But what she really planned to do was prepare for the next kill and the one after that.

She'd already checked out DI Laura Jefferson's house in Balham, but she intended to have another look this afternoon before returning much later to carry out the execution. And Roy Slack had sent her details late last night of someone else he wanted taken out. The name wasn't on his list but he'd stressed that he wanted the job done asap.

It wasn't a big deal. Rosa had been given the target's home address and fortunately it wasn't far from where she was right now. So she would recce it after her visit to Balham.

The wall-mounted TV came on as Rosa pointed the remote at it. The first thing they saw was the outside of Marion Nash's bookshop in Clapham. Then it cut to a photo of her with her detective husband.

After that there was a short clip of CCTV footage that showed a figure in a dark overcoat and baseball cap entering the shop. The reporter said that the person was believed to be the killer.

Rosa had to bite her bottom lip to keep from smiling. The

sequence would be completely useless as far as the investigation went because she couldn't possibly be identified from it.

'I hope whoever that is rots in hell,' Alice said. 'If I could send him there myself I would.'

Rosa had already been to hell and back but she couldn't tell Alice that. In fact she couldn't tell Alice anything about herself. She could only lie. It was what she always did.

'Will I see you tonight?' Alice asked.

They were both dressed and ready to leave the apartment.

Rosa pouted her lips. 'Are you sure you're not fed up with me?'

Alice grinned. 'What do you think?'

Rosa reached out and stroked Alice's cheek.

'I think we should make the most of these two weeks,' she said. 'And I want you to know that I'm having the time of my life.'

Alice was clearly delighted. She grabbed Rosa's arm, pulled her close, and gave her a long, hard kiss on the mouth.

Rosa felt something stir inside her. It was a feeling she wasn't accustomed to and she wasn't even able to identify it.

Was it a genuine crush? Or perhaps a more subtle form of affection for a woman who made her heart race?

Whatever it was, it felt good as well as strange.

'We should do something different tonight then,' Alice said. 'Why don't we have dinner together? I know this lovely restaurant. It's near here and it's cosy and romantic and—'

'It's a date,' Rosa said.

'Fantastic. I'll make the reservation for eight o'clock. Would that be OK?'

Rosa nodded. 'It should be.'

'Well, if you're held up just call me.'

But Rosa was determined that she wouldn't be late for the first dinner date she'd had in years. And to help ensure that she'd be on time she decided to visit Laura Jefferson's house earlier than she had planned to.

If the detective wasn't home by then, she would simply kill the boyfriend instead. He was bound to be there.

35

Laura

So Roy Slack apparently referred to the death of Terry Malone as 'the final straw'.

Naturally this had got me wondering. The first call I made was to the detective in the NCA who had mentioned it in his report.

His name was Julian Wheeler and he confirmed that his informant had been adamant that Slack had said it at Malone's wake. He added that the guy was one of his most reliable snouts.

I chose not to believe that it was simply an off-the-cuff remark. It was too loaded. Too full of menace. It was what people said when they'd had enough of a situation or a sequence of events and had decided to do something about it.

So the questions I now wanted answers to were:

Did the death of Terry Malone at the hands of a police officer trigger an angry reaction from Roy Slack?

Did he regard it as the latest in a catalogue of grievances against the police?

And did he decide to vent his fury, first by arranging for the officer in question to be kidnapped or killed, and then through a final, desperate act of vengeance against the Met itself before the cancer claimed him?

It would certainly explain why the task force had been targeted and we'd received that absurd ultimatum. He would have known that the Met wouldn't dare close the unit down or allow the detectives to step back from it. But he would also have known that we'd be put in an invidious position once the killings began.

Jesus.

It might have been a pretty far-fetched theory but that didn't mean it wasn't entirely plausible. And the more I studied Slack's file the more convinced I became that I was onto something.

The old villain was on record as saying that he held the police responsible for the deaths of his wife and father.

His wife died after she crashed her car into a bus on the way to see him at a police station after he was arrested. According to the detectives who broke the news to him, Slack flew into a rage and blamed them.

Then after his father was stabbed to death in prison he told a newspaper that it was the fault of the police. He claimed his dad was serving time only because detectives had planted evidence against him in order to get a conviction.

My thoughts were racing now and I kept coming back to the phrase that Slack had allegedly used at Malone's funeral wake.

The final straw.

Did it mean that Terry Malone was more to Slack than just a low-level employee? Was that why he attended his funeral and said what he did? And was it also why the copper who had killed Malone in the raid had suddenly and mysteriously disappeared?

I spent the next hour finding out as much as I could about Terry Malone. He'd been on the scene for a few years apparently. He had worked as a drugs dealer for the Romanians in North

London before the task force snared his bosses. He'd then been recruited by Slack's South London firm, ostensibly to work as a bouncer at one of his night clubs.

He had a girlfriend, Amy, and she was pregnant with his baby before she had the miscarriage on the night he was shot.

His mother had died about eight months ago and there was no record of his father.

I realised that I needed to know more about him if I was going to establish whether or not his death had indeed played a part in triggering the nightmare that was now engulfing us.

I decided to start by talking to his girlfriend. It took me half an hour to track her down. She was now living with her sister in Leeds but I managed to get her on the phone.

She wasn't very helpful, though. She said that as far as she knew Terry had not had a particularly close relationship with Slack.

'He was just his boss,' she said. 'He had a lot of respect for Terry and Roy was good to him. He paid him well and Terry enjoyed working for the firm.'

She then revealed something that I hadn't been aware of – that Terry had returned home late on the night he was shot because he'd had a meeting with Slack at one of his clubs.

'Terry was a bit tipsy because they'd been drinking champagne,' she said. 'And that stuff never agreed with him.'

'Were they celebrating something?' I asked.

'I don't know. Terry didn't say. He just got into bed and that was when those crazy coppers barged in and shot him. And there was no need to. He wasn't armed and he wasn't a threat.'

She was choking up so I brought the conversation to an end with a final question. Was there anyone else I could speak to who would know more about Terry?

'You should try Eddie Fowler,' she said. 'He lived with Terry's mum, Chloe. They were together for twelve years and he helped bring Terry up. They were pretty close.'

'Any idea how I can contact him?'

'Last I heard he was still at Chloe's place in Stratford.'

It didn't take me long to get an address and phone number for Eddie Fowler. Or to discover that the bloke had form. A criminal records check revealed that while in his early thirties he did a stint in prison for burglary. He was now sixty-one and on benefits. So I wasn't surprised that he answered when I rang him on his home phone.

I told him I was gathering information on Terry Malone and asked him if I could come and see him.

'What exactly do you want to know?' he said, and his voice had a northern lilt.

'Anything you can tell me – in particular the nature of his relationship to the man he was working for at the time of his death.'

'You mean Roy Slack?'

'I do.'

I sensed a moment's hesitation before he said, 'When were you thinking of coming?'

'Right away if that's possible. I can be there in half an hour.'

'I'll be waiting then.'

I went straight to Drummond to tell him where I was going and what line of inquiry I was following.

'I'm not sure where it will lead, guv,' I said. 'But nobody else has spoken to Eddie Fowler as far as I know. So he might be able to shed light on why Slack regarded Terry Malone's death as the final straw.'

'Go for it,' Drummond said. 'We've got sod all else in the way of leads. And get Marsden to go with you. DS Chappell is tied up making some calls on my behalf.'

Tony Marsden was on his best behaviour as we headed towards East London in the back of a police patrol car for our own protection. He refrained from making any crude remarks or insensitive observations and listened intently as I filled him in on why we were going to see Eddie Fowler.

'You told us yesterday that you thought it possible that Slack had decided to go out with a bang,' he said. 'So maybe you were right and it's what this is all about.'

'Well, I think it's more believable than a bid to shut down the work of the task force,' I said. 'The guy's no fool. He'll know well enough that however many cops are killed we'll still go all out to break up his empire and collar the scum who work for him.'

We were still discussing it when we arrived at the rundown council estate where Eddie Fowler lived on the ground floor.

He answered the door to us in his dressing gown and I wasn't sure he was wearing anything underneath.

'I was having a lazy day,' he said as he led us into a small, untidy living room that stank of cigarette smoke.

We introduced ourselves and he asked us why we were suddenly interested in Terry, and I told him we were with the task force that had become the target of a killer.

'We strongly suspect that Terry's former boss, Roy Slack, might be behind it,' I said. 'And if so then it's possible that he decided to do what he's doing because of what happened to Terry.'

Fowler was a thin man who looked as though his best days were far behind him. His face had an orange tint and his eyes were patterned with broken veins.

But he seemed pleasant enough, and after inviting us to sit down he explained that he was with Chloe Malone for twelve years and during that time got quite close to Terry.

'He was always a bit of a handful,' he said. 'But I liked him. Both me and his mum tried to persuade him not to get into villainy but he didn't listen. He enjoyed making easy money, and I could relate to that because I went down that same road when I was younger.'

'We understand that Terry joined Slack's firm soon after Chloe died,' I said. 'Is that correct?'

He nodded. 'At the time he was at a loose end. Your people had effectively cost him his job with the Romanians.'

'And do you know if he approached Slack or Slack approached him?'

There was a flicker of hesitation on his face. His eyes moved from me to Marsden and back to me.

'What is it, Mr Fowler?' I said. 'Do you have information that you're not sure you should share with us?'

He cleared his throat and swallowed.

'I can assure you that whatever you say will stay between us,' I said. 'This conversation is confidential.'

He licked his lips. 'OK, well, it was Slack who approached Terry because Chloe asked him to.'

'Really? When was this?'

'Three days before she died,' he said. 'She called him from the hospital and got him to go and see her.'

I cocked an eyebrow. 'Does that mean that Chloe knew him?'

Another nod. 'They went out together for a few months over twenty-five years ago.'

'So did they stay in touch?'

'No, they didn't.'

'So why did Slack feel obliged to do as she asked?'

Fowler sucked in a breath. 'Because she said she had something to tell him. Something she'd kept from him all those years. You see she never intended to break her silence but she wanted him to look out for Terry after she'd gone.'

I felt my stomach muscles clench because I suddenly realised where this was going.

'What was it, Mr Fowler?' I said. 'What was it she told him?'

He left it a couple of beats before responding.

'She told him that he was Terry's father. And she gave him a letter that she wanted him to give to their son if he decided to step up to the plate and look out for the lad.'

36

Slack

He was enjoying the view again, the one from his apartment balcony. The storm clouds had gone and the rain had eased to a fine drizzle.

London was looking grey and damp. It was on days like this that Julie used to try to persuade him to move to somewhere abroad where it was always sunny and warm and the cops didn't keep hassling them.

He wished now with all his heart that he had taken her. They could have had many more years together. And she would have given him a reason to live now. A reason to fight the cancer and stay alive for even a few extra months.

But she wasn't here and neither was Terry, the son he had known for only the shortest time.

Who wouldn't be bitter in his shoes? Who wouldn't be getting off on the mayhem and suffering he was causing?

He imagined with glee the panic inside Scotland Yard, home of the Metropolitan Police. The top brass would be in a right old state and with every killing the pressure would mount. As they tried to hold things together the minions would be running around like headless chickens.

They might well be convinced that he was responsible, but without proof there was fuck all they could do about it. And they weren't going to get any proof. Just like they weren't going to stop the bloodshed.

Rosa Lopez, The Slayer, was too clever by half. She was making it seem so easy. He understood why Carlos Cruz described her as the best in the business. She was in a league of her own, streets ahead of all the other contract killers he'd had dealings with over the years. Those guys would probably have been reluctant to take on a job like this where there were multiple, high-profile targets.

But Rosa Lopez had honed her skills in a country where mass murders were a feature of everyday life. Where assassins were tasked with killing entire families and large groups of people, including cops.

So to her this assignment wasn't so daunting, and he could not help but admire the business-like way she was going about it.

The CCTV footage of her in the overcoat and baseball cap had made him laugh out loud. The Old Bill would be scratching their heads, unable to determine whether it was a man or a woman.

He decided to call her up and tell her that she was doing a fantastic job. And to ask her how quickly she could eliminate the person whose name he had just added to the list. He was keen for it to happen as quickly as possible, but he appreciated that she would need time to plan it. He didn't want her to rush it and risk making a mistake.

She answered on the third ring and he said, 'I just wanted to let you know that you're doing a terrific job, Rosa. Keep up the good work and I'll make sure there's an extra bonus in it for you.'

'That's good to hear,' Rosa said. 'Is that the only reason you called me?'

'No it isn't.'

'Then I'm guessing it's about the name you sent to me last night. The one you want added to the list.'

'That's right,' he said.

'Well, I'm about to recce the target's home. Once I've done that I'll put a plan together with the aim of doing it tomorrow. Tonight's hit is all worked out and in hand. It'll happen in a matter of hours.'

'You're a star, Rosa,' he said. 'If there's anything more you need then just let me know.'

'I'll do that,' she said.

She hung up first and he went back inside, closing the balcony door behind him.

He checked the time. One o'clock. He hadn't yet decided how to spend the rest of the day. He was in no mood to do anything work-related. In fact he had already lost interest in everything other than his vendetta against the Old Bill.

He could get Mike to drive him over to Jasmin's place for a raunchy session with her. Or he could go and treat himself to a long lunch at one of his restaurants.

But after giving it some thought he decided to hang around the apartment and watch the news reports of how the cops were struggling to deal with the crisis.

A crisis that was set to get a whole lot worse over the weekend when Rosa delivered what would be a crushing blow to the very heart of the Met.

37

Laura

It came as quite a shock to discover that Terry Malone had been Roy Slack's son. But I had a feeling that it would have come as a much bigger shock to Malone himself.

'According to Eddie Fowler, Chloe Malone broke her silence after all those years as soon as she learned she might have only a few days to live after her stroke,' I told Drummond and the team when we returned to the office. 'Fowler didn't even know himself until she confessed to him in the hospital. She'd always insisted to him that she didn't know who Terry's father was.'

'So why not take the secret to her grave?' Drummond asked.

'Because she was desperately worried about her son. She knew he'd never give up his life of crime and she felt he needed protection. And who better to provide it than the biggest face in the London underworld?'

'So Slack just took her word for it that Terry Malone was her son?'

'Not quite,' I said. 'He obtained a sample of the lad's DNA and got it checked out. And it confirmed what Chloe had said.'

'How do you know this?'

'It was one of the things that came up in a conversation between Fowler and Slack at Malone's funeral.'

Fowler had explained to us that he approached Slack at the funeral to ask him if he'd revealed to Malone that he was his father.

'Slack told him he'd broken the news just a couple of hours before Malone was shot,' I said. 'That was why they'd been drinking champagne at Slack's club in the West End. He wanted Malone to look on it as a cause for celebration. He told the lad that when Amy gave birth to his grandchild he would make sure the family was well provided for. He also told Malone that he wanted him to be heir to his illicit empire.'

'The timing is significant if you think about it,' Tony Marsden said. 'Malone was killed about the time Slack was diagnosed with terminal cancer. That's probably why Slack decided to come clean when he did.'

It made sense and was enough to convince me that we were right to focus on Slack as our main suspect.

First he discovers he has a son and is about to become a grandfather. Then he finds out he's not long for this world, which prompts him to tell Malone that he's his dad. But on that very night Malone is gunned down by a police officer during a raid on his home.

All this was piled on top of a pathological hatred for the police that had been built up over many years.

The final straw.

Drummond and the rest of the team now believed, as I did, that the case against Slack was stacking up. That it was looking increasingly likely that he had decided to seek revenge against the police following Malone's death and Amy's miscarriage.

But Drummond was at pains to point out that we still had no hard evidence.

'I'm reluctant to bring him in again just to tell him that we know that Malone was his son,' he said. 'There's an argument that he should have told us when he was questioned about the disappearance of the officer who shot Malone. But it's not nearly enough to bring charges against him.'

And that was the problem. Slack's fat lawyer would walk rings around us if we sought to prosecute Slack with nothing but circumstantial evidence.

'We need much more,' Drummond told us. 'Find out who the killer is and link him to Slack. Prove that it's Slack or one of his people who is sending out those text messages. Get someone to grass him up. Without some solid evidence we can't touch the bastard and he knows it.'

Marsden and I pulled together a detailed account of our interview with Eddie Fowler. After feeding it into the system, Drummond told us both to go home and get some rest.

'I'm quite happy to stay for a couple more hours, guv,' I said. 'There's still a lot to go through in Slack's file, especially the personal stuff. If I can just find—'

'That can wait,' he said. 'You look knackered, and I've told you before that you can't survive on adrenalin alone. Besides, I want everyone in bright and early tomorrow morning even though it's Saturday.'

It was four o'clock and already dark outside. I was glad I didn't have to join the hordes of commuters on the tube. A few security measures had kicked in and one was that wherever possible we had to travel around London in marked police vehicles.

On the way home I phoned Mum and was pleased to hear that

219

she had arrived safely at Sylvia's house in Ringwood, and they were now sharing a bottle of wine.

'It's very festive here,' she said. 'Sylvia has already put up her tree and decorations.'

I was reminded that in just under three weeks we were due to fly to Spain to spend Christmas with Aidan's parents. I honestly didn't think that would happen now, even if by some miracle this nightmare ended suddenly. I mentioned it to Aidan when I arrived home and he suggested we leave it a week before cancelling the flights.

He started preparing a light meal for us. Cheese on toast with lashings of brown sauce. It was one of my favourites, and as I started digging in I realised I hadn't eaten all day.

'I got a call from Balham police station this afternoon,' he said. 'They asked if I had any concerns about security and then arranged to give me a lift home from school. It was weird.'

'But necessary,' I said. 'The car that's parked out front will now be there until there's no longer a threat.'

'Well, I have to admit that I do feel safer knowing that it's there.'

I told him that I was concerned we hadn't done enough to secure the house.

'I think we should call a locksmith and get them to fix stronger locks on the front and back doors,' I said. 'And we should install some motion-sensor lights as well.'

He agreed and said he would sort it over the weekend as I had to go to work.

The conversation was somewhat stilted because I was tired and Aidan was understandably nervous and uncomfortable. The strain was getting to us both and it was impossible to relax.

I couldn't stop thinking about Dave Prentiss and Marion Nash. And those vile text messages.

'Do you think there will be another murder tonight?' Aidan asked me.

It was the same question every copper in London would be asking themselves. There had been two killings over two days. Did that mean the perp was planning to carry on at that rate?

'I just don't know,' I said truthfully. 'But it must be less likely now that there's some form of protection for all those who've been threatened.'

But no amount of protection could stop anyone from falling victim to a determined hitman. I knew that and I was sure that Aidan did as well. But I chose not to say it out loud.

Instead I told him about our conversation with Eddie Fowler and what he'd revealed to us about Roy Slack.

But I was sorry I did because it provoked an angry reaction.

'I can't believe you haven't locked the bastard up,' he seethed. 'If you think he's the one behind this then you should have arrested him.'

'It's not as straightforward as that,' I said. 'We need proof and we don't have it.'

'You lock up suspected terrorists without proof,' he said. 'So what's the difference?'

'The difference is we know that Slack is not committing these murders. He's under continued surveillance. And placing him in custody probably wouldn't stop the killings or the threats anyway.'

'Then how are you going to bring all this to an end, Laura? How high does the body count have to go before the police take some serious fucking action?'

I didn't want to get into an argument so I stood up and started clearing the dishes. Aidan went to the fridge, took out a bottle of wine and poured some into a glass, which he carried into the living room. He was fuming and I didn't blame him.

I decided to give him time to calm down before joining him. I filled the bowl with warm water and began washing up by hand since we'd only used a couple of plates.

And that was when I thought I heard something outside. It sounded like an object had been knocked over in the garden. My first thought was that next door's cat had come through the fence and was skulking around again.

But then I suddenly experienced a twist of alarm. Supposing it wasn't the cat? Supposing there was someone out there?

I felt every muscle in my body go stiff as I stepped quickly across the room to switch off the light, plunging the kitchen into darkness.

A few more steps and I was at the sliding glass door which gave access to the garden.

I looked outside and at the same time turned on the patio light. Doing that probably saved my life because the person who was out there on the lawn and pointing a gun at me was momentarily blinded.

He had to cover his eyes as he pulled the trigger, which buggered up his aim. The bullet tore into the door, shattering the glass, but it missed me.

My reaction was all instinct and panic. I threw myself back across the room to where I'd left my pistol lying on the worktop.

I grabbed it and spun round just as the patio light was extinguished.

Without a moment's hesitation I fired three shots in quick succession into the garden.

I heard the door behind me open and then Aidan's voice.

'Stay back,' I screamed. 'There's someone out there.'

I saw flashes of light outside from the muzzle of a gun. I heard a bullet hit the cupboard door behind me. Another crashed into the front of the dishwasher.

The assailant couldn't see me and was just firing into the darkness. So I crouched down behind the table and fired back. More glass shattered and the noise was deafening.

But suddenly I realised I was pulling the trigger on an empty weapon and that the assailant had retreated.

I gripped my fear and stood up. Then stepped forward cautiously. My shoes crunched on shards of glass and when I reached the door I peered outside and saw that there was nobody in the garden.

I heard shouting behind me and the sound of the front door being forced open. I assumed the two officers who'd been sitting out front in the patrol car were coming through. And I wondered why Aidan hadn't let them in.

I got my answer a second later when two uniforms burst into the kitchen and one of them switched on the light.

I saw Aidan before they did. He was lying on his back on the floor and there was a big red stain on the front of his shirt where one of the bullets had entered his body.

38

Rosa

She was cursing out loud as she ran at full sprint along the alley.

'Fuck, fuck, fuck.'

She could not believe what had just happened. Or how close she'd come to catching a bullet.

'Fuck.'

Her breath thundered in her ears and hot bile burned in her throat.

'Fuck.'

It should have been so easy. She'd checked it out two hours ago when the house had been empty. She'd discovered for herself that there were no sensor lights and no barking dogs to make things difficult.

She had then gone on to recce the location of the next hit. And in hindsight that had been a mistake because when she returned she vaulted over the wall at a different spot and landed on a pile of clay pots that had crashed to the ground and alerted Laura Jefferson to her presence.

So instead of creeping up to the kitchen and shooting the

woman as she moved around inside, Rosa had been caught in the glare of the patio light.

It had distracted her, and as she fired that first shot she'd known it would miss the target. So she'd fired more but she hadn't anticipated that Jefferson would herself be armed and able to return fire.

'*Fuck.*'

So now she was having to run for her life back to where she'd left the bike, and she knew the cops wouldn't be far behind. The two who'd been sitting in the car in front of the house would have been alerted and they would already be calling for backup.

The short alley opened out onto a residential street with lots of parked cars and thankfully no pedestrians that she could see. Rosa veered to the left and picked up speed along the sidewalk. Her breath came in short, painful gasps, and the blood thundered in her ears.

By running she knew she'd be drawing attention to herself, especially in her cycle leathers and woollen hat. But she had no choice. She had to get to the bike as quickly as possible.

If anyone was unfortunate enough to see her face then she would have to kill them. But she didn't want to be forced to do that because she'd already made a big enough mess of things. And that was something she wasn't accustomed to. She rarely made mistakes, which was why she was so highly rated. *The best in the business.*

But what had happened this evening would do nothing for her reputation. She had fucked up, and that had never happened before.

Luckily she reached the bike before encountering anyone. She jumped on it without bothering to get the helmet from the saddlebag.

A car drove slowly by as she started the engine, but she was pretty sure the driver didn't look her way.

A second later she was on the move and sirens were shrieking from all directions as she sped through the unfamiliar back streets of Balham.

She fixed her jaw like a metal clamp and gave the road ahead her full attention.

Suddenly there were more cars and more people as she approached the main drag. She had to swerve to avoid a red bus. Then she was forced to mount the pavement when a van braked hard in front of her. Several people leapt out of her way and a woman screamed.

She steered back onto the road, darting between slow-moving vehicles. Horns blared and people shouted, but she kept going until the road ahead was clear.

She eased off the throttle, feeling safer, knowing that all she had to do was disappear down a quiet street where she could pull over and catch her breath. She would also check her phone to get her bearings, and then look for the quickest way back to Vauxhall and the hotel.

There were traffic lights up ahead, showing green. But just before she reached them they changed to orange, then red. Rosa did not want to stop so she gave it some revs and tore into the junction. But it proved to be a costly mistake on a day of costly mistakes.

A sleek black Mercedes sports car shot out from the road on the left as though from a racetrack grid.

Rosa didn't see it until it was too late. She tried to veer away from it but the front fender caught her rear wheel and sent her into a wild spin.

A cry erupted from her throat as the bike hit the kerb and she was flung into the air.

She landed on the road with a painful thud right into the path of a pair of fiercely bright headlights that were bearing down on her.

39

Laura

I finally stopped screaming, but only because I suddenly realised that Aidan wasn't dead.

The bullet had gone clean through his left shoulder, making a large hole and producing lots of blood.

But he was still breathing, still conscious.

'You need to stay awake,' I pleaded with him. 'I'm with you. You're going to be OK. An ambulance is on its way.'

It seemed obvious, even to my untrained eye, that no vital organs had been damaged. But the loss of blood worried me. It needed to be stemmed, and quickly.

I was on my knees cradling his head in my lap. His eyes were open and he was looking up at me, but I could tell they weren't focused.

He tried to speak but no words came out. The panic was swelling in my chest, and awful scenarios were racing through my mind.

I couldn't believe that this was happening. That the man I loved had been shot, hit by a bullet that had been meant for me.

I was only half aware of the commotion that was going on

around me. Shoes stamping across the kitchen lino. Loud, strident voices. Police radio static.

My mind flashed on an image of the assailant in the garden as the patio light came on.

It had been so fleeting that very little had registered. Just what looked like a shiny black body suit and dark woollen hat pulled down across the assailant's ears and forehead.

And the revolver that had been held in both hands and aimed at the kitchen door. And me.

The two officers from the patrol car had run into the garden and then climbed over the wall into the alley. But by then the assailant had fled into the labyrinth of streets on this side of Balham High Road.

Had an accomplice been waiting around the corner in a car? Was that car now speeding away from the area?

Why the hell was Aidan lying on the floor with a bullet in him and not me?

An officer told me that a fast-response paramedic had arrived outside. Another knelt beside me and talked to Aidan, urging him to keep his eyes open while holding onto his hand.

A third officer leaned over me and said that units were converging on the area and could I give him a description of the assailant?

It wasn't easy. My thoughts were swimming in feverish circles and I was desperately fearful that Aidan was losing too much blood. But I tried because I knew it was important. I closed my eyes and seized on the image again.

'I saw a figure standing in the garden just beyond the patio,' I said. 'But only for a fraction of a second. There was a revolver and it was pointing at the window.'

'What was he wearing?' the officer pressed.

'Something black, like a body suit or motorcycle leathers. And a hat. A woollen hat.'

'And the face? Did you see the assailant's face?'

I squinted in concentration, searching for definition in the smudge of flesh I'd seen beneath the hat.

And then it hit me and my eyes snapped open and I said, 'I can't be sure but I think . . . I think it might have been a woman.'

40

Rosa

She was lucky to be alive and she knew it. Watching those head-lights bearing down on her had been like staring death in the face. She really hadn't expected to survive.

But, miraculously, the car had skidded to a halt just inches from where Rosa was lying on the road.

She was battered and bruised, and the pain was beating through her body. But it would have been much worse if she'd landed on her head or face instead of her left shoulder.

It was the fourth time she had come off a bike in the nine years she'd been riding them, and once again it was down to her own recklessness. She should have seen the sports car coming from the left. She shouldn't have jumped the red light. It had been careless. Stupid.

'Are you all right, miss?' a man asked. 'Can you move?'

She was sure that she could so she went for it, rolling carefully onto her back and forcing herself to sit up. It hurt like hell and she had to stifle a cry. But it convinced her that no bones were broken.

'Thank goodness you're OK,' the man said.

She raised her head and saw a middle-aged guy with a short, grey beard.

'I really didn't think I'd be able to stop when you fell in front of me,' he added.

He must be the driver behind the headlights, she thought. The man whose quick thinking had probably saved her life.

But she had neither the time nor the inclination to show her gratitude. She needed to get up and away from here. But she wasn't sure how easy that was going to be.

She could see other faces now, hear more voices, as people were being drawn to the scene of the accident.

'*Fuck.*'

'Perhaps you should stay where you are until an ambulance gets here,' someone else said. A woman this time.

Rosa managed to shake her head. 'No. No ambulance. I'm fine.'

And then she struggled to get up, but it proved difficult because she was disoriented and in shock.

'Please help me,' she said. 'I need to go.'

She felt hands on her arms, helping her to her feet. Her head was spinning, but at least her legs didn't give way beneath her, and that came as a relief.

She felt a little giddy and stars fell past her eyes. She took a deep breath. Then another.

She straightened her back, moved her neck from side to side. Flexed her arms. Satisfied herself that all her parts were still in working order.

Then she looked around and realised that at least three pairs of eyes were watching her. The bearded man started speaking again but the voice was drowned out by the sound of a siren. Was it an ambulance or a police car? She couldn't be sure. She hadn't been in London long enough to distinguish between the two.

She took a step forward, shoving the man out of the way. She needed to locate the bike and get going before the emergency vehicle arrived. Or before these people tried to stop her.

She saw the bike lying on its side against the kerb a few metres away. It appeared that the engine had cut out but she didn't see any damage to the wheels or frame.

Rosa pushed herself towards it, her limbs protesting every step of the way.

'You can't just leave the scene of an accident,' someone said behind her. 'The police will want to talk to you and you're in no fit state to ride a motorcycle.'

She was still wearing the hat but it had shifted upwards, revealing her ears and strands of hair that fell across her forehead.

As she approached the bike she felt a hand on her left shoulder and it caused an explosive pain.

She whirled round and stared at the bearded man who was shaking his head at her.

'The police will be here any second, miss,' he said. 'They'll want to talk to you.'

She opened her mouth to warn him off, but at that moment she saw the flashing blue light of the police car speeding towards them.

'Fuck.'

She turned and rushed towards the bike and somehow she found the strength to pull it up off the kerb.

She threw herself onto the seat, praying to a God that she had never believed in that it would start up. But the first attempt to kick the engine into life failed. And so did the second.

'Stop her going,' someone shouted.

233

She turned as the bearded man grabbed her sleeve. But he let go when she rammed her elbow into his face.

Suddenly the wail of the siren filled her head as the police car drew up just behind her.

Two uniformed cops leapt out, and Rosa knew then that there was only one way she was going to be able to get out of this mess.

She withdrew the pistol from inside her jacket and with lightning speed she took aim and fired twice.

The cops were so close she couldn't have missed them even if she'd tried.

One of them was blown backwards against the front of the patrol car and the other staggered sideways clutching at his stomach.

There were gasps and screams all around as Rosa fired another shot into the air to deter anyone from coming at her.

She decided to have one last go at starting the bike and if it didn't work then she would leap off and run for it. But this time, to her great relief, the engine ticked over.

A moment later she was roaring away from the scene and from the two cops who were shedding blood onto the road.

41

Laura

The paramedic managed to stem the blood pouring from Aidan's wound. He also confirmed what I'd suspected – that the bullet had not struck any vital organs.

'A couple of inches over and it would have hit his heart,' he said. 'So in that sense he's a very lucky man.'

I broke down then and the tears were pushed out by huge, racking sobs.

Aidan squeezed my fingers, and I was sure that if he'd been able to speak he would have told me not to cry. But he was only half-conscious, having been given drugs for the shock and pain.

I stayed right there on the floor with him until the ambulance arrived and he was put on a stretcher. Then I pulled myself together, autopilot taking over, and followed the medics outside where the street was filled with police cars and uniforms.

It was very bright and noisy and it reminded me of all the crime scenes I'd attended over the years, never dreaming that one day my own home would become one.

I continued to hold Aidan's hand in the back of the ambulance, while trying desperately to stay calm.

But it was far from easy, especially when almost at once we encountered gridlock on Balham High Road, which I knew would delay us getting to the hospital.

The medic told me he'd heard there had been another incident in which shots were fired, and I immediately jumped to the conclusion that it must be connected to what had happened to us. Surely it couldn't just be a coincidence.

Had the assailant been caught or shot? Or had she shot someone else while making her escape?

By now I was convinced that the shooter was a woman and that I hadn't imagined it. The more I conjured up the image of the person I saw fleetingly in the garden, the clearer it seemed to become.

And it wasn't so much the face. It was more the hourglass figure. The defined waist. The curved hips. No man was shaped like that.

These things must have registered in my sub-conscious in that moment of sheer terror. And now they were coming to the forefront of my mind, details emerging through a mist whipped up by shock and panic.

A female assassin, for Christ's sake.

The same person no doubt who had murdered Dave Prentiss and Marion Nash.

I had been the next target on her list. Only she'd cocked up and shot Aidan instead.

That told me something really important about the bitch. It told me she wasn't nearly as clever as she thought she was.

42

Rosa

Rosa got quickly lost in the streets of South London. But that was OK because it gave her time to regain her equilibrium and refocus her mind.

She stuck to the side roads as much as possible to avoid traffic cameras.

She made her first stop soon after leaving Balham. She put on the helmet and took one of the fake stick-on number plates from the saddlebag and stuck it on the bike. A short while later she stopped again to replace the plate with another.

Her aim was to make it impossible for her progress to be recorded on CCTV and number plate recognition cameras.

She stopped a third time and used her phone to pinpoint her location. She was in Putney, about five miles from Vauxhall. She worked out the best route to the hotel and got moving again.

It was almost seven o'clock and the city was still full of life. Sirens wailed constantly and several police cars whizzed past her with their lights flashing.

It had been a close call but she'd survived it. There would be time later to analyse her mistakes and berate herself for making them. But right now her priority was to get back to the hotel as fast as possible.

She needed to assess her injuries and decide if they were the kind that would mend by themselves. She suspected they were. Already the pain in her neck and left leg was subsiding. But her shoulder remained extremely sore. She wouldn't know if she'd sustained any superficial injuries until she was able to strip off.

Adrenalin continued to surge through her body as she rode and it helped to ease her discomfort.

Her thoughts eventually turned to Alice and their dinner date. They were due to meet up in an hour at Alice's apartment and from there they were planning to walk to the restaurant.

Rosa was still desperate to go, but she wondered if it would be too much for her battered body. She would have to come up with a lie to explain away the pain and any cuts and bruises that would show up on her body.

She could say she was hit by a car or knocked to the ground by a mugger who tried to steal her bag. Or she could simply say that she had a bad fall outside the hotel.

The lie wouldn't be a problem. It would come easily enough. But Rosa knew that it wouldn't be so easy to relax and enjoy herself. Partly because of the pain racking her body. And partly because she was furious with herself for failing to kill DI Laura Jefferson.

She got to Vauxhall by seven fifteen and returned the motorcycle to the garage behind the pub.

On the walk to the hotel she purchased several packets of strong painkillers from a pharmacy, along with some ointment to reduce the swelling.

As soon as she entered her room, she took off her clothes and studied her reflection in the full-length mirror behind the door.

There were bruises on her left shoulder, right thigh and left knee. Her right elbow was badly grazed and so too was the back of her left hand. But at least her face and torso had escaped injury in the fall from the bike.

It was another reminder, as if she needed one, that luck had been with her. Without it she'd be dead now or sitting in the back of a police car with her wrists cuffed.

She decided to keep her date with Alice, but as time was pressing she sent her a text to say she would meet her at the restaurant at eight thirty. Alice replied straight away saying no problem. And since Rosa didn't know the location of the restaurant Alice sent her the address.

Rosa then took some of the painkillers and had a quick shower to ease her swollen muscles and joints.

While waiting for the water to heat up she switched on the TV. Once again her exploits were dominating the news channels.

News was breaking of two shooting incidents in Balham, which had taken place within minutes of each other. In one incident on Balham High Road two police officers had been shot and it was believed that one of them had been killed.

The other incident took place at a house close by and one person was apparently gunned down. However, the victim hadn't yet been identified and it wasn't known how serious his or her injuries were.

There was no footage as yet from either scene but a reporter, speaking over the phone while on his way to Balham, said, 'A police source has told me that the shootings are already being linked to the threats against members of Scotland Yard's organised crime task force and the murders of detective Dave Prentiss and Mrs Marion Nash, the wife of another detective on the force.'

Rosa felt her spirits lift with the news that one of the bullets she had fired into the darkened kitchen at Laura Jefferson's house had found a target.

Was it the detective herself or her boyfriend? She would have to wait to find out.

But in the meantime she could console herself with the knowledge that the mission hadn't been an unmitigated disaster after all.

43

Laura

We made it to the hospital in good time despite the traffic snarl-ups.

Aidan was rushed straight into surgery where a trauma team went to work on him.

I was told that his condition was serious but not life-threatening.

It came as such a huge relief that I broke down again and cried into the shoulder of one of the two armed officers who were sent to provide me with protection.

He led me into a private waiting room and told me that my colleagues from the task force were on their way. He wasn't able to tell me if the shooter had been apprehended, though.

I sat on a small leather sofa and drew my legs up to my chest, hugging my arms around my knees. My body was still shaking and it felt like I was under water, struggling for breath.

At the same time I became aware of a dull ache in my stomach, which I assumed was the muscles contracting.

I turned my thoughts to my mother and I was so glad she'd gone to Ringwood this morning. But I now faced the task of telling her before she heard it on the news. And then, of course, there were Aidan's parents in Spain. They also needed to be informed that their son had been shot by a sadistic contract killer.

I'd had the presence of mind to pick up my bag before I left the house. My mobile phone was inside with the Taser gun. I took it out but had to wait for my tears to dry up before making the calls.

I rang my mother first and broke the news to her in a slow, measured voice. She was so shocked that she couldn't speak for several seconds.

'He's going to be all right, Mum,' I said. 'He was lucky.'

'My God this is terrible,' she said, her voice shaking. 'I'll come straight home.'

'No you won't, Mum. You'll stay put. I don't want to have to worry about you.'

She started to object but I became insistent and she finally agreed to stay with Sylvia. She made me promise to provide her with regular updates on Aidan.

'And stay safe yourself, Laura. Please. You have the key to my house so move in there.'

I ended the call after telling her I had to get in touch with Aidan's parents.

It was his father who answered the phone and I became tearful explaining what had happened.

'I've seen plenty of shoulder wounds,' he said. 'If they stopped the bleeding and he's already in surgery then he should be OK. I'm sure of it.'

I'd forgotten that Tom Bray was a former soldier who had served in various conflicts and been awarded medals for bravery. His words gave me a tiny crumb of comfort.

'We'll catch the first flight we can to the UK,' he said after I gave him the hospital details. 'But it might not be until tomorrow.'

As soon as I hung up the waiting room door opened and DCS Drummond appeared with two other men, neither of whom I recognised.

'Thank God you're OK, Laura,' Drummond said and walked straight over to me. His face was ashen and the sinews in his neck were stretched tight.

I stood up and let him hug me, and this time there were no tears because I was all cried out and the fear and despair had turned to anger.

I pulled back from him and said, 'It was a woman who shot Aidan. I'm sure of it. Please tell me the bitch is dead or in custody. I heard about the other shooting on the High Road.'

He shook his head and I felt my heart drop into my stomach.

'You're right about it being a woman, Laura,' he said. 'But I'm afraid she got away.'

An icy dread flowed through me and my breath started thumping in my ears.

'Sit down,' Drummond said. 'I'll tell you everything we know.'

He gestured towards the two men. 'These are detectives Bannion and Flynn from Balham CID. They need you to describe what happened back at the house. They were briefed by the uniforms but they want to hear it from you.'

I sat down and closed my eyes, breathing deeply through my nostrils. When I opened them again I saw that the three men were seated and one of the detectives had his notebook out.

'First tell me about the other shooting,' I said. 'Was that her?'

Drummond nodded. 'Almost certainly. A woman came off her motorcycle after jumping a red light. Her description matches the one you gave. She was wearing a dark leather suit and woollen hat. She wasn't badly injured and as she tried to leave the scene a police patrol car pulled up. She produced a pistol and shot both of them.'

I shook my head. 'Oh Jesus.'

'One officer was declared dead at the scene,' Drummond said. 'He was shot in the chest. The other was shot in the stomach and is receiving treatment in this very hospital.'

I tried to speak but a sob lodged in my throat.

Drummond continued. 'We'll be comparing the bullets from Aidan and the officers. And we'll cross check-them with those taken from Dave Prentiss and Detective Nash's wife.'

'What about the street camera footage from Clapham?' I said. 'That looked like a man in an overcoat.'

'It was obviously a disguise,' he said. 'But it had us all fooled.'

I then told them what had happened at the house. I stayed sitting as I spoke, all hunched up, my hands held tightly in my lap.

When I was finished, Detective Flynn filled in some of the gaps.

'We suspect the noise that alerted you to an intruder in the garden was the sound of her knocking over some terracotta pots that were piled against the back wall,' he said. 'The patio light you switched on was extinguished by a bullet. We believe she then fired blindly into the kitchen five or six times. One of the bullets struck your partner.'

He added that so far no witnesses had come forward to say they had seen the woman flee along the alley.

'The motorcycle must have been parked close by,' he said. 'But in her panic to get away she caused an accident on the High Road. We'll hopefully have some CCTV footage pretty soon.'

He also told me that my pistol had been retrieved at the scene.

'I'd be dead now if I hadn't had it with me,' I said. 'I'm assuming the bitch didn't expect me to be armed.'

There were more questions I wanted to ask but just then the stomach pain I had experienced earlier returned with a vengeance. This time accompanied by a sudden bout of nausea. I had to excuse myself and rush to the loo, and Drummond said he would call me later.

In the toilet I shut myself in a cubicle and threw up into the basin. That was bad enough, but when I sat down to relieve myself I was in for another shock.

It wasn't just pee that poured out of me. There was also a disturbing amount of blood.

'I'm afraid you've had an early-stage miscarriage, Miss Jefferson.'

The doctor's words burned into my brain. It was another shock to the system. Another blow from which I knew I would never fully recover.

'B . . . but how is that possible?' I asked him. 'I didn't even know I was pregnant. I haven't missed a period.'

He gave a gentle shrug. 'It happens, I'm afraid, and far more often than you might imagine.'

The sight of the blood in the toilet and the severity of the pain in my gut had prompted me to tell a nurse and before I knew it I was in a trauma suite being prodded, poked and tested. I'd expected them to say that I was having a severe period, a reaction to what had happened to me. Not in my wildest dreams had I expected to be told that I had lost the baby that Aidan and I been desperately trying to conceive. Surely it wasn't possible. It had to be a mistake.

'I know it's hard to accept,' the doctor said, and his voice oozed sympathy. 'But you were at least seven weeks pregnant and I'm guessing you've not had any symptoms.'

He was right. I'd had no reason to suspect. I hadn't missed a period and the next one wasn't due for another week. And I hadn't experienced morning sickness, swollen breasts or cravings. Nothing to signal that a new life was forming inside me.

Jesus.

The tears came then, gushing out of me like scorching water from a tap. I wanted to curl up in a ball and die, or at least wallow in grief and self-pity until I was strong enough to face up to what I'd lost.

But I couldn't do that because I had Aidan to think about. He was my priority now, and the thought of having to tell him filled me with despair.

44

Rosa

The lie she told Alice was a simple one.

'I had an accident this afternoon,' she said as she walked into the small Italian restaurant at just after eight thirty. 'I fell down the stairs at the hotel. It was really stupid of me. I managed to hurt my shoulder and bruise myself in a few places.'

She held up her arm to show the graze on her elbow.

Alice was mortified. 'Oh, you poor thing, that's awful. You really shouldn't have come out. I'd have understood.'

'I wanted to see you,' Rosa said. 'I wasn't going to pass on our date just because of a little pain.'

Alice fell for it just as Rosa knew she would. Her expression was one of concern and not suspicion.

As soon as they were seated at a cosy table near the window, Rosa was glad she'd come. The painkillers were working their magic and she was no longer berating herself. After all, the mission hadn't been a total failure. She'd killed one cop and wounded another. And according to the latest news reports, she'd also shot Detective Laura Jefferson's partner, who was now in hospital.

With any luck he would die. But if he did survive then she would apologise to Roy Slack and at the same time assure him that she wouldn't miss the next target.

The fact was she couldn't afford to. Not if she wanted to restore her reputation as the best *sicaria* in the business.

Rosa found it such a joy to be with Alice. The evening flew by and for much of the time she was oblivious to her own discomfort.

Alice was so considerate, so understanding, that Rosa felt almost guilty for deceiving her. It was yet another emotion she had rarely experienced and she was beginning to wonder what was happening to her. It was like a light had come on in her life, suddenly changing everything from sepia to full-colour.

'I'm so glad you decided to come despite what happened to you,' Alice said after she insisted on paying the bill. 'I know it can't have been easy. You are such a dear.'

'A fall down the stairs was never going to stop me,' Rosa said. 'I've been looking forward to seeing you all day.'

Alice reached across the table, took Rosa's hand and squeezed it.

'Then you won't mind me telling you that I've been counting the minutes,' she said. 'I couldn't concentrate at work. I just kept thinking about making love to you again.'

They looked into each other's eyes, and Rosa knew that what passed between them, unspoken, was something meaningful. It made her want to tell Alice everything about herself, to open up her soul for the first time in her life.

No other woman had ever made her feel this way and it scared her. She'd known for years that she had nothing to offer when it came to relationships because of who she was and what she did. She'd therefore resigned herself to always being alone.

So far it had suited her. She'd gone from one sexual tryst to another. She'd never felt vulnerable, or exposed, and she'd never had to deal with a maelstrom of conflicting emotions.

Until now.

Alice Green had got under her skin after only three nights. Rosa found everything about her intoxicating. Her beauty. Her eyes. Her gentleness. Her silky smooth flesh.

Rosa had heard about people being swept off their feet, but she'd never thought it would happen to her.

But it had, because Alice knew how to get inside her head. She did it by being herself. And by being genuine and affectionate and real. These were traits that Rosa wasn't used to. Traits that were sweet and warm and irresistible – and so very dangerous because they were having such an effect on her. She was losing control of her emotions and that was unsettling. How long, she wondered, before she started having doubts about who she was and what she did.

But Rosa was determined not to worry about it or allow it to spoil the rest of the evening. Instead she decided to embrace the feeling, and she even imagined herself sharing more with Alice than just a few nights in London.

'When we get back to the apartment I'm going to give you a nice gentle massage to help ease those aching muscles,' Alice said.

It put a spring in Rosa's step as they walked from the restaurant back to the flat. And it stopped her mind from drifting back to what had happened in Balham. She needed to push that behind her and live in the moment again.

She had a glorious night to look forward to in Alice's bed. And then tomorrow she'd redeem herself with a killing that people would talk about for years to come.

45

Laura

There was nothing the doctor could do for me except to give me tablets to ease the pain in my stomach. I wasn't ill or injured or cursed with a physical disability. What I had was a broken heart and that couldn't be treated or cured with any medication.

Nonetheless the pain was immeasurable. And I decided that I was going to have to suffer in silence. I felt that in the circumstances it really wouldn't be fair to tell Aidan and our parents about the miscarriage. It would have to wait. Or perhaps they would never have to know. After all I could keep it to myself. Pretend that it had never happened in order to spare them the mental anguish.

At least I knew now that I was able to conceive. I wasn't infertile, which was something I'd feared. So there was no reason to believe that I wouldn't become pregnant again. And it was highly unlikely that next time a ruthless assassin would force me to miscarry.

But telling myself all this did not stop the tears from coursing down my cheeks. And it didn't stop me from wondering if my child had been a boy or a girl.

I spent an endless, sleepless night sitting next to Aidan's bed. He remained unconscious for most of the time after the surgeons carried out an operation on his shoulder.

They stitched up the wound, replenished the blood, and told me what I already knew: that it came close to being very much worse. But there were complications – the bullet had splintered a bone and caused significant muscle damage. It could be months before he was able to use his arm properly. And there was even a chance that it would remain permanently damaged.

He looked awful. His skin was grey and there were dark pouches beneath his eyes. He was lying on his back and an intravenous drip was pumping a saline solution into his arm from a bag.

I kept staring at him, while thinking how lucky I was not to have lost him. Dave Prentiss's wife hadn't been so lucky, and neither had Graham Nash.

Naturally guilt reared its ugly head and I told myself I should have done more to protect him. Should have reacted more forcefully to the fears that he and my mother had expressed.

But I also knew it'd be wrong to direct my anger inwards when those who were really responsible were still out there. And in all probability stalking another victim.

There was the assassin in the motorcycle leathers, who nobody believed was acting alone. And there was the evil shit who was surely paying her to do what he didn't have the guts or the skills to do himself.

Roy Slack.

Of course I still couldn't be one hundred per cent sure that it was him. But all my instincts were telling me it was. And since becoming a police officer all those years ago I'd learned to trust them because they were usually right.

I wondered if he'd drawn up a list of those to be murdered.

Or had he left it to his bitch assassin? Were we being targeted in any particular order? If so why was I chosen as the third victim?

Another yet-to-be-answered question was who had given them all the information on us? Our personal details. Addresses. Phone numbers. The names of our loved ones.

Was it one of my colleagues on the task force? A bent copper? A piece of scum of the highest order? And if so did that person have a hand in the decision-making process?

Images from the last few days were flying around inside my head. Dave Prentiss's blood-spattered body. His distraught wife. Graham Nash's shocked expression as he was led out of the office. The smirk on Roy Slack's face when I questioned him. Our kitchen door being shattered by the impact of that first bullet. The dark, disturbing figure aiming a gun at me from the garden. Aidan lying on the floor with a bullet wound. And that doctor's face as he told me that I'd suffered a miscarriage.

Jesus.

Suddenly the rage was rampant in my mind. This couldn't go on. It had to stop. It was an unprecedented assault on the Met, and a murderous, unwarranted attack on individuals.

But right now there seemed no way of stopping it. Not unless the bitch in black made another mistake. Or we managed to collar Slack and got him to call a halt to the killing spree.

But how likely was that? I was willing to bet the bastard was enjoying himself. He was getting his own back. Making sure he went out with a bang.

It was a sick, deafening swansong from a man who appeared to blame others for the bad things that had happened in his life.

A man who now felt he had a final score to settle.

* * *

I saw the woman who killed my unborn baby when I left Aidan and went to get myself a coffee.

The drinks machine was in the waiting room and next to it was a television on the wall. I switched it on and tuned into the BBC news channel.

It was nearly dawn outside so the media had had plenty of time to get across the story. They were reporting that a huge hunt was underway across London for a woman who was believed to be a professional assassin. She had struck early the previous evening at the home in Balham of DI Laura Jefferson, who was attached to the organised crime task force.

The woman had climbed into the back garden and tried to shoot Jefferson through the kitchen window. But the detective had been armed and returned fire, causing the woman to run away. However, the detective's partner, Aidan Bray, had been hit by a bullet and was recovering in hospital.

The assailant had then tried to flee on a motorbike but came off it when she collided with a car at traffic lights on Balham High Road.

She then opened fire with a revolver on two police officers who arrived in a patrol car. One was killed, the other wounded.

'The woman managed to escape on the bike and her current whereabouts are unknown,' the reporter said. 'But Scotland Yard has just released video footage of the woman and are appealing for anyone who has seen her to come forward.'

Grey CCTV images flicked across the screen showing a leather-clad rider on a motorbike. There were three short clips from different cameras but in none of them could her face be seen.

I felt my breath stall as I stared at the television, and a blind fury welled up inside me.

The reporter explained that there was no video of what happened at the traffic lights because the camera positioned there wasn't working. He also said that police were convinced that the woman was responsible for the murders of Dave Prentiss and Mrs Nash.

There followed a couple of interviews with eye witnesses to the accident, one of them a guy with a beard who tried to stop the woman leaving the scene. His name was Martin Dacre and he described her as being in her late twenties or early thirties.

'She's rather pretty and has an accent,' he said. 'She also has dark hair and some of it was poking out from under her hat.'

Young and pretty, he'd said. I found it hard to believe he was describing a heartless murderer. But then killers these days came in every shape, size and gender. We lived in a world where children carried out terrorist attacks, deranged nurses slaughtered their patients, and young, intelligent men deliberately drove vans into crowds of people.

During the next couple of hours I took calls from several of my colleagues, including Janet Dean and Kate Chappell. They were anxious to know how I was. Kate said she would try to come along to the hospital.

I desperately wanted to tell her about the miscarriage. I wanted her to know that I had lost my baby. But I held back because I decided it was a bad idea.

To everyone else what had happened to me was just collateral damage. In the scheme of things it wasn't significant. After all, my baby had been a mere embryo, the size of a blueberry apparently, its internal organs not even developed.

So how could that compare – in their eyes – to the murders of Dave Prentiss and Marion Nash?

I phoned my mother and Aidan's parents to update them on his condition. They'd all seen the news on the TV and were finding it impossible to comprehend what was happening.

This time I spoke to Aidan's mum, Veronica, and for the first time since I'd known her I heard her cry. I tried to reassure her that her son was going to be all right, but when I told her about the complications it was my turn to break down and sob.

I'd been trying to hold it in, but I wasn't strong enough. The tears burned tracks down my cheeks and for at least a minute I couldn't speak.

When finally I was back in control, I said, 'I'm sitting with Aidan now and he's sleeping soundly. He should be awake soon and I'll tell him you're on your way here.'

The couple had managed to get seats on a morning flight from Alicante and were hoping to arrive at the hospital early afternoon.

Aidan emerged from his drug-induced slumber at 7am and could only vaguely remember what had happened to him. The first words out of his mouth were, 'My shoulder really hurts.'

'It won't for long,' I said. 'I'll get the nurse to give you more medicine for the pain.'

I kissed him on the lips and told him that I loved him. When he smiled up at me the tears threatened again, but this time I held them back.

A doctor was summoned to check him over and she told him that he was responding well to treatment. But she also explained about the complications and I could tell he didn't fully understand that it could make his life hellishly difficult for months to come.

I then told him what had happened back at the house and held nothing back. As I spoke a frown puckered his forehead and his sad eyes glistened.

'I'm glad it was me who got shot and not you,' he said. 'Thank Christ the crazy bitch fucked up.'

He was dismayed to learn that she had got away and had shot

255

two police officers in the process. He then implored me to stop working for the task force and to state publicly that I had.

'If you don't then she might come after you again,' he said.

I chose not to respond to that because I hadn't had time to decide what I was going to do. The truth was I had no idea. For one brief moment I was tempted to tell him about the baby, but I pulled back, knowing it wouldn't be right to add to his suffering.

It would have to remain a secret. My burden. My own personal hell. At least for now.

Aidan managed to stay awake for about ten minutes. When he was back under I went to the toilet to pee and freshen up. My eyes were dry and sore, as though filled with sand, and I felt depleted.

I washed my face and applied a bit of make-up from my bag in an attempt to conceal the redness around my eyes. But I couldn't conceal Aidan's blood, which stained my beige blouse.

The doctor suggested I go home and change, but I didn't want to leave Aidan, and, besides, the house was still a crime scene and I probably wouldn't be able to stay there until much later.

I returned to the waiting room and got myself another coffee. Kate Chappell turned up at nine o'clock and I was glad to see her.

She was wearing a dark suit with padded shoulders and her face was taut and sullen. As she embraced me I could feel the tension in her body.

'I can't begin to describe how relieved I am that you're all right,' she said. 'But please tell me that Aidan is out of danger.'

'He is,' I said, and then filled her in.

'I came as soon as I could get away,' she said. 'It's sheer chaos out there. And we're all wondering who'll be next.'

'It's fucking scary,' I said.

'You're not kidding. Nobody knows what to do. It seems the

only way to stay safe is to lock ourselves away but that's not practical. I came here in a car with two armed minders, for God's sake.'

I shook my head. 'It's all so unreal. We're the police. We shouldn't need protection. What's more, every officer who's assigned to protect us is putting his or her life on the line as well.'

I stopped talking and let the silence fill the room. Kate dropped onto the chair opposite me, and her hands fell onto her knees, fisting anxiously.

For long seconds it was as though we were both paralysed by our thoughts. We just stared at each other, and the only sound was our own heavy breathing. But then came another sound. The all-too-familiar sound of a text arriving on our phones at the same time. Moments later we were both reading the message. It consisted of just three short sentences.

And it contained a threat that was every bit as sinister as the first one we'd all received.

46

Slack

As soon as he woke up, he started to curse the cancer that was going to shorten his life.

The symptoms were getting worse, and last night had been the most difficult so far. The nausea, the gut pain, the ache in his head that even the pills couldn't drive away. The doctors had warned him to expect this and had told him how bad it would get.

He'd been fine before going to bed and had spent a pleasant evening by himself drinking Scotch while flicking between the news channels.

As soon as the story broke about the shootings in Balham he'd known it was the work of Rosa Lopez. He had to wait an anxious couple of hours before he received a text from her confirming that she hadn't been arrested and apologising for missing the target. She'd ended the message with the words: *It won't happen again.* And for some reason he believed her.

He felt she'd already made up for her mistake by bringing down two uniforms and the partner of detective Laura Jefferson, the smart-arsed cow who had interviewed him. It was a shame she wasn't dead but that didn't mean she wouldn't be within a few days.

Before going to bed, Slack had sent Danny another text that he wanted forwarded to all the detectives on the organised crime task force. They'd have received it by now, and he knew it would prompt them to come and see him again.

They'd want to ask a whole bunch of new questions, including why he had never told them that he was Terry Malone's father. He knew they were now aware of it because he'd been tipped off last night by his mole on the inside.

But it wasn't a huge deal. He was only surprised it had taken them so long to find it out.

No doubt it would strengthen their conviction that he was behind the threats and killings, and that he'd had a hand in the disappearance of firearms officer Hugh Wallis.

But so what? Without any evidence they were fucked. The Met, his long-time nemesis, was virtually paralysed by despair and frustration. Every copper across every rank would be feeling the pain. And that was exactly the position he'd hoped they'd be in when he'd put his plan together. He'd wanted to hurt them, punish them, deliver a blow that would enable him to claim when the end came that he'd beaten the bastards.

After all, it was all he had to live for now. In the coming weeks and months the cancer would take from him everything that he still found pleasurable. He'd have to stop drinking Scotch and having sex. He'd find it harder to keep food down and just leaving the apartment was going to become an ordeal.

Was it any wonder then that he felt so bitter? And not just with the Old Bill. He'd been dealt a shitty hand. He was still only fifty-seven, for fuck's sake. Until fairly recently he'd been enjoying the trappings of his success. All-night sessions at his clubs, drug-fuelled orgies in fancy hotel suites, long days at the races, blowout meals at London's most expensive restaurants.

Now he had neither the stamina nor the inclination to even try to have fun.

So that was why this meant so much to him. And why he was loving every minute of it.

Another appearance on the TV by the Met's top dog brought a smile to his face. Commissioner John Saunders was trying to convince the public that his band of Keystone Cops hadn't lost control of the situation.

Addressing reporters outside Scotland Yard, he said, 'We believe that the woman who's committing these murders is being paid to do so by someone else. It's part of a heinous plot to destabilise law enforcement in the capital. But it won't work. Every one of my officers and support staff will stand firm, and we will reject all demands that come from the perpetrators. Meanwhile, I'm confident that we'll soon be closing in on this woman and those who are involved with her.'

They ran the CCTV footage again that showed Rosa on the motorbike. But at no time was her face visible.

There was no mention of the latest text message that had been sent to the detectives. Maybe that was because the Commissioner hadn't seen it yet. Or perhaps they were intending to keep quiet about it. The thought made him chuckle.

On the table in front of him was the phone he used to communicate with Danny. He picked it up and called him.

'Time to send the new message on to the media,' he said.

'Will do, boss,' Danny replied. 'How are you feeling?'

'Better than I did last night. But I won't be doing much today so you look after things and call me if there are any problems.'

They talked briefly about events in Balham and he told Danny not to be concerned, that Rosa was still on top of things and the Old Bill had no idea who or where she was.

'But brace yourself for another visit from them,' Slack said. 'What Rosa does next will trigger a wave of arrests the like of which this city has never seen.'

Slack ended the call, but before switching off the phone he re-read his latest message and it thrilled him to think that it would cause even more panic within the Met.

I made it clear that the killings won't stop until you and your colleagues resign from the task force. But your superiors say it won't happen because it'll set a dangerous precedent. So I'm going to do something that will make them reconsider their position.

His lawyer called at eleven o'clock to say that the police wanted to question him again.

'They want you to go to the nick,' Darren Peacock added.

'Are they arresting me?' Slack asked.

'No. It'll be voluntary.'

'In that case tell them to get stuffed. If they want to harass me they can come here and do it. I'm not feeling well.'

Peacock called back thirty minutes later to say the coppers would be arriving at midday.

'Don't let them in until I get there,' he said. 'I'm on my way.'

Before getting dressed, Slack gathered up the phones he used exclusively for making contact with Rosa and Danny and put them back in the safe that was hidden behind wall tiles in the kitchen.

Then he made himself another cup of coffee and waited for the Old Bill to turn up.

They arrived at the same time as the lawyer and there were two of them. The detective who did all the talking was a cocky sod named Marsden. The other was a thin woman with short hair named Gloria Stanford. Slack recognised the names from the list he'd given to Rosa.

'I understand from your lawyer that you're not feeling too good,' Marsden said when he was seated in the living room.

Slack stared at him, his eyes unflinching and fierce. The cop reminded him of a stumpy little pimp he'd beaten to death two years ago for trying to fleece him. For that reason he took an instant dislike to the guy.

'If you want to know why it's because I've got cancer,' he said. 'So I'd be grateful if you don't waste too much of my time.'

Marsden nodded. 'I'm aware of your condition, Roy. I was—'

'Only my friends call me Roy,' Slack cut in. 'And since you're not my friend you can show me some fucking respect and call me Mr Slack. Or even sir.'

The detective's jaw tightened and bulged, and Slack wound him up still further by grinning broadly.

'I'm glad you think this is funny because I don't,' Marsden snapped. 'Three more people were shot last evening and one of them, a police officer, is dead.'

Slack shrugged. 'So I heard. But don't tell me that you think it was me in that sexy leather outfit riding the motorbike?'

'We're not stupid,' Marsden said. 'We know that your grimy hands are all over this, despite your denials.'

'Is that right? Then I take it you're here because you've come up with the evidence to charge me.'

Marsden gritted his teeth. 'We will eventually. Make no mistake about that.'

'Well, you need to get a move on,' Slack said. 'I'll be dead and buried in a matter of months.'

The detective looked as though he was going to lose his temper. His eyes flared and his bottom lip trembled.

His colleague put a hand on his arm and murmured something in his ear.

The lawyer took this as his cue to intervene, and said, 'I'd like to remind you officers that my client is allowing himself to be interviewed voluntarily even though it's the fourth time in just over a week that you've questioned him. So unless you get on with it I'm going to advise him to ask you to leave.'

Marsden sat there fuming while Detective Stanford began the interview. The first question was: 'Why didn't you inform us that Terry Malone was your son?'

Slack feigned surprise. 'How did you find out about that?'

'That's not important. You should have told us.'

'Why?'

'Because it's relevant. You're a suspect in the disappearance of the police officer who shot him.'

'And I've already told you that I know nothing about that.'

'We don't believe you,' Marsden piped up, his tone aggressive. 'You were Malone's dad. It's bleeding obvious that you decided to get revenge.'

'Revenge is a mug's game, and I'm not a mug,' Slack said. 'But if you reckon I've lied to you then feel free to produce the evidence.'

For the two detectives it was all downhill from then on. They pressed him again about the text messages sent to members of the task force and their families. And about the murders of Dave Prentiss and Marion Nash, and the shootings in Balham.

'And I'll repeat what I told you before,' he said. 'It's got nothing to do with me.'

'We know you blame us for the deaths of your wife and father,' Marsden said. 'And you told someone at your son's funeral that his death was the last straw. That's given rise to speculation that you've decided to wage war against the Met, your aim being to cause a lot of harm before you bow out.'

He laughed. 'That's total bollocks. I'll admit I hate coppers with a vengeance, just like other people hate blacks and Muslims and gays. But that doesn't mean I'd pay someone to go out and kill a bunch of them.'

'It's also an outrageous allegation to make,' Peacock said. 'Especially since you don't have a single piece of evidence to back it up.'

And that was why Slack was able to sit there feeling so supremely confident. It didn't matter what the stupid cunts believed or suspected. Without proof they couldn't touch him and they knew it.

It took them another half an hour to accept that they weren't going to get anything out of him. They asked him a range of questions relating to his business interests and his private life. To some of them his answer was a firm: no comment.

He could have called a halt sooner, but he liked to see them struggling. They were desperate to get him to incriminate himself in some way, but that was never going to happen.

In the end they left frustrated and dispirited, and Marsden's parting words were: 'I'll be seeing you again, Roy. And when I do I'll make sure I wipe that fucking smile off your ugly face.'

47

Laura

The morning dragged after Kate left. I spent most of the time at Aidan's bedside and I spoke to him even when I knew he was asleep.

My mind was in turmoil, and my heart was in overdrive because I was drinking so much coffee.

The latest text message to arrive on our phones had given me something else to think about, other than Aidan and the fact that I'd miscarried even though I hadn't known I was pregnant.

. . . I'm going to do something that will make them reconsider their position.

It sounded so ominous. What the hell did it mean? What was going to happen? And could it really be any worse than what had happened already?

I wondered if the leather-clad assassin was poised to commit another despicable act. Perhaps Roy Slack had instructed her to step up her game. Or maybe she wasn't the only one whose strings he was pulling.

It was an appalling thought that there might be more than one contract killer out there, but the Commissioner himself cast doubt on that when a reporter put it to him during one of several appearances on camera.

'We certainly hope that isn't the case, but of course we can't rule it out,' John Saunders said. 'However, the evidence does seem to suggest otherwise. I've just received a forensics report on the bullets used in the murders of DI Dave Prentiss, Marion Nash and Warren Christie, the officer shot in Balham High Road yesterday evening. It confirms that they all came from the same weapon. And they're also a match for the bullet that wounded Mr Aidan Bray in his home.'

The story dominated the airwaves. It was as though there was nothing else happening in the world.

There was so much for broadcasters to get their teeth into. The human-interest angles. The implications for law and order across the country. The fact that it was proving so easy for someone to cause so much chaos and confusion. And the continued specula-tion as to who it might be.

Politicians were lining up to condemn the killings. Most insisted that the Met must not close down the task force operations. But there was one who called for them to be suspended temporarily in view of how much blood had already been shed.

I had not seen this kind of hysteria since London was last targeted by terrorists. Then the coverage was focused entirely on the victims, the carnage, the ISIS suicide bombers who were known to have been responsible.

But this was different. These weren't random attacks. Police officers and their loved ones were being targeted. And the killer was a mysterious woman who, according to witnesses, was more like a model than a murderer. So in many ways it was a far more interesting story.

For the news media it was manna from heaven: a story that just kept on giving. But for the rest of us it was a ghastly nightmare that showed no sign of ending any time soon.

Aidan was awake when his parents arrived earlier than expected at 1pm. He was able to talk, which came as such a relief to them and to me.

They had lots of questions and I answered them as best I could. But describing what had happened back at the house – and keeping schtum about the miscarriage – was a real challenge and I kept choking on my words.

And it was just as bad when I ran through what the doctor had told me about the damage to Aidan's shoulder, including the fact that he might never regain full use of his arm.

Aidan held it together better than I did, and pointed out that at least he wasn't dead, which made me smile.

After he fell asleep we retreated to the waiting room where I switched on the TV and his parents saw for themselves what was going on.

His mother, Veronica, was beside herself.

'How the bloody hell has she managed to get away?' she said, referring to the assassin on the motorcycle. 'All those cameras. And the witnesses. It's ridiculous.'

And it was, of course. But for me the real question was where was the bitch now? And what was she planning to do next?

48

Rosa

It was 2pm when she arrived at her destination – the towering Sky Reach Hotel on London's Cromwell Road, close to the Natural History Museum.

She was carrying the black briefcase that Roy Slack had left in the garage behind the pub. It contained the component parts of the sniper rifle that could be assembled in thirty seconds.

She'd spotted the hotel while checking out the home of her next target. As soon as she'd realised that the line of fire was perfect she'd gone ahead and booked a room, insisting it be East facing and on or above the fifteenth floor of the twenty-two storey building.

She used a fake credit card to check in and the name on it was Maria Santos.

The receptionist was a young man with ginger hair whose eyes lingered on her face for longer than was necessary, before his gaze dropped to her cleavage.

She was wearing a V-neck T-shirt under a new black raincoat, and a blonde wig that was one of two she carried with her when she travelled.

She'd already located the security cameras on her first visit to the hotel so she was careful not to look at them.

'You're in room 712,' the receptionist said. 'As requested it's on the fifteenth floor. I do hope you enjoy your stay, Miss Santos. If there's anything you need then don't hesitate to call us.'

All she really needed was some luck. Tonight's mission could only be carried out if the target arrived back at his house, as was expected. Her window of opportunity would last for only seconds. But that wasn't so unusual, especially with high-profile targets who were deemed to be at risk and therefore had a personal security detail who ushered them in and out of places.

The room was larger than she'd expected and much smarter than the one she was staying in over in Vauxhall.

She closed and locked the door behind her, placed the briefcase on the bed, and went straight to the window.

It offered a fabulous view of London, and it took her just a few seconds to locate Appleton Mews and the house with the blue door. According to Slack's source inside Scotland Yard it was where the target lived with his wife and two teenage daughters.

It had a small balcony and an attached garage. There was a street light close to it and she knew that it would work to her advantage if, as expected, she was still waiting here when it got dark in a couple of hours.

The mews was about five hundred metres away, well within the range of the rifle Slack had provided. Through the telescopic lens it would look almost close enough to touch.

Rosa was an expert marksman, having acquired her sniper skills over many years. She'd killed eleven people back in Mexico using a rifle from a distance, including two politicians and three senior police officers. And she was proud of the fact that she had never missed a shot.

The window opened only about six inches, presumably to stop guests from jumping out, but it was plenty wide enough for the barrel of the gun.

Having satisfied herself that she had chosen a great position, she went back to the bed and opened up the briefcase.

Minutes later she was sitting on a chair next to the window and the rifle was resting on the ledge. The television was on behind her, providing a running commentary on the hunt for the woman on the motorcycle.

Rosa stared down at Appleton Mews, ready to spring into action the moment a vehicle turned into it.

But she knew it was probably going to be a long wait.

49

Laura

I decided to go home just after 3pm. By that time Aidan was sitting up in bed and his parents were with him.

Two armed officers accompanied me and we travelled in a marked car.

It was only a short drive to the house and when we got there it was still a crime scene. Police vehicles were parked outside and a group of people, consisting mostly of our neighbours, were gathered on the pavement.

There were also a couple of press photographers who started taking pictures the moment I stepped out of the car.

I was greeted at the front door by Josh Miller, the crime scene manager, who I'd known for years. He'd been expecting me, and he asked me how Aidan was.

'He's recovering, thankfully,' I said.

'That's good to know, Laura. We've all been worried.'

It was weird entering the house. It felt cold and abandoned, and my muscles stiffened.

'We'll soon be finished here,' Miller said. 'But I'm afraid it's still

271

a mess. We've had the front door repaired but the kitchen window isn't yet fixed. I strongly suggest you stay somewhere else tonight.'

'I'm going to,' I said. 'My mother's house isn't far away. I just need to get some things.'

I'd known what to expect, but it still came as a shock when I walked into the kitchen. There was Aidan's dried blood on the floor and yellow stickers marking the spots where bullets had struck, including the front of the dishwasher and two cupboard doors.

'The woman fired no less than eight bullets into the house,' Miller said. 'You're so lucky you were able to return fire.'

Without the glass door, the cold air from outside made me shiver. But despite that I just stood there, feeling the tears well up as my mind carried me back to the previous evening. The sound of gunfire. The breaking glass. The figure in the garden shooting into the kitchen. Me on the floor with Aidan's head in my lap and his blood on my hands and blouse.

When did it happen? I wondered. That precise moment when my pregnancy was terminated. When the baby died in the womb before I knew that he or she was even there.

'Are you OK?' Miller asked me, and I suddenly realised that my chest was pumping for oxygen.

I nodded. 'It's just a shock coming back to all this.'

'I can imagine. But rest assured that when you next return it will be almost like it was before. The glass is being replaced later and we'll give it a good clean.'

'Thanks, Josh.'

I didn't need to pick much up. A change of clothes, some toiletries and some things for Aidan. I only anticipated staying at my mother's house for one night.

But as I packed my small case I wondered if it would be better not to return until Aidan was discharged from the hospital. The thought of sleeping here alone filled me with dread. It made me think about some of the victims of crime I had dealt with over the years. The ones who'd become mental wrecks after their homes had been violated.

Would Aidan and I ever be able to get over it and continue to live here? Cooking in the same kitchen that had been shot up like a saloon in a western movie? Walking over the spot where Aidan's blood had been spilled? Relaxing in the garden from where the killer had launched her violent attack?

There were wider questions too. How would this impact on our lives in general? Our future together? Our ability to eventually find peace of mind?

And what if I was wrong to assume that I would conceive again? What would it do to me? To us? It was a thought too horrible to contemplate.

I felt my body start to shake so I sat on the bed and put my face in my hands. Just then my mobile phone rang, making me jump.

It was DCS Drummond, calling to see how I was and to update me.

I told him about Aidan's condition and said I was feeling better in myself.

'The doctor said I was sick because of the shock,' I lied.

He informed me that the woman who had shot him was still on the loose. It made me angry. Scared. I felt blood pounding behind my eyes.

'We need to find her, guv,' I said.

'We're doing everything we can,' he replied. 'The people who saw her after she came off the bike are going through pictures we have on file. But in all honesty there aren't many females in the system who match the description or the MO. I'm beginning to think that maybe she's a hired gun who was imported from abroad.'

'What about Roy Slack?' I asked. 'Is he still in the frame?'

'He is and I sent Tony Marsden to see him. But he's still pleading ignorance and if we can't link the bastard to what's going on we're buggered.'

'Have you stepped up protection for everyone else?' I asked.

'As much as we can. But we're under strict instructions not to wind down the operation. So it means that every member of the team is going around with armed minders.'

'Does that include you, guv?' I asked.

'It does. But as you know it's no protection against a seasoned pro like this girl obviously is.'

'What about family members and loved ones?'

'Everyone who received the texts has now been assigned personal bodyguards. And we're advising them to move to other addresses or stay indoors.'

'My mum's gone to her friend's place in Ringwood.'

'I know. We've contacted her and there are two officers outside the house already.'

'What about your family, guv?'

I knew he had a wife and two children and lived in London, but I wasn't sure where.

'They left for her brother's house in Wigan last night. I'm staying put, though. In fact I'll be going home soon to have a shower and get a change of clothes.'

'Well, be careful,' I said. 'And thank the team for all their kind messages and tell them to take care.'

But even as I spoke I knew that none of us had any control over our own destiny. And that the psychotic cow on the motorbike hadn't yet finished destroying our lives.

50

Rosa

It was early evening and already dark outside. The target hadn't yet arrived and Rosa was still in position next to the window of her hotel room. Still waiting patiently to commit another murder.

Appleton Mews was bathed in an orange glow from the street lamps and she'd seen various cars and people come and go. But nobody had entered or left the house with the blue door.

She was hoping she would see the target soon, though, so that she'd still have time to meet up with Alice. She'd told her that she was attending an all-day seminar that would probably finish late. Alice had understood, of course, and had said to come to her apartment whenever she could. Rosa was anxious not to disappoint her, or herself.

Despite everything that was going on it was Alice who kept invading her thoughts. Rosa couldn't wait to hold her in her arms again. To kiss her. To lick her. To feel her breath on her face. To taste the juice from between her thighs.

It was a craving like none she had ever experienced. And it was getting stronger. Becoming more of a distraction.

In the past she had always managed to compartmentalise her feelings and the mental anguish that had blighted her childhood. But now she was struggling with that. The barriers were down and her thoughts were out of control.

She was finding it harder to focus on the job. Harder still to keep Alice's face out of her mind's eye.

When Rosa had left the apartment this morning, Alice had stayed in bed.

'I'm having lunch with my dad and then I'm going shopping,' she'd said. 'I might even buy you a present.'

She was probably back home by now, Rosa thought. Getting ready for this evening. They were going to spend it making plans for tomorrow's tour of London.

Rosa wondered if Alice had seen the CCTV footage of the woman on the motorcycle. Had she heard the man with the beard describe the woman as being attractive and having a slight accent?

If it had been in Mexico the media coverage would have been more muted, the story far less sensational.

It was an added pressure, along with the ridiculously high number of street surveillance cameras, and the fact that all of those people on the kill list knew that they were potential targets. So they could take precautions, change their routines, never let their guard drop, arm themselves just as Laura Jefferson had done.

For Rosa the scenario she found herself in was challenging rather than intimidating. It meant she had to be sharp, creative, fast-thinking, patient.

And lucky.

So far her luck had held up, and when seven o'clock came she discovered that it still hadn't deserted her.

Dead on the hour two cars entered Appleton Mews and Rosa knew instinctively that her target would be in one of them.

It had been a long wait, but at last it was over.

She leaned forward towards the window, the rifle pressed into her good shoulder, the telescopic lens tight against her right eye.

The two black unmarked cars pulled up in front of the house with the blue door.

Rosa inhaled deeply and held the breath in her lungs. She stilled her body and felt the anticipation grow as she watched two men get out of each car. They were wearing dark suits and it was obvious to Rosa that they were cops. They looked around them as though searching for signs of danger.

After a few moments the rear door of the first vehicle opened and another man got out.

Rosa saw immediately that he was the man she'd come here to kill. The target.

And he made it easy for her by standing under the glow of the street lamp nearest to the house while he spoke to the other men.

She centred the crosshairs on his face, which loomed large in the magnified lens.

The first bullet pummelled into the centre of his forehead and sent him flying backwards against the front door. The second hit him in the throat as he slid to the ground. And the third struck him in the chest.

As his bodyguards dived for cover, Rosa pulled the rifle back through the window into the darkened room.

Within sixty seconds the weapon was disassembled and back in the briefcase, and she was closing the room door behind her.

She knew she didn't have much time, that the cops would close in quickly on all the most likely sniper locations, including the tall hotel.

And that was all the more reason to remain calm and avoid attracting attention.

Rosa went down in the lift and then walked calmly through the busy reception area and onto the street.

She did not encounter any problems or resistance because everyone she passed was blissfully unaware of what had just happened. The cops in Appleton Mews would still be struggling to get their act together. Screaming into radios while desperately trying to avoid being shot at themselves.

Imagining the chaos she'd just caused filled Rosa with a sense of accomplishment as she walked quickly away from the hotel.

She felt good because the mission had been successful. There was no way the victim would survive the three bullets she had pumped into him. And she was excited because she could now spend the rest of the evening with Alice.

Four streets on, she hailed a taxi and climbed in.

'London Bridge railway station,' she said to the driver and made herself comfortable in the back.

At the station she would enter one of the public toilets, take off the wig and stuff it in her shoulder bag. She would also dump the raincoat. Then she'd lose herself in the crowd before getting another taxi to the hotel in Vauxhall. No way would the cops be able to track her.

As the taxi carried her away from the scene of her latest assignment, she sat back and closed her eyes to reflect on what she had just done.

Once again she'd shown how easy it is to kill someone. The target had been easy to get to despite having four burly cops with him for protection. It served as a warning to everyone from prime ministers to presidents that they were as good as dead when a price was put on their head.

Rosa knew that this particular killing was going to have a profound impact on the city. There was going to be a strong and immediate reaction, and the hunt for the assassin would be stepped up.

But she remained confident in her ability to stay one step ahead of the cops, no matter how many of them were assigned to the task of finding her.

She opened her eyes and looked out at the streets that were filled with people and traffic. The sounds of voices and engines were drowned out by the high-pitched wail of multiple sirens. It signalled to everyone that something serious had happened. Something bad.

Rosa wondered how long it would be before the news got out that the Commissioner of the Metropolitan Police had been shot dead outside his home in West London.

51

Laura

News of the Commissioner's murder reached me an hour after it happened.

Aidan had just settled down for the night and I was about to leave the hospital to go to my mother's house.

Sergeant Ray Wilks, one of the armed officer's who'd been assigned to protect me, came into the room and said, 'I'm sorry to disturb you but there's something you need to know.'

He told me when we got to the waiting room and my insides turned to ice.

'It just came through on the radio,' he said. 'It seems he was shot by a sniper outside his home in Kensington.'

His words sliced through me like a rotablade, and my lungs were suddenly clutching for air.

I wanted to believe that it wasn't true, that it was fake news spread by a mischievous creep with access to the police radio frequencies.

I crossed the room and switched on the television.

'I don't think the media's aware of it yet,' Sergeant Wilks said.

And he was right. The news channels were still leading with the Balham shootings and the hunt for the woman on the motorcycle.

I grabbed my mobile phone from my pocket and jabbed at it. DCS Drummond answered straight away.

'Hello, Laura,' he said, before I spoke. 'I can guess why you're calling.'

'Is it true, guv? Has the Commissioner been killed?'

'I'm afraid so, but the details are sketchy. There's still a lot of activity at the scene. I'm on my way there now.'

'Was it just him or was anyone else shot?'

'He was the only victim, although he had four armed officers with him at the time. Word is he was shot with a high-velocity sniper rifle so the area around his house is being closed down.'

'Do we assume it's the same woman?' I said.

'I think we have to. That last message stated that something would be done to make us reconsider our position. This must be it.'

I wanted to ask more questions, but Drummond said he had more calls coming through and would ring me later.

When I came off the phone it felt as if my heart was flinging itself against the wall of my chest.

'Sit down and let me get you a cup of coffee,' Sergeant Wilks said, so I nodded and sat down on the sofa.

The assassination of John Saunders was a staggering development. And totally unexpected. He wasn't just another detective investigating organised crime. He was – or had been – the highest-ranking police officer in the country. The Commissioner of the Met, no less. The man in charge of a force that consisted of more than 40,000 staff, including 33,000 regular police officers.

The job didn't just entail leading the fight against crime in the capital. The Commissioner was also responsible for counter-terrorism and the protection of the Royal Family and senior government ministers.

His death at the hands of an assassin would have huge ramifications and be headline news around the world. It was going to spark a major debate about protection for senior officers and politicians. And it would plunge morale within the Met to an all-time low.

Sergeant Wilks handed me a Styrofoam cup filled with steaming black coffee, then told me he was going to resume his position in the corridor.

'I won't be leaving here just yet,' I told him, having changed my mind about going to my mother's house. 'I don't know how long I'll be staying.'

After he had left the room I was consumed by a strong sense of unease. I remained seated on the sofa, not moving even to drink my coffee. My muscles felt as though they'd been injected with lead, which was probably my body reacting to yet another shocking event.

I was convinced now that this wasn't just about the organised crime task force. I suspected the killings would continue even if the Met closed it down. This was aimed at every police officer in London, and the death toll was certain to rise.

So who would be next? Another detective? A family member? My mother? Me? Or would it be someone like the Mayor of London, to whom the Commissioner reported on matters relating to crime and policing?

The more I thought about it the harder it was to keep from screaming out loud. It got to the point after about twenty minutes where it seemed like the walls were closing in on me.

I set my untouched coffee on the table and got up to return

to Aidan's room, where I'd now decided to spend another night. I couldn't bear the thought of leaving him by himself, even though he was on the road to recovery.

But just as I was heading for the door the newsreader on the television grabbed my attention with the words: 'Reports are coming in that John Saunders, the Commissioner of the Metropolitan Police, has been shot and killed close to his home in West London.'

I stayed in the waiting room for another two hours watching the story unfold on the TV.

I learned that Saunders was shot three times when he stepped out of a car in front of his house.

He was returning home from another hellish day during which he'd given five interviews and fronted two press conferences at the Yard.

It was believed he was the victim of a sniper who targeted him with a long-range rifle.

The search for the assassin was centred on the nearby Sky Reach Hotel on Cromwell Road. It towered above the area, and from the upper floors there was a clear view of the Commissioner's house.

'Mr Saunders leaves a wife and two teenage daughters,' the newsreader said. 'It's understood they moved out of the house early this morning and are staying at their other property in Sussex. They have been informed.'

My heart ached for his wife and kids and I could only imagine what a terrible shock it was for them. It put things in perspective for me. The loss of an unborn baby couldn't possible compare with the loss of a husband and father. Could it?

I was familiar with the Sky Reach Hotel, a contemporary landmark in that part of the capital. I'd had no idea that the Commissioner lived in its shadow and I'd never heard of Appleton Mews.

A picture of the house, which had a blue door, appeared on the screen and the newsreader pointed out that the family owned it and it wasn't a grace-and-favour property that went with the Commissioner's job.

The Assistant Commissioner, a middle-aged woman named Geena Donaldson, read out a statement beneath the revolving sign outside Scotland Yard.

She confirmed that the Commissioner had died at the scene and it was believed he was murdered by the same woman who had carried out the other killings during the past week.

'This is a sad day for the Metropolitan police and for London,' she said. 'John Saunders was a fine man and an excellent Commissioner.' She had to pause there because her voice broke and it appeared that she might lose it.

But after clearing her throat, she went on, 'I spoke to his wife Janet by phone a few minutes ago and I've promised her that we will track down her husband's killer. It's a promise I intend to keep, no matter how long it takes.'

She ended the statement by revealing that the Prime Minster would be chairing a meeting of the government's emergency committee, COBRA, the following morning.

COBRA, an acronym for Cabinet Office Briefing Room A, was a mechanism whereby ministers, senior police officers and security officials could meet in response to major events and emergencies such as terrorist attacks.

It was obviously a sensible move and a necessary development. And it would take the hunt for those responsible to a whole new level.

But I feared it would not be enough to stop the murder spree. Or to snare the wicked witch with the deadly armoury and the heart of stone.

52

Rosa

She was in a taxi on her way to Alice's apartment when her phone rang. It was Roy Slack, and he slurred his words as he spoke, which made her wonder if he'd been drinking.

'I want to congratulate you, Rosa,' he said. 'You've surpassed my expectations.'

'I'm glad you think so,' she replied.

'It's all over the news. We've created chaos, and every copper in London is shedding a tear. This is exactly what I was hoping for when I added his name to the mix. You did well considering how little time you had.'

'Most jobs don't require that much planning,' she said. 'Locations can be studied via the web and people are much easier to track with new technology. Plus, every target steps into the line of fire sooner or later.'

'You're being modest,' Slack said. 'You pulled off a blinder and I've already been in touch with Carlos Cruz to tell him that I think you're a fucking legend.'

Now she was certain he was drunk and she was keen for the conversation to end.

'Do you want me to continue?' she asked him.

'I do indeed,' he said. 'I'm having too much fun to stop now. But I'm going to make it easier for you because it'll be harder from today to get to those people on the list. So you have my blessing to kill any copper at random, plain clothes or in uniform. I want a few more of the bastards taken out so that means you staying in London into next week.'

It was the kind of thing that the cartel bosses in Mexico would say. And that included Carlos Cruz. Killing gave them a buzz, especially when it was carried out as an act of vengeance.

It occurred to Rosa that Roy Slack would have been right at home in Tijuana or Acapulco. He had exactly what it took to survive and prosper. He was cruel and sadistic, and quite mad. He also had a huge sense of entitlement.

'And I want you to know that you're well on course to earn yourself that bonus I mentioned,' he said. 'Carlos told me he's paying you half a million dollars. Well, I'll give you the same amount if you carry on delivering. How does that sound?'

'Terrific,' she said, and resisted the urge to ask him how much he was paying Carlos for her services.

'Well, just make sure they don't get their hands on you,' he said. 'So far they haven't got a fucking clue who you are and I want it to stay that way. OK?'

'OK,' she said.

She put the phone back in her bag and allowed herself a smile. So her reward for completing the assignment was now going to be a cool million. And she didn't even have to pre-plan the hits. She could go up to any cop in the street and blow his or her brains out. What could be simpler?

Her thoughts turned to what to do with the money – and whether she should use it to embark on a new chapter in her life. One that wasn't just about death and destruction and a series of meaningless one-night stands.

Alice had opened her eyes and mind to the possibility of something better and more fulfilling. But it would mean leaving Mexico and turning her back on everything she knew. The Slayer would cease to exist and she would have to re-invent herself.

It wouldn't be easy, of course. And it would entail a huge amount of risk. But there was no reason it couldn't be done by developing a careful exit plan. She knew where to go to get fake documents – everything from visas to birth certificates. She could obtain all the paperwork she needed to set herself up here in London.

She would open new bank accounts to move her savings. Take out new credit cards. Ensure she didn't leave a trail for others to follow. She would erase all trace of The Slayer and become someone who was so very, very different.

When the elevator door opened, Alice was standing there, wearing a big, bright smile and a knock-out black dress that revealed more of her body than it covered up.

She flew straight into Rosa's arms and gave her a long, passionate kiss on the lips.

'That was because I missed you so much today,' Alice said, stepping back. 'And I was really worried that you wouldn't be able to make it tonight.'

Alice took Rosa's hand and led her along the corridor to her apartment.

'You look stunning,' Rosa said. 'That's such a beautiful dress.'

'Not as beautiful as you are,' Alice replied.

Once inside the apartment, Rosa shed her coat and followed Alice into the kitchen. There was a tray of snack food on the breakfast bar and a bottle of champagne in an ice bucket.

'I wasn't sure you'd have had time to eat,' Alice said. 'And since you have tomorrow off I was hoping you'd drink with me tonight.'

'Of course I will,' she said, smiling. 'I don't want to be as sober as a judge on my first Saturday night in London.'

They both laughed and Alice poured two glasses of champagne. As she handed one to Rosa, she said, 'How are you feeling now? Is your shoulder still painful?'

Rosa shook her head. 'I'm almost as good as new and that's thanks to what you did to me with your fingers last night.'

'Well, I was glad to be of service,' Alice said. 'Now come into the lounge. I've got a surprise for you.'

Rosa took a sip of champagne and it felt good. She was breaking her own rule about never drinking alcohol on an assignment, but what the hell? She put it down to the Alice Green effect and it raised a smile.

The first thing Rosa noticed when she entered the lounge was that the TV was on and showing a photo of the man she had murdered just under three hours ago.

She felt her body stiffen and a rush of heat burned in her chest.

'I bought you a little gift,' Alice said. 'I saw it in Harrods and I just couldn't resist it.'

Rosa wrenched her eyes away from the screen to where Alice stood next to the coffee table. She'd picked up a small blue box with a red ribbon around it.

She held it towards Rosa and said, 'I hope you like it.'

Rosa was taken aback. No one other than her parents had ever given her a present.

'You shouldn't have,' she said as she stepped forward.

Alice shrugged. 'Why ever not? I'm the happiest I've been in years and that's thanks to you.'

Rosa took the box and gently removed the ribbon. She already knew that what was inside would have been expensive. From what she'd heard nothing sold in Harrods was cheap.

She gasped involuntarily when she saw what Alice had bought her. It was an exquisite chain friendship bracelet with a silver bar studded with tiny diamonds and chains twisted to create the illusion of rope.

'It's by Monica Vinader,' Alice said. 'She's my all-time favourite jewellery designer.'

Rosa was speechless, but her heart was pounding. Once again Alice had surprised her with a wonderful gesture of affection and generosity.

'This is so lovely,' she said, finding her voice. 'It must have cost a small fortune.'

'Not nearly as much as you might think,' Alice said. 'But what I paid for it isn't important. I just hope that when you wear it you'll think of me.'

Rosa felt a wave of emotion that almost reduced her to tears. She gave the bracelet to Alice and asked her to put it on her wrist.

'I'm going to wear it every second of every day from now on,' she said. 'So that means I'll always be thinking about you.'

They made love there and then on the sofa, and even the sound from the TV did not lessen the intensity of the experience for Rosa. She lost herself in the moment and it seemed as if Alice did too.

It was as though they had been made for each other. The perfect fit. Two women who'd been destined to be together. Sharing something that was real and special and sublime.

Rosa knew now that she was going to do whatever it took to keep this perfect woman in her life.

She would lie and cheat and kill anyone who stood in her way.

It was time to accept that her life had changed because against all the odds she had fallen in love.

After making love they showered together and then drank more champagne.

It was going to Rosa's head but she didn't care. She was feeling better and happier than she'd felt in a long time.

There was an awkward moment when Alice drew her attention to the TV and said, 'Have you seen this? It's terrible. Another policeman has been murdered. The top guy this time. They say it's that bitch who rides the motorbike and that she's being paid to do it.'

'I heard about it just before I left the hotel,' Rosa said. 'I didn't realise that this was such a violent city. It's like home from home.'

'I think we should turn the television off so it doesn't dampen our mood,' Alice said.

Rosa nodded. 'That's a good idea.'

Alice replaced the rolling news bulletin with soft background music.

Rosa immediately relaxed again, and the rest of the evening was pure bliss. They drew up a list of the places they would visit the following day, including Buckingham Palace, Oxford Street and Trafalgar Square.

And then they went to bed early so that they could make love again.

Before she fell asleep, Rosa told herself that she had made the right call. This would be her last assignment as a contract killer. It was time The Slayer went into retirement and she embarked on a new and more rewarding life.

53

Slack

He was well and truly pissed. During the course of the evening he'd put away half a bottle of Glenfiddich and three glasses of one of his finest wines.

It was enough to make his doctor have a seizure because of the strong links between alcohol abuse and pancreatic cancer.

But what better way to celebrate the death of the Met's top dog? The biggest cunt of them all. The leader of the pack. The man responsible for setting up the organised crime task force.

On the day it began operating, John Saunders said, 'The men who run these gangs are revolting creatures who prey on the weaknesses of others. They're an ugly stain on this great city of ours and the job of this task force is to put them where they belong – behind bars.'

It was well past midnight now and the BBC were showing the last interview the man gave before setting off on his date with destiny.

The prick talked about the hunt for the female assassin on the motorbike, and he offered his condolences to the officer shot dead on Balham High Road. He even said that it was believed she was killing coppers on behalf of a gangster with a grudge against the Met.

Slack raised his glass of Scotch at the TV and said, 'You were right about that, mate.'

The BBC then switched to an exterior shot of the Commissioner's house and the camera swung up to show the hotel that overlooked it. The newsreader said that it was thought the sniper had fired from one of the rooms on an upper floor.

The location of the hotel had been a stroke of luck. Rosa had done well to seize on it. She'd shown great initiative, and he was full of admiration for the way she'd bounced back so spectacularly after the cock-up the night before in Balham.

It hadn't been his intention to target the Commissioner. But it had struck him as a good idea after the bastard kept insisting that the task force would carry on with its operations. It was like saying you can kill as many of us as you want to but we will never let you win.

And that had been a big mistake on his part because it had seemed to Slack like a challenge – one that he'd felt compelled to respond to.

He chugged back more Scotch and let out an enormous burp. At that moment his landline rang for the umpteenth time. He knew it would be one of his people, calling to check that he was aware of what had happened or to ask him if he'd had anything to do with it.

The first few calls he had answered, but now he was no longer bothering to because talking to the lads took up too much time. He wanted some peace and quite so that he could wallow in the success of his mission.

After all, there was nothing more satisfying than revenge. The thought of how much pain he was inflicting on the Old Bill filled him with a warm glow. This was Retribution with a capital R. Payback with a capital P.

His old man would have been proud of him. And so would Julie. And he was sure that his only son Terry would have been lapping it up if the fuckers hadn't gunned him down.

It was one in the morning when he finally sloped off to bed. He knew he'd sleep like a log, and not just because he was drunk.

For the first time in ages he was happy rather than sad. And he actually felt glad to be alive because he now knew that he was going to even the score with the Met – and in doing so fulfil his dying wish.

PART THREE

54

Laura

Sunday dawned cold and bright. From the window of Aidan's room it looked like the start of a summer's day. There wasn't a cloud in the sky, and it was difficult to believe that Christmas was fast approaching. And what a wretched Christmas it was going to be.

Fortunately I'd managed to sleep for a couple of hours sitting up in the chair. My troubled thoughts tried to keep me awake, but they were no match for the wave of sheer exhaustion that eventually pulled me under.

I had time to go to the loo and rinse my face before Aidan surfaced. He looked much better. Some colour had returned to his cheeks and he seemed more alert. But at the same time he was clearly feeling sorry for himself. It made me glad that I hadn't yet told him about the miscarriage.

I called his parents who were staying in a nearby Premier Inn and got him to talk to them. He asked them to bring him some chocolate when they came to visit and it made me smile. It was a sure sign that he was on the mend.

I didn't break the news to him about the murder of the Commissioner until the nurse had changed his dressing and the doctor had examined his wound.

The news shocked him, of course, and he asked me lots of questions, most of which I couldn't answer.

'It's why I stayed here all night again,' I said. 'I just couldn't bring myself to leave you.'

I told him about going to the house and the extent of the damage.

'I'll pop back today to see what's changed,' I said. 'But I intend to bed down at mum's, at least until you're discharged.'

I phoned my mother while Aidan drank a cup of tea and ate a biscuit. The latest murder had upset her deeply and she began to sob.

'I know what his poor family is going through,' she said. 'We went through it ourselves after your father was killed.'

My brain took me back to the weeks and months after Dad died and I remembered what a nightmare it was. The grief and pain and anger that made it so hard to function.

'I'm so scared, Laura,' my mother said. 'For myself, for you, for everyone. Surely the police with all their people and resources should be able to stop it.'

I told her that I was confident it wouldn't be long now before we caught the assassin and the creature who was paying her to wreak havoc. But it was a lie. I knew we weren't making any progress and we wouldn't unless we found that chink in Roy Slack's armour.

And it was going to be just as difficult to find the assassin. There were thousands of motorcycle riders in London, most of them wearing leathers and helmets. If we started flagging them down randomly we'd just cause major chaos.

I told my mother I'd call her back later in the day and just as I put the phone away Sergeant Wilks popped his head in. He said he was going off duty and a new security detail had taken up position in the corridor.

It should have reassured me, made me feel safer, but instead it sparked a fresh surge of anger. My chest started to feel tight, and a red mist clouded my vision.

'What are you thinking, Laura?' Aidan asked me.

I took a slow breath and said, 'I'm thinking how much easier it would be to stop this if we didn't have to abide by the law.'

Aidan frowned. 'And if you were given free reign what would you do?'

I didn't have to think about it. 'I'd put thumb screws on Roy Slack and the heavies who protect him and I'd squeeze until they coughed up.'

If only to avenge the death of our unborn baby.

'So why don't your lot do just that if you're so convinced he's behind it – instead of spouting a load of bullshit about lack of evidence?'

'Because we're coppers, Aidan. Not criminals. And that's a hard truth that villains like Roy Slack have been exploiting for decades.'

'But it's ridiculous. What if he's too clever for you and you don't find any proof? What then? Do you just accept that there's nothing you can do about it? Christ, Laura, three police officers have already been murdered along with a woman whose only crime was being married to one. Another officer was shot and wounded just like me. And yet the bloke you believe hired the killer is free to orchestrate more carnage. It makes no bloody sense.'

To the general public, especially those who'd been victims of crime, it didn't make much sense. It was the reason that as police officers we were often asked why men we knew to be major criminals were allowed to go on flaunting the law for years. They didn't appreciate that reasonable suspicion and probable cause were not enough. In the UK you were presumed innocent until proven guilty.

One of the most frustrating cases I'd dealt with was that of a drug baron named Leon Fawkes who was acquitted of three gang-land murders even though we knew he'd committed them. Each case fell apart because we failed to come up with sufficient evidence to convince the juries.

That was where we stood with Roy Slack. It was why I feared that there might be only one way to stop the killings – and that was for someone to take the law into their own hands.

I was also pretty sure that I wasn't the only copper in the Met who was coming to the same conclusion in the wake of the Commissioner's murder.

At 8am I went to the waiting room to check on the news.

I quickly discovered that quite a lot had happened overnight.

Detectives had established with a high degree of certainty that the sniper was indeed a woman, and that she had fired on Appleton Mews from a room on the fifteenth floor of the Sky Reach Hotel.

There was even security footage from inside the hotel of her walking up to reception and checking in. Predictably she kept her head down and avoided looking at the camera. But I didn't need to see her face to know that she was the same woman who had shot Aidan. She had simply swapped her motorbike leathers for a dark raincoat, which she wore with the collar up.

There was also something not quite right about the blonde hair, which led me and others to believe that it was a wig.

A DCI Maurice Longford was interviewed by reporters outside

the hotel and made an appeal for anyone who had seen the mystery woman to come forward.

'A number of factors lead us to believe that she's the assassin,' he said. 'She checked into the hotel a few hours before the Commissioner was shot and requested a room on the fifteenth floor facing Appleton Mews. She then vacated the room directly after the shooting and was seen leaving the hotel. We now know that the credit card that she used at check-in was a fake and the address she gave does not exist.'

I switched between the news channels. On Sky a reporter did a piece-to-camera outside 10 Downing Street and explained that the COBRA emergency committee would be meeting there soon to discuss how to deal with what was happening.

CNN carried an interview with the Mayor of London who described the death of the Commissioner as devastating.

'This sustained attack on the Metropolitan Police is without precedent,' he said. 'The investigation into the shootings and the threats that have been made is now the biggest of its kind ever undertaken in London. During the night, officers carried out raids on dozens of homes and a number of arrests were made. We're confident that inquiries will lead to the apprehension of the assassin and whoever she's working with.'

I sat there, burning over his words, knowing that they gave false hope. Just because people had been arrested, it didn't mean they'd be charged. They'd be questioned and held for a time before being released. And those with any connection to Roy Slack would be browbeaten and bribed.

But I was betting that Slack was playing this one close to his chest and that even most of his own people had been kept in the dark. It was almost certainly why no one had grassed him up despite the problems this was causing for the whole of the London underworld. The gangs had never been under so much pressure. They were all in the spotlight like never before. The disruption to their operations was costing them millions.

So surely if even a few knew the identity of the assassin at least one of them would have tipped the police off by now. Likewise if they could have provided us with evidence of Slack's involvement we would have seen it already.

A number of senior Scotland Yard officers and politicians appeared on screen to pay tribute to the Commissioner. A statement was read out on behalf of his wife who said her grief was painful beyond words. And she described John Saunders as a devoted husband and loving father to their two daughters.

As I watched and listened, I could feel the anger building inside me, dangerously electric. I was the partner of one of the victims so I was expected to take time off and stay away from the investigation. But I now realised that there was no chance of that happening. Not in view of the miscarriage. And not with Aidan lying in a hospital bed, his life possibly changed forever by an assassin's bullet.

I needed to get right back into the thick of it. Help find the woman responsible and the bastard who was paying her.

My original brief from DCS Drummond had been to go after Slack. So that was exactly what I would do – whether I was allowed to or not.

55

Rosa

They began their tour of London with a light breakfast at a café in Covent Garden. The sun was bright in the sky and it lifted the temperature a few degrees. It meant they were able to sit at an outside table.

Rosa was wearing one of Alice's coats – a bright-red knee-length number with a designer label. Alice had also loaned her a scarf so she was more than comfortable.

Alice herself looked striking in a pale-blue puffer jacket and black jeans.

Rosa had never felt so content. This was a whole new experience and she was loving every minute of it.

Up to this point her life had been devoid of friendship and intimacy. She'd been a loner who had always preferred her own company. But now, for the first time, she realised what she'd been missing.

Already this morning she had done something that had blown her mind – it was the simple act of walking hand in hand with another woman. She'd never done it before because she'd never had a girlfriend. Never openly displayed her sexuality. Never felt the need to spend her spare time with anyone but herself.

Dispassionate sex in anonymous hotel rooms had always seemed enough, along with the thrill she got from her work.

It meant she had never had to lose control or have anyone discover the weaknesses that defined her. She'd adopted a simple philosophy early on and that was to embrace the fact that she wasn't like most people. She was different. She had a lack of empathy for others, and no moral boundaries. It followed, therefore, that she had never been able to trust anyone.

But now she was on the verge of doing just that. It felt both strange and exhilarating.

She looked across the table at Alice, who was nibbling delicately on a slice of buttered toast. Right now there was nowhere in the world she would rather have been. And no one she would rather have been with.

This woman with the boyish haircut and beautiful eyes had captured her heart and made her realise that she could be more than just a killing machine – that deep inside there was a whole range of feelings and emotions that had either been ignored or supressed for many years.

At last they were finding their way to the surface, but in so doing they presented Rosa with the biggest challenge she had ever faced.

'First stop, Trafalgar Square,' Alice said after they had finished breakfast. 'Then we'll walk along The Mall to Buck Palace. From there we'll go to Oxford Street and I know a lovely restaurant where we can have some lunch. This afternoon we'll visit the South Bank. How does that sound?'

'Perfect,' Rosa said. 'And thank you for showing me around. I really appreciate it.'

'Don't be daft,' Alice said. 'It's my absolute pleasure.'

They held hands again as they walked from Covent Garden to Trafalgar Square. Rosa drank in the sights and sounds of London with all her senses.

Before coming here she could never have imagined herself doing something like this. But then she was no longer the same woman who had arrived from Acapulco a few days ago.

Then the only thing on her mind had been the assignment. How many people was she going to kill? How hard was it going to be? How soon could she return to Mexico?

Now she was focused on the future and the questions it raised were far more difficult to answer.

Was her love for Alice reciprocated? Would she be able to convince her that she was someone she wasn't? Would Carlos Cruz try to stop her walking away from the cartel? And, if so, how should she react?

She tried to stop thinking about it and to just enjoy being with Alice. But it was like trying to push back against the tide.

Rosa fell in love again that morning, this time with London itself. The city had been growing on her since she first arrived.

Her initial impression had been less than favourable, but her opinion had changed. And as she walked through the West End she realised that she would like to live here.

It was such a diverse and vibrant city, drenched in history and teeming with life. There was no place in Mexico to match it.

Rosa was thrilled at the prospect of living here with Alice. What a time they would have together. There would be so much to do, to see, to share. The bars, the restaurants, the clubs, the stores. The very idea was enough to make her salivate.

'Are you having a good time?' Alice asked her as they approached Trafalgar Square.

Rosa laughed. 'You may not believe this but it's already turning into the best day of my life so far.'

Alice blushed, then pulled Rosa to a stop so that she could kiss her. It was meant to be a small kiss, a peck on the lips. But it lasted a good thirty seconds and drew attention from some of the people around them, including a uniformed police officer who actually stopped to look at them.

Rosa felt her body tense and for a moment she thought she might have to reach for the pistol that was concealed in her bag and use it before she'd planned to.

But then the cop smiled and went on his way, and Rosa breathed a huge sigh of relief.

She knew that he was just one of many cops she would see during the course of the day on the streets of London. All of them were potential targets, and one of them would soon become her next victim.

All Rosa had to do was seize the opportunity the moment it presented itself. And she was fully confident that it would at some point in the day.

56

Slack

He spent the morning nursing a hangover. But it wasn't so bad that it stopped him gloating over the shitstorm he was causing.

It was all over the news. The tears, the grief, the shock, the chaos. It filled him with pride to think that he was responsible.

Over the years he had achieved a great many things. He'd built a criminal empire, made a fortune, avoided going to prison, dispensed with most of his enemies. But in terms of sheer satisfaction nothing compared to this.

It was the purest and sweetest form of revenge because it was on a grand scale. It would impact on every copper in the country. Cause widespread suffering. Make the bastards regret what they had done to his son, his grandchild, his wife, his father. And to him.

He could easily stop now and know that he had done what he'd set out to do. One call to the murderer from Mexico would put an end to it. But he'd been completely honest with her when he'd said he was having too much fun. He wanted to enjoy the last rollercoaster ride of his life for just a little longer. A few days maybe, or a week at the most. Then it'd be time to bow out.

He didn't care that in the meantime his businesses would go on suffering, along with those of the other London firms. They were losing money big time as the Old Bill took out their anger and frustration on every villain in the capital.

Slack had already been contacted by several of the other bosses who had begged him to stop what he was doing. It was clear that none of them believed him when he'd said he had nothing to do with it.

He didn't give a shit what they thought, though. They weren't his friends and he didn't owe them anything. It actually amused him to think that once Rosa started killing cops at random the pressure on the other outfits would probably increase tenfold.

He saw it as an inspired move on his part. Extending the bloodbath beyond the organised crime task force would generate even more panic and confusion.

On Sundays he always went to the restaurant below the office in Rotherhithe for a slap-up lunch. As far as he was concerned their roasts were the best in South London.

He arranged for Mike to pick him up at twelve o'clock. Then he had a shower and got dressed.

When he checked himself in the mirror he saw that his eyes were booze red and the pouches beneath them were darker than ever.

The hangover was all but gone, but the cancer was giving him some grief again. There was a gnawing ache in his stomach and lower back, and it felt like the blood was boiling in his veins.

He would try to ignore it as usual, but it was becoming increasingly more difficult even with the medication.

He called Danny to make sure he'd be joining him at the restaurant. Sunday was when he and his most loyal lieutenant got together to discuss any issues that had cropped up during the previous week. But today they'd be talking about things other than business.

'The lads don't know whether they're coming or going,' Danny said. 'What happened to the Commissioner has freaked them out. They say everyone is pointing the finger at you, boss.'

'So what have you told them?'

'That it's bollocks. I've said you wouldn't be stupid enough to sanction such a high-profile hit that would cause enough heat to burn all our businesses to the ground.'

'Well done, mate,' Slack said. 'I don't know what I'd do without you.'

'You'd be in trouble,' Danny said. 'Right now I'm the only friend you've got.'

'And I appreciate it, Danny boy. I knew I could trust you, which was why I got you involved. And it's why I want you to leave the country as soon as you can get yourself sorted. This'll be over in a little while and I don't want you around to take any of the flak. I'll be transferring the other half million I promised into your offshore account tomorrow.'

'Are you sure about that, boss?'

'One hundred per cent. We can talk about it over lunch. But first there's one final message I want you to send out. Have you got a pen.'

After dictating the message to Danny, Slack went out onto the balcony while waiting for Mike to arrive in the car.

It was a beautiful day. The air was cold and thin, sharp in his lungs, but the sun was shining with a vengeance.

He knew he wouldn't see many more days like this. But that was OK because he was ready to close the curtains on his life before his deteriorating health made it insufferable.

As he looked out over London, he thought about the contents of his hidden safe. The suicide note and the gun. Ready and waiting for him to make his move.

He was quietly confident that when the time came he wouldn't hesitate to put the pistol to his head and pull the trigger. It'd be quick and painless and would add to the mess he was going to leave behind.

It was a shame he wasn't going to live to a ripe old age so that he could continue to enjoy the fruits of his labours – the fucking, drinking, gambling and lording it over his empire.

But fate had conspired against him and he'd been put on notice. Fortunately he still had control over the time and manner of his exit from the world. And at least that was something to be grateful for.

He started making a mental list of the things he wanted to do in the days ahead, such as visit his son's grave and the park where his wife's ashes were scattered. Shag Jasmine at least one more time. Have a final drink with Danny at one of the clubs. Write a letter in which he'd reveal that he killed Hugh Wallis in revenge for what he did to Terry.

That was as far as he'd got before Mike phoned him to say he was waiting downstairs.

Slack put on his overcoat and went down in the lift to the lobby. Samuel, the ageing concierge, bid him a good day. So did the burly doorman who received a regular retainer from Slack for tipping him off about anyone behaving suspiciously in or around the building.

Mike had the grey Merc today and he was standing next to it with the rear door open.

Slack paused on the pavement before getting in, squinting against the sun as he looked around for any sign of police surveillance. But he didn't see anything and it made him wonder if they had given up the ghost. It wouldn't have surprised him since they would have desperately needed the manpower elsewhere.

'How are you doing, boss?' Mike asked him.

He grinned. 'As always I'm feeling the pressure, Mikey. But as always I'm coping.'

He climbed in the back and Mike closed the door.

It might have been a Sunday but the traffic was still heavy. It would probably take them twenty minutes or more to get to Rotherhithe across the river.

He was looking forward to a good old roast. As usual he'd skipped breakfast so he was ravenous.

There was a time when he got them to pile up his plate with meat and potatoes, but not anymore. The cancer affected his appetite, so these days he could only manage small portions.

They were across the river and into the back streets of Rotherhithe when his phone went off. The ringtone told him it was his mole inside the task force, the person who had provided him with the personal details of all the detectives, plus the home address of the Commissioner.

He thought about not answering because he was in no mood to listen to another rant about how things had gone too far. But he decided he couldn't take the chance in case it was something important.

So he swiped the green icon and said, 'If you're gonna have a moan then I'm fucking hanging up.'

'No, don't.' The voice that barked in his ear was loud and anxious and he felt a frisson of unease.

'What is it?' he said.

'You need to stay at home, Roy. Don't go out. You won't be safe. I've got wind of a plot to—'

But that was all he got to hear because at that moment Mike slammed hard on the brakes and he was thrown forward. He dropped the phone onto the floor between his feet and his face rammed the back of Mike's seat.

'What the fuck?' he yelled.

The Merc had skidded to a halt because a black van had swerved into its path. At once the van's rear doors were thrown open and two men wearing balaclavas jumped out.

Mike was slow to react. He was still trying to slam the car into reverse when his door was wrenched open and a revolver was shoved up against his face.

'If you move I'll blow your fucking head off,' a deep male voice screamed at him.

At the same time the back door was yanked open and the other guy told Slack to get out.

Slack didn't move, so the guy reached in, grabbed his arm and pulled him onto the road.

'Who the hell are you?' Slack shouted.

'We're your worst fucking nightmare,' the man said.

The guy with the gun smashed it against Mike's head, rendering him unconscious. Both men then dragged Slack over to the van and ordered him to get in the back.

He refused so the gun was pushed up against his back and the man holding it said, 'You have five seconds to do as you're told and if you're still standing here then you're a dead man.'

Three seconds later Slack was in the back of the van and he heard the engine roar as it accelerated forward.

He was told to lie on the floor between the two men, who were sitting on fixed benches.

When he tried to speak the one with the gun, the taller of the two, kicked him hard in the ribs, which sent a blast of pain through his entire body.

'Speak only when you're spoken to,' the guy said sharply.

He knew better than to argue. These blokes meant business, and he sensed that all they needed was an excuse to beat the shit out of him.

So he just lay there, his left cheek pressed against the cold, hard floor, his breath thumping in his ears.

He wondered if Mike had regained consciousness and had raised the alarm. Who would he call first? Danny probably. But there wasn't much Danny could do, not without more information.

It was unlikely Mike had noted the van's registration number, and Slack hadn't spotted any onlookers when he was pulled from the car.

The ambush had taken place in a quiet street, one that he knew pretty well. There weren't any houses or flats. Just some drab commercial units and a disused factory. Chances were no one saw what happened.

The kidnappers had chosen a good spot, and he guessed they must have followed the Merc from the apartment building. He cursed Mike for not spotting them. But then the traffic was heavy until they left the main roads.

The two men remained silent so all he could hear were his own thoughts and the chugging of the engine.

The tables had certainly been turned on him. He couldn't even hazard a guess as to how many times he had ordered the same stunt to be pulled on men he wanted to punish. It must have run into dozens.

So was that their intention? To punish him?

The warning from the mole inside the task force had come too late.

Don't go out. You won't be safe. I've got wind of a plot to...

If it had been just minutes earlier he would have stayed in the apartment or arranged for a tooled-up crew to accompany him to the restaurant.

But he had lucked out, and now he was at the mercy of these men in masks. And he had no idea where they were taking him.

57

Laura

I waited until Aidan's parents arrived before I left the hospital. The plan was for me to go home and get changed before going to the Yard.

Aidan was happy for me to return to work if Drummond was prepared to let me. In fact he positively encouraged it.

'They need all the help they can get,' he told me. 'You're wasted sitting here with me. I'm fine. You know that. So get back into the game, for everyone's sake. And find the fucking bitch who did this to me, even if you have to break the rules to do so.'

There was fire in his eyes as he spoke and his words were like slaps to my face. They prompted me to think the unthinkable – that perhaps the only way to bring this whole thing to an end was to break the rules.

I was taken home in an unmarked police car with two armed officers. The forensic technicians had finished their work and our house was in a much better state. The kitchen doors had been replaced and most of the mess cleared up. But there was still a fair amount of damage that would have to be repaired in the coming weeks either by us or the landlord. We'd need a new dishwasher for one thing, and a new patio light.

However, I still wasn't sure I wanted to go on living there even if the interior were to be given a complete makeover. It just didn't feel the same anymore and I doubted that it ever would.

I showered and put on a beige sweater and grey trousers, which I wore under a black wool trench coat. I then got my armed escort to take me to the Yard.

We drove north through Clapham and Lambeth, and as usual the streets were heaving. London always came to life on a Sunday. Tourists and day-trippers turned out in force and now they were being joined by Christmas shoppers.

The way life was carrying on made it seem like the city wasn't in the midst of a crisis. But it was. A crisis that had already cost the lives of four people.

It had started out as an investigation by the task force into Roy Slack's criminal empire. Now it was much more than that. Murders had been committed. Threats made. The police, whose job it was to protect the people of London, could no longer protect themselves. It was a terrible state of affairs.

And for me it was also personal. I'd lost a baby. My boyfriend was lying in hospital with a bullet wound. One of my colleagues was dead. My mother was living in fear. And my house had been shot up.

So naturally I was angry. In fact a rage I had never known had taken hold of every cell in my body.

And it was directed at two people. One was Roy Slack, the man who was seeking a brutal revenge against the Met.

And the other was the bloodthirsty bitch who was helping him.

*   *   *

316

I arrived at the New Scotland Yard building just before two o'clock. The car dropped me outside the entrance on the Victoria Embankment.

The sight that greeted me brought tears to my eyes. The paving slabs around the entrance were covered with flowers that had been laid as a tribute to those who'd been killed, including the Commissioner, John Saunders.

Some of the bunches were stacked beneath the famous revolving sign carrying the words New Scotland Yard. Others spilled over onto the pavement.

There were dozens of people around and some of them looked visibly upset. I also saw two TV camera crews who were filming what was going on.

I quickly entered the building so they didn't spot me. The atmosphere inside was understandably tense and muted. Most people were still in shock. They spoke quietly, eyes downcast, grief etched into their features. I'd expected this but it was still difficult to take.

Upstairs in the task force office, the team were hard at it. Rushing around. Talking into phones. Tapping furiously at keyboards. There were some people I didn't recognise, no doubt drafted in from other departments.

Several of my colleagues stopped what they were doing when they saw me walk in and two of them – Kate Chappell and Janet Dean – came over to see how I was.

'Laura,' Kate bellowed as she approached. 'What are you doing here? Shouldn't you be with Aidan?'

'I was,' I said. 'But his parents are with him right now and he's doing well. We both thought that I'd be more useful here.'

Janet pulled a face. 'That goes against protocol, love. You're the girlfriend of one of the victims.'

I shrugged. 'I'm sure that won't be an issue considering how bad things are.'

'Well, Drummond's in his office,' Janet said. 'Let me know how you get on. Perhaps we can have a coffee downstairs.'

'So have there been any developments?'

Janet shook her head. 'Sadly, no. We're working in tandem with other divisions, but the truth is we're still chasing our tails.'

'What about the woman? I saw the latest security footage from the hotel.'

It was Kate who answered. 'Well, it won't surprise you to learn that she's vanished. We're now waiting for her to resurface and strike again. And at the same time we're praying that she won't.'

'So we don't know where she went after leaving the hotel?'

'We've heard from a taxi driver who thinks he gave her a lift to London Bridge station. A couple of guys are now trawling through the CCTV tapes from there.'

'That's not very encouraging. What's the latest on Roy Slack? Did we bring him in again?'

'Drummond decided there was no point and I have to agree.' This from Janet. 'He won't change his story and his lawyer has already lodged a formal complaint saying that we're harassing him. We even pulled the surveillance crew away from his home last night because there's a desperate shortage of people now.'

'This is crazy,' I said. 'We know he's behind this.'

'But we don't know for sure, Laura,' Janet said. 'And that's the problem.'

My temper sparked. 'Don't tell me the bastard has convinced you that our suspicions are misplaced and he's really just a poor innocent sod who's dying of cancer.'

'Not at all,' Janet said with an expansive shrug. 'He's still a suspect. But there's absolutely nothing to tie him to the killings except the idea that he's getting revenge against the Met.'

'It's more than just an idea, Janet. It's fucking obvious.'

'Not to me it isn't. And Drummond's been taking stick for focusing too much time and effort on Slack. The Commissioner himself raised it with him before he was shot.'

I shook my head and the indignation rose within me.

'This is bollocks,' I said, and it came out louder than I'd intended.

'Hey, calm down, Laura,' Janet responded. 'I know you're upset, but we're coppers. We're supposed to deal in evidence, not conjecture.'

I felt my heart heat up. 'Fuck me, Janet. It sounds like you want the bastard to get away with it. And he will if we don't go after him.'

Anger flared in Janet's eyes. 'How dare you say that? The fact is we've drawn a big fat blank where Slack is concerned. So maybe you've convinced yourself it's him because you want it to be. And that's dangerous and unprofessional.'

'You're talking rubbish,' I said.

'Am I?

'Yes, and you bloody well know it.'

As we stared at each other a startling thought occurred to me. Was it possible that Janet Dean was the bent copper inside the task force? Was that why she was springing to Slack's defence?

I wanted to ask her. To blurt it out.

Are you on his payroll?

Is that how you can afford a posh house and a boat?

Did you provide him with our personal details?

But I resisted, knowing that I was probably wrong. Knowing too that if I said it I couldn't take it back.

Instead I turned sharply and stormed across the room towards Drummond's office.

His door was open and I could see him at his desk watching the TV. When he saw me approach he stood up and waved me inside.

'You're not supposed to be here,' he said. 'I told you to take all the time off you need to be with Aidan.'

'I don't need any more time off, guv,' I said. 'Aidan is much better and he's being well looked after. I'll be more useful helping out on the investigation.'

He gestured for me to sit down and then shook his head as he perched himself on the edge of the desk.

'That's not an option, Laura,' he said. 'You're in no fit state mentally to be working. You've had an awful shock and we can't ignore the fact that one of the victims is your partner.'

'But I'm all right, guv. Honestly. And you can't possibly have enough people to cope with what's happening.'

He thought about it while chewing on the inside of his cheek.

Drummond had never been a stickler for rules and protocol so I was hoping that he wouldn't make a big thing of it and would just give me the go-ahead to return to duty.

After a few seconds he opened his mouth to speak, but then his attention was suddenly drawn to the television screen.

'Hang on,' he said. 'I want to hear this.'

He grabbed the remote from his desk and turned up the volume. Then together we watched the Prime Minister step up to a lectern outside 10 Downing Street.

She then made a short statement about the COBRA meeting that had just finished and which she'd chaired. Her face was glum and her voice strained as she spoke into a microphone.

'I called the COBRA meeting following the murder of the

Metropolitan Police Commissioner, John Saunders,' she said. 'He was the latest victim of a campaign of terror against police officers and their families. This morning we agreed ways to step up our response. The measures include transferring officers from other constabularies into London. The security services and the Counter Terrorism Command will play a more active role. They'll work alongside those teams already involved in the various investigations.'

She went on to describe what was happening as appalling and despicable, and she named all the victims, including Aidan.

She then commended what she said was the courage of the officers on the organised crime task force who had been directly threatened in the anonymous text messages.

'Those detectives deserve our full support and respect for continuing to work despite the risks to themselves,' she said.

After reading the statement she declined to take questions from reporters and went back inside her official residence.

Drummond then muted the sound and shook his head at the screen. His eyes were puffy and red, and his dark hair was uncombed. He suddenly looked much older than his forty-eight years and it was obvious that the pressure was getting to him.

I waited for him to say something, but he seemed lost in his thoughts so I cleared my throat to get his attention. When that didn't work, I said, 'Are you all right, guv?'

He snapped his head towards me, as though coming out of a trance.

'Of course,' he said. 'Sorry. I was just thinking about the last time I saw the Commissioner. He came down here yesterday afternoon, sat exactly where you're sitting now.'

Another shake of the head, and then he rubbed his face, as though trying to erase the stress.

'Who's in charge?' I asked him. 'I mean until a new Commissioner is appointed.'

'The Assistant Commissioner, Geena Donaldson,' he said. 'She's giving a press conference in an hour.'

'A good choice,' I said.

Drummond nodded. 'In time she'll probably get the job, but it won't happen until this nightmare comes to an end. And none of us knows when that will be.'

After a beat, I said, 'I've just been told that—'

I didn't get to finish the sentence because Detective Gloria Stanford burst into the office at this point with news of a development. And it hit me for six.

'We've had a call, sir,' she said. 'It's about Roy Slack. He's apparently been abducted.'

58

Slack

'Who the fuck are you guys and what do you want with me?'

It was the same question he'd been asking for half an hour. But his abductors continued to ignore him.

There were three of them now, including the van driver. They stood together over by the big double doors, looking outside anxiously while talking to each other in whispers. He got the impression that they were almost as nervous as he was.

The tall one had put his gun back inside his leather jacket and had replaced it in his right hand with a cigarette, which he drew on every couple of seconds.

Slack watched them from the chair they'd tied him to using duct tape. His wrists were secured behind his back and his ankles to the front legs of the chair.

They were in a car mechanic's workshop, and the only window had a thick curtain across it. A fluorescent strip light hummed and stuttered on the ceiling above him.

It had taken them about fifteen minutes to get here after they'd snatched him, so he reckoned he was somewhere in South or East London.

He didn't see the exterior of the building because they backed the van up against the doors before dragging him out. Once inside, they'd forced him onto the chair in the centre of the workshop and warned him to be quiet.

'So what happens now?' he'd asked them.

'We wait,' one of them had replied.

'What for?'

'The man who wants to ask you some questions.'

He was sure that whoever they were waiting for was going to do more than just ask questions.

He sat up straight, shoulders pushed back, tried not to let them see how scared he was. But he couldn't stop his body from shaking or droplets of sweat from sprouting on his forehead.

He'd never been in a situation like this before and it was a real eye-opener. He now knew what it had been like for all those unlucky pricks he'd brought to places like this to be tortured and murdered.

He'd laughed at those who had pissed and shit themselves. And he had mocked those who had begged him to let them go.

He was determined not to be so pathetic and weak. He'd rather die than disgrace himself like that.

The place stank of petrol and various other unpleasant odours. It was cramped compared with other workshops he'd been in and it was packed to the rafters with repair equipment, including tool chests, battery chargers, car creepers and transmission jacks.

Most of the London gangs owned at least a couple of garages and he wondered who this one belonged to. Was it one of the slags who had phoned him? Jack Smythe or Willy Norman perhaps. They were both convinced that he was responsible for the cop killings and they were both headcases. So maybe it was one of those guys who was about to turn up in the hope of persuading him to pull off his shooter. If it was one of them then it was unlikely he would walk away from this.

'Here we go,' one of the blokes said.

Slack heard a car pull up outside and his heart did a drum roll.

He lifted his head and clenched his jaw as he stared at the doorway. Two of the men went outside and he heard voices. A few moments later they came back in and they were standing either side of a man who wasn't wearing a balaclava.

Slack recognised him at once and the breath lurched out of his chest.

'I don't fucking believe it,' he gasped. 'The last person I expected to see coming in here was a copper.'

Slack saw it as a bad sign, the fact that DS Tony Marsden hadn't bothered to conceal his identity behind a balaclava like the others.

It could mean only one thing – that he would ensure that nobody but him and his hooded companions would ever know what happened here.

Slack recalled what the short-arsed plod had said as he'd left the apartment after grilling him.

'I'll be seeing you again, Roy. And when I do I'll make sure I wipe that fucking smile off your ugly face.'

Marsden walked slowly towards him, his eyes pinpricks of rage, while the others spread themselves out around the workshop. Slack assumed they were lower rank coppers and felt either too guilty or too scared to show their faces.

'So I take it that this is not an official follow-up interview,' Slack said, his voice laced with sarcasm.

'Doing things by the book has got us nowhere,' Marsden replied.

'So we've decided that the only way to stop this murder binge of yours is to go down the unofficial route.'

The first punch caught Slack off guard. Marsden's fist crashed against his chin, snapping his head backwards and sending his bottom teeth into his tongue. The blow also drove the air from his lungs, and his vision blurred with pain.

Through the tears he watched as the detective took off his suit jacket and threw it onto a nearby bench. He then pulled up his shirtsleeves and flexed his biceps.

Slack straightened himself in the chair and spat blood from his mouth onto the floor.

Then he let out a bark of laughter and said, 'Is that the best you've got, you poison fucking dwarf? I know girls who can hit harder than that.'

Marsden snorted, a phlegmy, back-of-the-throat, sound.

'I told you that I'd wipe that smile off your face, Slack, and I will. And I'm also gonna make you tell me who's doing your dirty work for you.'

Slack shook his head. 'So you think you can beat a confession out of me? Well, forget it. I won't confess to something I haven't done.'

'You can deny it until you're blue in the face,' Marsden said. 'But everything points to you. Only someone who's on death's doorstep or has a fucking death wish would take on every copper in this city. And you're the only person I know who has a big enough motive.'

'Oh, that's right,' Slack said, his voice glacial cold. 'You think I want revenge because of what you arseholes did to my wife, my son, my father and my unborn grandchild. Well, I won't deny that I'd like to see you all rot in hell. But you've got the wrong man. That's why you don't have any proof. Because there isn't any.'

Marsden turned to his three companions. 'Hear that, lads? The stupid cunt doesn't realise that it's gone way beyond the point where we need proof. He still thinks he can hide behind the law.'

'Then let's get on with it, Tony,' one of them replied from beneath his balaclava. 'Get the bastard to spill his guts and then we can have some fun.'

Marsden turned back to Slack. His face was contorted, hateful, and his brow started collecting moisture.

'What we're about to do will have the blessing of every police officer in the country,' he said through gritted teeth.

Slack forced a sardonic grin. 'Do you seriously believe they'll want a moron like you taking on the role of judge, jury and executioner?'

Marsden slammed his open palm against Slack's right cheek, then followed through with a hard punch to the gut.

Slack pitched forward with a loud shriek. The pain was such that it felt like his insides were suddenly on fire.

The detective then grabbed him by the hair and pulled his head back.

As he spoke, a line of saliva stretched between his lips. 'You seem to think that you're still the big time gangster who everyone is afraid of. Well I've got news for you, Slack. You're just a disease-ridden old crock who nobody gives a fuck about.'

Marsden then hawked and spat a dollop of phlegm into Slack's face.

Slack's spine grew rigid, and he took in a deep breath through his nostrils. He tried to gather strength from the voice in his head, which kept repeating the mantra: *When you have nothing to lose, death no longer holds any fear.*

But he wasn't ready to die just yet. And when the time came he wanted it to be on his terms. These renegade cops were going to fuck up his plan, spoil the grand finale.

If he died here then Rosa Lopez would go home, her job unfinished, and his suicide letter would probably never be discovered. And even if he did confess now he was sure there'd be a cover-up and he wouldn't be given the credit he deserved.

'I want the answers to three questions,' Marsden said. 'Who is the woman carrying out the killings on your behalf, and where can we find her? And what have you done with the firearms officer who shot Terry Malone?'

Slack swallowed hard, his face hot with pain. He was breathing heavily now, panting, and his body was a mass of tightening knots.

There was no way out of this. He could see that they were going to kill him for two reasons. The first was because they knew what he'd done and they hated him for it. And the second was because they couldn't afford to let him go. They had crossed a line themselves and if it got out they'd end up in prison.

'You should make it bloody easy on yourself and answer the questions,' Marsden said.

'I can't tell you something I don't know,' Slack told him. 'And beating me up won't change that.'

Marsden whacked him again. A back-hander this time across the left side of his head.

'Where's the woman, Slack?' he demanded. 'And what happened to officer Wallis? You might as well tell us now because you will eventually. I guarantee it.'

'Do yourself a favour and let me go,' Slack said. 'If it ends now I won't say anything to anyone. You have my word.'

Marsden shook his head. 'You're in no position to make deals, you scummy piece of low-life. Take a look around you. See all those tools hanging from the walls? I'm sure you know from experience that most of them can be used to cause a lot of pain. Well, if you don't tell us what we want to know you'll soon find out what it feels like to have your teeth pulled out with pliers and your knees crushed with a hammer.'

For a fleeting moment, Slack was tempted to tell them everything, but he resisted. There was no point because they were going to hurt him no matter what he said or didn't say.

This was their chance to get revenge for what had happened to their colleagues and the Commissioner. Their chance to show him that no villain was a match for the mighty Met.

And yet there was an irony here that would be lost on them. He was sure of that. It wouldn't occur to them that their actions would only serve to justify what he had done to them.

It showed that they represented an institution that was rotten to the core, peopled by an army of bent coppers who were prepared to break the laws they were meant to uphold whenever it suited them. And this scrawny little shit of a detective who was trying to act tough was a prime example of those who deserved to suffer a whole lot of pain and humiliation.

'Tell you what, detective,' he said. 'Why don't you get one of those hammers down from the wall and shove it up your arse? Or better still get one of those idiots in their stupid masks to get a set of pliers and cut off your limp, little cock?'

Marsden let rip then. He drove two more punches into Slack's face and one into his stomach. As Slack yelped in pain, the detective stepped back. But there was no respite because one of Marsden's accomplices then struck from behind, slamming his knuckles into the back of Slack's neck.

None of the blows was hard enough to knock him out, which meant he had to endure excruciating pain and the feeling that his head was flying off into orbit.

Blood filled his mouth and he could feel the flesh around his eyes swelling up.

Marsden started shouting at him. 'There's worse to come if you don't speak up you cunt. The pain I'll inflict will make the cancer seem like a mild irritation.'

Slack managed to lift his chin off his chest and stare up into Marsden's angry face. He had nothing but contempt for the detective and he thought it a great pity that the guy hadn't been at the top of Rosa's list. It was more than likely now that she wouldn't get around to killing him.

'You made a big mistake bringing me here, copper,' he said, and each word propelled a spot of blood from his mouth. 'It won't stop the killings and it's bound to backfire on you big time.'

That earned him another slap around the face. He squeezed his eyes shut and compressed his lips against the pain. His head swam and all he wanted to do was pass out.

He heard Marsden bark an order, but he couldn't make out the words. He kept his eyes closed and focused on controlling his breathing, which had become shallow and ragged.

Then something hard was pressed against his chest and his eyes flew open.

'It's time to get serious,' Marsden said. 'I'll start with the little finger on the right hand and work my way up.'

Slack stared at the object that was being waved in front of his face. It was a large adjustable wrench. He'd used one just like it himself once to snap off the fingers of a villain who had given him problems.

The fear was thick inside him now and he tried to speak, but his throat was paralysed.

'Let's untie his hands,' the detective said. 'I want him to see what I'm . . .'

His voice suddenly dried up mid-flow and his body stiffened.

'Oh, Christ,' he said, and only then did Slack realise why he was so alarmed.

Familiar sounds were coming from outside. Tyres screeching to a halt. Car doors slamming shut. Raised voices announcing the arrival of the police.

Slack felt a wave of relief flood through him.

'Looks like your mates have arrived in the nick of time,' he said, and managed a weak smile even though it hurt like hell.

59

Laura

The news that Roy Slack had been kidnapped was shocking enough. But I experienced an icy shiver when we received a tip from an anonymous caller claiming that detective Tony Marsden was the kidnapper.

The first call alerting us to the abduction came from Slack's driver, Mike Walker. He rang the three nines after their car was ambushed in Rotherhithe, close to Slack's headquarters.

Walker claimed that two men had jumped from the back of a van and attacked him before snatching Slack and making off.

Soon after that the second call came from someone who refused to give their name but said that Marsden and several other police officers had carried out the kidnapping.

Naturally all hell broke loose. Drummond tried to call Marsden but his mobile was switched off. He was among a bunch of officers who had worked through the night and had gone home to get some sleep. But when Drummond called his wife, she said he'd been out since this morning and she'd assumed he was at the office.

After that efforts were made to determine his whereabouts, and it didn't take long. The GPS tracking on his car pinpointed its location in Peckham, just a couple of miles from Rotherhithe.

The assumption was made that if his car was there then so was he. Within minutes a rapid response team was deployed and Drummond hurried out of the office to go there himself. In his wake he left a team aghast at the extraordinary turn of events.

We all hoped that it wasn't true, that Marsden hadn't gone rogue. But I had a bad feeling that he might well have done. I recalled what he had said to me the morning after Marion Nash was murdered in her bookshop.

'My money's on Roy Slack . . . If it was up to me I'd do what the scumbag obviously did to that firearms officer, Hugh Wallis. Just lift him off the street and make him disappear.'

I agonised for a few minutes over whether to tell Drummond, but decided to keep it to myself out of a sense of misplaced loyalty.

I then discovered that he'd also made his feelings known to a few of the other detectives, including Janet Dean.

'After the news came in about the Commissioner he really flipped,' she said. 'He started ranting about how Slack was making us look like a bunch of amateurs and that he shouldn't be allowed to get away with it.'

'So do you reckon he's actually gone and done it?'

She shrugged. 'I suppose we'll know soon enough.'

We were still waiting for an update from Peckham, which was expected at any time. I decided to stick around even though Drummond hadn't said I could return to work.

I sat at my desk, unsure what to do next. The office was suddenly much quieter. It was as though a heavy cloud had descended, stifling discussion and dampening the enthusiasm of every member of the team.

But they carried on working. Some were on their phones chasing down leads, while others were searching online for clues and information.

This latest development would complicate matters no end. It would ensure that Roy Slack remained firmly in the frame, but for the wrong reasons. And if he had been harmed in any way it might even garner him some sympathy from the public. It was a ghastly thought and it provoked an uneasy turn in the pit of my stomach.

I couldn't see it as anything other than a serious setback because it would make the powers-that-be even less inclined to pursue him.

A ferocious anger rose up inside me and my internal dialogue got stuck on: 'Shit, shit, shit.'

I turned on the desk PC and pulled up Slack's file. Saw that nothing had been added to it during the past twenty-four hours except a note of the interview that Kate and Marsden had conducted with him, and the fact that surveillance on him had been discontinued. It was all very disappointing.

I then ran through the files on the other main suspects, primarily Slack's top team and other London gang leaders. There was nothing to excite me on any of them, and no links to the murders or the threatening messages that had been sent to us.

But one short note caught my attention and related to Slack's top enforcer, Danny Carver, otherwise known as The Rottweiler.

A member of the tech team had examined his phone and laptop and concluded that there was nothing incriminating on either. However, he'd thought it worth mentioning that in his opinion Carver was a bit of a computer wizard.

'This observation is based on the sophisticated software on his laptop and phone, and the high-tech nature of the various applications that have been installed,' he wrote. 'It suggests that Mr Carver has much more than a basic understanding of computers and would therefore know how to send emails and text messages that can't be traced.'

The technician added that both the laptop and phone were still in our possession and would be subjected to more tests.

There was a note below this from Drummond saying that he wanted Carver to be questioned again, but it seemed that this hadn't yet been actioned. In view of what had been happening, and the widespread hysteria, it didn't surprise me that it wasn't considered a priority.

And yet perhaps it should have been. Danny Carver was Slack's right-hand man, after all. The pair was roughly the same age and had known each other for years.

Carver was a former mercenary with a fearsome reputation as a man of violence. It was hard to believe that he wasn't involved in his boss's revenge mission.

I read through the transcript of the interview he'd had with detectives. He'd denied all knowledge of the text messages and the murders, and nothing had been found at his home in Streatham.

It struck me that formally interviewing him again wouldn't get us any further. But that didn't mean he shouldn't remain a prime suspect along with Slack himself. And if so then there had to be a way to find out what he really knew. A way to prove that The Rottweiler was lying through his fucking canine teeth.

But right now I couldn't see a way – not unless we followed Tony Marsden's example and broke all the rules in the book.

The news from Peckham was worse than bad. It came through at two o'clock in a phone call from DCS Drummond that was put on speaker so that we could all listen in.

'This is a fucking clusterfuck,' he seethed. 'DS Marsden has been arrested along with two of his pals from Wandsworth CID and another who's attached to the firearms unit. They took Slack to a car mechanic's workshop with the aim of torturing a confession out of him. Luckily the response team arrived before they got down to the heavy stuff, but he was roughed up and is at the hospital. And before anyone asks, no, he didn't confess to anything. He continued to deny being responsible for what's going on.'

This wasn't what any of us wanted to hear. When the news got out it was going to be a public relations disaster for the Met. It wouldn't matter that Marsden and his crew had acted out of desperation following the Commissioner's murder. They had broken the law in a big way and had brought disgrace on themselves and the rest of us.

It wouldn't have been so terrible if they'd got him to fess up. They'd still be in trouble but it would have been worth it. Now, though, everyone lost out.

There was going to be enormous pressure to leave Slack alone. And valuable time and effort was going to be wasted pursuing other suspects while Slack's hired gun continued her merciless killing spree.

There was a mixed reaction in the office. Some of the detectives condemned Marsden's actions, including Janet Dean, who said there was no excuse for what he'd done.

'It's not our job to act as judge and jury,' she said. 'The prick has shamed us all.'

The discussion also triggered speculation as to who had betrayed him. And once again Janet's reaction to what he'd done got me wondering if it was her. Was she the person who had given Slack all our personal details? The bent copper who was obviously working for the gang boss?

We all knew that corruption was still endemic in the Met despite all the crackdowns. But this was more than an officer turning a blind eye to a gang-related enterprise. This was someone who was effectively colluding with a killer. Someone who even now was prepared to help Slack out of a tight spot.

I told myself I was reading too much into what Janet was saying. That my suspicions had to be unfounded. She was a good cop. A decent cop. She would never stoop so low.

I blamed the fact that my head was all over the place. I couldn't shake off the rage that was making it hard for me to think straight. It was like trying to wriggle out of a straightjacket.

Then just as I was telling myself that things could not get any worse, we all received another text message on our phones.

And the pressure was ramped up yet again.

The message contained another threat, and it caused the panic and anxiety inside me to grow into a flaming ball.

You had your chance to stop this and you didn't take it. Now it's just about teaching you all a lesson. So from today every copper in London is a potential target, including those on the street and in their cars. And remember – as the bodies pile up you only have yourselves to blame.

Any one of our suspects could have sent it, even Slack if he knew how to deliver messages on a time delay.

But for me the most likely candidate was Danny Carver, who had been described by a member of the tech team as a computer wizard.

To someone like him sending multiple text messages and remaining anonymous would be a piece of cake. The problem we had was that his house had been searched and his phone and laptop examined.

But that didn't mean they were the only ones he had. In fact there was a strong possibility that he had several more of each.

I put my thoughts to work on it while everyone else was working themselves up into a lather over the latest text.

My rational self was telling me that I should wait for Drummond to return and push for him to stay on Slack's case and to go after Danny Carver with renewed vigour. But what if he told me to go home? That because of what Marsden had done he didn't want anyone else to breach the rules or ignore protocol.

I decided I couldn't have that. I was too fired up. Too angry. And at the same time I was convinced that I was onto something.

Find the fucking bitch who did this to me even if you have to break the rules to do so.

I took a determined breath to stiffen my resolve. Told myself that I had no choice now but to follow Tony Marsden's lead and go it alone. Desperate times called for desperate measures. And it wasn't just a knee-jerk reaction to what Aidan had said. From where I stood we weren't going to achieve anything by doing things by the book. We'd face restrictions. Solicitors. The law would work against us and more of my fellow officers would be murdered.

I thought about involving someone else but decided against it. I didn't want to place them in a difficult position or have them insist I tell Drummond.

I had to do this by myself and if it didn't pan out I'd be the only one in trouble.

Suddenly my dad, my hero, was inside me head, barking orders and telling me to go for it and to hell with the consequences.

And then, as if I needed further incentive, I saw Aidan in my mind's eye lying on our kitchen floor. Followed by the blood-drenched bodies of Dave Prentiss and Marion Nash. And I thought about the baby who had been taken away from me. The most innocent of innocent victims.

I asked myself if it was right that the people responsible might escape justice. The answer, of course, was an emphatic *no*. I therefore decided that I had to go with my gut.

Returning to my desk, I printed off a few pages from Danny Carver's file.

Including his address.

60

Rosa

She was having the time of her life and she didn't want the day to end.

They were now passing the Houses of Parliament on their way to the famous riverside area known as the South Bank.

'You'll love it there,' Alice said. 'If the queues aren't too long we can go up on the London Eye. It has terrific views over the city. Then we'll get some cocktails at one of the swanky bars before going for dinner somewhere really nice.'

Alice was so excited she could barely contain herself, and Rosa loved her all the more for it. There was no longer any doubt in her mind that she wanted Alice to be a part of her future. A big part.

She couldn't imagine going back to Mexico. To her soulless apartment and the life that she now realised was devoid of fun and purpose.

Before today she had never experienced the joy of sharing things. Or the thrill of knowing that someone enjoyed spending time with her. It had never occurred to her that she'd been lonely.

Just alone. And until today that had been enough. But not anymore.

'Ahead of us is Westminster Bridge,' Alice said, pointing. 'In a minute we'll cross that to get to the South Bank. But first there's another building I want to show you just to the left here along the embankment.'

Rosa was still mesmerised by all the sights. She could now see the giant Ferris wheel they called the London Eye. Alice had already told her that it cost seventy million pounds to erect and was the most popular paid attraction in the country.

Rosa had never been on a Ferris wheel. And she'd never been to a fairground either. She remembered her father telling her that he was going to take her to one. But that was a week or so before he was murdered alongside her mother, so it never happened.

Rosa noticed a crowd of people up ahead. There were also several police officers in yellow jackets.

'This is the place,' Alice said. 'It's called New Scotland Yard and is probably the most famous police headquarters in the world.'

Rosa felt her back stiffen.

'It's not usually like this, though,' Alice said. 'I wonder why . . .'

And then they saw the flowers and the television camera crews and it dawned on both of them what was going on.

'Oh God, these flowers are tributes to the Commissioner who was shot yesterday and those other policemen,' Alice said. 'Don't they look beautiful?'

Rosa opened her mouth to speak, then snapped it shut. She wasn't sure what to say or how to react. But she did know that she had to remain calm, that there was no need to get anxious.

Alice pulled on her hand so that they could have a closer look.

Rosa was surprised at how many flowers had been laid here

and at the number of people who had come to look at them. She guessed there were over a hundred, and some were in tears.

The building itself also surprised her. It had an art deco façade and looked more like a luxury hotel than a huge police HQ.

Alice let go of her hand and crouched down to read some of the cards that people had attached to the flowers.

While she did that, Rosa looked around, and it occurred to her that she was responsible for all of this. It didn't make her feel guilty. Just strange.

She had killed more than fifty people in total and had never stayed around long enough to see first-hand the grief she'd left behind. This was another new and sobering experience.

Alice stood up, took a tissue from her bag, and dabbed at her eyes.

'It's easy to forget what's happening when you're not watching the telly or listening to the radio,' she said. 'I feel like I'm at a funeral.'

Rosa put an arm around her and pulled her close. Then she turned to kiss her forehead. As she did, she happened to catch sight of a woman who had just walked out of the building through the glass doors. She had brown hair and was wearing a black trench coat.

Rosa recognised her from her photos and her heart quickened. The last time she'd seen Laura Jefferson had been two nights ago when she'd tried to kill her at her home in Balham.

Now the detective was striding purposefully towards where she stood. And the look in her eyes was one of grim determination.

Rosa was suddenly alert, but not unduly alarmed. This is nothing more than a wicked coincidence, she told herself. It can't be anything else.

Nevertheless she went very still as Jefferson walked towards her through the crowd. She looked to be in a hurry and paid no attention to the flowers on the ground.

Rosa unzipped her bag, ready to grab the pistol inside if necessary.

'Time to go, I think,' Alice said, squeezing Rosa's hand. 'If I stay here any longer I'll probably start crying.'

Rosa didn't move because at that moment Jefferson walked past them. Their eyes locked for a fraction of a second, but in the detective's there was no sign of recognition.

Rosa let out a breath she didn't know she'd been holding, and then allowed Alice to lead her away from the forecourt and onto the pavement.

But Rosa's eyes followed Laura Jefferson, who walked up to the edge of the kerb and flagged down a black taxi.

The chance encounter had lasted only a few seconds, but it took much longer for the tension to leave Rosa's body.

What were the odds on that happening? she wondered. Ten million to one maybe. And what would she have done if the woman had recognised her? It was something that didn't bear thinking about.

The detective was the first target that Rosa had missed, and for that reason the woman intrigued her. She made a mental note to find out more about her. Purely out of interest. She wondered how long she had been a police officer. Whether she had children. If she had ever killed anyone.

And for some reason that Rosa couldn't explain she was glad that Laura Jefferson was still alive.

Perhaps it was because two nights ago she had proved to be such a worthy adversary.

The South Bank was throbbing with people, mostly tourists and groups of students. And there were quite a few uniformed cops.

343

But unsurprisingly Rosa was in no position to take any of them out.

It wasn't a problem, though, because she was prepared to bide her time. She was sure that sooner or later she would see an opportunity and be able to slip away from Alice. It wouldn't take long or be that difficult to shoot an unsuspecting cop. She would just have to make sure that she wasn't seen or caught on camera.

The pistol had a suppressor attached so there wouldn't be a loud bang. Just a muted crack as the bullet left the barrel. It was going to be risky. Of that she had no doubt. But Rosa did not intend to let her client down just because she had decided to go out and enjoy herself.

She'd agreed that she would aim to carry out a killing a day and she was determined to do so. This was going to be The Slayer's final assignment, after all, and she had every intention of ending on a high note.

The queues for the London Eye were too long to consider joining, so they didn't bother. Instead they went to a trendy bar in a hotel overlooking the Thames.

They drank Tequila Sunrise cocktails, and Rosa pushed Laura Jefferson from her thoughts. It wasn't difficult while she was with Alice. The woman made everything else seem irrelevant.

'You know what scares me?' Alice said. 'It's that this week is going so fast. Before we know it you'll be heading home to Mexico, and I'm going to miss you so much.'

Rosa saw this as an opportunity to test the water. To see if Alice was as love-struck as she was.

'I could always try to extend my stay,' she said.

Alice beamed. 'You really mean that?'

Rosa nodded. 'I wouldn't say it if I didn't.'

'My God that would be wonderful. You could check out of the hotel and stay with me in the apartment.'

It was Rosa's turn to smile like a cat who's got the milk. 'You'd let me do that?'

'Are you kidding? It'd be like having Christmas come early.'

There followed a five-minute display of mutual affection. They hugged and kissed and whispered endearments to one another. And they didn't care that they were attracting attention from the other people in the bar.

Rosa was on cloud nine. It seemed to her that this day just kept getting better.

'I've been telling my parents about you,' Alice said. 'They'd like to meet you.'

Rosa felt her stomach contract. 'Really?' It was all she could think of saying.

Alice laughed. 'Well, you don't have to look so worried. They won't bite.'

'But why do they want to meet me?'

'Because they're curious. They know I'm besotted with you and they want to see the person who's making me so happy.'

Rosa was flattered, delighted and alarmed in equal measure. Delighted that Alice had used the word besotted and alarmed at the prospect of meeting her parents.

It would, of course, be necessary at some point if she and Alice stayed together. But she wasn't ready to take such a giant step. They were bound to ask questions about her job, her past, her family. And she hadn't had time yet to get her story together. To re-invent herself.

If they became suspicious they might make enquiries. They could find out that her name wasn't really Maria Rodriquez. And that she didn't work for the Mexican government's tourism department. They might even alert the police in order to protect their daughter.

'They've invited us both over to dinner any evening this week,' Alice said. 'They live in Chelsea. Please say yes. It'd mean a lot to them and to me.'

Rosa didn't want to disappoint Alice so she nodded and smiled and said, 'Of course I'll come. But the latter part of the week would be best for me.'

That would give her time to either work on her story or come up with a good excuse not to go.

Alice was overjoyed. 'You'll love them. I promise. And they'll love you.'

Only if they don't see through the lies, Rosa thought.

'In fact I'll call them now and suggest that we arrange it for Thursday or Friday,' Alice said.

Rosa stood up. 'And while you do that I'm going to the restroom.'

It was an excuse to slip away so that Alice wouldn't notice that the smile plastered on her face was a false one. A short toilet break would give her time to collect her thoughts and stop the panic from swelling in her chest.

But that wasn't how it turned out because on the way to the ladies she saw someone who gave her much more to worry about than meeting Alice's parents.

It was Roy Slack, the man she was working for.

He was looking down at her from the TV screen on the wall above the bar. His face was battered and bruised and he was telling a reporter that he'd been kidnapped by a group of police officers.

61

Slack

He hadn't expected a camera crew to be waiting outside the hospital's A & E department. Someone must have tipped them off.

Under any other circumstance he would have told them to get lost. But now he was keen to let the world know what those coppers had done to him.

'So were the police officers known to you?' the reporter asked.

'Only one of them,' Slack said. 'The others were wearing balaclavas.'

'What can you tell us about him?'

Slack grimaced and rubbed a knuckle into both eyes. Then he shifted his weight and looked directly at the camera.

'I've been told not to say anything, but to hell with that. These cuts and bruises on my face are courtesy of a detective sergeant Tony Marsden. He's with Scotland Yard's organised crime task force and he made it clear that he was going to torture me and then kill me. If the other bunch of coppers hadn't turned up when they did I'd be dead.'

'So were you told why they kidnapped you?'

'For sure. The Old Bill are in a panic. They don't know who's behind the murders of the Commissioner and those other people. They've come up with a list of suspects and I'm one of them. I've protested my innocence but they don't believe me even though they've got no evidence proving I'm involved.'

'That's a strong accusation to make, Mr Slack.'

'But it's true. They've had it in for me for years. They say I'm a crook, but they've never been able to prove it and they don't like it.'

'So you're denying you had anything to do with the Commissioner's death and the threats against the other officers.'

Slack nodded. 'I am. I'm a legit businessmen, not some kind of Mafia godfather who gets his rocks off by paying for coppers to be killed.'

The reporter had told him that the interview was going out live on the BBC. That was good because it meant they couldn't edit his words or bleep out Marsden's name. It would infuriate the Met and that made it all the more satisfying.

He decided to take a couple more questions even though he was anxious to get home. His head was pounding and the tablets he'd been given to dull the pain in his stomach hadn't yet kicked in.

But there was also something he wanted to get out into the open. Something that would make what Marsden had done all the more unpalatable in the eyes of the public.

'I understand that your injuries have been treated, Mr Slack,' the reporter said. 'But why are you going against the doctor's advice to stay here overnight?'

'There's nothing more they can do for me,' Slack said. 'I've told them to use the bed for someone who's worse off than I am.'

'And what about your driver, Mr Walker? We're told he was also injured.'

'He was clobbered with a gun when they ambushed us,' Slack said. 'He's got a bad wound to the back of his head and will have to stay in. His wife is at his bedside.'

'So is there anything else you'd like to tell us about what happened today?' the reporter asked.

Slack pulled another face to show that he was still in pain. Then he said, 'What's really sickening is that Detective Marsden and all his colleagues know that I'm not a well man. I have pancreatic cancer and I've been given only a few months to live.'

He wanted to smile because he knew that the revelation would pile further pressure and embarrassment on the Met, and hopefully win him some public support.

He didn't answer any more questions after that and signalled for Danny to escort him to the car.

Physically he felt like shit, and he knew that he should have probably let them keep him in. But he hated hospitals almost as much as he hated coppers. They made him feel weak and vulnerable and brought back painful memories of the two days and nights he spent at his wife's bedside after she crashed her car. She never regained consciousness and died slowly, her body broken, her face badly disfigured.

'You sure you're up to going home, boss?' Danny asked him.

He nodded as he shuffled towards the car.

'I need a stiff drink and a cigar more than I need a bunch of nurses fussing over me,' he said.

He sat by himself on the back seat of Danny's car. Danny had come straight to the hospital after Slack had got them to phone him as his next of kin.

'I still can't get my head around it,' Danny said as he gunned the engine. 'I was convinced you'd been grabbed by one of the other outfits. It never even entered my head that it might be the Old Bill.'

'Mine neither until Marsden walked in,' Slack said. 'But there's an upside because the bastard has fucked himself good and proper. He'll still be doing time long after I'm dead and buried.'

'And what you said back there about the cancer won't help his case any,' Danny said.

Slack grinned. 'That's exactly why I decided to say it.'

'I gathered that, boss. But the lads will be pissed off that you hadn't already told them. And they'll start to panic about what's going to happen to the firm. I'm sure our phones will start ringing any minute.'

'I get that,' Slack said. 'But it won't matter now anyway. Time's running out, Danny. A few days from now I'm checking out. I've done what I set out to do and it's worked out well. You'd better get on your bike too.'

'I'm planning to, boss. Just got a few things to sort.'

Danny reached into his jacket pocket and pulled out a mobile phone, which he held up for Slack to take.

'Mike found it on the floor of the car and gave it to me when I turned up there,' he said. 'I figured you wouldn't want the Old Bill to get their hands on it.'

'Good thinking,' Slack said.

Mike had only been unconscious for a few minutes after the guy slugged him with the gun. As soon as he came around he called Danny before phoning the police. The car was now being subjected to forensic examination, along with the mechanic's workshop in Peckham.

In addition four London coppers were being questioned on

suspicion of kidnap, causing grievous bodily harm and conspiracy to commit murder.

For Slack it was proof that every dark cloud had a silver lining.

They arrived at Slack's apartment twenty minutes after leaving the hospital.

'Don't bother to come up,' he told Danny. 'I'll be all right. I want you to go home and call the lads. Tell them not to hassle me tonight on pain of death. And arrange a meeting for tomorrow. I'll answer all their questions then.'

Before Danny drove off, Slack asked him if he'd sent the latest text message.

'I put it on a timer,' Danny said. 'It went out when we were supposed to be having lunch. Just like you wanted.'

It was seven o'clock when he entered his apartment – six hours after he was abducted.

A drum was beating in his head, and he was sore all over. He checked himself in the mirror and saw that he still looked as bad as he felt. His bottom lip was swollen, and there was a large bruise beneath his left eye. His mind flashed back to just before the cops came bursting through the doors of the workshop. Marsden had been threatening to snap his fingers off with an adjustable wrench. And that would have been just the start. God only knew what else the cunt would have done.

So he could hardly complain about a few bruises and a tender gut, especially when the cancer was eating away at his insides anyway.

He stripped off, took a shower, then slipped on his dressing gown. While he was doing this, his phone rang several times and he heard the pings of incoming text messages.

He didn't bother to find out who had tried to get in touch

351

until he was sitting in front of the telly with a large Scotch and a Cuban cigar.

By now the pain in his head had lulled to a dull, persistent throb, and he was glad he hadn't stayed at the hospital. At least here he could do what he usually did to relax and think. And there was a lot to think about. Like when to acknowledge that he'd achieved his objective. When to tell Rosa Lopez she could go home. When to take the gun from the safe and use it to put himself out of his misery.

He checked his missed calls and text messages. Frank Piper had phoned and so had Clive Miller, two of his top lieutenants. But they hadn't left messages or voicemails.

His mole inside the task force had left a message, though, and it answered a question that had been bugging him.

It was me who tipped off the team as soon as we were cut off. Glad they got there in time.

Slack: *How did you know what Marsden was going to do?*

Mole: *Overheard him talking on phone. Pure luck.*

Slack then opened the next text message, which had come from Jasmine.

Tried to call you babe. Been so worried. If you want me to come straight over just say the word.

But sex was the last thing on his mind, and he didn't want her company because although she was a tasty piece of arse she was also as thick as two planks.

He just wanted to be alone so that he could drink, smoke and watch the news on the television. There was plenty there to keep him entertained.

He laughed as a shame-faced detective was forced to say that no police officer should take the law into his or her own hands. He cringed at his own ugly mug being interviewed in front of the hospital. And he listened with interest as one newsreader laboured the point that alleged London crime boss Roy Slack had been detained and released no fewer than four times during the past week or so.

He had to laugh. It was like icing on the fucking cake. It would have been enough to hurt the Old Bill with the murders. But now they faced a major self-inflicted scandal that would tarnish them for years to come.

It was an unexpected bonus and well worth the pain he'd suffered at the hands of that maverick detective.

A montage of photos appeared on the screen and his thoughts switched immediately to Rosa Lopez. The photos were of the four people she had killed. Detective Inspector Dave Prentiss, Marion Nash, the copper shot on Balham High Road, and the Commissioner, John Saunders.

He wondered why he hadn't heard from her. Maybe she hadn't seen the news. Or maybe she took the view that as he'd been released it was going to be business as usual.

She certainly wasn't the type to panic. She had nerves of steel, that one. And the job she was doing for him was surely much easier than most of those she'd been tasked with in the past. Now it was set to get even simpler. All she had to do was cruise the streets on the bike and gun down any copper on the beat. Or she could fire directly into the windscreen of a patrol car. Or play safe and take aim from a distance using the sniper rifle. The Slayer was a true pro so the next few days were going to be a doddle for her.

He decided to send her a text to reassure her that he wasn't about to pull the plug.

I'm still alive and kicking. Carry on the good work until you hear from me.

He thought about her while he waited for a response. The woman intrigued him. She had to be the hottest contract killer out there. The kind you see in the movies. In Mexico – a country filled with assassins – she must have outshone all the others.

Her boss, Carlos Cruz, had told him a few interesting things about her during their last phone conversation.

'She's an enigma even to us, my friend,' he'd said. 'Most of the guys in the cartel would love to fuck her, but unfortunately she prefers women to men. And that doesn't surprise me because as a little girl she was badly abused by her adoptive father and his paedophile friends.'

Cruz also said that Rosa's parents were murdered and she took revenge on the man who killed them.

'Soon after that we became her family,' he'd added. 'She's been a loyal member of the cartel since then, and our most accomplished *sicaria*. We're all she has and all she needs. I can't imagine her ever leaving the fold.'

It was 7.30pm when Rosa replied to his text. She didn't bother with any pleasantries or even say that she was glad he was still alive.

She simply wrote: *OK.*

62

Laura

The taxi had dropped me off at home an hour ago and I was still here because I was having second thoughts. The enormity of what I was planning to do had hit me suddenly, like a harsh wake-up call that gives you a fright.

It didn't help that I hadn't really thought it through. I was being driven by an unbridled anger and a burning sense of injustice. The same emotional triggers that had caused Tony Marsden and three other police officers to put their careers – and their lives – at risk.

Did I have it in me to step over the line? To break the rules. It was a question I had never had to ask myself. But then I'd never faced a situation where the law was desperately failing the victims of a brutal murderer.

Now the threat went beyond the organised crime task force. All police officers in London were potential targets, and there didn't seem to be a damn thing we could do to stop it.

It was an alarming change of strategy aimed at 'teaching you all a lesson'. It also illustrated yet again the startling ease with which a crazy person with a weapon can strike terror across a whole city or country.

We'd had it before, many times, with jihadists who let off bombs and attacked innocent people with knives. Now it was the turn of an assassin who was doing it, not for some radical cause, but because the gangster paying her wanted revenge on an entire police force.

I'd spent the last hour sitting on the sofa trying to work up the courage to go and confront the man I believed was heavily involved in what was happening. And to use brute force if necessary to get him to come clean.

I kept asking myself how I would feel if I chickened out now and another officer was killed tonight or tomorrow. Or what if the bitch came looking for me again? Or even went to the hospital to finish Aidan off?

It was entirely possible that Danny Carver was actually in touch with the woman. That he was the middleman between her and Slack. And if so, then maybe, just maybe, I could get to her through him.

Weighed against that were the dire consequences for me if it went belly up, like it had for Tony Marsden and his crew.

Anxiety clawed at my chest as I agonised over it. I started pacing up and down the length of the living room, clutching the sheet of paper with Carver's address on it.

Once again images cascaded through my mind. Images with unwelcome clarity that were driving me towards committing a criminal act. Aidan in that hospital bed. Dave Prentiss lying dead in his own hallway. Marion Nash's body on the floor of her shop. And the blood that poured out of me into the toilet pan as my own baby's life was extinguished.

When the phone rang the acid churned in my stomach. I thought it might be one of the police bodyguards, ringing to see where I'd gone to without them.

But it was my mother, and I spent five minutes reassuring her that I was fine. She sounded terrified, though, and I yearned to reach out and give her a hug.

'When will this end, Laura?' she sobbed. 'Surely it can't go on. It's so awful and sad. Why can't the police stop it?'

'We're trying, Mum,' I said. 'Believe me we are.'

I told her where I was and gave her an update on Aidan's condition, then said I'd contact her first thing in the morning.

While I still had the phone in my hand I called the hospital and they told me that Aidan was asleep and his parents were still with him.

A headache began to rage between my temples and my thoughts continued to burn like a fuse.

I checked my watch, saw it was eight o'clock already and time to make up my mind either way.

My heart was beating its way out of my chest so I sat down and switched on the TV. I wanted to know if there had been any further developments since I'd left the office.

I happened to catch the start of a recorded interview with Roy Slack, who looked as though he'd been trampled under a herd of buffalo.

As I listened I scowled my hatred at the screen and felt my pulse escalate. The bastard was clearly in his element, acting like he was an innocent victim while slagging off the police.

But his face betrayed him. There was the smug expression that he was trying hard to conceal. And there was the glint of amusement in his eyes.

He thought he was untouchable. That the law was powerless to stop his grotesque killing spree, especially after what had happened to him. But this sick, arrogant performance was surely enough to drive any copper to breaking point.

Including me.

I grunted out a bitter laugh and said aloud, 'You've made up my mind for me, you evil fucker. I'll do whatever it takes now to put you and that psycho bitch away.'

I spent the next fifteen minutes working out what I was going to do, while praying that Danny Carver would be in and alone when I got to his house.

Then having come up with the bare bones of a plan, I hurried upstairs to change into a dark polo sweater, jeans and a hooded windcheater jacket.

Back downstairs I grabbed my scarf and gloves from the table in the hall and made sure my shoulder bag contained the Taser gun, a set of handcuffs and the car keys.

I then stormed out of the front door, ready and willing to break the law in the name of justice.

Aidan and I shared an ageing Peugeot 307. It didn't get much use because driving in London was usually a nightmare and it was much easier to take the bus or tube.

But I didn't anticipate the roads would be very busy this evening and it was only two miles from Balham to Streatham. I put Danny Carver's address into the satnav and got going.

I was glad I didn't still have the gun with me because there was a good chance I'd be tempted to us it. But I did have the police regulation Taser X2, and I felt safer knowing I had it. After all, the guy I was going to see was a violent psychopath. He'd spent twelve years in prison for stabbing a man to death and then two years as a mercenary in the Middle East before going to work as an enforcer for Roy Slack.

Since then he'd earned a reputation that was as ugly as he himself was. By all accounts he'd killed half a dozen people and crippled a few more. But like his boss he'd managed to avoid prosecution.

It was always the same story. There was never enough evidence to get a conviction and nobody was ever brave enough to testify against him.

Villains like Danny Carver weren't easily intimidated, and they knew how to work the system. That was why going through the formal interrogation process with him would be a complete waste of time. If he knew more than he was letting on then the only way to get it out of him was to play by his rules.

There was a limit to how far I'd be prepared to go, of course. But until I reached it I wouldn't know where it was.

I'd never been a shrinking violet. And I'd be the first to admit that I had a fierce temper that had got me into trouble on more than one occasion.

But this was the first time I'd allowed myself to get worked up into such a frenzy, though I felt it was justified in view of what had happened to Aidan and to the baby that had been growing inside me.

Carver's house was in one of those streets that didn't look very impressive, but where properties were worth a fortune.

It was end-of-terrace, with a small, enclosed front garden and a short driveway on which stood a smart BMW 7 Series.

I parked across the street and saw that there were lights on inside, both upstairs and down. I switched off the engine and sat there in the dark for a while, trying not to acknowledge the nerves that were raging inside me.

According to Danny Carver's file he lived alone and wasn't married. But that didn't mean he was by himself in the house.

For all I knew he was spending the evening with a girlfriend or a couple of his gangster pals.

So that was the first problem to confront me. The first unknown.

My intention was to ring the doorbell and step out of sight until he answered it. And then I'd attack him with the Taser, delivering fifty thousand volts to his body and incapacitating him for up to five seconds. Enough time to put the cuffs on his wrists.

I would then ascertain whether or not he was alone. If he wasn't, I'd scarper. But if he was I'd do all that I could to get him to reveal the whereabouts of the assassin.

I turned my phone onto silent and wrapped the scarf around my face, covering my nose and mouth. Then I lifted up my jacket hood and pulled it tight so that only my eyes were visible.

In the rear-view mirror I looked like someone the police would stop and search without a moment's hesitation.

It was a quiet residential street and there was no one about. They were all inside their homes having dinner, watching television and doing whatever else they did behind their closed doors.

I told myself again that I was doing the right thing. I was doing what had to be done. If I didn't do it the carnage would continue. And those responsible for my miscarriage could go unpunished.

I removed the key from the ignition and took a deep breath. *Stay calm*, I told myself. And stay focused.

My heart thumped against my ribcage as I started to get out of the car.

But then I stopped suddenly because I saw Carver's front door open and light from inside spill onto the driveway.

He closed the door behind him and I thought he would climb into the BMW. But he didn't. Instead he walked past it onto the pavement.

And then he started to cross the road in my direction.

63

Rosa

Rosa's patience was rewarded when they left the hotel bar. They were on their way to a well-known tourist attraction that Alice wanted her to see.

'It's a full-scale replica of Sir Francis Drake's sixteenth-century sailing galleon,' she said excitedly. 'And right next to it there's a really cute pub that does smashing cocktails.'

But just before they reached their destination Rosa spotted the police patrol car. It was parked at the kerb in a quiet, unlit street next to an apartment block overlooking the Thames.

This is it, she told herself. The opportunity I've been waiting for.

'Oh my God,' she yelped suddenly as she made a big thing of delving into her bag. 'My purse isn't here. I must have left it on the seat back at the hotel.'

'Don't worry,' Alice said. 'We can go back and get it.'

Rosa shook her head. 'There's no need for you to come. I'll dash back while you go over there to the pub and get the drinks in.'

'Are you sure?'

'Of course. It'll only take me a couple of minutes.'

What followed was so simple. So straightforward.

Alice headed for the pub and Rosa turned and walked in the opposite direction. When she looked back and saw that Alice had disappeared inside, she stopped and took stock of the situation.

The police car was still there and there was only one occupant – a woman officer in the driver's seat. She was perhaps taking time out or waiting for a colleague to appear. But from Rosa's point of view she was the proverbial sitting duck.

Rosa looked around, noting that there were no CCTV cameras focused on the immediate area. The few people who were around were simply passing by and none of them seemed to even notice the police car that was parked about ten metres back from the riverside walkway with only its side lights on.

Rosa dipped her hand into her bag as she strode purposefully towards the car. When she drew level with it she stopped and turned and was glad to see that the walkway was now clear, although she could hear voices.

She had approached targets in exactly this way before. The secret of success was to act natural but at the same time move with the speed of a striking cobra.

She peered through the passenger-side window and saw that the cop was looking at her cell phone. When Rosa tapped on the glass the woman turned sharply and a frown creased her brow.

She appeared to be in her thirties and was rather pretty.

Rosa didn't try to open the door because she knew instinctively that there was no need. The cop did not perceive her to be a threat and proceeded to lower the window.

And that proved to be the last mistake she would ever make.

'What's the problem, miss?' the cop asked her.

Rosa glanced quickly around and saw there was nobody watching. Then she whipped the pistol from her bag, thrust it through the open window and fired three shots into the woman's body.

The shock registered on the cop's face but only for a split second. And she didn't make a sound other than to expel a lungful of air.

Then she slumped sideways across the passenger seat from where she couldn't be seen from a distance.

Rosa swiftly withdrew the gun and slipped it back into her bag. She stepped back and checked again that she wasn't being watched. The walkway and the street were both still empty.

As she walked away from the car she knew that it could not have gone any better. It had been a slick, clean hit. Easy and effortless, which was usually the case with random executions. There was no need to plan them. No need to agonise over the approach or the exit route. All you had to do was seize an opportunity and that was exactly what she had done.

Before she got to the pub where Alice was waiting she sent a text message to Roy Slack to let him know that she was continuing to hit her target of one kill a day.

64

Laura

I couldn't be sure that Carver had spotted me. But as he walked towards the car, I reached into my bag for the Taser. Just in case I was about to be confronted.

I was lucky that I wasn't parked under or near to a street lamp. But if he looked through the windscreen he'd be sure to see the dark figure sitting behind the wheel.

Fortunately he didn't look through the windscreen or the side window as he walked behind the car and onto the pavement.

Relieved, I let go of the Taser and exhaled as a jolt of adrenalin spiked through me.

I watched him in the wing mirror walking away from me along the pavement, so I decided I had little choice but to follow him. I didn't think he'd be going too far without his car and it seemed too cold for a leisurely evening walk. He wasn't even wearing a coat. Just a loose sweater over jeans.

So maybe he was going to the local pub for a drink, or to a restaurant for something to eat.

As it turned out he went as far as a small corner store where I held back and watched him go inside.

Through the window I saw a young female assistant reach up and pluck a pack of cigarettes from the shelf behind her.

As Carver paid her, I retraced my steps along the street so that I'd be a safe distance ahead of him if he returned home. And that was exactly what he did.

I seized the opportunity to get there before him and ducked down behind a pair of wheelie bins to the right of the front door.

A few seconds later I heard him step onto the driveway and I got a whiff of the cigarette he'd sparked up during his short walk back.

And then I heard him insert his key in the lock. As he pushed the front door open, I made my move, leaping out from behind the bins with the Taser in my outstretched hand.

He heard me and whirled around and as he did so I pulled the trigger, hitting him just below the chest with a fierce jolt of electricity that sent him sprawling backwards into his hallway.

He lay there on the carpet, his whole body shaking dramatically, his mouth wide open in shock.

I knew that I had to move fast, that he would soon stabilise and regain control of his muscles and senses.

So I whipped the cuffs from my bag and rushed through the doorway. I had to grab his arms and pull him away from the door so that I could kick it shut.

Then I knelt down, pushed him over onto his front, and cuffed his hands behind his back.

'This is a two-shot Taser,' I told him and held it in front of his face that was pressed against the carpet. 'If you don't do as I say I'll give you another blast.'

I put my knee against the small of his back and let him feel the weight of me. His body went still and he began to mumble incoherently.

I got up off him and hauled him to his feet where he wobbled unsteadily. Then I gripped the cuffs with one hand and shoved the Taser into his back with the other.

'Is there anyone else here?' I said.

'What the hell is going on?' he spluttered back at me. 'Who are you?'

'Just answer the question, Carver. Are you alone?'

He threw himself against the wall and tried to turn to face me. But I responded by yanking his arms up behind his back, which made him scream.

'OK, OK,' he yelped. 'There's no one else here, for Christ's sake.'

I pushed him along the hall to the first open door, which led into a large, modern kitchen. Once inside, I fired the second shot from the Taser. This time the point of impact was midway between his shoulder blades, and he went crashing to the floor.

While he reacted again like he was having a fit, I took his belt from his jeans and used it to secure his ankles together.

By the time I'd done that the vessels were throbbing at my temples and the breath was roaring in my ears. But I'd managed to bring down the notorious Rottweiler in less than two minutes. And I felt good about that.

So now the bastard was completely at my mercy, and the first stage of my plan was complete.

Oh, how the mighty fall!

That was my initial reaction as I looked down on the trussed-up figure of one of the most feared men in the London underworld.

'You don't look so tough now,' I said. 'I can't imagine why they call you The Rottweiler. A poodle would be more fitting.'

He rolled onto his side and stared up at me, confusion writ large on his face.

'Do I know you?' he snarled.

'I'll ask the questions,' I said, speaking through my linen scarf while trying to make my voice sound gruff. 'It's why I'm here. And why I'm going to hurt you if you don't answer them.'

He narrowed his shark-like eyes. 'Have you just escaped from a fucking mad house? If not then that's where you belong.'

I lifted my right shoe and brought it down hard on his chest. He screwed up his face and let out a sharp grunt of pain. He was lucky that I was wearing flats and not heels.

'You don't know me but I know all about you.' I said. 'You're Roy Slack's right-hand man, and you're a murdering bastard. You've also lied to the police about knowing nothing about his revenge attacks on officers.'

His eyes stretched wide and he shook his head. 'Are you serious? That's what this is about.'

'I'm deadly serious,' I said. 'In fact I reckon you're the one who's been sending those text messages to the detectives on the task force. I hear you're some kind of computer nerd, so that kind of thing is right up your street.'

'You're talking bollocks.'

'I don't think so. You're in this shit right up to your neck. And you're going to tell me all about it. Starting with everything you know about the woman who's carrying out the killings on Slack's behalf.'

That was the moment he realised I was a copper. He curled his lower lip and his eyes took on a fiery intensity.

'I don't fucking believe it,' he blurted. 'You're Old Bill. First you snatch Roy and now me. Jesus, you pigs must be desperate.'

I kicked him in the crotch this time and the agony that contorted his features was a sight to behold. I realised suddenly that I was actually enjoying myself.

While he twisted his body and moaned, I looked around the kitchen. Marble worktops. Shiny grey units. All the mod cons. There was an island in the centre of the room and a table with four chairs. Clearly he'd spent a lot of his ill-gotten gains on it.

'This can go on all night,' I said. 'And you won't be as lucky as your boss was because there's no team of coppers on their way here to rescue you.'

His complexion was pallid and sickly, but he was a tough brute and I didn't get the sense that he was ready to start talking. It was a shame that I couldn't just reach my hand into his brain and pull out the information.

'There's something else you're going to tell me before the night is over,' I said. 'The firm has someone working for them inside the task force. Someone who must have given you the personal details of the detectives. I want to know who it is.'

If somebody had asked me a week ago if I'd be able to do what I was now doing I would have told them absolutely not. No way could I ever resort to torturing anyone, even a low-life thug like Danny Carver. But it's amazing how events can change people and make them act out of character.

Right now I was way out of my comfort zone. A renegade copper. A law breaker. But I didn't feel uncomfortable. And I didn't feel any guilt or shame. It might have been different if I'd been willing to accept the possibility that Slack had been telling the truth all along and he didn't know anything. But I wasn't because I'd convinced myself that it couldn't be anyone but him. And nothing I'd seen or heard had caused me to change my mind.

'It's just come to me,' Carver said. 'You're the bird who turned up at the office. Jefferson. It was your bloke who was shot in Balham. The teacher.'

He made it sound like it was no big deal. And that made the anger tremble inside me. So I kicked him again. In the stomach. And as he writhed on the floor, I said, 'Tell me what you know, Carver. Or so help me I will . . .'

He screwed his face into a snarl. 'You'll what, copper? Kill me? I don't fucking think so. You ain't got the bottle.'

I pulled back my coat hood and ripped off my scarf. I'd hoped that I'd be able to do this without revealing my identity, but now I didn't care if he saw my face. In fact I suddenly wanted him to.

'You have no idea what I'm capable of,' I roared at him. 'Your boss tried to have me murdered. He got someone to assassinate the Commissioner and kill one of my colleagues. So do you really think I'd balk at putting you six feet under? Especially since nobody knows I'm here and every cop in this city would give me an alibi if I needed one.'

His jaw tightened as he continued to stare at me without blinking. He was sizing me up, trying to work out if I was angry enough and reckless enough to take this much further.

I held his steely gaze, determined not to show any weakness or hesitation. I wanted him to know that I wasn't about to lose my nerve. That I'd been pushed beyond reason and didn't care about the consequences of my actions.

'You won't get me to admit to anything,' he said after a few seconds. 'And this psycho act is wasted on me. I can see you have a temper like most bitches. But you don't have the stomach to see this through. It takes a certain kind of person to torture a confession out of someone. You have to be like me, and you're not.'

'This false bravado won't wash,' I said. 'We both know that

369

when the pain gets bad enough you'll open up. And I'm more than prepared to inflict it even though I don't regard myself as a complete psychopath.'

I left him where he was and walked around the kitchen, opening drawers. I found what I was looking for in the one below the sink. A large, sharp kitchen knife. I would use it to scare him. Not to hurt him. At least that was what I told myself as I held it up for him to see.

'Four people have already been murdered,' I said. 'And two others – my partner and a police officer – are in hospital with bullet wounds. You need to understand that this is not just about stopping further bloodshed. This is also about me getting sweet revenge. So do you really think that I'm going to pass up this opportunity to do exactly that?'

I didn't tell him about my miscarriage because I feared that if he shrugged it off I would slit his throat.

I bent over and put the tip of the blade against his left cheek, just hard enough to pierce the skin and produce some blood.

'This is what's going to happen,' I said. 'I'm going to have a look around your house to give you time to think this through. If you've got any sense you'll conclude that there's no point holding back. Not only will you save yourself a lot of grief, but it'll also work in your favour when you face your day in court.'

I threw the knife on the nearest worktop and started to take off my belt.

'First I need to ensure that you won't make a noise and try to roll around,' I said.

Something close to panic seized his expression. 'Your people have already searched the house. There's nothing to find. They took my laptop and phones and—'

I shut him up by grabbing a tea towel from a holder on the

wall behind me and stuffing it into his mouth. I secured it behind his head and then used my belt to hog-tie him by attaching it to the cuffs and to his own belt.

'I get the impression you don't want me to look around,' I said once he was completely immobilised. 'I'm guessing that's because you've got something to hide.'

I took a pair of disposable gloves from my bag and put them on. Then I went upstairs first. There were three bedrooms and a bathroom. None of them yielded anything of interest, and they were all pretty bland and lacking in warmth and colour.

The living room had more character. There was a brown leather sofa with two matching chairs, a cream shagpile carpet, and a huge flat-screen TV that seemed to fill up half of one wall.

But my eyes were immediately drawn to the opposite wall, which was lined with three floor-to-ceiling bookcases. The middle bookcase was open like a door and beyond it was a small room with a desk inside.

I'd read about these hidden rooms in a magazine article quite recently. Although they were as old as the hills, they were now in vogue and becoming a common feature in large homes across London.

My interest piqued as I stepped towards it and saw that inside it was more like a really big cupboard than a proper room. However, there was space enough for a desk with a chair and book shelves on all three sides.

There was a computer on the desk and the sight of it caused the air to lock in my chest.

This one obviously hadn't been discovered during the police search. And there had been no mention in the report of a secret room.

I realised suddenly why Carver had become panicky just now

when I'd said I was going to look around the house. He'd left the door to his secret room open, no doubt because he'd been working in there before going out for some fags.

As I stepped inside I wondered if I had stumbled onto something significant. Was it from this tiny cubbyhole that Carver had sent out the threatening text messages?

I looked at the computer keyboard and screen, then reached out and touched the mouse to see if it had been left on. When the screen came to life I couldn't believe my luck.

I sat on the chair with a view to delving into his files. But first I studied the icons on the desktop, and noted he was using Google Chrome as a browser. I thought that would be a good place to start.

I went straight to the history list to see what Carver had been looking up online. There'd been surprisingly little activity over the past couple of days. But five days ago – on the Tuesday – he'd searched for information on someone known as *La Asesina*.

As soon as I opened up the first site he'd visited I saw that *La Asesina* was the name that had been given to a woman who was reckoned to be among the most ruthless assassins in Mexico. The English translation was *The Slayer*.

And instinct told me that she was the same woman who had crossed the Atlantic in order to bring terror to London.

65

Rosa

They were still in the pub when they heard the sirens.

'It sounds like there's something going on close by,' Alice said.

When they left the pub they saw that a small crowd had gathered on the walkway. The street where the cop lay dead in her patrol car had been cordoned off. Two other police cars were parked next to it, and there were lots of officers around in high visibility jackets.

'I wonder what's happened,' Rosa said, and then added, 'I think it's probably best that we don't hang around.'

They walked quickly away from the scene arm in arm and went for dinner at a restaurant near the Millennium Bridge. As usual Rosa was able to move her thoughts on from the murder she had just committed. However, she was still hyper from the rush of adrenalin and it took two vodkas to ease the tension in her bones.

But after that she was even more relaxed than before because she was no longer under pressure to seek out a victim. The job was done and she didn't have to look for another target until tomorrow, which meant she could focus all her attention on Alice.

The place they were in was already adorned with Christmas decorations, and there was even a large, brightly lit Christmas tree in one corner. It prompted Alice to ask Rosa where she would be spending Christmas.

Rosa simply said that she hadn't decided. Then, to deflect any follow-up questions, she launched into a spiel about how Mexicans celebrated the festive season.

'In my country Christmas is called *Las Posadas*,' she explained. 'We stage lots of festivals, and the holiday runs from December the twelfth to January the sixteenth. And, of course, the weather is warm. Not like here.'

Rosa hadn't celebrated Christmas for many years. Even though she'd been born into a religious family, the significance of it meant nothing to her. Three years ago she executed a journalist on Christmas day because Carlos Cruz did not like an article he'd written about the Sinaloa cartel. The man was taking part in a procession at the time with his wife and two children when she rode past on her motorbike and shot him in the head.

'It's a pity you can't be here for Christmas,' Alice was saying. 'We could have a great time together.'

Rosa felt a tingle of excitement. 'Maybe I can be here,' she said. 'If you really want me to be.'

They'd been exchanging teasing remarks like this throughout the day. Trying to gauge each other's reaction. Fishing for compliments or a sign that they were both hoping the relationship would continue beyond the end of next week.

'Of course I'd like you to be here,' Alice said. 'Or if you can't then perhaps we can meet somewhere in between. I can get time off work. No problem.'

They talked about it as they left the restaurant and walked arm in arm back along the South Bank towards Westminster Bridge.

It was a beautiful evening, full of people and colour. Above the city the dark sky was crowded with needles of frozen light.

It had been a day that Rosa knew she would remember and cherish for the rest of her life. There hadn't been a dull moment. From seeing the palatial home of the Queen of England to spotting detective Laura Jefferson leaving New Scotland Yard. From strolling along the famous Oxford Street to watching Roy Slack tell the story of his abduction live on television.

And, of course, there'd been execution number five. What a result that had been. The cop in the patrol car had been there for the taking. She'd been in the wrong place at the wrong time. And she had paid the price.

Rosa had gathered so many memories and it wasn't over yet. They decided to walk back to Alice's apartment rather than take a cab. And on the way they were going to stop for more drinks and peruse the lighted shop windows that were packed with Christmas goods.

For Rosa it almost seemed as though she had already adopted her new persona. Maria Rodriquez was no longer merely one of the many fake names she'd been using. Maria Rodriquez was the woman she was about to become.

Alice Green had triggered what Rosa now viewed as an irreversible transformation. Sure, she was still a work in progress, like an unfinished portrait. But soon all the component parts would be in place, and the lies she would have to tell forever would be embedded on her psyche.

Plus, the paid assassin known as The Slayer would be consigned to history.

66

Laura

My throat was almost too tight to swallow as I stared at Danny Carver's computer screen.

He had visited no less than seven online sites in his search for information on the notorious female assassin they called The Slayer.

She apparently worked for the infamous Sinaloa drugs cartel in Mexico and was credited with killing more than fifty people, including police officers, politicians and journalists, as well as rival cartel members.

But in every other sense she was a mystery. The police and the media did not know her true identity or what she looked like. However, rumour had it that she was young and attractive and rode around on a motorbike.

She was by no means the only woman who was making a living as a contract killer in Mexico, which I knew to be one of the most violent countries on earth. There were several others, and their monikers were just as striking – 'The Angel of Death,' 'The Shadow,' 'The Devil's Daughter.'

But it was The Slayer who Carver had been interested in. And I could think of only one reason why that would be.

There was a printer on the desk so I switched it on and selected a page to print off. It was an online news feature about the murder six months ago of a town mayor in the state of Sinaloa, on the west coast of Mexico. The headline read: *New Mayor Shot Dead*, and it told how the young, idealistic politician, Gisela Serrano, was gunned down outside her home just three weeks after she pledged to root out dishonest government staff and expunge corrupt contracts in lucrative public services. Two bullets were fired into her body by an assassin who rode by on a motorbike.

Police suspected the killing was carried out by *La Asesina* on the orders of the Sinaloa cartel who feared the mayor's policies would impact on their businesses.

Once the page was printed I rushed back into the kitchen with it. I removed the tea towel from around Carver's head and held the sheet of paper in front of his face.

'Is this the woman who's working for Slack?' I said. 'The co-called Slayer.'

His voice came out in a wheeze. 'I don't know what you're talking about.'

'Is that right? Then tell me why you've been searching online for information about her. I checked the Google history on your computer. The one you keep hidden in that secret little office that my colleagues obviously failed to discover.'

He shut his eyes and exhaled, as if blowing out candles on a birthday cake.

'You've been rumbled, Carver,' I said. 'This woman they call The Slayer rides a motorbike. So does the bitch who shot my partner. She also works for the Sinaloa cartel, which we know has

377

a business arrangement with the firm. You lot distribute drugs for them in the UK.'

He opened his eyes, shook his head, said, 'You had no fucking right to go on my computer. You don't have a warrant. Whatever I've been doing online is my business.'

I felt a surge of anger, but repressed it.

Instead, I said, 'I'm about to call this in. So in a little while this house will be swarming with officers, including techies who will seek out whatever you've got hidden on that computer and on those phones that you didn't tell us about.'

I'd found three smartphones in the desk drawer. They were all locked, and passwords were needed to open them. But I couldn't help thinking, and hoping, that at least one of them had been used to send the threatening text messages.

'You won't get away with this,' Carver screamed at me.

'I already have,' I said. 'So there's no point holding back. Just tell me if Slack did a deal with the cartel to use this woman. And where is she?'

He was shaking now, sweating, and it must have been obvious to him that the game was up. He'd been both unlucky and careless. He should have closed the door to his secret room when he went to get a fresh pack of cigarettes. But, of course, he hadn't expected me to turn up and zap him with a Taser gun.

'I'm not saying another word until I speak to a lawyer,' he said.

The urge to kick him again was strong, but I resisted.

'Suit yourself,' I said.

I dashed back into the living room and called DCS Drummond. He answered on the second ring but before I could get a word in he told me that another police officer had been murdered. The news hit me hard, but I was more angry than shocked.

'WPC Leah Campbell was shot while sitting in a patrol car along the South Bank,' he said. 'I'm at the scene now and it's not pretty. Three bullets were fired into her body from close range, most likely by someone leaning through the side window.'

'Christ almighty.'

'She was parked up while waiting for her partner, who, believe it or not, was paying a visit to his girlfriend in a nearby block of flats. He discovered her body when he returned to the car.'

'And you reckon she's another victim of our assassin?'

'I'd put money on it,' he said. 'The last text warned us that every cop in London was a potential target, including those on the street and in patrol cars.'

I then told him that I was at Danny Carver's house in Streatham.

'What in God's name are you doing there?'

'I came to ask him some questions.'

'But you're not—'

'Just listen, guv,' I cut in. 'You need to get here as quickly as you can. And bring someone who's computer savvy.'

'Why? What's going on?'

'I think I know who the assassin is,' I said.

'Jesus. Have you got a name?'

'Not as such. But it looks like she's a well-known killer and was imported from Mexico to do the job for Slack.'

'How did you find this out?'

'I went on Carver's computer.'

'But his computer is with forensics.'

'He has more than one, guv. And he keeps this one in a secret little room that wasn't found during a search of the house.'

'Holy shit. Give me the address and I'll get there as soon as I can.'

* * *

379

Drummond turned up at Carver's house fifteen minutes later along with a bunch of uniformed officers.

By then I had taken steps to protect myself against accusations of assault. I'd put the knife back in the drawer, removed my belt, which I'd used to hog-tie him, and made up a story about what had happened here.

'I know that strictly speaking I shouldn't have come here, guv,' I said to Drummond as he followed me into Carver's kitchen where the man was still lying on the floor. 'But after I read the forensic report that described this guy as a computer wizard I suspected he might have been the one who sent the text messages. So I decided to drop in here on the way home. He was just arriving back himself when I approached him on the doorstep and said I wanted to ask him a few questions.

'But he started threatening me straight away and then became violent so I was forced to use the Taser and then restrain him with the cuffs. I was about to call for back-up when I stumbled on the secret room.'

'The bitch is lying,' Carver shouted from the floor. 'She attacked me for no reason. She was going to torture me.'

Drummond rolled his eyes. 'Save it, Carver. Detective Jefferson is a fine, upstanding officer and there's no way she would do something like that.'

He instructed the uniforms to take Carver outside and told me to show him what I'd found.

As we walked along the hall to the living room, he put a hand on my shoulder and said, 'Tell me the truth, Laura. Did you attack him? And were you planning to torture him? I've already got enough on my plate dealing with the fallout from what your colleague Marsden did. And now this other shooting.'

I shook my head and the lie came easily. 'Of course not, guv.

It happened just like I said it did. You have to believe that.'

He gave me a hard stare. 'I want to, Laura. I really do.'

'Well, you can rest assured that I didn't step over the line, guv. I acted in self-defence. I know I shouldn't have come here but I'm glad I did. And you will be too when you see what I've found.'

A moment later Drummond followed me into the hidden room and then stood behind me as I sat down at the desk and scrolled through the online sites on Carver's computer that referenced The Slayer.

'I'm convinced it's her, guv,' I said. 'This woman, The Slayer, also rides a motorbike and I don't reckon that's a coincidence.'

'We need to involve the other law enforcement agencies,' he said. 'And the Mexican embassy here in London. We also have to put the squeeze on Carver.'

'He's clammed up and wants a lawyer,' I said.

'Then we'll push him hard.' Drummond took out his mobile phone. 'The techies are supposed to be on their way but I'm going to chase them up. I want those smartphones unlocked and I want to see everything that's hidden on that computer.'

'We should check all flights from Mexico in the days before Dave Prentiss was shot,' I said. 'If she is our assassin then I'm guessing that was when she flew in.'

'I'll get on it,' he said as he stepped out of the room and started talking on the phone.

I remained sitting at the desk. My mind was on fire, and when I rubbed the back of my neck I realised that I was sweating.

I found it easy to imagine how Danny Carver must have spent hours in this room. It was cramped, but cosy, and for a computer geek it was the perfect sanctuary.

There were four shelves on the wall above me and they

contained a collection of unlabelled CDs, books on computers and a pile of glossy magazines on computing and technology.

In the past it would have struck me as odd that a thug like Carver would be interested in this stuff. But these days criminals saw it as a way to enhance their repertoire. And I didn't doubt that Carver had used his skills to help Slack generate business and make the firm's lines of communication more secure.

A few other items were on the desk in addition to the computer and printer. There was a half-full can of Carlsberg, an empty pack of Marlboro cigarettes and a spiral-bound notepad and pen.

I picked up the pad to see if there was anything written inside, but all the pages were blank. However, experience had taught me to always check for indentation writing.

And sure enough there was an impression on the first page that would have been created by the pressure of the pen on the page that had been above it.

I couldn't quite make it out so I went in search of a pencil. I found one in a kitchen drawer and rested the pad on the worktop while I gently rubbed the lead tip over the indentation marks to bring out the contrast.

The letters and numbers that appeared as if by magic sent a cold rush of blood through my veins.

They also made me believe that we might at last be closing in on the killer.

67

Laura

Danny Carver looked mortified when I held up the notepad to show him what the pencil had revealed.

'The top sheet might have been torn out but this is what you wrote on it,' I said. 'So it's time to stop fucking us around.'

'Go screw yourself,' he snapped. 'And while you're at it, call my brief. I've given the number to that twat over there in the uniform.'

Carver had been hauled back into the house from the patrol car he'd been put in outside. He was now sitting at the kitchen table, his hands still cuffed behind his back.

Drummond, who was standing next to me, pointed a rigid finger at Carver and said, 'Were you sent to pick the woman up from the airport? Is that why you scribbled on the pad?'

Carver ignored him and raised his eyes to the ceiling.

'What does Bridges mean?' Drummond persisted. 'Is it someone's name or the name of a road or house?'

But the villain remained tight-lipped and was obviously determined not to say anything without getting advice from his solicitor first.

'Get this piece of scum out of here,' Drummond told the uniforms who were standing in the doorway.

His phone buzzed at the same time and he snatched it out of his pocket to answer it. The gaffer had made two calls in quick succession after I'd shown him what I'd found on the pad. The first had been to the office where the team were told to check out what Carver had scribbled on the pad. The second had been to the Assistant Commissioner who had asked to be informed of any significant developments. And this was most definitely that.

I placed the pad on the worktop and studied it again.

Maria Rodriquez
Flight BA242
Terminal 5

Bridges

I'd discovered through a quick online check that BA242 was a scheduled service that ran most days between Mexico City and Heathrow. It departed late at night and, with the time difference, arrived in London just after four o'clock in the evening the following day.

Officers were now onto British Airways to find out if and when a Maria Rodriquez had been a passenger.

It might not have been conclusive evidence, but my gut was telling me that Maria Rodriquez must be The Slayer, and that she had come here at the behest of Roy Slack.

In a way it made perfect sense because he wouldn't have wanted to recruit someone who might be on the radars of UK and European law enforcement agencies.

It was my guess he had exploited his links with the Sinaloa

cartel to enlist the services of a seasoned professional. Someone who wouldn't flinch at the idea of killing police officers.

And the woman known as The Slayer fitted the bill. From what I'd read online she was the stuff that legends were made of.

Had she really killed more than fifty people? If so then she was obviously a bloodthirsty psychopath. And she clearly enjoyed what she did because she must have been doing it for years.

I was well aware of how bad things were in Mexico and how the sheer scale of violence and corruption was beyond belief. I also knew that the wars between the various cartels had encouraged a large number of people, mostly men, to become contract killers.

But it was still hard for me to understand how any woman could embark on a career that entailed slaughtering dozens of strangers.

Maria Rodriquez clearly wasn't her real name and we'd probably find that she had entered the country on a false passport.

So what was her real name? Who was The Slayer? Was she a wife? A mother? How old was she? What made her become a killer in the first place? The questions were snowballing in my head.

Drummond came off the phone and said, 'That was the office. British Airways have confirmed that a Maria Rodriquez was on flight 242 that arrived at Heathrow from Mexico City on Tuesday. We've contacted the Border Agency and passport and landing card details are being sent over.'

'Tuesday was when we received the first text message,' I said. 'And the day before Dave Prentiss was shot.'

He nodded. 'It's looking like the risk you took in coming here is paying off, Laura.'

'Let's hope so, guv. I just wish we could get Carver to open up. He must know we've got him bang to rights.'

'And that's the problem. He's afraid of digging a deeper hole for himself. I'm having him sent back to the Yard. He might be forthcoming once he's talked to his lawyer.'

'What about the word Bridges?' I said. 'We still don't know what it refers to.'

'The team are all over it. They're checking roads, houses, firms and names. I've told them to get back to me the moment they get a sniff of something.'

'So what do we do in the meantime?'

He waved his hand. 'We turn this place inside out. See what else we can find.'

Within half an hour the house was packed with people. More uniforms arrived along with scene of crime officers and techies from the cyber-crime unit, who got straight to work on Carver's smartphones and computer.

When I realised it was almost eleven o'clock I felt a sudden pang of guilt and rushed outside to phone the hospital. Thankfully Aidan was awake, having slept for most of the evening, and he assured me that there was no need to apologise for not calling sooner.

'I've heard about the police woman who was shot tonight on the South Bank,' he said. 'They're saying on the news that it's believed to be the same killer.'

'That's right,' I said. 'It's dreadful. But at least we're closing in.'

I filled him in on what had happened, skipping the gory details, and he said he was proud of me for using my own initiative.

I would have carried on talking but a uniformed officer appeared at my side and told me that DCS Drummond wanted me to go back into the house.

'I have to go, Aidan,' I said. 'Please try to get a good night's sleep and I'll see you tomorrow.'

'I love you, Laura,' he said.

'And I love you too.'

Drummond was waiting for me in the kitchen and I could see from his face that he was gagging to tell me something. He held up a plastic evidence bag containing what looked like one of Carver's smartphones.

'We've got the bastard,' he said, a triumphant note in his voice. 'The text messages to us were sent from this phone, which we've managed to get into. Carver hasn't bothered to delete them and I suspect that was because he didn't think this would ever fall into our hands.'

'Is there any evidence to suggest that Slack put him up to it?' I asked.

'Not yet, but if we don't find it I'm sure we can persuade Carver to rat on his boss. He won't want to take the fall by himself.'

Drummond's own phone rang again and he answered it. As he listened, I watched how his features tightened and his posture changed. I wondered if he was being given good or bad news.

When he hung up, he looked at me and said, 'The team have had a result with the word Bridges. It's not a person or a house. It's a hotel called Bridges over in Vauxhall. It came up in an online search and someone had the good sense to ring the place to see if they had any guests named Maria Rodriquez. And they do.'

'My God.'

'We have to go straight there,' he said. 'You come with me. Leave your car here and you can pick it up later.'

68

Rosa

'There's something I need to tell you,' Rosa said. 'I can't hold it in any longer.'

Alice rolled over on the bed so that they were facing each other.

'I'm all ears, babe,' she said, smiling. 'What is it?'

They were both breathing heavily, and their naked bodies glistened with perspiration. That was because they'd been going at it since they'd arrived back at the apartment an hour ago. Another blast of sensational sex that had left them both satisfied but exhausted.

It was now almost midnight, and Rosa felt she couldn't let the day end without saying what she'd wanted to say all evening. She knew it was a risk and that it might cause the most wonderful day of her life to end in disaster.

But she had to get it off her chest because if she didn't she knew that she wouldn't be able to sleep.

'So come on, babe,' Alice said, her smile faltering. 'What is it you want to tell me?'

Rosa put a hand against Alice's cheek, and as she did so she felt the skin tighten at the back of her neck.

'I've fallen in love with you, Alice,' she said. 'I realise we've only known each other for a few days and that's why I've been afraid to tell you. But it's driving me crazy wondering if you feel the same or if for you this is no more than a short fling.'

Rosa steeled herself for Alice's response, and the nerves fluttered in her stomach.

For several seconds Alice said nothing, and Rosa feared that she had made a terrible mistake.

But then Alice spoke, her voice a soft whisper. 'I can't imagine why you look so worried, Maria. Surely it must be bloody obvious that I feel the same way about you.'

Rosa's heart exploded. 'Do you really mean that?'

Alice laughed. 'I've been smitten from the moment we met. I've never felt like this with anyone. And it's scaring me because I've always been led to believe that it can't happen so quickly.'

'Then we have to decide whether we should trust our feelings,' Rosa said.

'Well, I can only tell you that if feels right to me. And if it feels right to both of us then surely that's all that matters.'

Rosa felt the breath of Alice's words on her face, the faint whisper of something sweet.

'I thought I was in love once before,' Alice continued. 'But it wasn't like this. I feel like I'm under your spell.'

Rosa grinned. 'That's because I'm a wicked witch.'

Alice shook her head. 'I like to think I'm a good judge of character and I can tell you're a kind and generous person. You don't have a wicked bone in your body.'

'But you don't really know me,' Rosa said.

'So what? I see that as a good thing. It means there's so much more for me to find out.'

And none of it will be the truth, Alice. Everything you're going to learn about Maria Rodriquez will be a lie. It can't be any other way. You can never know who or what I really am. I can't tell you about the people I've killed or the lives I've destroyed. Or about the abuse I suffered as a little girl and what I did to the man who adopted me.

If you knew all that then there's no way you would ever love me or want to be with me. You would probably hate me and I couldn't bear that. So we'll both have to live with the lies if this is to work.

But it won't be a problem, Alice, because what you don't know can't hurt you.

'So what now?' Alice said as she snuggled closer to Rosa. 'We've declared our love for each other and that's fantastic. We now have to decide where we go from here.'

'Actually I've already given that a lot of thought,' Rosa said. 'And I've decided to leave my job and move to London.'

Alice couldn't believe it. She started shedding tears of joy as Rosa pulled her close and held her against her chest.

After a few minutes Rosa felt hot tears break free from her own eyes. She hadn't cried in years and she saw it as yet another sign that she was becoming a different person thanks to Alice.

69

Laura

Bridges Hotel occupied a nondescript building on Kennington Lane, close to Vauxhall Bridge.

We arrived at the same time as an armed tactical support team. Officers wearing combat helmets and visors, and carrying automatic weapons, emerged from the back of an armoured van. They trooped along the pavement and into the hotel in a matter of seconds. Drummond and I followed them inside after they gave us the all-clear.

It was a typical no-frills establishment, providing three-star accommodation for tourists and business people on a budget. There was a small reception desk and behind it stood a young man wearing a smart white shirt and a shocked expression.

The officers spread themselves out around the room – in front of the lift, at the bottom of the stairs, next to a door leading to a dining area. There was no sign of any guests and that was a relief.

Drummond marched straight up to the desk and showed the receptionist his ID.

'I'm Detective Chief Superintendent Drummond,' he said. 'What's your name?'

'Lionel Wren, sir. I'm the night manager.'

'Well, I'm sorry we've alarmed you, Mr Wren, but we're here to arrest one of your guests. Her name is Maria Rodriquez. She's dangerous and possibly armed. So tell me which room she's in.'

Lionel Wren just stood there with his mouth open, his eyes out on stalks.

Drummond raised his voice and brought his fist down on the desk.

'Please answer me, Mr Wren. Maria Rodriquez. Which room?'

Wren snapped to attention and said, 'It's room twenty-two on the fourth floor. But I don't think she's in. I haven't seen her since I came on at five o'clock. Plus Miss Rodriquez instructed us not to go into her room, even to clean it, during her stay.'

'Which is for how long?'

'She told us she's not sure but the room has been booked and paid for in advance for two weeks.'

'OK. Now I need a key to room twenty-two.'

Wren produced a master key card from a drawer below the desk and handed it over.

Drummond then said, 'In sixty seconds I want you to call the room and let it ring until someone answers. It'll either be Maria Rodriquez or one of us. Have you got that?'

Wren nodded.

I stepped forward and pointed to a security camera high up on the wall to the right of the desk.

'How long do you keep the footage from the camera?' I asked him.

'A week,' Wren said.

'In that case while we're upstairs we'd like you to look through the tape and cue it up on a shot of Maria Rodriquez. Can you do that?'

'Sure.'

Drummond then turned to the officer leading the tactical unit, gave him the key card and said, 'Over to you. Fourth floor. Room twenty-two.'

The firearms team went about their task with military efficiency. Four of them hurried up the stairs and Drummond and I followed. The rest of the team remained in the reception area.

On the fourth floor the officers moved quietly along the corridor and arrived at room twenty-two just as the phone started to ring inside.

It continued ringing for a full minute before the team leader signalled that he was going in.

He inserted the key in the slot and pressed down on the handle. Then he pushed the door open and stepped back while shouting, 'Police, police! Stay where you are!'

There was no response from inside, and the only sound was the phone ringing.

The team leader peered into the room and then stepped inside and turned on the light. The rest were right behind him.

'All clear,' one of them called out almost immediately as the phone was picked up to stop it ringing.

I entered the room behind Drummond just as other guests started to appear in the corridor and the officers had to tell them to go back inside their rooms.

Room twenty-two was pretty basic. A double bed, fitted wardrobe, TV, dressing table and en-suite bathroom. The bed hadn't been made properly but it didn't look as though it had been slept in recently.

We donned our latex gloves and started looking around. And

it wasn't long before we discovered what Maria Rodriquez looked like.

We also found proof that she was indeed the female assassin who had brought terror to London.

70

Laura

It didn't take us long to carry out a thorough search of the room. But the first thing that struck us was what was actually missing from it. There were no toiletries or make-up and no toothbrush in the bathroom.

But there were clothes in the wardrobe, along with a travel bag on wheels. It made us believe that the woman was sleeping elsewhere but planned to return before checking out.

'Maybe she's staying overnight with someone she knows,' Drummond said. 'Might even be in a hotel or apartment down near the South Bank, which is why she came across the officer in the patrol car.'

We didn't dwell on this because our attention became focused on the small safe resting on one of the shelves in the wardrobe. It was locked and a combination number was needed to open it.

The night manager was summoned, and he unlocked it using an override code. That was when things became really interesting.

The safe contained an Apple iPad, three passports, two wigs, a key on a ring and a white envelope.

The passport photos were all the same and of an attractive woman with long black hair. But there were three different names, one of which was Maria Rodriquez.

I had to admit she was a stunner. She reminded me of those hot Latina girls who often graced the covers of fashion magazines. She had soft features, olive skin, full lips and sultry eyes. It was beyond me why someone lucky enough to be so beautiful would choose to become a contract killer.

And the evidence to prove that she was indeed the woman we were looking for was laid bare on a sheet of paper inside the envelope.

It was a typewritten list of names, addresses and contact details of all the detectives on the organised crime task force, along with many of our relatives, wives, husbands and partners. My name was there and so was Drummond's. And there were ink lines through two of the names – Dave Prentiss and Marion Nash. However, the Commissioner's name wasn't on the list and I wondered if it had been added as an afterthought.

Also, there was nothing to indicate who the next victim was going to be.

'I'm assuming this was provided by the mole inside the Met,' I said. 'It's terrifying to think that she was planning to work her way through it.'

At the bottom of the list was a web address. Drummond opened up the iPad, which wasn't locked, and typed the address into the search engine.

What appeared shocked us both. There were several pages of photographs of most of those on the list, including me, Drummond, Aidan and my mother. It seemed they'd been copied from various social media sites and in the case of some of the detectives, from newspaper features.

The iPad also revealed that she had used Google Maps to check out the addresses, including my home in Balham. It was all very disturbing. I had to close my eyes and will myself to think clearly.

'There's still nothing to link the bitch to Roy Slack,' Drummond said. 'Except Danny Carver.'

'I reckon this is enough to be getting on with, guv,' I said. 'Evidence will turn up, I'm sure.'

The investigation had taken a huge leap forward. The assassin was still out there, perhaps stalking her next victim, but we knew who she was. And what she looked like.

'Why do you think she has this?' Drummond said, holding up the key ring from the safe.

The plastic fob enclosed a photo of the outside of a pub and the words *Three Crowns, Vauxhall.*

The name rang a bell with me. 'We drove past that pub on the way here, guv. It's about two hundred yards along the road.'

'Then we should check it out. She'd have had this for a reason. It could be that she was booked into this hotel because of its proximity to the pub.'

We went back downstairs. By now more police had arrived, including detectives and uniforms from the local division who asked Drummond to put them in the picture. He did so in the back office while we all viewed the CCTV footage of Maria Rodriquez, or whatever her name was, on a monitor.

'This was when she arrived at the hotel last Tuesday,' the night manager said. 'As you can see she was accompanied by a gentleman. He's the one who made the reservation over the phone and popped in earlier that day to pay up front in cash for two weeks.'

The man was Danny Carver, and he stood to one side as the woman showed her passport and checked in.

The picture quality was excellent and so we had a very clear shot of her face. We got the manager to freeze it as she approached the desk.

Maria Rodriquez was indeed a looker and had a figure to match. She wore a leather jacket, torn jeans and a tight brown sweater, and I realised that her passport photo did not do her justice.

'We have to make a decision,' Drummond said. 'Do we release this to the media or keep it to ourselves and wait here for her to show.'

'We have to get it out there, guv,' I said. 'For one thing we can't be sure she'll come back here. And we don't know if Slack will be tipped off by his mole, in which case she'll be gone.'

He nodded. 'I agree.'

He turned to one of the other detectives and told them to sort it.

'I want a photo and video clip across every TV news bulletin as soon as possible,' he said. 'And see if we can get something in the late editions of the morning papers.'

After a quick conflab it was decided that forensics would move into room twenty-two, but that we'd maintain a low profile outside the hotel.

'We watch and wait just in case she turns up,' Drummond said.

Several armed officers were told to remain inside the hotel while others were instructed to take up discreet positions outside.

'The rest of us are going down the pub,' he added.

The Three Crowns was a typical London pub and looked as though it had been around for years. There were lights on inside even though it was almost one thirty on Monday morning.

The main entrance faced onto Kennington Lane and there was another entrance around the back. The team covered all bases before knocking on the door. They couldn't take any chances because of the possibility that Maria Rodriquez was inside.

In the event the only people on the premises were the landlord, whose name was Jack Pickering, and his wife Mandy. They were still clearing up after a long day.

They were both middle-aged and plump. He had a hard, lined face and a beer belly, and she was painfully thin with skin that sat in folds beneath her eyes.

Drummond made them sit in the bar as officers searched the place. He then piled in with questions while they were still reeling from the shock.

They both denied knowing anyone named Maria Rodriquez. But the husband flinched slightly when he was shown the woman's passport photo.

'Think carefully before you answer, Mr Pickering,' Drummond warned him. 'The woman is wanted on multiple counts of murder. She claimed her latest victim – another police officer – earlier this evening not too far from here. If we find out later that you lied to us you'll be in deep, deep trouble.'

Pickering hesitated, then looked at his wife before he spoke. 'She was here a few days ago. But only the one time.'

'Who was she with?'

He swallowed, took a deep breath, said, 'Whatever's going on I've not been involved. I just run this pub.'

'So who was she with, Mr Pickering?'

He looked at his wife again, and this time she grabbed his arm and said, 'Tell them, Jack. Don't let that bastard drag you into something as bad as this.'

Pickering nodded and turned back to Drummond.

'She was here with Roy and Danny,' he said.

'You mean Roy Slack and Danny Carver?'

He nodded again. 'Roy owns this boozer. I just work for him. He was here alone and then she arrived with Danny. They were only here for about forty-five minutes.'

'And then where did they go?'

He shrugged. 'I dunno. They left.'

Drummond held up the key ring taken from the hotel safe. 'The woman had this with her. What does it open?'

Pickering frowned. 'It's the key to the garage out back. I'm under strict orders never to go in there. So I don't.'

I didn't believe him, but that was something we'd come back to later. First we needed to look inside that garage.

The contents of the garage came as a shock to all of us. It was an assassin's lair, and it caused a wave of nausea to wash over me.

'This is fucking unbelievable,' Drummond said, and he wasn't wrong.

The motorbike took up much of the space, but my eyes moved directly beyond it to a large table. On it there was a semi-automatic sniper rifle, no doubt the one used to kill the Commissioner. There was also a large commando knife, a garrotte and three mobile phones.

The only thing missing was the person who had been making use of them.

'There's enough stuff here to keep forensics busy for a month,' Drummond said.

But we didn't need forensics to tell us that we'd hit the jackpot. We now had all the evidence we needed to arrest and charge Roy Slack and to make sure that he spent the last days of his life banged up in a prison cell.

'Let's go collar the lying bastard,' Drummond said. 'And if we get really lucky we might find that he's shacked up with the biker bitch.'

71

Slack

He was dreaming about Terry Malone, the son he had scarcely known. They were sitting next to the pool at the villa in Spain, sipping beers while Terry's wife Amy frolicked in the water with the baby.

They were having such a great time, away from killer cancers and trigger-happy coppers.

He was telling the boy about his life, about his wife Julie, about his mum and dad, and about how he had built his vast criminal empire from scratch.

'This villa will be yours one day, Terry,' he was saying. 'Along with the firm and everything else I own. And you can pass it all on to my grandchild.'

But as with most of his dreams it ended suddenly and unpleasantly.

He heard Amy scream, and darkness replaced the sunlight. Then he saw himself standing over Terry's grave as the coffin was being lowered into the ground. He felt the anger rise up inside him and the tears gush from his eyes.

And then he was lying in a hospital bed, surrounded by coppers in uniform who were laughing at him, taking the piss, telling him he'd got what he deserved and they hoped his cancer-riddled body would rot in hell.

But in response he just sat back against the pillows and smiled at them, because in the end he knew that he would have the last laugh.

The ringing of the phone woke him, and he was surprised to find that he was still on the armchair in the living room. The lights and the TV were on and his dressing gown was sprinkled with ash from the cigar he'd smoked before falling asleep.

On the coffee table in front of him was an empty glass and the bottle of Scotch with the top still off.

He looked at his watch and groaned when he saw that it was only one thirty in the morning.

The phone was on the carpet next to the chair so he had to lean over to get it and stretching send a bolt of pain shooting up his arm and across his shoulders.

He realised then that he hadn't done himself any favours by dozing off in the chair soon after Rosa had messaged him to say that she'd taken out another cop. He should have gone to bed, stretched out, and made himself as comfortable as possible.

'Hello,' he barked into the phone.

'It's me, Roy. Thank God you answered.'

It was his mole in the Met and he felt a burst of irritation.

'Do you know what fucking time it is?' he ranted.

'Just listen to me, Roy. They're on their way to arrest you. They know everything.'

Slack felt his heart plunge in his chest.

'What do you mean by everything?'

'They've taken Danny Carver in and they know who you hired

to carry out the killings. They raided her hotel room in Vauxhall and they found her bike and weapons in a garage next to a pub that you own.'

'Has she been nabbed as well?'

'No. They don't know where she is.'

'Well, that's something at least.'

'Look, Roy, I'm begging you to keep me out of it. I've done everything you asked me to. So please don't drop me in it.'

'Do you think I give a fuck about you?' he raged. 'You're one of them. You're a copper and you're as fucking corrupt as they come. So I'm gonna make sure that it all comes out, including the fact that you got me to kill someone for you.'

'Roy, please. Don't. I can't—'

He cut the connection. He wasn't prepared to listen to any more pathetic drivel. There were more important things to concern him now. If they were coming for him then this was it. Time to bow out. He felt sorry for Danny and he was curious to know how the Old Bill had put it all together. How the fuck had they traced Rosa to the hotel in Vauxhall? And how had they found their way to the pub?

It was a bummer, but at the end of the day it didn't really matter. He'd got his revenge on the Met and that had been his aim.

He decided to use his phone one last time and sent a brief message to Rosa.

The police are onto you. Good luck and thanks for everything. Sorry you won't get the bonus I promised. Suggest you disappear.

He went out onto the balcony and hurled the phone into the Thames so that the police wouldn't get their hands on it.

Next he hurried into the bedroom and put on his most expensive shirt and a pair of smart trousers. He then went into the kitchen and opened the safe hidden behind the tiles.

He took out the gun and two envelopes. He left his knuckle-duster inside, along with a plastic folder with documents pertaining to all the properties he owned, some of which the cops knew nothing about.

Finally he returned to the living room and placed the gun and the envelopes on the coffee table.

Before sitting back in the armchair he picked up the framed photo of his late wife from on top of the drinks cabinet and gave her a kiss.

'I'll be with you soon, sweetheart,' he said.

When he was seated again, he held the photo in one hand and the gun in the other.

And waited for the filth to arrive.

72

Laura

Our convoy of police vehicles covered the six miles from Vauxhall to Canary Wharf in just fifteen minutes.

My blood began to race in anticipation as we approached Roy Slack's luxury apartment building overlooking the Thames.

I was praying that the woman would be there with him so that we could seize them both in one fell swoop and prevent further bloodshed.

But I wasn't overly optimistic because I just couldn't imagine someone who looked like Maria Rodriquez sharing a bed with a slug like Roy Slack.

There was no messing about when we arrived at our destination. Officers armed with assault rifles and pistols immediately sealed off the building and entered through imposing front doors with stained-glass panels.

The concierge and a liveried doorman were asked about Slack and both confirmed that he was his apartment on the top floor. When shown the passport picture of Maria Rodriquez they both said they hadn't seen her, and it sounded to me like they were telling the truth.

There were two lifts and we used them to carry us up through thirty floors to the top.

A plan of action had already been agreed – which was to batter down the door and burst right in. In the best-case scenario he'd be in bed and wouldn't put up any resistance. If he wasn't then they would have to react to whatever situation presented itself.

I drew a tremulous breath when we stepped out of the lift into the corridor on the thirtieth floor. Then as I watched the team take up positions, my heart started drumming frantically.

This was the moment I'd been waiting for. When we finally came calling on London's most ruthless gangster with enough evidence to put him away.

But we weren't there yet, and until we put the cuffs on him I feared it could all still go wrong.

'We move on three,' the team leader said quietly.

An officer with a steel battering ram stepped up to the door and on the count of three he swung it against the metal lock. It took two blows to force the door open and officers stormed in, yelling at the tops of their voices.

Then suddenly they fell silent and I thought that was because they'd caught Slack unawares and he was being restrained.

But I was wrong. After a few seconds word came back to us that a stand-off situation had developed.

Drummond was asked to go into the apartment and I simply followed behind. We walked along a tastefully furnished hallway to the living room where two officers stood just inside the doorway.

My stomach clenched as tight as a knot when I saw that they were pointing their rifles at Roy Slack.

He was sitting on an armchair with the muzzle of a pistol pressed against his chin. And he was grinning.

'Seems to me that you lot are making a habit of barging into homes uninvited,' Slack said, and his lungs sounded rusty.

'We've come to talk to you, Roy,' Drummond said. 'So be sensible and put the gun down.'

'Now why would I do a stupid thing like that? I've been told that you've finally got the evidence you've been looking for, which means that if I go with you now I'll end up dying in prison. And that was never part of the plan.'

'So what was the plan, Roy?'

Slack ignored the question and looked at me. I noticed then that he appeared worn out, as though he'd been drained of energy and emotion. His eyes were dull and opaque, and blood vessels were throbbing at his temples.

'I wondered if I would ever see you again, Detective Inspector Jefferson,' he said. 'You made such an impression on me when you came to the office the other day that I really felt like giving you a slap.'

I chose not to react other than to give a small, tight smile, which he didn't seem to like. His face became taut suddenly, brimming with hate.

'I bet you weren't smiling when that boyfriend of yours took a bullet,' he said. 'I thought it was a bloody shame that it didn't kill him.'

I didn't rise to the bait for fear of making a bad situation much worse. So we stared at each other for a short while before he shifted his gaze back to Drummond and said, 'For your information this was always part of the plan, although I didn't imagine I'd have an audience.'

'Where is she, Slack?' Drummond said. 'Where is Maria Rodriquez?'

He laughed. 'You mean The Slayer. Well, you must know that's not her real name.'

'Then what is?'

'I have no fucking idea.'

'But you do know where she is.'

He shook his head. 'I don't actually, but I suspect she's out celebrating her latest kill, which I'm sure you know all about by now. A bitch copper this time, I gather.'

'We've seized the weapons that were in the garage behind the pub.'

'Well, obviously she's still armed and still has unfinished business.'

One of the armed officers stepped to one side, prompting Slack to tighten his grip on the gun.

'I'm sure you wouldn't want me to blow my brains out before you've heard my confession,' he said.

Everybody froze, and the tension in the room became stifling.

'I thought not,' Slack said. 'So here goes. I believe you've sussed already that this was all about revenge. It was never about stopping the task force from probing my affairs. I just started with that to make it more interesting. No, this was me getting my own back on you lot for what you did to my son, my wife, my dad and my unborn grandchild.'

It felt like a fist was clenching my heart, squeezing it tight. I thought about the baby I'd lost and wanted to tell him. But I didn't because I knew he'd be pleased that he'd done to me what the police had done to his son's girlfriend.

So I bit down on my lip and listened to the bastard try to justify his actions.

'The Old Bill fucked up my life good and proper,' he went on. 'When I was told I only had months to live I decided to make you pay. I knew I had nothing to lose so I reckoned it could be my swansong.'

He pointed to the envelopes on the table in front of him.

'One of them contains my suicide note which spells it all out. When you read it you'll understand why I hate you all so much. The other envelope contains a little surprise for you guys.'

'Please put the gun down, Roy,' Drummond said. 'Let's have a proper conversation. You don't want to take your own life. Surely.'

'But I do. I thought I'd just made that clear. I've got fuck all to live for. I was only delaying this moment so that I could punish you lot of parasites and I'm satisfied that I've done just that.'

With his free hand he picked up the photo frame that had been lying on his lap.

'It's time I was reunited with my Julie,' he said.

He looked at the picture and his nostrils flared like he'd picked up a scent.

I was sure I wasn't the only one who considered rushing across the room to wrest the gun from him. But he was a good five metres away and that made it too risky.

Tramlines gathered on his forehead and he said, 'There's one other thing I want you to know. That copper who murdered my boy Terry is dead. I killed him myself. I don't know where the lads dumped his body and even if I did I wouldn't tell you.'

He then held the photo frame to his chest and it struck me that the expression that came over his face was one of pure contentment.

The last thing he did before pulling the trigger was to close his eyes and smile.

The bullet blew a hole through his head, shattering his brain before exiting through the top of his skull and slamming into the ceiling where it left a big red mark.

The room was showered with blood and bits of flesh and bone. It was a horrible thing to witness, and for some seconds I stopped breathing and it felt like I was swirling in currents.

Then I clutched at my stomach and rushed out of the room into the hallway where I dry-retched violently and felt sharp tears prick at my eyes.

The next ten minutes passed as if in slow motion. I stood in Slack's kitchen feeling dizzy and nauseous, while mentally rewinding what had happened.

Drummond eventually came to join me, his face pale and drawn.

'It's probably already obvious to you but he's just been certified dead,' he said.

I nodded. 'I'd have preferred it if he'd died slowly and painfully of cancer.'

'Me too. But at least he's finally gone and the world's a better place for it.'

'His gun-toting bitch is still out there, though,' I said. 'And we still don't know where she is.'

'There's something else you have to know, Laura,' he said. 'I've read Slack's suicide note, which basically says what he told us before he topped himself. But I've also opened the other envelope. The one he said contained a surprise for us.'

'And?'

His expression darkened. 'Well, it's more than just a surprise, Laura. It's a gut-wrenching shock.'

73

Laura

I could tell that she knew. It was obvious from the look in her eyes as Drummond and I strode towards her across the office, followed by a detective and two uniforms.

A fierce rage was burning in me, but I stamped on it, pushed it down, because Drummond had warned me not to lose the plot. But it was a real struggle because I wanted to wring her neck and tear her eyes out.

The bitch had blood on her hands. The blood of Dave Prentiss, Marion Nash, the Metropolitan Police Commissioner and my Aidan.

She was the one who had given Slack all our personal and confidential details. The one who'd been leaking information to him for years. The rat. The mole. The animal who, according to Slack, had persuaded him to arrange for the murder of the detective husband who'd dumped her for a younger woman.

She should have known at the time that one day Slack would use it against her. And that it was probably the only reason he had agreed to do it.

She was sitting at her desk and it looked to me as though she had already been crying. She stood up when we reached her, and fragments of memory flashed through my mind. The jobs we went on together, the drinks we shared, the conversations we had.

It was painful to know that she'd betrayed me and the rest of her colleagues. And it had been the worst kind of betrayal because she'd been a party to murder.

'You need to come with us, Detective Chappell,' Drummond said, and as he proceeded to caution her she turned to me and her face seemed to fold in on itself.

I thought she might ask what was going on, to brazen it out, but she didn't and for me that confirmed her guilt. She probably knew that it wouldn't take us long to substantiate the claims that Slack had made in his note. He'd stitched her up because even those corrupt coppers on his payroll were his enemies, and he hated them with a vengeance.

'How could you, Kate?' I said. 'What you did was despicable.'

Tears exploded at the corners of her eyes and a hot flush infused her face.

'I'm so very sorry,' she sobbed. 'I swear I didn't know he was going to do what he did. That's the truth.'

The tears streaked down her cheeks but I had no sympathy for her.

'You gave Slack our names and addresses,' I said. 'And you stayed silent when the killings began. That makes you an accessory to murder. I hope you spend the rest of your life in prison.'

They were the last words I spoke to her. But as she was led away I stared at her back, my eyes burning holes in the air. And I wondered how she had managed to fool us so well, and for so long.

Several other detectives witnessed what had just happened,

including Janet Dean, who stepped up to me and said, 'Well, for the life of me I never saw that one coming. This has been one hell of a week for surprises.'

I looked at Janet and felt a shiver of guilt for believing that she and not Kate had been the bad apple on the team.

74

Rosa

She was humming a tune to herself as she got dressed. She felt deliriously happy, and the last thing she wanted to do was go out and kill someone else.

She would have preferred to spend another day with Alice. They could have stayed in bed, or gone for a walk, or just sat on the sofa and talked about their future together.

But it wasn't possible, and not only because Alice had to go to work. Rosa had her own job to do and it was the only way she would get her money and keep Roy Slack and Carlos Cruz happy while she secretly put in motion the plan to shed the skin of The Slayer and begin her new life with Alice.

It was 8am and it occurred to her that she hadn't yet checked her messages. It was something she usually did as soon as she woke up but this morning she'd been distracted. Plus, her phone was still in her bag and her bag was in the kitchen where she'd left it last night.

It wasn't a problem, though, because she was almost ready to join Alice who was out there making coffee and toast.

They had intended to get out of bed earlier, but when they

awoke at six they hadn't been able to keep their hands off one another. Their lovemaking had lasted forty-five minutes and had ended with them declaring their love for one another.

Rosa had stayed on top of the bed, basking naked in the post-coital dream state, while Alice showered first. Even now Rosa was still feeling light-headed from the waves of pleasure that had washed through her body.

After she pulled on her jeans she walked over to the bedroom window and gazed out over London, the city she would soon be calling home. It looked set to be another fine day, and the clear-blue sky enhanced her mood.

It's now official, she told herself. Alice and I are an item. She's my girlfriend. The love of my life. The person I intend to grow old with.

During what had been a restless night, Rosa had thought long and hard about the process of transformation from Rosa Lopez, contract killer, to Maria Rodriquez, former government tourism executive.

Not much could happen until her work here was finished. Then she would return to Mexico, collect her half million dollars from Cruz, and add it to her savings. She'd then settle her affairs, which would include a quick sale of her home.

She wasn't sure if it was a good idea to tell Cruz that she was leaving the cartel and moving to London. He was bound to be angry and might even try to stop her.

So maybe it would be best not to tell him. She could just vanish, fake her own death perhaps. She couldn't even be sure that he would bother looking for her.

But one thing she was sure of was that the path she had chosen to take was the right one. Alice was her future now and that future was looking brighter than ever.

At least it was until she finished dressing and walked out of the bedroom and into the kitchen.

Rosa sensed straight away that something was wrong.

Alice was standing next to the sink with a stricken expression on her face, while clutching her mobile phone close to her chest.

She stared across the room at Rosa, her eyes shimmering with tears, her whole body trembling. It looked for all the world as though she had suffered a terrible shock.

'Dear God, Alice,' Rosa exclaimed. 'What's the matter?'

But Alice didn't respond. She seemed frozen to the spot, and this sparked an ugly fear in Rosa's gut.

She took a step forward, but Alice shook her head and said, 'Please don't come any closer.'

Rosa felt the blood stir inside her, a hot flush through her veins.

'I don't understand,' she said. 'Why are you like this?'

Alice's eyes flicked to the left and Rosa followed her eyeline. Only then did she become aware of the television, and she stared in total disbelief at an image of herself on the screen.

The news anchor's voice struck her like a knife through the heart.

'This is the woman police believe is the assassin. She was caught on a security camera at the hotel in South London where she's been staying since she arrived from Mexico on Tuesday. Police found weapons and a motorbike in a garage nearby to which it's known she had a key. The woman, named as Maria Rodriquez, is wanted in connection with five murders, the latest of which was committed last night.'

A silent wail of desperation rose in Rosa's throat, and a cold chill slid over her flesh.

She turned slowly to look at Alice, and when their eyes met she knew that her dream of a new beginning had been shattered.

'You didn't leave your purse in the hotel, did you?' Alice said.

Rosa couldn't speak so Alice carried on.

'You used that as an excuse to slip away from me and murder that officer in the patrol car near the pub.'

Rosa's mind was thumping out of control. She screwed up her eyes, trying to stop the tears squeezing out.

'I can't believe I fell in love with you,' Alice said, her voice breaking. 'You're a monster. You kill people for money.'

'But I love you, Alice,' Rosa said. 'You must believe that.'

'I don't care. You're not who I thought you were. And I'm scared of you.'

'But there's no need to be. I would never hurt you, Alice. Ever. You mean so much to me. We can still . . .'

Alice shook her head and held up her phone for Rosa to see.

'I just called the police,' she said. 'They'll be here any minute. I was about to leave the apartment when you came into the kitchen.'

Alice's words gave way to uncontrollable sobs. Her face crumbled and she dropped her phone on the floor.

Rosa rushed across the kitchen to comfort her, but Alice backed away, clearly terrified.

'Please don't touch me,' she wailed. 'I beg you. Please.'

Rosa stopped and burst into tears herself, her mind and body racked by a crushing despair.

But at the same time the survival instinct kicked in and a voice deep inside told her to grieve later for what she'd lost. Right now she had to save herself and that meant fleeing the apartment before the police arrived.

'Please forgive me,' was all she said to Alice as she turned and ran back into the bedroom where she collected her things.

She picked up her bag, slipped on her coat, and rushed out of the apartment without saying another word.

417

Going down in the lift she took out her phone to call Roy Slack because she was going to need his help. But that was when she saw his message, which ended with the words 'suggest you disappear'.

75

Laura

The events leading up to my confrontation with one of the world's most prolific killers went like this.

I was in a patrol car when the alert came over the radio. Someone had called the three nines to say that Maria Rodriquez, the woman wanted by the police, had spent the night in her apartment and was still there.

The caller's name was Alice Green, and she claimed she'd been seeing Rodriquez since she arrived in the UK. According to the emergency operator she was distressed and feared for her life.

We had just left Scotland Yard and the patrol car driver was giving me a lift to Streatham so I could pick up my own car from outside Danny Carver's house where I'd left it the previous evening. The plan was for me to then go to the hospital to see Aidan.

But I told the driver to change course, turn on the siren, and head for Knightsbridge where Alice Green's apartment was situated overlooking Hyde Park.

The address went out to all units, and teams of officers headed there from across London. But the rush hour traffic was kinder to us than everyone else, and for that reason we got there first.

It was why I was the one who spotted The Slayer as she came tearing out of the building. I was lucky and she wasn't. It was as simple as that.

We were just pulling into the kerb when I saw her. She was instantly recognisable in her leather jacket and with that eye-catching mane of glossy black hair.

The sight of her sent a chill flushing through my body. In that split second I thought about the lives the bitch had destroyed. Dave Prentiss. Marion Nash. The patrol officers in Balham and on the South Bank. The Commissioner. My unborn baby.

And I thought about the dreadful wounds she'd inflicted on Aidan's body and mind. Wounds that would have an impact on the rest of his life. On our lives.

She looked anxiously about her, as though trying to decide in which direction to go. And that was when she spotted the patrol car and took flight.

She turned left and headed east towards Piccadilly, and it threw us because the car was facing the other way and the traffic made it impossible to execute a speedy U-turn.

There was only one thing for it and that was for me to go after her on foot. No way could I let her get away now that I was so close. So I opened the door and jumped out.

She had a lead on me of about twenty metres. I screamed out for her to stop but of course she ignored me and ran for all she was worth.

The street was busy and pedestrians stared at us both, startled. Those who got in our way were unceremoniously shoved aside. As I ran my face was clenched with murderous fury. I had never in my life felt so worked up. So driven. So determined.

I was totally consumed by a visceral hatred for the woman I

was chasing. I had to stop her causing any more pain and suffering. And I had to make her pay for the damage she'd already done.

I could hear sirens shrieking from all directions, getting closer, drowning out the other city sounds.

My breath rasped in my throat as I hurtled along the road. But I wasn't gaining ground. The muscles in my legs burned as I hammered my feet on the pavement. The woman was fit and fast, and I was terrified I was going to lose her.

But I knew that if I did I would never forgive myself. This might be the closest we would ever get to bringing her down. I was the only thing that stood between the bitch and freedom. If she managed to give me the slip then she would find it easy to disappear in a city with a population of nearly nine million people.

Suddenly she veered to the right and sprinted across the road between the slow-moving traffic. A young man coming the opposite way was pushed to the ground, and a bus driver had to slam on his brakes to avoid running him over.

Somehow I managed to keep pace with her, although it was a struggle. I could barely breathe now and my chest felt as though it was going to explode. But a voice in my head was screaming at me to keep going. To ignore the pain. For Aidan. For mum. For my dead colleagues. For Dave Prentiss's child who would never know his father thanks to the she-devil up ahead. And for the life she had effectively ripped out of my own womb.

After another half minute of hot pursuit my perseverance paid off when she tried to jostle her way through a cluster of tourists and lost her balance, stumbling into the road.

Luck deserted her again because at that very moment a motorcycle was overtaking on the inside and it struck her side-on with a sickening thud. She was thrown back onto the pavement and into the group of tourists. I heard her cry out and saw her hit the ground.

The group dispersed and I rushed forward, my wheezing breath loud in my ears. Suddenly I was looking down on the woman they called The Slayer. And I felt a pang of disappointment that she was still conscious and not covered in blood.

She was lying on her side and struggling to breathe. Her eyes were dazed and startled at the same time, her mouth twisted into an ugly grimace. Clearly she was in pain but her injuries weren't visible.

I took out my ID and waved it in the air. 'I'm a police officer,' I shouted while panting for breath. 'Stay back and give us space. This woman is under arrest.'

As I spoke she rolled on her side and reached for her bag, which was lying next to her. It made me think that she might have a gun so I dropped to the ground and flung my body over hers.

'Forget it, bitch!' I screamed into her face. 'Your number's up and you're nicked.'

I forced her onto her back and she gave a groan of agony. She wasn't so pretty now, or so threatening. The Slayer had been subdued and she looked pathetic. I could barely believe that she was the woman who had terrorised the city. The cold-blooded killing machine from Mexico. Her heart may have been made of stone but her body, as it turned out, was as fragile as mine.

I searched her bag and sure enough there was a pistol inside with a silencer attached to the barrel. I had no doubt that it had been used to kill WPC Campbell.

As she looked up at me her face curled into a frown.

'I know you,' she said. 'You're that detective.'

I nodded, blinking furiously at the sweat stinging my eyes.

'That's right,' I said. 'You tried to kill me and you messed up.

You shot my man instead. And the fact that I'm the one who's collared you has made my day.'

She tried to lift her arm to strike me but it was obviously hurt and the pain of movement made her yelp.

'You don't deserve to live,' I told her. 'But you deserve to fucking suffer. And believe me you will.'

There was so much I wanted to do to the bitch, so much harm I wanted to inflict. But I couldn't because people were watching and the sirens were fast approaching.

So instead I leaned over and whispered in her ear. 'You know what's really funny, you evil fucking cow. It's that in the end it was a ruddy motorbike that brought you down. I find that beautifully ironic.'

It turned out she had a broken arm and a fractured thighbone. So in that respect she was fortunate. The motorbike that ran into her could have caused so much more damage.

She was taken to hospital in an ambulance with an armed police escort.

I watched from the pavement as they sped off. I was drenched in sweat and my lungs were aching from exhaustion. But at the same time I was feeling mightily pleased with myself.

Thanks to me Roy Slack was gone and his hired assassin was under arrest. There'd be no more threats. No more murders. Their reign of terror had been short-lived, but it had been devastating. Five dead. Six if you included my child. Two wounded. And many lives destroyed.

As I stood there being gawped at by strangers I felt a tide of emotion rise up through my body. I couldn't believe that it was over. The threats. The shootings. The bloodshed. The abject fear that had gripped us all.

I wanted to cry. To let it all come pouring out. But I forced myself not to, and instead sent a text to Aidan and my mother in which I wrote: *At last it's over.*

When Drummond arrived on the scene he was full of praise for what I'd done.

'You've played a blinder, Laura,' he said. 'We'll probably never know if she would have carried on killing but at least we do know that now she won't be able to.'

I asked him if he had spoken to Alice Green, the woman who had tipped us off.

'I'm calling on her next,' he said. 'You should go home or to the hospital to be with Aidan.'

But curiosity got the better of me and I insisted on going with him to interview her.

Alice Green was in pieces when we arrived at her apartment and I felt sorry for her. She told us how she had met the hot Latina chick at a West End club and how they'd fallen in love with each other.

'I know it was ridiculously quick, but it was real,' she sobbed. 'She seemed so kind and so . . . normal.'

Alice confirmed that they had spent last night together on the South Bank and that Maria had sneaked off to shoot the police officer.

'I swear I had no idea what she was going to do,' she said. 'She gave no clue, even after she did it. She joined me in the pub and then we had dinner. And I had no reason to suspect that anything had happened. Or that she was carrying a gun in her bag.'

It was such a sad story that I found myself fighting back tears. I wondered if The Slayer had really meant it when she told Alice that she intended to leave Mexico and move to London. Or had it merely been a cruel lie just so that she could have a sexual partner during her stay here?

It was one of the questions that we would put to her in the days ahead, along with what her real name was and who else she'd been in contact with since arriving in London.

But there was no knowing if she would bother to answer any of them. After all, there was nothing she could tell us that would encourage a judge to show even the slightest degree of leniency when it came to sentencing.

This woman was going to face the full force of the law. She had murdered four coppers, including the Metropolitan Police Commissioner. It was my guess she'd receive multiple life sentences and never be released from prison.

And throughout her incarceration she'd always be looking over her shoulder, wondering if her former boss in the cartel had put a price on her head for fear that one day she would reveal everything she knew about them.

76

Laura

A lot happened in the weeks following The Slayer's arrest. She was remanded in custody, charged with various offences, including five counts of murder.

While she languished in jail, thousands of people lined the streets of London for the funerals of her victims. I was among them and so was Aidan who insisted on going along each time to pay his respects.

Roy Slack's funeral was a much quieter affair and only a handful of people turned up. This was because many of those who had worked for the firm had been arrested or had fled abroad.

Danny Carver was among those facing long spells in prison. Others included two villains named Johnny Devonshire and Pat Knowles, who we discovered had been nearby when Roy Slack had battered to death the firearms officer Hugh Wallis.

They were then tasked with making arrangements to get rid of the body, which was put in a boat and attached to weights. It was dropped in the sea off the Sussex coast at night so they weren't able to provide a location.

The pair were exposed as a result of a folder found in Slack's hidden safe, which contained the deeds to a number of properties we didn't know he'd owned, including one in Dulwich.

A detailed forensic search of the property uncovered traces of Wallis's DNA and blood in the basement. The subsequent investigation led to Johnny Devonshire confessing to what he and Knowles had done.

It proved much quicker and easier to extract confessions from Tony Marsden and Kate Chappell. Marsden and three other police officers pleaded guilty to kidnapping Roy Slack. And Kate Chappell admitted taking bribes from the gangster over a number of years and providing him with confidential details about detectives on the task force. She also owned up to asking him to arrange for her husband to be run down by a car and killed after he walked out on her.

They were all now awaiting trial.

Needless to say Aidan and I didn't manage to get away at Christmas. Instead we spent it at home with my mother and his parents who flew in from Spain.

And it proved to be a joyous occasion. There was an overwhelming sense of happiness and relief. We knew we had a lot to be thankful for. We were all together as a family and Aidan was alive and recovering well. The doctors were now saying that they were confident he would regain full use of his arm within months, or perhaps even weeks.

I even felt the strong presence of my father and I could almost hear him telling me how proud he was of me for bringing the nightmare to an end, even though I'd crossed a line in order to do so.

I still hadn't told anyone, including Aidan, about the miscarriage. Maybe in time I would, but I didn't think they needed to know just yet. It was something I hadn't yet come to terms with myself.

On Christmas morning we exchanged gifts, and the one that Aidan gave to me lifted my spirits still further. It was an engagement ring, and it came with a bended-knee proposal.

'I want us to get married, Laura,' he said. 'We've put it off long enough. But what's happened has made me realise that it's time we tied the knot and started a family.'

This, of course, was music to my mother's ears and when I said yes she started to cry.

It made me realise that this was the start of our journey back to normality. It was going to be long, hard and painful, but I had every confidence that we would get there in the end.

EPILOGUE

The Sinaloa cartel struck two months after Christmas.

Rosa Lopez was returning to her cell from a meeting with her lawyer at which she'd been told that a date had been set for her trial.

The news added to the weight of her depression and made her want to spew up her guts.

She was still finding it hard to accept that her life was over and that she would never be free again.

Prison life had already taken its toll. She'd lost a stone in weight and her skin had become tight and pasty. Even so she was still the most attractive woman on the high-risk wing. The others were mostly fat old hags or ugly young bitches with crude manners.

Some of them were hanging around on the landing as Rosa walked back to her cell. As usual she drew comments and wolf whistles.

One woman who was on remand for killing her baby son asked Rosa if she wanted her pussy licked. Another said, 'You're our hero, gorgeous. Shame you didn't kill more fucking coppers.'

Rosa had so far preferred to keep to herself. She'd spent most of her time lying on her bed thinking about Alice Green and the life she could have had with her.

She didn't blame Alice for calling the police that morning three months ago. She could only imagine how shocked the poor woman was when she saw the news and realised that her new girlfriend was an infamous killer.

Despite what happened, Rosa knew that Alice would forever have a place in her heart.

When she got back to her cell she sat on the edge of her bed and buried her head in her hands.

An image of Alice flared in her mind and she thought about the first time they'd made love. Before long she was sobbing loudly and her face was wet with tears.

'Cheer up, luvvie,' someone said, and Rosa looked up to see a fellow inmate standing in the doorway with her hands behind her back.

The woman's name was Olivia Todd and she'd been part of a notorious drug smuggling gang before being locked up for murder.

Rosa's heart lurched, not because she was scared of the woman, but because a bunch of other inmates were gathered on the landing right outside her door. And whenever that happened it usually spelled trouble.

Rosa sprang to her feet, but before she could prepare to defend herself, Todd was across the cell and ramming into her, shoulder first.

Rosa fell back against the wall and her legs gave way. In the split second before she fell to the floor she glimpsed the makeshift knife in Todd's right hand and felt the blade being plunged into her side.

'It's a gift from the cartel,' Todd said. 'Carlos Cruz wanted you to know that he hadn't forgotten you.'

Rosa drifted in and out of consciousness. She was aware of her assailant running out of the cell and the group outside suddenly dispersing, having provided cover for the attack.

The cell door had been left open and she was dragging herself towards it when the guards appeared.

The next thing she knew she was on a stretcher and could hear snippets of a conversation.

'An ambulance is on its way. It'll need an armed escort.'

'It's a knife wound. She's losing blood.'

'The wing has been locked down, but I guarantee we won't find the knife or any witnesses to what happened.'

She blacked out for a while then and when she regained consciousness she was in an ambulance. A paramedic was treating her wound and she could hear the siren blaring. Thankfully the pain in her side had been dulled by drugs.

'We're about to arrive at the hospital,' the paramedic said. What seemed like just a few seconds later the ambulance stopped and the back door was opened.

She managed to stay awake as she was stretchered out of the ambulance.

She saw the entrance to the hospital's emergency department and there were two armed cops standing in front of it.

When the shooting started she watched as they both fell to the ground. Screams rang out and there were more shots and a lot of shouting.

She heard a man's voice order the paramedics to step away from the stretcher. As she turned her head towards the voice she glimpsed a figure in a balaclava holding a sawn-off shotgun.

She wasn't so far gone that she didn't know what was happening. The ambulance was being ambushed and she was being snatched. But why and by whom?

The questions hung in the air as she was picked up off the stretcher by a pair of strong hands. She was carried a short way and placed on a mattress in the back of a van. Two women wearing what looked like surgical gowns sat either side of the mattress.

Rosa tried to speak, but one of the women told her to stay quiet and then started to examine her wound.

At the same time the van jolted forward and it was immediately obvious to Rosa that it was speeding away from the hospital.

She lay on the mattress, her mind reeling as she tried to make sense of what was happening.

Then suddenly a needle was injected into her arm and she fell into a deep, dark pit.

She awoke to find that she was no longer in the back of the van. She was on a bed in a room with white walls and soft lighting.

It was a moment before she realised that her arm was attached to a drip and a man in a white coat was standing next to the bed holding a clipboard. He was tall and middle-aged with jet-black hair and olive skin like hers.

'Hello, Miss Lopez,' he said, with an accent that convinced her he was Mexican. 'My name is Antonio. I've been waiting for you to wake up. How do you feel?'

She swallowed and blinked away the crust from her eyes.

'Confused,' she said. 'Where am I?'

'A very private facility,' he replied. 'The authorities don't know you're here and let me reassure you that we've tended to your wound and you're going to be fine. You lost a significant amount of blood but no organs were damaged. The knife penetrated the soft tissue at the side of your torso below the ribs and above the hip. That's precisely where your attacker was told to place it so as not to cause a life-threatening injury. You'll have a scar, but it's a small price to pay for your freedom. You'll soon be up and about and on your way back to Mexico.'

For a moment Rosa thought she was dreaming. She closed her eyes briefly and when she opened them the man who called himself Antonio was still standing there, smiling.

'I don't understand,' she said.

He reached out and gently touched her arm. 'The cartel mounted the operation in order to spring you from jail, Miss Lopez. Your attacker was paid to stab you so that you would have to be sent to hospital. Our team were on stand-by and as soon as you arrived there they launched an ambush. It was easier than we thought it would be. Two police officers were shot, but naturally we won't be shedding any tears for them.'

Rosa was stunned. She'd thought the cartel might arrange for her to be killed to stop her talking, but she hadn't considered the possibility of a rescue mission.

'I've been asked to pass on a message from Mr Cruz,' the man said. 'He wants you to know that he never had any intention of abandoning you. He told me to tell you that you're a valued member of the cartel family and that we always look after our own. He's got a bottle of champagne on ice for when we eventually get you back to Mexico. And he'd like you to carry on working for him as long as you are able. As far as he is concerned you are his best *sicaria* and he doesn't want to lose you.'

It was enough to make Rosa smile. The thought of going back to her old life was suddenly quite appealing, and was certainly preferable to wasting away in a prison cell.

It wasn't as if she had been unhappy before coming to London.

She'd enjoyed working for the cartel, and had been content doing a job that paid so well.

Alice Green, bless her, had offered something different. Something better. Safer.

But a future with Alice was no longer an option. And neither was going it alone.

Right now Rosa needed the cartel more than they needed her. And despite everything she knew that without them she would struggle to survive.

'Can you inform Mr Cruz that I am very grateful to him,' she said to Antonio. 'And tell him that The Slayer will soon be back in business.'

ACKNOWLEDGEMENTS

Once again my thanks to the team at Avon/HarperCollins for all their support during the writing of this novel. But a special thank you goes to my editor, Victoria Oundjian. Her insightful input turned *The Rebel* into a far better book than it would otherwise have been. The changes she suggested made such a big difference to the storyline and the development of the characters. And for that I'm really grateful.

Women always
uncover the truth....

The MADAM

JAIME RAVEN

Murder, loyalty and vengeance collide in a gritty read perfect
for fans of Martina Cole and Kimberley Chambers.

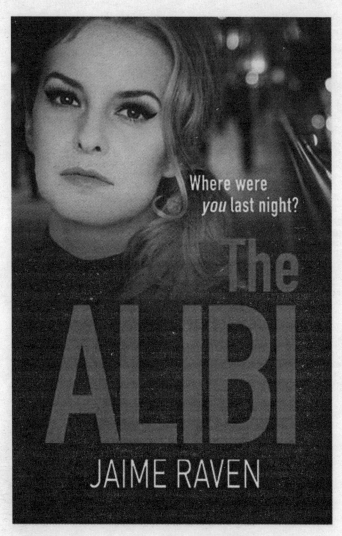

Where were *you* last night?

The
ALIBI

JAIME RAVEN

A perfect crime needs a perfect alibi . . .

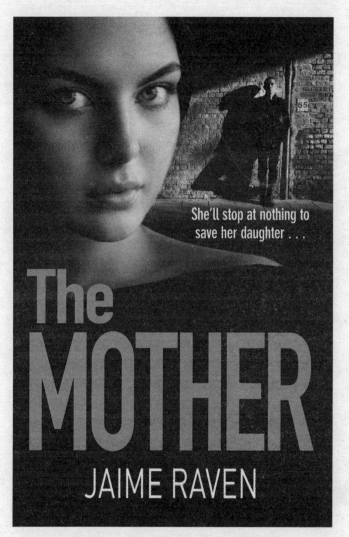

She'll stop at nothing to
save her daughter . . .

The
MOTHER

JAIME RAVEN

She'll stop at nothing to save her daughter . . .